'There have been moments throughout the history of ... ...re
writing when a writer sl... ...hat
keep nature and society ... ...ogical
truth but also a self-fulfi... ...aring
and at times beautifully v... ...
This *is* what will happen.

'A fascinating novel of radical ideas and what-if scenarios.'
LAURA MARNEY

'Haggith's evocation of landscape and wildlife is lyrical and
vivid, written with a poet's eye for detail. Her characters
convince and entertain. This ambitious, visionary novel belongs
to no single genre but encompasses romance, drama, comedy
and literary fiction. *Bear Witness* is a big-hearted book [that]
will make a significant contribution to the debate about the
future of Scotland's wilderness.' LINDA GILLARD

'A passionate and subversive book, written with a poet's touch.'
JASON DONALD

'*Bear Witness* takes you deep into thickets where government
policy, science and environmental activism collide with one
woman's passion. A "what if?" with an emotional heart.'
LINDA CRACKNELL

'A wonderful storyteller... Science, politics, romance and nature
observation combine as [Mandy Haggith] explores re-wilding
of both individual and land. This is a book with bite, relevant to
contemporary debate about large predators but also a source of
many other pleasures and surprises.' KENNY TAYLOR

Also by Mandy Haggith

Fiction
The Last Bear

Poetry
Castings

letting light in

Non-fiction
Paper Trails: From Trees to Trash,
the True Cost of Paper

BEAR WITNESS

Mandy Haggith

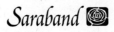

Saraband

Published by Saraband
Suite 202, 98 Woodlands Road
Glasgow, G3 6HB, Scotland
www.saraband.net

ISBN: 978-190864329-2
ebook: 978-190864330-8

Printed in the EU on 100% post-consumer-waste recycled paper,
made without optical brighteners or bleaches.

Layout by Jo Morley

1   3   5   7   9   10   8   6   4   2

For Bill and all the bears

Described by *The Scotsman* as a 'backwoods philosopher', Mandy Haggith lives on a wooded croft in Assynt, Sutherland. Originally from Northumberland, she spent a decade in artificial intelligence research before quitting academia for a freelance career as a forest activist and writer. Her first poetry collection was published in 2005 to broad acclaim; her non-fiction book on the environmental impact of the paper industry was called 'compelling and terrifying' by *The Observer*, and she scooped a national literary prize in 2009 for her first novel, *The Last Bear*. She co-ordinates the European Environmental Paper Network.

I have spotted footprints in the snow and scratches on trees, so I know they're here, but I don't actually expect to see one. After centuries of persecution, it is understandable that bears are shy.

I'm out walking early this morning. It's not that long after the spring equinox but already the days seem to be stretching towards that white, endless light of the Nordic summers, so when I woke it was light enough to want to get out. I can't get enough of these woods, this breathtaking place.

At night you could believe it's still winter. The cold is biting and the snow is still a metre deep. Icicles hang from the roof of the *hytte*, dripping a little each day in the sunshine. We've even seen the Northern Lights, a ghostly green veil, like an algal bloom – just like in all the pictures you see, only colder. The air at night is nostril-shocking. It's dangerous to be out in it too long. All your exposed skin starts sending alarm signals to your brain and you feel your nose getting colder and colder until you have to breathe through your mouth and freeze your tonsils for a while instead.

But as soon as the sun rises, it's all so different. Magical. There's heat in the sun, real bodily comfort, and such incredible sights out here in the forest. Endless patterns of snow, ice and frost. Carvings made by just-melting streams. The animal footprints are dialogues written on snow: loping triangles made by a hare followed by the trot-trot-trot line of a fox on its trail; beautiful feather imprints and claw-etchings left by ptarmigan, tracked about by a lynx's spoor; and of course the huge punctures in the drifts made by elk, their giant two-toed legs plunging into the depths with each great stride, and behind them the hungry paw prints of a bear.

I stop beside the river, tired. I wish I'd learned to ski because tramping in the deep snow is hard going. Where snowmobiles have compacted the snow it's relatively walkable but anywhere else it's a matter of lunge and flounder, up to my knees or thighs each step.

There are signs of beaver here: young birch trees gnawed right through. It's hard to tell how long ago they were felled. Did I disturb the beaver preparing an extension to its lodge, or was it here a week ago, going after the juicy shoots, full of the rising sap? I'm entranced by the teethmarks on the wound, and when I look up I can't quite make out the scale of the brown animal crossing the river.

Then I see that it's a big creature, up at the first bend of the river, where the water is shallow. It's a bear! The wind is blowing in my face and the river's conversational babble is an aural shield between us. I think of trying to get out my binoculars but I know the only thing I can do is to stay stock still. Any movement at all may give me away.

She is halfway across the river. She looks over her shoulder and a cub bounds, splashing, into the water after her, calling out, I imagine, in complaint. I can't hear it, but I can see that the cub's mouth is open as it follows its mother's lead into the snow-melt gushing river. It must be freezing, poor thing. Two big steps for the adult, a couple of jumps and a scramble for the cub, and they are gone, into the dark spruce shadows on the other side.

I'm staring and staring but I can't get another glimpse. They're away, invisible again. Safe. But oh my, wow, I've seen bears! Mother and cub – it doesn't get more special than that.

I guess she didn't know I was here. Just like I didn't know they were here, on my side of the river, while I was immersed in beaver signs. I might have bumped into her on the track, or more likely got close enough that she would have heard my crunching footsteps or smelled me coming and hidden herself and her young one in the shelter of the forest. She wouldn't have shown herself to me if she knew I was here. Or would she? Knowing she was putting the river between us, did that make her confident? No, it couldn't be. What if I'd had a gun? She would never put herself in range like that, would she?

I thank my aptitude for bumbling, lazily, curiously. I thank the luck that I was stock still at that moment. I thank the beaver for catching my attention. I thank the snow for making me tired enough to stop. It is a blessing. I don't believe in anything that might choose to bless me, nor can I imagine why I might deserve any such thing, but I thank it anyway, whoever or whatever it is that gave me the benison of a bear cub on this spring morning.

I feel so many confusing things. Sheer joy, of course, but tempered by so many other sensations. It almost seems a bit naff to try to write them down, they sound so abstract. There is fear, the innate terror of the predator, which is a kind of bodily, visceral thrill. There's frustration that it's so brief, so fleeting, the encounter. How long had it lasted? Seconds only. I wish it had been longer. I wish I had my camera there, ready to catch the shot. I could have had a prizewinner. Yet of course it's imprinted in my mind as deeply as the footprints in the snow, and though I'm disappointed not to have a picture, I also know there's something truer in my sighting for having been unaided by technology. Yet I am left with no proof, and the scientist in me knows that the evidence of my eyes only is no evidence at all, really.

When the next wave of emotion bites, I get up and set off back to the *hytte*. The wish that I had someone with whom to share such moments is unavoidable. I suppose it's called loneliness. It's familiar, anyway, and it washes through me. Then it gives way to the strongest sensation of all: a kind of hunger, a greed, triggered by those few seconds – to do it again, to repeat the thrill, to see more bears.

Part *One*

It was the coconut smell that alerted Callis to Yuri standing beside her – that strange shampoo he used. She lifted her head from the microscope and flinched at his tense grey eyes, too close, as if he were about to kiss her. She glanced around. Had anybody seen? She tried to limit any physical sign of her recoil, but knew he must have registered it.

She hit the button on her phone and pulled the plugs from her ears. The music of Arvo Pärt was replaced by lab clatter. 'Sorry,' she said. It seemed to have become her default greeting.

'Your father has just called,' he said. 'He couldn't reach you. He says it's urgent.'

There were two missed calls on her phone. She always kept it on silent and must have been too engrossed to notice them coming in. Her father could only have bad news. 'What's happened?' she asked, sliding down off her stool, fumbling to put the slides back into their case.

'You must call him.'

She looked about at the interrupted work.

'We'll tidy up. Go.' He waved over a technician.

She stuffed her headphones back into her ears, slung her bag over her shoulder and started dialling as she left the lab. Out in the wood-lined corridor she heard the familiar policeman's telephone voice.

'MacArthur.'

'It's me Dad, what's up?'

'Cally. Thanks.' His voice shot up a register, as if he were choking.

'What's happened?'

He said nothing.

'Is something up with Mum?'

There was just the sound of his breath. Then, 'She's dead.'

'What?' She held the phone away from her and frowned at it, then ripped the plugs from her ears and put the device to her head, as if holding it by her ear in the old-fashioned way would make it more likely to tell the truth, or somehow take her closer to her father.

'Dad?' she said. 'Sorry. What are you saying?'

'In the night. She just was gone, this morning, in bed. I couldn't wake her.'

She could hear him sobbing. She had never known him to cry. Men like him don't, not in Aberdeenshire, not anywhere, really. Except of course they do, really, when their lifelong love is a corpse in the bed beside them.

'What happened?'

'I told you. She was just there. She died in her sleep.'

The strips of the parquet floor stretched long and thin in converging lines.

'Have you called an ambulance?'

'Aye. There's nothing they can do. They'll do a post-mortem, find out, you know… But we know already.'

'What do you mean?'

'It was a brain tumour. We found out about a month ago.'

Callis slid down the wall into a crouch.

'That's not fair,' she said. Impotent I-want-my-mammy tears welled up into her eyes. She heard herself squeaking. 'She never said. You didn't tell me.'

'She meant to. She was going to, love, she was. We didn't think it'd be so sudden.'

Callis felt the floor melting beneath her. 'I'll get the ferry.' She surprised herself by how calm her voice sounded.

'If you want to fly…?'

6

'You know I don't fly.'

'No, I know. But if you want to, I'll pay.'

'No. I wouldn't dream of it.' She knew he couldn't really afford it, not these days, and anyway she had staked her career on her knowledge of climate change. It was ideological. Apart from which, the ferry meant time to think. An aeroplane would be far too rushed. 'I'll get the boat tomorrow, if I can get a ticket. I should be home by Sunday night.'

'I'll pick you up. You'll let me know when you get in.'

'Will you be all right?'

'Aye, don't worry about me. Just you get the ferry now.'

She heaved herself to her feet, sliding her phone into the pocket of her white lab coat. She knew some of the other Institute staff joked about her uniform behind her back, as a British affectation, but she didn't want acid on her clothes. Even though today she had only been identifying pollen grains from a soil sample, which carried no risk of splashes whatsoever, it was still lab work and it felt right to don the coat. It made her feel the part. That and the music – sacred choral works to block out the background chat. What part did it make her feel, exactly? Was it an act, this job? Surely not. It was Science.

Suddenly, the walls of the corridor were too smooth, the shiny wood too polished. She pushed open the half-closed lab door and made her feet tread across to her workstation, where Yuri was peering at her slide rack and notes. She wondered if his coming in person with the message was just a ruse to scrutinise her work.

He looked up as she approached and she saw his eyes, darting, and understood just how much her rejection of him had soured their friendship. Behind his face, painted with concern, the predatory question was still there in his eyes.

She stopped a few feet away, shielding herself with her bag.

He stepped forward into her space, the repellent waft of coconut shampoo forcing her on to her back foot.

'My mother's dead,' she said, not believing how matter-of-fact it sounded. 'I need to go home.'

7

'Of course.' His hands stretched towards her. Then, as if realising she had placed herself out of arm's reach, he put his palms together and pointed his fingers towards her like a priest making a blessing. 'I'm sorry.'

She nodded. Paul, the technician, was already clearing her work into files. 'I'll get my things. I'll be away until after the funeral. Maybe a week?'

'I understand. Compassionate leave. It's not a problem. Send me a message when you know your return.'

She turned away from him, the hunger in his eyes setting her rigid, but as she walked towards the door, his voice stopped her.

'Callis.'

She looked over her shoulder. His hands had separated, opening out, as if beseeching her. 'My sorrow to your father.'

She nodded again, hitched her bag on to her shoulder and closed the door behind her.

🐾 🐾

Early the next morning, six-ish, it was light in that bright April daylight-all-the-time Nordic way. A part of Callis was calm, and she had already begun to gather objects into a bag, packing things she knew she needed (clothes and toiletries, money and passport). But the rest of her was going into meltdown, grabbing things almost at random: books she had never even opened yet; the knitting she had abandoned two winters back, sick of the pink; three skirts for the funeral, none of which she had worn in ages. A teddy bear went in, then came back out again. Her camera kit likewise. Years ago she had mastered travelling light, but that day nothing that she had mastered mattered.

Her phone was on the counter, filling the kitchen with chart music. The weather report was the usual saga of flooding. The news came on and the gunman told his tale. She stood with a bowl of muesli going soggy and started to cry, then put the cereal down and sat right there on the cold slab floor, like Alice, ready to drown in a sea of her own tears.

The farmer on the radio told how he had shot the mother bear and captured the cub, and as an act of symbolism, a reminder to the Norwegian people of their roots as the tamers of the wild, he had taken the little animal into Trondheim, and at the foot of St Olav's statue, he had taken his gun, rested it on brown fur and pulled the trigger.

An onlooker described how he had heard a bang and realised it was a gunshot, and then he'd noticed a man standing shouting in the middle of the roundabout where Kongens gate meets Munkegata. He said blood and bits of the cub's body were splattered all over the base of the patron saint's statue and the farmer was bellowing about the right to protect oneself from predators.

Callis wasn't sure if she was crying for the bear cub, or for her mother, or for both. Perhaps with fury for not having been told about the tumour. Perhaps just for herself, alone in a hopeless place. She was leaving that morning anyway. She only wished she had been at home to say goodbye. She hadn't said goodbye. She hadn't said anything that really mattered. And now, barely a mile from where she worked, some bastard had shot a bear cub. For all she knew, perhaps it was the very one she'd seen only a couple of weeks ago.

The radio said that scientists were reporting that the bear was possibly the last denning female in Norway. Callis hadn't realised they were that rare. The announcer introduced a Professor Scazia from Romania, spokesperson for the International Conservation Union. 'It is a tragic day for bears,' a deep voice said in English.

Some blockage had burst in her. Something happened on that kitchen floor she never could explain: as if, on hearing of the death of the bear, a new life-force surged inside her.

The deep radio voice continued. 'The bear numbers in Norway have already been drastically reduced in recent years by Aujeszky's disease, also known as pseudorabies. We cannot allow conservation efforts to be thwarted by the barbarity of a few individuals. We must not let this year be a year only of loss. I ask the people of Norway not to give up hope.'

She picked herself up, packed a few last things: a pen, some jewellery, sensible shoes and waterproofs. She remembered her keys, then left. Halfway down the street, she turned, went back, got her oldest, most worn-out-with-love teddy bear and strapped it to her rucksack, apologising to it about the rain, then had to run to the station to catch the tram.

That was the start of it. A quick tram journey down into Trondheim, a short walk to the terminal and twenty-four hours of ferry to chew over her life. She was tired and emotional and yes, had had a bit too much gin as well. She was glad to have a berth to herself. She could not have handled conversation.

She got out the last letter from her mother thanking her for the birthday gift cookery book. She had written, as always, about the weather. Spring was coming late, the trees were slow to put on leaves. What gales! What frosts! The cherry blossom ruined!

Perhaps she should have guessed how ill her mother was that night she had dreamed about her, after she had phoned not wanting anything in particular, just wondering if all was well. Now Callis realised she should have wondered in return, but instead she had kept her head too firmly in her pollen counts and the paper for the Warsaw conference on pine.

Cancer. Her mother had been unable to say the word, could not commit it to paper, but perhaps she might have whispered it, or used some euphemistic phrase, if Callis had only called her back in time. At least it took her fast. Should she be thankful for that?

She cried a bit more, then had another gin, and sat watching her life spool past in her mind like a box of cotton bobbins, spilled and tangling, unravelling into a drunken stupor.

She stumbled into her bunk and lay awake, with her teddy bear tucked under her chin, thinking ahead to her father alone in his bed. The house would be full of memories, her mother's presence everywhere from the front door to the big loft, the best thing about their Scandinavian-style wooden house. She had always loved it up there: it was perpetually warm, full of her father's wine, rows of demijohns with their furtive bubbles, burping through the winter, as if each glass jar had its own invisible frog-genie.

She remembered when she was little she had made a hibernation den in one corner and taken her teddy bears up into it, having heard that this was what bears liked to do at the first onset of snow. Her mother had helped her up with a huge cardboard box, which she had turned on its side, in the corner of the room. It took several trips up and down the stairs to bring all her bears up. She had installed them all in their cave, making sure they were each snuggled comfortably, then wished them good night, until the spring.

That night she had woken in the dark, her empty bedroom scary without its furry inhabitants. She must have cried because her mother had appeared in her nightie and told her that although brown bears slept all winter, she wasn't sure that polar bears did. She offered to find out if one of them might still be awake. Callis lay listening to the creak of the loft stairs, a pause, then the padding of slippered feet back down. Her mother reappeared with Berg, her fluffiest polar bear, who was not hibernating. Sleep, presumably, returned to normal.

She had spent a lot of time that winter in the loft, she seemed to remember, checking on the bears in their burrow, snoozing to their chorus of wine-frogs. At some point, spring no doubt had come and the box of bears had emptied. She had no memory of that. She just recalled the warm brown cave full of sleeping bears, who moved over to let her curl up among them, one or two of whom might wake from time to time and growl or shuffle over for a cuddle and to listen to what she had to say.

Back in the present, in the last vestiges of this short spring night, she imagined herself curling up in the den of a real sleeping bear, feeling the hushing lap of breath against her cheek, sinking into fur. She must have slept eventually, the roll of the boat like the rhythm of air in lungs, the engine-growl of sleep droning her to a dreamless place.

Waking for a pee, her head scrubbed clear of everything but self-loathing on account of the gin, it was obvious what to do.

She couldn't bring her mother back, but bears were a different matter.

🐾 🐾

Her father was standing at the arrivals door and at first she didn't recognise him. Her own father, grown so old, so suddenly. Perhaps it had been coming for some time. She hadn't really looked at him, she supposed, for ages; he was just the shadow behind her mother. It was nearly a year since she'd been back: she had stayed in Norway on her own at Christmas, gone to a local New Year party, avoiding Hogmanay at home, with all the rituals she had long outgrown.

He reached out to her and she let him hug her. Still wearing uniform blue slacks and fleece, but his straight, tall body had shrunk, somehow, or slumped, as if an internal wall had collapsed. His eyes were vacant, deep in, and there was a manner about him she couldn't place at first, then it struck her. He was in policeman mode. On guard. He tried to take her bag, and she tried to stop him, then gave in: the rucksack on her back had all the weight in it.

She followed him outside. He had parked in a disabled bay, right beside the entrance, and when she gave him a questioning look he waved at the windscreen. 'Disabled sticker. Got it for your mum.'

She slung the rucksack in the back seat, then got in the front.

'So,' he said, as she buckled up. He reversed out of the space and joined the flow of traffic. She waited for him to continue speaking. 'How's the job?'

First things first, she thought. She toyed with various answers: I slept with my boss and now he reminds me of a lizard; almost as boring as being a policeman; well paid but soulless. 'It was an easy crossing,' she said.

He glanced at her. 'You smell of drink.'

'Did you hear about the bear?' she said.

Nobody told her Malcolm Johnstone would be at the funeral. Not long after the service started she turned to catch the eye of Diana, who was sitting with Frances and Stig a few rows back on the other side of the crematorium chapel. Her friends smiled at her, and Diana held up a camera and pointed at it questioningly. Callis shook her head. Her father had expressly said no pictures. She saw Frances nudge Stig on her left and he winked a greeting. Nice of Stig to come, Callis thought. He had spent a lot of time with her mum while she and Frances had been playing girly games together. And there just behind him was Malcolm, a big well-groomed presence in the crowd.

She hated crematoria. Why her mother had chosen to be burned she couldn't imagine. It wasn't exactly a religious service, that would have been too inappropriate for an ardent atheist like her mother, but she had loved to sing, so there were hymns. What else do you sing? Auld Lang Syne? It sure as hell wasn't Hogmanay.

Callis stood on the front row beside her father. He looked so frail, as if his wife had been keeping him firm, pumped up, and now he had deflated overnight. The woman cleric who was leading the service claimed to have been an old classmate of Flora Scott – as she'd been called before she married Derek MacArthur – but from the nonsense she spoke, Callis thought she mustn't have seen her mother since they'd left school forty years ago. She stood wishing she had a sister, someone to stand beside, to conspire with over what to do with their father, someone to share the mourning with. Though maybe, she thought, maybe grief is such a private thing it can't be shared. There was only her and her father now. The stable leg of the family tripod was gone.

On her other side was Aunt Marjory, whose hands were trembling so hard that Callis eventually grabbed the one nearest to her and held on. They smiled at each other through tears. Marjory's make-up was a mess. They might not have been as close as they could, but being family seemed somehow enough for now.

As the coffin disappeared into the hole in the wall, organ music started up, a Bach toccata. Oh Dad, thought Callis, did you not see further than the first thing on the list?

It was odd that Malcolm was there. As the congregation filed up the aisle towards the door, their eyes met. Hers were dry again, but smarting, raw; his seemed brown and friendly.

Callis and her father stood at the porch door, thanking people for coming, asking how they were, muttering embarrassed noises at their sympathies and trying not to baulk at crassness and pity. Callis wished that she did not have to be there at all.

Malcolm shook her father's hand first. 'You won't remember me,' he said.

'Of course I do. You're Maureen Mason's boy: Donald, isn't it? No.' Her father shook his head, knowing he'd got it wrong.

'Malcolm.' They both said it together and smiled.

'Look, love!' He turned to Callis as Malcolm reached his hand towards her. 'It's wee Malcolm from the old school house. You haven't changed a bit, son. Thanks for coming!' He turned to the next person emerging from the chapel's doorway.

Callis felt her right hand enveloped by strong fingers, and looked down to see her thumb and knuckles covered by a second palm. Her other hand involuntarily joined the many-fingered clasp.

'Long time, no see,' she said.

'I'm sorry about your mum.'

'Thanks. So am I.' And before she knew what she was saying, it came out: 'I didn't get to say goodbye.'

She was crying again. She looked outside to gravel, yew trees, overblown tulips and gaudy primroses every colour of the rainbow bar the pale, watery-sunshine yellow they should naturally be. More people were trying to be polite and all she wanted was to run away. Malcolm took a hand from hers and made a stroking gesture on her upper arm, then wrapped his arm round her, hugging her so she found herself sobbing on to his black coat. The fabric was rough against her cheek. Scratchy and dark and smelling of smoke and mothballs.

She pulled herself away and swallowed, reaching for a hankie. 'Sorry. Where did you come from today?'

'Not far. Near Inverness.'

'Far enough.'

'I heard you came from Norway.'

She nodded. 'Can you stay for lunch? We're going to the Point.'

'Yeah, that would be good. I'm starving. Had an early start.' He smiled and his eyes were shiny as melting chocolate.

'Speak to you later. Thanks for coming.'

All the rest was a stream of hands and mouths and words about her mother that Callis didn't want to hear. Memories shattered over and over on to the paving slabs and gravel, reforming and splintering again, cutting into her with each platitude spoken and answered outside the grey, fuming building.

Eventually Callis turned to her father. 'Let's go and eat.' She felt sick.

He nodded mutely, his face like quartzite.

'Do you need a drink as much as I do?' she asked.

He shook his head. She wasn't sure he had heard her.

🐾 🐾

Callis sat at a table with Diana, Frances and Stig, Frances' twin brother. Her father's table seemed to be monopolised by old police colleagues of his, or maybe they were from the football club, she didn't really know any of them. There were some friends of her mother too, who had indicated she would be welcome with them, but it seemed easier to join her own pals.

The lunch was one of those dreadful pub back room buffets with potato salad out of a tin and chicken drumsticks. Callis and her father had quickly dismissed the idea of having people back to the house, but now she regretted it. Her mother deserved something a bit less tacky.

Callis was on what she called 'cooking lager', the weakest at the bar, not her favourite drink but working on the basis, drummed into her by her father, that you should only let your drinks get stronger as the day goes on. This looked like it might be a marathon. She would have rather had a gin and tonic or a dry white wine but, wanting to stay in control for once, hoped a lager might spin out for longer.

'Are you OK?' Frances asked.

'I haven't a clue,' said Callis. She found she couldn't tell her what she'd said so easily to Malcolm. Frances had been her best friend since they were teenagers, but right then Callis was not prepared to pour her feelings out on to the table with the vol-au-vents and deep fried onion balls.

Diana pulled her camera out of her big leather bag. 'Is it OK if I take some shots now?'

Callis shook her head. 'Dad said no pictures.'

'What, not even now? There are some great faces here.'

'Sorry. He hates what he calls "the paparazzi".' Callis tried to sound conciliatory.

'You could ask him, maybe, if I could just take a few?' She leaned forwards, trying to get Callis to look at her.

Callis sighed. She didn't want to seem unreasonable. 'Look, I know he'll just say no.'

Diana put her camera back in her bag with a pout and a shrug. Callis looked at Frances for help.

'Who's the red-haired wifey with your Dad?' Stig asked. She could have kissed him.

'That's his little sister, Marjory. Runs a sauna in Dundee. She's the family's naughty lady.'

'She sure looks the part,' he grinned. She did stand out. As usual, she had seized the opportunity to take dressing up a few steps further than the rest of the family.

'She's an inspiration to us all,' said Diana. 'Glamorous and independent-minded. And a fabulous model! One of my photos of her won the Women's Photography Prize a few years back.'

'My father always said she should have been on the stage,' Callis said. 'Apparently she spent her childhood dressing up and stripping off and never lost the knack. She's an old softie, really. But she's had some life.'

Her red hair was natural, Marjory claimed, just enhanced a little. But she made the best of those red locks, and today they were sculpted up into a kind of beehive on top of her emphatically painted face. She had done a bit of retouching since the ceremony, Callis noted. Her black gown – it was far too fulsome to be described merely as a dress – glittered. Her laugh, as big as her figure, drew everyone's attention.

'And the fella beside her?' asked Stig. Marjory was flanked by a sea captain, complete with leather-elbowed navy jacket and hoary beard.

'That's her man, Jack. He runs a ship's chandler business, has shops in a few coastal towns in the northeast, and he does what he calls "jobs on the water", whatever they are. The lad on the other side of my dad is my wee cousin, Donnie,' Callis said. 'No. Cousin's son. Whatever that makes him. He's a star at Dad's football club.'

'Is he still coaching?'

'Yeah. I think most of the guys along that end of Dad's table are from the club.' She took in the row of well-muscled whisky-drinkers. 'I recognise some of them, but most of them, no idea.'

'I assumed they were all colleagues of his,' said Frances. 'They look like policemen to me.'

'How did your dad get on being a copper and having a sister who runs a sauna?' asked Stig.

'Don't ask!' Callis laughed. 'He refuses to speak to her most of the time, but my mum and her got on like a house on fire, so he had to be civil. She's not one to be ignored, isn't my Aunt Marjory.'

'Families, eh?' Stig smiled.

'And who's your lonely watcher at the bar?' asked Frances.

Callis looked behind her, into those brown eyes. She waved him over.

'Malcolm, meet Frances. We've been friends since before university. And this is Diana, and Stig. Grab a chair.'

He put his pint down, reached forward and gave each of the three a brief, business-like handshake. Then he pulled a red-velvet upholstered seat over from an empty table, and slung his coat over its back. Stig shuffled his chair aside to let Malcolm settle in beside Callis. She smiled at him, at a loss for words.

He lifted his pint and took a swig, then licked the moustache of foam away. It reminded Callis of how he looked eating ice cream, the boy still there in him, just a whole lot bigger. She noticed Frances and Diana exchanging glances.

'How do you know Callis?' asked Frances.

'We walked to school together from the age of six.'

'Five,' Callis corrected.

'Hand in hand,' he said, grabbing hers and swinging it. Callis laughed then for the first time in days. Or was it months? She could see Frances adding two and two and making five and she found she didn't care, just wanted him not to let go. It was such a big hand, with fingers as rough as tweed.

Callis and Malcolm hadn't been particularly friendly at school until the day she went with her mum to the local dairy to watch the cows being milked. She had been shy of the farmer but enthralled by the bulky swaggering cows with their udders dangling, pushing into the milking parlour. Malcolm had been there with a stick, slapping the cows, not fiercely but enough to direct them into their stalls. She had been shy of him, too. He had nodded to her like a man, then ignored her like a man, but she had watched him.

To her surprise the next time she saw him at school he had been friendly to her. He was a boy again. He was going to be a farmer. He explained to her all about the cows and she was impressed by what he knew. It wasn't school knowledge, it wouldn't help him in English or Maths, but it was real and she knew, somehow, it mattered more than most of the things they learned in Science and Nature. Malcolm knew about cows and milk and, it turned out, he knew about grass and hay, barley and wheat, soil and rain. He knew more than you would guess just by looking at him.

'Was she besotted with bears back then?' Frances asked him.

'I don't know, were you?'

Callis tipped her head, thinking back. 'Yeah, I guess I was.'

'Why? What is it with bears anyway?' Diana said.

'I'm not sure. It's something to do with the way they're portrayed in all those kids' books, like Pooh and Paddington, as dotty old softies, and then in reality a mother bear will knock your head off with one paw if you threaten her babies. They seem to have a lot of possibilities – cuddly but dangerous. For some reason that appeals to me!' She stopped. Diana was nodding as if this explained something profound, and Malcolm had a teasing grin on his face.

'I could probably tell you all kinds of other things about her she'd rather you didn't know,' he said to Frances.

'Me too,' said Frances. Callis gave her a hard stare and she smirked back. 'Later.'

'And how about you?' Malcolm asked Diana.

'Well, I've known both these lovely ladies since they joined my secret society at Edinburgh.'

'Secret society?'

'Not *that* secret, I guess. We met at Fe-Phi-Pho...'

Malcolm frowned, 'As in?'

'A group of right-minded women with a flair for photography.' Diana looked around, checking she had everyone's attention. 'We met every Thursday evening in the back room of Bannerman's in the Cowgate, to plot the revolution, or at least a revolution in imagery of women.'

Frances and Callis grinned at each other; they'd heard this version of the story a thousand times. But Diana's attention was squarely on Malcolm, to whom it was all new.

'From pornography to supermodels, from music videos to advertising, we chewed over all the ways our society manipulates women's ways of seeing themselves. We were all mad on photography of course, took endless pictures, tried to afford the latest and best equipment, and we ran some, I have to say, brilliant campaigns trying to change the way woman are shown in everything from university websites to the *Sunday Herald*'s colour supplements.'

'Why fe-fi-fo?' asked Malcolm. 'Were you cannibals as well?'

'Aye, definitely,' said Callis. 'We had a ritual Englishman bar-becue at every meeting.'

Frances guffawed.

Diana smiled at Malcolm indulgently. 'Our full name was "The Feminist Philosophical Photographic Society". We were inspired by a book by Louise du Pont called *A Feminist Philosophy of Photography* and most of us have adopted her ethic of independence, real independence, I mean, not this nationalistic nonsense we've had thrust upon us...'

'Some of us voted "Yes", Di, you'd better watch what you say!' Frances knocked on the table as if to make a point of order.

'Oh please, can we agree not to discuss the referendum?' Callis said. 'Not today. We'll only argue and it'll get nasty. It's over. Carry on about du Pont.'

'All right. Where was I? Oh yes, the kind of independence that du Pont advocated and which we *all* agree about...' – she made a sweeping, inclusive gesture towards Frances – 'is eschewing relationships with men on the basis that they're exploitative and demeaning to women.'

She stopped and looked at Frances, who nodded. Then she turned to Malcolm and smiled. 'Not that we have anything against men per se, many of you are perfectly delicious. But relationships, marriage, all that crap, it's a recipe for humiliation. Anyway, to cut a long story short, I was elected Chair of Fe-Phi-Pho the year Callis and Frances joined, and I, well, I took her under my wing, didn't I?' She tapped Callis twice on the hand, as if in warning, while still looking at Malcolm. 'And then Callis and I worked together, ooh, six years back now?'

'Six and a half. I started in October, straight after uni.'

'I taught her to split hairs,' she said. 'Literally and metaphor-ically, as you can tell.'

'You can talk! Ms Pedantic,' Callis said.

'Literally?' Malcolm asked.

'We worked in a lab analysing chemical contamination in animals from persistent pollutants like PCBs, dioxins, stuff like that. We had to do masses of tests on animal hairs, checking them out under an electron microscope. Fiddly stuff, repetitive, very boring. Only a total nitpicker can survive. Callis was born to the job.'

'Thanks, Di!'

'So is that what you do in Norway?' Malcolm asked Callis.

'Kind of. I've been doing a lot of counting pollen grains from archaeological soil samples recently, working out how ecosystems have changed over time. So, different questions, but I still spend a stupid amount of time craned over a microscope or a computer screen.'

'No rude remarks about pains in the neck then?' Diana grinned.

'No thanks!'

'My dad says I do this job because it's the only kind of wildlife I get to see since I can't sit still. He used to take me to the woods near home at night to watch badgers come out of their sets, but I would fidget too much. Fidget, wriggle, scuffle, scuffle. The badgers wouldn't come. They must have run out of a back door or maybe they just stayed in, wondering what this big gallumphing thing was scratching around outside. Anyway, like I said, Dad says this is why I just get to look down a microscope – whatever's on the slide is oblivious to how much shuffling I'm doing.'

Everyone laughed along at her outpouring, then after a pause, Malcolm turned to Diana. 'So do you work in a lab as well?'

'No, no. Admin, admin and more admin, nothing worthwhile I'm afraid,' said Diana.

'Keeping the health service running doesn't count as worthwhile?' Frances said.

'OK. It might be worthy but it's not exactly interesting unless you happen to be into spreadsheets, which of course I am: I love my spreadsheets, they are magnificent spreadsheets.' She made a theatrical flourish with her arms to emphasise their ironic magnificence, winning a laugh from her audience. 'But I appreciate not everyone shares my passion. If you want real excitement, Stig's the one.'

They all looked expectantly at the man in question, Frances' brother Steven, known to everyone for as long as they could remember as Stig. Callis recalled the times when he and Frances had visited during university holidays and how he used to gravitate to the kitchen, spending hours chatting with her mother while she and Frances hung out together in her bedroom. Stig and Frances had lost their own mother when they were in their teens, and for a while Flora had filled the gap for Stig. Now, he was stroking his goatee beard watching Jack and Marjory giggling together in the corner. Diana dug him in the ribs.

'He's at the Scottish Land Institute. Tell them what you do.'

'I'm a research scientist.'

'Yes, but tell them about your project.'

'I'm running a lynx reintroduction study.'

Callis put the pint down on the table without taking a swig. 'Are you really?'

'Aye.' He gave her a shy grin, but she could see he was proud.

They were interrupted by a perfumed flourish. 'Can I get any of you young folks a drink fae the bar?' Aunt Marjory gave Callis a squeeze on her shoulder, reaching her other arm out, with a sweep of velvet, to touch Diana on the lower arm. Her scarlet-painted nails stroked the black-lace cuff of Diana's dress-jacket. 'Divine as ever, Diana.'

With heads and hand gestures, they all indicated enough in their glasses. 'I think we're fine, thanks,' said Callis.

'You're looking fantastic yourself, Marj.' Diana's eyes twinkled.

'And this is Frances? Aye. And you're still hanging out with your brother. Have you no got yourself a man, quine? Don't tell me you're like Callis.'

'I'm independent and proud of it.' Frances tossed her hair.

'It's all your doing, Diana. You're a bad influence. What these skinny lassies need is a bit of action on the love front, that's what I think.'

Diana threw her head back laughing. 'You know my motto, Marj. Love's a noose…'

Callis and Frances chimed in, '…for a goose.'

The madame raised her eyes to the ceiling, then stepped to stand behind Malcolm, who turned his head and gave her a baffled smile. 'Good luck, son,' she said. 'They've hearts of stone, these three.'

Marjory swept off and Callis turned to Stig. 'You heard about the bears in Norway?'

'Aye, terrible.'

'What?' asked Frances.

'They're shooting all the bears,' Callis said.

'You what?'

'The morning I left, there was this awful thing on the news. A farmer from the Lierne region hunted down one of the few female bears denning in Norway, maybe even the last one, then captured her cub and brought it to Trondheim and shot it in the centre of town as some kind of idiotic protest.'

'That's dreadful,' said Frances.

'Bloody farmers. Don't get me started,' Callis said. She didn't say anything about her sighting in the snow, as if speaking about it might tarnish the memory.

'How do they know it was the last one?' asked Malcolm.

'They're all radio tagged, or were,' said Stig.

'Yes, but surely there are plenty more of them lurking in the mountains.'

'Don't think so,' said Stig. 'The monitoring has been pretty serious these past few years. Of course individuals wander over the border from Sweden, but they've watched the numbers actually denning in Norway drop steadily year by year. They eventually put a hunting ban in place but there are still people who want to kill them. Farmers mostly, poisoning them, shooting them. And pseudorabies took a lot, once the population got too small to be viable.'

'There should be an outcry,' said Frances.

'Are you involved with animals as well?' Malcolm asked her.

'No, sadly, I'm in marketing, for a publishing house. But I am about to learn the art of making teddy bears. Does that count?'

Laughs all round. 'Actually, Cally, you should come along. It's a weekend course at a big house in Moray, this weekend, it looks lovely. I think I've persuaded Diana and if you came too it'd be a real reunion of the sisterhood.'

Callis looked at Diana, who gave a shrug of encouragement. 'The house looks fantastic. The soft toy bit's just an excuse for a weekend living in style in the country. I thought I might get some interesting photo opportunities. Plus hot tub and mansion rather appeals!'

Frances touched Callis on the sleeve. 'No need to make your mind up straight away, I'll call you.' She turned back to Malcolm. 'And you? What's your line of work?'

'I'm a farmer,' he said, looking Callis straight in the eye.

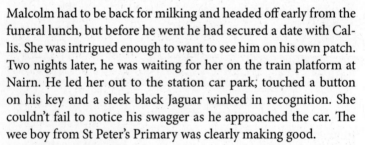

Malcolm had to be back for milking and headed off early from the funeral lunch, but before he went he had secured a date with Callis. She was intrigued enough to want to see him on his own patch. Two nights later, he was waiting for her on the train platform at Nairn. He led her out to the station car park, touched a button on his key and a sleek black Jaguar winked in recognition. She couldn't fail to notice his swagger as he approached the car. The wee boy from St Peter's Primary was clearly making good.

'Nice car,' she said.

'This? It's just my runaround.' He looked at her sideways and grinned.

'You're kidding.'

'Not really. My real car's a Citroen Flying 15.'

Callis hoped she didn't look as blank as she was. 'I take it I should be impressed by that. This one's swanky enough, I assure you.'

'Nah but the Citroen's a beauty. It's a bit of a hobby of mine, fixing vintage cars. I make a pound on the side, doing up Daimlers, people love them for weddings and that. I wouldn't drive one myself, but it funds me to tinker with the real classics.'

He drove her to a country inn three miles out of town. As the oak door swung to behind them, a tall bald barman nodded to Malcolm, 'Evening, Sir. Usual?'

'Aye,' he said. 'Driving juice.' Turning to Callis. 'What'll you have?'

'G & T, please.'

'Are you eating tonight, Sir?' the barman asked, adding fancily-cut lemon to a glass.

'Aye.'

'I'll put them on your tab, then.'

They took their drinks to a corner seat, and when the proprietor came to take them to their table in the restaurant he shook hands deferentially with Malcolm and positioned a chair for Callis as if she were a visiting dignitary.

She took the leather-bound tome offered to her and, once he was out of earshot, said, 'Are they like this to everyone, or are you top dog around here?' She glanced through the menu. The set meal price was high enough to raise expectations.

'It's my local,' Malcolm smiled, 'and I work for the man who owns it.'

'Who pays well, clearly.'

'Oh, I've got pretty low overheads – I get a house with the job – so most of what I earn can go on toys and treats. This is my treat, by the way.'

'No way, we'll go Dutch. I get a Norwegian salary, remember. And I'm an independent woman.'

He shrugged. 'If you insist.'

'I insist.'

The food fulfilled the promise of the menu. Ornate edifices of shitake mushrooms with sculptured garnishes were followed by a grapefruit sorbet before they tucked into venison cooked to perfection with side dishes of herby mashed root vegetables. It was all served up in an atmosphere of calm prowess. The wine glasses were huge and Callis found herself talking too much, heading off down a conversational highway – government agriculture subsidies – that was bound to go nowhere constructive, but she couldn't seem to stop herself acting as if a political discussion was all that she wanted from the evening.

As they shared the fruit-and-cheese board, Callis missed the last train and wasn't sorry. They went back to Malcolm's house. It was the end cottage in a terrace of four, with a big garage on the side, where he played with his cars. It was just a field away from the farm. He could go out of the gate at the bottom of the garden and walk with the cows across to the dairy, he said, uncorking a bottle from a French chateau Callis had never heard of.

She sank into the huge leather sofa and wondered if she would be able to raise herself from it ever again. She was astounded at the neatness of the place. An impressive hi-fi filled one corner, like an altar. Malcolm waved a remote control at it until it produced something bluesy and American.

He watched her taking in the decor. 'I do like it tidy,' he said. They talked domestic habits for a while. He always washed up after each meal, he said. It was a habit he had picked up on his gap year in Australia, living in a farm cabin infested with cockroaches. The only way to keep their numbers down was to leave them no food.

Callis thought of her house back in Trondheim: the scatter of books and magazines in the lounge; the way clothes tended towards heaps in the bedroom; the bathroom, well, she did clean it from time to time, blitzing it really thoroughly until everything gleamed, but normally, there were better things to do than housework. She didn't want to think what cockroaches might do in her kitchen.

He admitted to employing a cleaner. 'I love coming in from work when it's been cleaned, like the wee beeswax fairies have been.'

She giggled at the idea and he beamed. In the warm glow of wine, the idea of tidiness seemed almost spiritual, but the thought of employing someone to bring it about struck her as impossibly decadent.

'How do you afford it, but?' she asked.

'Lydia's dirt-cheap. Her husband Dima works on the farm and she's desperate for a bit more cash. They'll put up with a pittance, the Russians.' He emptied his glass and the conversation worked its way back to European food subsidies, less coherently than before. After wine, the age-old rules of drinking demanded nothing less than whisky. Malcolm had several malts.

'I won't regret this, will I? I'm a few ahead of you.'

He grinned, pouring amber liquid into tumblers. 'Don't worry, I'm catching up fast. Do you remember that time in the school playground when we let you girls play football?'

'Yeah, I do actually.'

'You were bloody good.'

'Was I?' She couldn't really recall it. 'Must have been beginner's luck.' She thought of herself with scabby knees and plimsolls, not exactly a seductive image, though school memories turned out to be a good source of laughs.

In a pause, she thought about mentioning bears, but something made her hold back.

He offered coffee, eventually, and went off to the galley kitchen to put it on – real coffee blasted in a Viennese pot on the back ring of the stove. The music chugged along. Tiredness washed over Callis. This place was so extraordinarily tidy, she thought, and the sofa so deep and comfortable. She stifled a yawn as Malcolm came through with two china mugs.

'You're tired. Not surprising, the funeral and all that must have been exhausting.' He put her coffee on a side table and sat back down opposite her in the leather armchair. She let her legs, tucked up under her until then, stretch out across the sofa, not sure if she was disappointed that he had not joined her there. No pass being made, then. Was she going to sleep down here? It was confusing all of a sudden. He had started talking about his father's funeral, but she was finding it hard to connect the movements of his mouth with words and what it might have to do with her, how she could keep awake to try to understand. She just wanted to sink into the cushions, let herself lie back and find darkness.

She half came to on the staircase.

Her feet banged on the narrow corner as the flight twisted back on itself. She'd been up here to the toilet earlier. Now she

27

was being carried, his arms under her legs, around her shoulders, her head flopping. She stiffened her neck and looked at him. 'Was appenin?'

'Time to tuck you up to sleep. You didn't look comfortable on the settee.'

'It was very comfy.'

'I've got a very comfy bed, too. Soon have you tucked up.'

She put her arm around his neck and closed her eyes. A turn through a doorway. She was lowered on to a bed. As her head settled on the pillow she looked up into those chocolate eyes, momentarily, then their mouths met, tongues explored, his body hanging over hers.

'Waking up now!' he grinned, shifting over her, pinioning her to the bed with his legs on either side of her body. She wondered if this was what she really wanted to be doing, but then he kissed her again and she did it anyway.

🐾 🐾

Callis woke with a dry mouth. She was lying at the edge of the bed, both arms above her head as if in surrender. Her hands were freezing, her temples taut with the after-effects of alcohol.

Malcolm lay spreadeagled, his right forearm under her neck, mouth open. His sleep looked untroubled.

Callis prised herself into a half-raised position and slipped out from under the covers. She grabbed the blue-and-red-striped flannel gown off the back of the door and slung it around her shoulders. The handle squeaked as it turned.

'Stealing ma bathrobe?'

She looked round. He seemed wide awake. 'It's Baltic in here,' she said. 'I need a pee.'

'Don't be long.' He rubbed his hand through his hair. 'I've got something for you.'

Her head rang, but there was a raw clarity in the tightness behind her eyes. Enough clarity to know that she didn't want what he had waiting for her.

The bathroom was even colder than the bedroom; the toilet seat was a punishment. She put a towel on the floor to stand on while she splashed water on her face, wondering what to do. She thought about all of the brain cells she had destroyed, all those neurons scorched by alcohol. She had a sudden fear that some of them might store memories of her mother. Even though she knew the brain didn't work like that, she felt as if a hand was grabbing at her throat. She sat back down on the toilet. Her mum's face, what was it like? Her hair and her padded coat, she could picture those; but no eyes, no mouth, nothing. She felt her own face begin to dissolve and reached for toilet roll to wipe the tears that rolled down her cheeks and streamed out of her nose, choking her.

Juddering gasps. Spasm. She held the wad of tissue over her mouth, trying to be silent. The feel of her mother's hand on her head, another spasm. Then misery. Little sobs of pure misery. She hadn't been able to say goodbye. Didn't say goodbye. Didn't say goodbye. She swallowed a throatful of sobs.

She had to stop this. She was in his house. He'd be able to hear her. She blew her nose as quietly as she could, threw the tissue into the bowl and reached for another few squares off the roll.

She forced herself to her feet, splashed more water on to her face and looked at the haggard visage in the mirror. Eyes like a mixie rabbit, she thought. Then the possibility of Malcolm, lying in bed with a morning erection. She ran the tap, lapped water from her hand, trying to stop it trembling. Please not that. Please not. She would have to explain. Just say she felt sick. No. Too raw. She started to cry again.

She lowered the toilet lid and sat again, taking deep shuddering breaths. A shiver racked her. She couldn't stay in here, she'd catch her death. She must pull herself together. Perhaps just a cuddle would be possible. She'd like a cuddle. He'd not force anything more, surely, would he? She couldn't bear it. Not just now. Maybe some other time. No, she was a Fe-Phi-Pho girl, she didn't do other times. She would add this night to her handful of other sexual experiences, filed away under 'disappointments', and just forget about it.

She got up and splashed water on her face for a third time, drank some more water and rubbed her teeth with her finger. She dabbed a bit of toothpaste on it and tried again. Her mouth felt toxic. Should she borrow his toothbrush? She knew all these AIDS phobias were irrational, but... Had they used any protection the night before? She struggled to remember. Her mind was failing. Then yes, the memory of a condom. No, she mustn't cry. She would just go into the bedroom and get her clothes and say she had to go. Brazen out the shame.

She gave her nose another blow and dried her face. The toilet flush was explosive.

As the cistern squealed, she crossed the landing and nudged open the bedroom door. The bed was empty, covers tidied, 'her' side folded back like in a hotel room. How tidy he is, she thought, for what seemed the hundredth time. She dressed in the clothes lying on the floor on her side of the bed, conscious of them being crumpled and more appropriate for dinner than for breakfast. She wished she had some make-up to disguise the stains of her grief, but she didn't. Tying her hair back and biting her lips would have to do.

Malcolm turned as Callis edged over the threshold and stood in the doorway between the living room and kitchen. It was a grey day. Out of the window the garden was dominated by a rectangle of soil, ploughed by the look of it, without a blade of vegetation. A particularly tidy vegetable patch or a zen gardening feature, she wondered. The field beyond was a meadow, grass cropped close to the ground with the brown stripes of a recent spreading of slurry.

The kitchen was all chrome and pine. Malcolm stood with his back to an incongruous Aga, which took up one entire wall of the room.

'Coffee? Or tea?'

'Coffee. Thanks.'

'No bother. Are y'all right?'

She breathed out but no words came. The lie was not possible. He sloshed coffee into two mugs, then wiped up the spillage and the bottom of both cups.

'Was it something I, or... your mum, or... Milk, sugar?'

Callis shook her head and reached for the proffered mug. She sipped. He added milk and two heaped sugars to his and stirred noisily.

'Look, I'm sorry, Callis, if I...'

'It's OK. I mean, it's not. I was not saying... It was my mum.' She swallowed and took another mouthful of coffee.

'Would a hug help?'

She nodded and set her mug on the worktop. She took a step towards him. He met her halfway, let her hide her face in his thick checked shirt. He smelt strong, and faintly of cattle. She let her hands come to rest on his back.

Diana picked Callis up from her father's house on Friday afternoon. Frances was already in the car, and Callis was glad to take the back seat. It was the first time in ages they'd been together, just the three of them.

The Teddy Bear Weekend was exactly Fran's sort of thing; fabric and needles and sewing were all second nature to her. She would no doubt grasp the fundamentals in no time and manufacture a precise copy of the bear in the pattern, complete with friendly expression on its face, leaving just enough time to tidy up before they had to leave. Diana would surely be as skillful at this as she was at everything else. She was bound to create some furry work of art. Callis, on the other hand, knew she would struggle and fret, striving for a perfect bear and cursing all the failings inevitable for a beginner. She didn't know why she had agreed to go.

They drove through sheeting rain, which slowed to a drizzle as they arrived at the Victorian mansion. They were greeted by a glamorous woman about their own age, wearing high-heeled cowboy boots, tight cream riding trousers and a frothy silk blouse. Her long blonde hair shone like a shampoo advert.

'Welcome to Fenwick House ladies. I'm Juliana.'

Diana stepped forward to shake hands. 'I'm Diana,' she said. Next to their glossy hostess, she looked almost shabby in her black pumps and long mohair cardigan. Callis was glad she had only brought jeans.

Diana turned to her and dragged her forward. 'This is Callis.' She stumbled on the doormat and dropped her hold-all.

'Let me help you with that.' Juliana turned her smile on Callis. 'What a pretty bag,' she said, standing it upright. It was an old carpet bag made out of upholstery material with wooden handles. Callis wanted to tell Juliana that it had been her mother's, that she had been going to throw it out because it was old-fashioned until Callis had saved it from her. But she said nothing and they just shook hands.

Frances stepped up with a charming smile. 'And I'm Frances.' She held her hand outstretched in greeting. 'Fantastic house!'

Their hostess looked gratified by this. 'Yes, isn't it! It's been in the family for four generations now, we're very lucky. Follow me, I'll show you to your rooms.' She lifted a clipboard from a polished wooden sideboard and checked down a list of names. 'Diana... Hunter?'

Diana tried to see what else was on the chart. 'That's me.'

'... and Frances Morrison, you're next to each other, sharing a bathroom, I hope that's all right. They're gorgeous rooms with a view down over the gardens. And Callis... what an unusual name, it's lovely, Callis MacArthur?'

Callis nodded.

'You're... oh, you're at the back, but you do have a bathroom of your own.'

Juliana swept up the staircase and the others followed along behind. At the first landing, she showed Diana to a big, bay-windowed, velvet-curtained room, which did indeed have magnificent views down not only over the garden but out to the hills beyond. Frances was delivered to the room next door.

Then Juliana ushered Callis out and back to the staircase. On the next landing she led off down to the end room. It was cozy, with Laura Ashley furnishings that suited the carpet bag.

'It's perfect,' Callis said.

'We'll gather at 5.30 for tea on the patio. I'll leave you to unpack.'

The door swung shut behind her. Callis sat on the bed. She wondered if the weekend would help her to stitch herself together or whether she would be overwhelmed by grief. Juliana seemed nice enough, if a bit posh.

What if she cried in public? She hated such shows of emotion. They embarrassed everyone. At least she had her own room. She was glad it was small.

At 5.35 she dragged herself downstairs, her footsteps muffled in thick carpet. The whole house smelled of hyacinths, two notches too sweet. She heard Diana and Frances before she saw them, laughing loudly on the patio. Frances had added a silk scarf to her standard outfit of black slacks and top, achieving her usual nonchalant elegance. Diana had put on a patchwork flamenco dress, and turned towards Callis as she approached. She looked into her face as if assessing what others could not see. 'Don't worry,' she said. 'I have gin.'

They stood around with cups of tea. Juliana mingled and got acquainted with everyone, finding out what people were hoping to make during the weekend, whether they had brought materials with them and what experience they had. She then gathered the group together in the big conservatory and introduced the plan for the weekend. They would choose fabrics and patterns and begin cutting out before dinner. She gestured to the tables up against the wall, strewn with rolls of furry cloth, felt, glass jars and Tupperware boxes of assorted haberdashery. 'On Saturday you'll complete cutting out, if you haven't already, and we'll spend the day sewing. Then we'll have all of Sunday for stuffing and finishing – eyes, ears, noses, tongues, claws, that sort of thing – so we'll hopefully all be finishing with a smile by Sunday teatime. Any questions?'

The group shook mute heads. Then the youngest of the group, a round-faced girl, who looked about seventeen and was squeezed into jeans at least a size too small, said, 'Is the fabric and all that included in the price, or do we have to pay for what we use?'

'Good point, Sally. It's all included, feel free to use whatever you want. That reminds me there are some things you can pay extra for if you'd like, some options for seeing some real animals, for example.' She swung a dazzling smile around the room like a searchlight. Then she launched into what was obviously a much-repeated spiel. 'We have lots of free options – walks to various spots on the estate where your chances of spotting animals is good. There's a lovely riverside path where there are chances of seeing fish jumping and always lots of birds. There's also a bird hide out beside the loch, we've a pine marten and badger feeding station, and if you're lucky you might spot capercaillie on the woodland walk. There's a map of those walks in your bedrooms. Alternatively, for a small extra charge, we can drive you out on to the moor to the south and see if we can spot any deer, or we can even take you to the wildlife reserve at Glenmathan to see if you can spot any of their big carnivores. That's for those of you who want to make your bears really realistic!!'

She had, of course, saved the best for last. Diana was straight on the case, enquiring about times and costs.

After a few questions Juliana said, 'You can make your plans during the course of this evening, ladies. For now, let's get started with the creative process. Gather around here, I've got fabrics and patterns laid out for you to make your choices.'

By dinnertime, Diana had begun a substantial polar bear and Frances was undertaking a grey cat, as close as she could get to a lynx, given the patterns and materials on offer. Callis had chosen a chocolate-brown velvet and was planning a small bear. The group was getting to know each other. The teenager turned out to be already planning to set up a toy business and was doing every relevant course she could find. The other participants were all women, mostly aunts and grandmothers aiming to make gifts for young children.

'I might have known it'd be full of grannies,' Diana grumbled to Callis. 'We're going to have to do something to avoid the zimmer frames.'

Over dinner and gin the three friends agreed to go on the Glenmathan drive at crack of dawn on Saturday. Frances was keen to get the morning light for photographs. 'Fe-Phi-Pho, here we go!' she said. 'It's been ages since the three of us went out snapping together.' Callis wished she could muster more enthusiasm.

'Better get some beauty sleep before the morning shoot,' Diana said.

Frances grimaced. 'Could they not arrange for dawn to be a bit later?'

Callis was already on her feet. Her mother had used the phrase 'beauty sleep' almost every night of her childhood. She needed the privacy of her room.

🐾 🐾

The alarm went at five and Callis dragged herself out of bed, dressed warmly and headed downstairs. They drank coffee out of thermos flasks from the dining room sideboard, then gathered in the grand hallway and waited for Juliana, who arrived in jodhpurs and tweed jacket as if she were about to ride out on a hunt.

'I'm not coming with you,' she said, leading them out of the front door, where a sleek 4x4 stood waiting. 'John will drive you. There's no one better at spotting animals – he can see a frog at half a mile.'

Diana muscled her faux-ex-army boots, black leather jacket and big camera into the front seat. John gave her a dismissive nod and faced straight ahead. He lacked cap and gloves but was otherwise playing the chauffeur role to a tee. Callis and Frances took the back seat and Frances began spreading out her photographic gear. Callis fingered the 'point and shoot' she had borrowed from her dad, wishing now she had brought her camera from Norway after all.

Juliana said, 'John will get you home for breakfast at about nine. Enjoy!' The door slammed shut and John pulled away.

'How far is Glenmathan?' Frances called from the back.

John took his time answering. 'Thirty miles, thereabouts.'

Frances was in taxi-driver chat mode. 'Have you been with the Fenwick estate for long?'

'Aye.'

John's reluctance to talk grew more apparent in his pauses until her interrogation let up.

They drove in silence past Inverness and across the Kessock Bridge. Dawn light marbled the water of the Moray Firth. The landscape beyond it was shrouded with cloud. There was little traffic and John barrelled along.

Frances and Diana talked camera kit for a while. Callis watched the Ross-shire fields and woods flow past. She spotted a roe deer on the edge of some trees, but didn't mention it to the others.

'What are they?' Diana gestured to a forestry plantation on the right. Two large birds of prey hung in the air above them, then one swooped down across a field as if down an ice-slide.

'Kites,' said Callis.

Frances craned over to see past her. 'Beautiful!'

The bird checked its descent and soared upwards. All three women tried to keep the birds in view until the last possible moment, their heads swivelling backwards as the vehicle curved round a long bend in the road. When Callis turned forwards, Diana was eyeing her.

'So, Cally, do tell. You're being very secretive about your brown-eyed date after the funeral.'

Callis felt the blood bloom up from her neck. She tried to keep eye contact with her friend but there was something too owlish in her face. 'No secret.' She looked down.

Frances nudged her. 'You're blushing.'

Diana swivelled her head round to face forwards again. Callis drilled her gaze into the back of the car seat.

At Glenmathan, John punched in a code and the eight-foot-high gate swung open. They puttered up the track, eyes peeled, cameras primed, peering into the tangle of young birches and willows. At a junction they met a red Land Rover and its occupant, a tall, leggy character in a tweed jacket and brogues, got out and strode over. John opened his window and shook hands with him.

'Hullo, John.' He bent down to look in at the passengers. 'Good morning, ladies. Welcome to Glenmathan. I'm Luke. I gather you're keen photographers and you're hoping for bears.'

Callis, Frances and Diana assented with gestured equipment, which their host noted with approval. 'I'm afraid the riverside road is pretty much a wash-out at the moment, so I suggest you take the upland track. It's your best bet for bears, anyway.'

The women all nodded. 'What are our chances, realistically?' said Diana.

'With John here, pretty good, I'd say, but of course there are no guarantees.' He grinned at John.

'When did they come out of hibernation?' asked Callis. Luke peered into the back of the car at her.

'Well, strictly speaking, they don't hibernate, and it's been such a ridiculously mild spring they've been out and about in good weather since February. They're full of beans just now. Keep your eyes open.'

'Are there any cubs?' Frances said.

'You bet. Four of the females have cubs, seven in total, and there are four one-year-olds still with their mothers from last year. We've lost a couple of young unfortunately; the males can be very aggressive to them, you know. So the mothers with young tend to be extremely shy. You can consider yourselves very lucky indeed if you see cubs. We saw one of the mothers up among the pines on top of that hill yesterday.' He gestured to the north. 'There's a feeding station there, so it's definitely worth a look. The mothers are hungry. You know where I mean?'

John nodded.

'Look, there's an elk!' Callis pointed down towards a patch of willows where an outsized coffee-coloured deer was browsing.

'Well spotted!' Luke tapped the vehicle roof. 'I'll leave you to it. Give me a tinkle if you spot anything interesting. Have a good morning, ladies, and good luck.'

John switched the engine into life and slid the vehicle forward for a clearer view of the elk.

'You scored the top man,' he volunteered. 'That was Luke Restil, owns the place.'

Diana nodded satisfaction. 'Nice enough man,' she said, 'though I'm getting tired of being "ladied".'

'Och, he's just being polite.' Frances took another shot of the elk and sat back.

Callis leaned forward towards John. 'That seemed a big hint about the feeding station by the pines.'

'Aye. We'll go there then?'

'Yes, please,' said Diana.

'Wherever you recommend. We're in your hands,' said Frances.

'I wonder what they feed them,' said Callis.

'Pig nuts,' said John.

'What on earth are they?' said Frances.

'Fish meal, corn.' John said. 'Plenty protein.'

The track wove up among birches, past a big rowan in smithereens.

'That's bears,' said John.

'That'll be them after the berries in autumn. Look at that! Devastation.' Callis was delighted, and even more so when John pointed out a large brown mound of bear turd.

By a grand oak, just coming into leaf, they forded a rushing burn. A roe deer bounded away into a tangle of holly and brambles. They were in thick woods now and under the shelter of a crag. Aspens stood tall and stately. More rowans hung from the rocks above.

'Delicious light,' said Frances, watching the peach morning glow through her lens.

'It's lucky we're here early in the year,' Diana said. 'Once the trees are all fully in leaf it must be impossible to see anything.'

'Hence the feeding stations, I suppose,' Callis said. 'It's probably as much about keeping us punters happy with a chance of spotting the wildlife as about feeding them.'

'Is that right?' Frances asked.

Diana looked at John. 'Bit o' both,' he said.

He slowed the car to a crawl as they approached the next bend and glided down towards a clearing, the motor ticking along, almost silent. He pointed left. 'There.'

In the shadows under a group of aspens, a brown form was head-down in a clump of wild garlic, front legs scraping up soil, snout rootling and licking.

'And a cub,' said John, rolling the car forward a couple of metres so they could see the little bundle snuffling in turned-over soil just beyond its mother. The telephoto lenses span, telescoping and sighting.

Callis put down her camera. The bear lifted her head and scanned, snout up. The cub tumbled towards her and tried to push under her body to suckle. Callis gazed, her throat choking, her eyes blurring over. The bear turned and pushed her cub away deeper into the cover of trees.

Callis took a deep breath and swallowed.

'I barely got them in focus and they were gone,' said Diana.

'But we saw them,' said Frances, jubilant. 'And according to Luke that means we're very lucky. Isn't that right, John?'

'Aye. They're shy. What now?'

'You're the guide,' said Diana. 'Take us wherever you think we might get some more wildlife.'

Callis said nothing. She felt as if she was tearing apart, as if she was splitting down the centre of her ribcage. She kept her face calm but inside she burned. Had the killing of the bear in Norway got to her that badly? She fought the urge to get out of the car and follow the bears into the woods. She had to bring bears back, it was as simple as that. She had no idea how, or even what the first step might be, but she had to do something to stop this gutted feeling. She breathed deeply until she felt herself relax again.

They drove on up into the hills, where the trees were less dense, keeping all eyes trained. A golden eagle soared above, against a spectacular backdrop of white water gushing down a bouldery slope. Low-angled sunshine underlit a bank of slate grey clouds. A group of stags struck Glen-monarch poses on the skyline. The women joked about shortbread tins and took the photos anyway. No lynx or wolves deigned to show themselves but the three photographers were well satisfied with their sightings.

At 8.30 John suggested a return to Fenwick for breakfast.

'My tummy's grumbling,' Frances said.

They all concurred.

Just before they reached the reserve gate, a female wild boar emerged from a tangle of last year's bracken and young birches on one side of the road. John stopped. Apparently oblivious to the vehicle, the sow trotted across the road, followed by five piglets, tails twirling like a procession of wind-up toys. They scuttled after their mother, vanishing into the vegetation on the other side of the track.

Diana was triumphant in the front seat, where she had had an unimpeded view out of the windscreen. She flicked through her shots, laughing at the perfect images of the pigs she had captured for posterity.

They drove back to Fenwick in high spirits. 'Good trip,' said Callis. 'I'm so glad we saw a bear.'

'Yes, I guess,' said Diana.

'My first ever,' said Frances. 'In the wild.'

'This isn't wild,' Callis snapped.

'Yeah, sorry, but you know what I mean. It seems pretty wild here. Have you seen them before?'

'Mm-hm. In Finland, and in Sweden a few times now. And I finally got a sighting in Norway, a few weeks back, which is rare.' She nearly said, 'That was a mother and cub, too,' but instead said, 'I just love them.' She wasn't sure why she needed to keep quiet about that moment in the snow and the other mother and cub. She remembered how she had felt so much more alive than she did now, as if she could be a different person, out there in the forest. It was nothing like this, trapped in a vehicle, the bears confined behind a fence.

'It's cats do it for me,' said Frances.

Callis fell quiet, cradling the image in her mind of the bear cub nudging its mother's snout. She didn't care that her photograph was blurred.

'What are you dreaming about?' Frances elbowed Callis gently on the arm.

'I was thinking about the bear, and wouldn't it be great if they really were wild.'

'I doubt your farmer would be very keen on that!' Frances laughed.

Diana turned round from the front seat. '*Your* farmer, is he now? So you had your wicked way and left him panting?'

Callis felt her hackles rising. 'It wasn't like that.'

'I suppose he was a fair enough piece of meat. Was he any good in bed?'

'Diana, you're outrageous,' said Frances.

'No, come on, I want to know.'

'To be honest, I was so pissed it's all a bit of a blur,' Callis tried to laugh.

'Oh Callis, for goodness sake, how old are you?'

Callis bristled, but said nothing.

'You can actually remember whether or not you had sex with him, I take it?'

'Yes, of course.'

'And?'

Callis felt something snap inside her, as if a bolt slid open. 'What's with the inquisition? We did, and it was great.'

Diana raised her eyebrows, but before her sarcastic comment could come, Callis, suddenly intrepid, continued, 'And I'm looking forward to the next time.'

Diana swivelled back round to the front, but not before Callis had seen her eyes widen into a glare. There was a pause. The engine hummed. John turned the car into the drive of Fenwick House.

Frances giggled. 'Naughty Callis, you know we're not allowed back for seconds.'

Callis sighed. 'Maybe I'm growing up.'

'And what is that supposed to mean?' Diana didn't turn round but the voice from the front made clear that her jaw was set and the issue was not likely to be dropped.

Juliana was there to welcome them back into the house and usher them into the dining room where the other women were already eating. She handed them a list of options and they all chose the hearty breakfast, then helped themselves to fruit and yoghurt from the lavish buffet. A couple of the other guests questioned them about their sightings, but at the first break in the conversation, Diana leaned in to Callis.

'You are joking about this farmer, right?'

Callis pulled at her hair. 'No,' she said. 'I mean... I don't know.'

Diana's chin jutted forward and her eyes narrowed. 'We have a pact.'

'I know.' Callis couldn't hold Diana's gaze.

'So you were joking.'

Callis looked past Diana and her eyes rested on a large gilt-framed painting. A man on a horse reached down with his hand outstretched, tenderly, to a woman standing just out of arm's reach, her back turned. She allowed herself to remember the feeling of Malcolm's hug. 'No, I wasn't,' she said. 'I'd like to see him again.'

'But you know where that leads. The pact – it's not just an idle promise, it's values. Independence, freedom, remember? Shackling yourself to a man is completely inconsistent with that.'

Callis took a gulp of tea. Their breakfast arrived and they ate in silence, cutlery rattling against plates. Callis chewed and swallowed, drank more tea, steadying herself.

'I've been thinking about my mum and dad. Seeing my dad at the funeral. Seeing all that... well, all that love. Love. That's another value too, like freedom.'

'Love.' Diana spoke the word as if it tasted foul in her mouth. 'What will you want next? Chivalry? Honour? This isn't the

Victorian era.' She looked round at the painting. 'This house must be getting to you. You'll be embroidering samplers and coats of arms before we know it.'

Frances was laughing along. 'It's just a crush, Callis, and you know what to do with them.'

'Crush them!' She and Diana high-fived.

Callis looked at her plate, not smiling. She speared a mushroom with her fork. 'I'm not saying I'm in love,' she said. 'I'm just saying that if I was, that might not be a bad thing.'

'Love is a fool's dream,' Diana snapped.

'You know it is, really,' said Frances.

Callis looked at her. 'I don't know what I know anymore.'

Diana gripped Callis by the forearm and Callis tried to shake her off. 'Let go of me.'

Diana's grip hardened. 'If women in the rich countries of the world do not assert their independence, what hope is there for the freedom of women in Africa, in Muslim countries?'

'Oh for crying out loud.' Callis tugged her hand loose, her knife clattering on to the plate. She shoved her chair back, eyes smarting, and half-ran out of the room, the first tears unloosing before she reached the door. Juliana was about to make another entrance as Callis barged past, breaking into a sobbing run as she hit the stairs, and not slowing down until her bedroom door closed behind her. She sat on her bed and pulled a hankie out of her pocket.

'Fucking bitch.'

🐾   🐾

By the time a tentative knock came on the door, the tear storm was over. Callis opened up to Juliana, who was holding a small tray.

'I thought you might like a cup of tea.'

Callis gave her a watery smile and took the cup, backing into the room, and sitting down on the bed. Juliana closed the door behind her and leaned on it.

'Is there anything I can do?'

Callis shook her head, then sipped. The cup jittered back on to the saucer. She looked studiously at the pastel-blue wall to Juliana's left, thinking it was almost the same shade as her bedroom in Trondheim, and realising it was a little too baby blue for comfort.

'Men?' Juliana said.

Callis shook her head. 'Kind of. Actually, the man is fine. It's my so-called friends.'

'I'm not prying. I just want everyone to have a nice time here.'

'I've broken our pact of spinsterism.' Callis wondered if she should feel guilty at this disloyalty.

'Spinsterism?'

'Since university we've been part of a group called Fe-Phi-Pho and we basically vowed not to get into relationships with men, to remain free and independent.'

'It sounds just like Diana's warrior maidens in the Greek myth. Did you know Callisto was one of them? I guess with your name you must know all about it.'

Callis stared at Juliana. 'I don't often meet people who know the story.'

Juliana stroked her hair. 'I read classics at university, though I have to admit I looked it up in Ovid last night after your name rang a bell. It's a fascinating story.'

'A classic tale of a woman who is raped and gets the blame. Though I always quite fancied being turned into a bear.'

Juliana smiled at her, as if humouring a child. 'It's just such a funny coincidence that you're in a group with Diana, and now you say you're all virgins!'

Callis shook her head. 'We're not that extreme. We haven't got anything against men per se, we're not against sex, far from it, one-night stands are very much allowed, but I'm, well, I don't seem to be willing to keep to the rule about not going back for more.'

'I see. The god tempts you back. And is he worth it?'

Callis looked down at her teacup. 'I don't know for sure. I hope so.'

'What does this god do for a living?'

'He's hardly a god. He's a foreman or something, on a farm. It's not far from here. Long something.' It was a relief to speak about it. She had another sup of tea.

'Longworth?' Juliana's voice was quiet.

'Aye, that rings a bell. But he doesn't really act like a farmer. He drives a Jaguar, for one thing. That's not exactly Old Mac-Donald, is it?'

Juliana shuffled as if she were getting bored, or restless. 'Mmm.'

Callis glanced up at her. 'You probably know him,' she said, not sure if she wanted anyone else in the world to know him.

Juliana was looking out of the window. 'Longworth is certainly part of the estate,' she said. Her air of friendly confidante had dissipated. 'Anyway, we'll be making a start soon, if you want to join us. When you're ready.' She turned. 'I'll leave you to it.'

She snapped the door behind her as she left and Callis heard her stride off down the corridor. The fire door banged. The cup trembled as Callis finished her tea.

There was little conversation between the three friends for the rest of the day. Diana and Frances took over a table and spread their polar bear and lynx fabrics out so much that there wasn't enough room left for Callis to share. She sat on her own and during breaks made a point of chatting with some of the other course participants, or going back to her room. The rest of the time she concentrated on sewing the seams of her bear, ignoring the glances from Diana and Frances. She slipped away early to bed after dinner.

When Callis came down for breakfast, Diana and Frances had gone out for an early morning walk, Juliana said. She sat next to an older woman from Pitlochry, who stroked the empty shell of her velvet bear and probed Callis in a gentle manner for an explanation of her evident discomfort. It was a relief to have someone to talk to about her mother, but when she felt the grief rising she changed topic, then excused herself.

'I'll try to finish my bear quite soon,' she said to Juliana, 'and if you don't mind, I'll leave early, once I'm done. It would be good to get back to my father.'

'That's fine.' Two figures walked past the window. 'Here are your friends now, I'd better get the stuffing and decorating materials ready.' She strode off to the conservatory.

Diana and Frances' laughter pealed from the grand hall. Callis tried to make a dash for the back staircase but Diana caught her coming out of the dining room.

'Morning Cally, can I have a word?'

Frances set off up the stairs. 'See you later, I'm off for a shower.'

Diana led Callis to the front porch, an elegant glass-roofed room with a stone slab floor and cushioned bench seats beneath ledges of fading hyacinths and newly potted geraniums, not yet in flower. They sat opposite each other. Callis rubbed her bear on her knee, sensing that an interrogation was about to begin, but to her surprise Diana started with an apology. Callis wasn't aware of ever having seen her shame-faced before, but that was how she appeared, her hands clasped in a pleading gesture in her lap, neck bent.

'I'm sorry I've not been at all sensitive or understanding this weekend. It must be awful for you at the moment. You must be missing your mother, I imagine, although I can't really. It must be dreadful.'

'Yeah. It's OK,' said Callis, 'I'm sorry I'm not very good company.'

'I'm serious, it's me that's the one to be sorry. It's not surprising you're a bit withdrawn. I should have been making more of an effort.'

Callis looked at the downcast figure opposite her. 'Thanks. I appreciate it. It is a bit tough.' She wanted off this topic. 'Time to stuff my bear.'

She started to get to her feet but Diana leaned over and pressed a hand on one leg to encourage her to sit back down.

'One other thing,' she said. 'About your farmer.'

Callis was interested. Another climbdown?

'Frances and I have talked about it and we agree that it's really important, and especially just now, while you're grieving. We can see that love and all that, goodness knows even marriage, might look different in such circumstances. And especially as you've known him since childhood, that must be… comforting?' She paused.

'Is there a "but" coming?' Callis had been listening for some tone that would stop her feeling she was on the edge of a steep bank of a fast-flowing river.

'Well yes, kind of.' Diana put her hands on the bench beside her and looked Callis straight in the eye. It was her greatest weapon, that direct gaze. It had won her every achievement of her life. 'It's precisely now, when you're off guard, that you need to be most vigilant, if that's not a contradiction. If you're not careful, in this moment of weakness you could get yourself embroiled in something that you'd never give in to in your right mind. So we're offering to be your protectors, if you like.'

'How do you mean?'

'Well, if you get any urges to see him again or anything, you can call us and we'll remind you why that's a bad idea.'

'Well, I won't need that, I'm off to Norway again in a few days. And my urges are my own business, anyway.'

'Oh Callis, you're exasperating. Think of all the things you can do: travel the world, run your own life, give as much or as little to your career, be as creative as you like, manage your own time. All that's completely hamstrung if you've got to take some other person into consideration all the time, especially a man, and before you know it, children would beckon and that's twenty years of your life, minimum, to the dogs.'

'But it's nothing like that. We've had one date. I'm not remotely contemplating any of that.'

'Not yet, maybe. But we all know where these things start, hence the pact. We can see the danger signs, Cally, that's all we're saying. Don't go there.'

Callis rubbed her head. 'I'm not going there.'

'Fine, so we're agreed.'

47

'No. Well… No. I'm not sure I want to be protected. That makes me feel… It's as if you're saying I'm unreliable. Not able to make my own decisions.'

'It's understandable.' She reached for Callis' bear, as if to stroke it, and Callis snatched it away. 'You're not thinking straight.'

'I'm sad, not deranged, you know. I may be on an emotional roller coaster. I am. But I'm not irrational. If anything I'm seeing things more clearly than for ages.'

'That's all part of it, trust us.'

'You're not listening, are you?'

'Cally, it's you that's not listening. We're offering to help you.' Diana's gaze bored into Callis as if force of eye contact was all that was required to convince her.

Callis knew that gaze and she wasn't going to let it intimidate her. She looked down at the floor, observing the deposition pattern in the sandstone. It had probably been laid down millions of years ago. Then she spoke. 'I want the freedom to meet Malcolm Johnstone again if I feel like it and not if I don't. We might turn out just to be good friends.'

'Well, friends is one thing.'

'And if we end up in the sack again, I want the freedom to do that.' She wasn't quite sure what was driving her to stick her neck out about this, but it felt true as she spoke the words.

'But that wouldn't be freedom, would it?' Diana uncrossed her legs and crossed them the other way. 'You surely don't need us to reiterate all that stuff about true freedom as restraint, liberation from the passions. Come on, Callis, that's Fe-Phi-Pho 101. Fallacy of the Appetites.'

Callis squirmed. It was true. This was basic doctrine. She had believed it all for so long. The ideal state of non-attachment had been irrefutable since she had thought it through, what, nearly ten years ago. It was completely irrational to be opposing it now. But the more Diana was adamant, the more Callis wanted to resist. She said nothing. She knew Diana was still looking her directly in the eye, monitoring. Eventually Callis met her gaze.

'And if I go ahead?'

'You mean reject our offer of help?'

Callis shook her head. 'No, if I sleep with Malcolm again?'

'Same difference.' Diana's jaw was set.

'Aw, come on. One shag.'

'It's the principle of the thing.'

'So it's not an offer of help at all, it's an order to submit to your control. It's an ultimatum.'

'You're very emotional just now, Cally. I think that's putting it a bit strongly. It's an offer made in friendship, and of course you can reject it if you choose to but that's, well, that's your choice.' She was sitting straight-backed now.

Callis found herself starting to cry. 'I don't think this is very fair,' she said, feeling the ground beneath her weakening. 'I just want...' She couldn't bring herself to speak the thought. Comfort. A hug.

Diana sat hard and silent opposite her while Callis blew her nose. 'I take it that's no, then?'

Callis shook her head, mutely.

Diana stood up. She paused. 'Goodbye, Callis.' The door swung behind her.

Callis clutched the flat bear in her lap. She ruffled the velvet fibres against the pile, then stroked them into shiny smoothness. The creature seemed to emanate resolve, a symbol of what she knew she needed to do – to make it real, to fill the idea of a bear with substance, not just to dream and play with toys and do her arid job and live her meaningless life.

She got to her feet and headed back to the conservatory. There, she selected two yellow eyes, a felt nose and a clump of kapok. She listened intently to Juliana's instructions and proceeded to stuff the bear, evenly, taking care not to pack it so tightly that it was stiff. The result was floppy and undeniably cute, and along with the stuffing it was full of wishes and determination.

Then she started making her goodbyes. 'I'm going to get the train home on my own,' she said to Diana, who was in the process of stuffing her polar bear.

49

She hardly looked up. 'I've said goodbye already.'

Frances' lynx was splendid, the first whisker being knotted into position. She, at least, got up to give Callis a hug and admire her bear. 'What'll you call it?' she asked.

'"Brown", probably,' said Callis. 'I'm not very strong on names.'

'"Brown" it is, then. Smile!' Frances pointed her phone at her and Callis grinned a false smile for the shot, trying to hide her face with the toy.

'Take care, and let us know if you change your mind,' Frances said.

Callis picked her bag up in the hall where Juliana was waiting with an evaluation form. 'I hope you've enjoyed the weekend despite everything,' she said, formal as a hotelier, no trace of her earlier warmth. Callis wondered what Diana had said to her.

She mustered one last smile and shook her head. 'It was all very nice, thank you. I'll fill this in at home.' She stuffed the form into the outer pocket of her bag.

'John's waiting. He'll take you to the station.' Juliana showed her to the door, with another, Callis thought, rather pointed 'goodbye'.

The word echoed around her head all the way home, the emphasis on 'bye'. *G'bye, G'bye, G'bye*, a voice in her head repeated, leaving her old self behind. Once on the train, east from Nairn, she got out her book, Simone de Beauvoir's *The Second Sex*, but left it unopened on the seat next to her. She sat stroking the velvet bear, her fingers delving in its fur for some answer, some sense of direction, something to fill the void that her life had become.

On the ferry back to Norway, the tiny cabin made Callis feel claustrophobic. She couldn't get her mother out of her mind, the thought of her touch, that cool hand on her forehead when she was sick as a child. She remembered sitting between her mother's knees after a bath, on the floor beside the bed, wearing her dressing gown, the comb gently tugging her hair, fingers untangling it from scalp to tip.

She went out on deck. The water frothed like a petticoat around the boat, the sea fresh as peppermint. The wake billowed up like meringue, like lace, like doilies on birthday party plates. She had a sudden taste memory of lemon meringue pie, so tart it made her cry. She said goodbye over and over, over and over. But nothing eased the failure to have said it when it mattered.

When Callis disembarked, Norway seemed an alien land, yet she could not put her finger on what had changed. She noticed that the clock on her phone had shifted forward by an hour to 12.30, remembering the joke that Norway was one hour and ten years ahead of Britain. From the headlines on the newsstand, the whole country seemed to be obsessed by the killing of the bear cub.

Callis bought a sandwich and munched it on the tram from the stop nearest the ferry terminal up to her flat at Vestmarka. Coming up the narrow path to the modern wooden house she had lived in for the past two years, she found herself imagining what it might look like to her friends in Scotland, to Malcolm even. Brashly coloured, she thought, though the ochre yellow colour hadn't struck like that before she went home. She clunked the deadlock and the door yawned open like a stranger. She dumped her bag and had a shower, but couldn't settle, so she set off again for the Institute.

Her in-tray was piled high, half from before she had left for the funeral, half unopened post. She sliced all the envelopes open, but barely glanced at the contents of most of them. One was a pollen analysis she had requested from one of the research assistants before she left. She sat at her desk, leafing through it, with a growing sense of disconnection. She knew why she had asked for it: the soil sample had come from an archaeological dig of an early Bronze Age settlement in the far north of the country, and she remembered that she had wondered what it would tell her about the climate and vegetation, and whether that would correlate with similar data from Scotland. She also distinctly remembered being excited by the possibility of making these comparisons. Now all she felt was numb.

She picked the analysis up and took it to the filing cabinet. She opened the top drawer. It was too full to add anything else. How often had she written 'weed filing cabinet' on her to-do list in recent months? Back at her desk, she plumped the analysis down on the top of the in-tray, sat down and powered up the computer. Her online inbox and filing system was in an even worse state than the paper version.

After a couple of hours of painful catch-up, Callis gave up for the day, and called Karl to ask him to invite her for a drink after work. Karl was her pal, 55, gay, as devoted to her as she was to bears. He ran a café-bar at the harbour and she had taken to drinking there. It was cheaper than most of the pubs in town and handy for the tram, plus there was always something interesting to watch as pleasure boats and fishing vessels plied back and forth between the fjord and the canal.

She arrived at 6pm. Karl had binoculars trained on a yacht making its way back from the fjord.

'Is that Michel out there?' she asked.

Karl nodded. 'It's a fine night for a sail. We haven't had many chances since she came out of the boat shed for the season. Michel's been at his salon all day and needed some fresh air after all that hair lacquer. I was going to get someone in to tend the bar and go too, but then you called.'

'I'm sorry,' she began.

'Don't be. I'm glad to see you.' He poured them both a glass of white wine from the fridge behind the bar. They took the drinks out on to the deck of the wooden building, enjoying the spring evening. They tried to ignore the huge yellow food processing factory further along the front, spoiling the view. Its fishy odour wasn't as bad as it could be some days. They watched as the bascule bridge swung open to allow a yacht to pass out from the sheltered canal into the fjord, then clunked closed again.

'Do you want to talk about your week at home?' he asked.

She shook her head.

'Books then?'

'Yeah, I'm reading a tome by Simone de Beauvoir and I'm totally bored by it. I need a bodice-ripper or something!'

'A what?'

'An easy-to-read historical romance.'

'I can't help you there.'

'Oh come on, Karl, you've always got great suggestions. You introduced me to Laxness and Pushkin and Sándor Márai. There must be something you can think of?'

Karl had appointed himself her guardian shortly after she arrived in the country two years previously. He had introduced himself in the library in Trondheim, telling her he admired her taste in books, and they got chatting, finding themselves kindred spirits in their love of good old-fashioned paper books.

'Perhaps you should try Dickens.'

'Dickens? Come off it. What are you reading at the moment?'

'A history of the Catholic Church.'

'OK, leave books. What about politics?'

'Well, it's been a hairy week here.'

'How so?'

'Norway has gone crazy about bears.'

'Cool. I saw a newspaper sign saying something like "*Thorsinn Backs Bear Bill*". What's that about?'

'Did you hear that a farmer shot a bear cub by St Olav's statue?'

'Yes, it was on the radio the morning I left.'

'Well, there's been uproar ever since. First children began writing to politicians from schools, then environmental organisations have been on the TV saying it's disgraceful. It turns out half our leaders sleep with toy bears and all of their children do. It has been like pressing some kind of button. People are horrified by the blood on our patron saint, and we Norwegians like to think we are in tune with nature. It's important to our, how would you say, "national psyche"? The bear is deep in legend, we have many stories.'

Callis was agog. 'Go on,' she said.

'It's our brother-creature. There are the macho men who want to hunt anything, of course, but for most people we prefer to think of hunting as a kind of sacred ritual, something traditional. Not brutal at all, almost a kind of worship. In the past we would thank the bear, the spirits, you know. Wiping out the last one is like killing a Brother-God. It has horrified our whole nation. We're full of shame and guilt and anger at the farmer: Boltzman, German name unfortunately for him. I gather he's taken refuge with relatives in Denmark. There were vigilantes at his house, calling for him to come out and face their guns. We have all gone quite crazy.'

'I'm glad to hear it.'

'Why?'

'I'm one of the ones who sleeps with a bear.'

'Well, I admit it, I have one, too.' They smiled, and clinked glasses.

'I was gutted when I heard the news that morning. I cried first about the bear, then about my mother. Somehow it seemed I was crying about the same thing.'

'The bear is very deep in our psyche. You Scots are a big part Viking, so you are maybe close enough to us to feel it, too. You know the way the mother bear goes to sleep in winter, burying herself away. It is like she dies. Then in spring she wakes up, she comes back from the dead with cubs, new life, like the earth is a womb. She is a sign...' he waved his hand in a circle, searching for a word.

'A symbol?' Callis suggested.

'Yes, a symbol of fertility. The bear is like the goddess of mothers, the spirit for making life. It's natural for us all to feel grief at her loss. And for you, two losses in one day. Poor Callis.'

'Are people saying this?'

'Perhaps not in so many words, but I think they feel it.'

'You should write it down. This is so important, to see it this way.'

'I could do that. Maybe I will write a letter to *Aftenposten*.'

'Go for it, Karl. Up the stakes. If bears are that symbol of rebirth then surely instead of killing them off we can bring them back again?'

'People here are saying this. Bring them back. Bring back the bears.'

'But won't they just be persecuted again?'

'That's where all the debate is now. That's the hot question. Hence the Bill – there's a private member's bill to bring some Swedish bears and set them free, put forward by Bakker. Bjørn Bakker, good name for it, huh? And the Prime Minister has said he'll support it, and I think it'll be hard to beat, and they'll give bears special status, making it a crime to kill them anywhere in the country. So it cannot happen again.'

'OK. But it's what we call locking the door after the horse has bolted.'

'It's a good step. I think we need something to make us all feel that we are not a nation of animal slayers. But of course everyone says there is no point having a bear protection law with no bears to protect. Logic demands we bring them back.'

Callis finished her wine and put it down, feeling it resonate, as if she could make it sing. 'I want to be in the ring.'

'In the ring?' Karl frowned incomprehension.

'Involved. I want to help. I want to help bring the bears back.' Hearing herself say it was like watching a compass needle settle on due north. 'If we can do it here, then maybe we can do something in Scotland, too. I found out when I was home that a friend of mine is doing a trial to reintroduce lynx. Anything's possible.'

'Maybe you should be reading Barry Lopez.'

'Who?'

'American nature writer, brilliant.'

She looked him up on her phone and nodded. 'Yeah, good recommendation.'

'More wine?'

'No.' For once she wanted to stay sober. 'I'm tired. Long ferry journey. Better go home.' She got up and in the ensuing flurry of air kisses, Michel appeared, as tall and elegant as Karl was not. Together, they always made her think of Gandalf and Frodo.

'Good sail?'

'Wonderful. Welcome back. You're not leaving?' He placed a slender hand on her arm.

Looking up, she saw his long face full of concern. 'I must. I'm sorry,' Callis said. 'I've got a lot of thinking to do.'

'We were so sorry to hear about your mother,' he said.

'Thanks, but it's not that. It's the bears.'

'The bears? Has there been another…?'

'Karl will fill you in. See you soon.'

She walked along the shore to the tram stop. Back at her flat she unpacked her bag and began tidying up. She had left the place in a mess before going to Scotland.

For a while it was steadying to impose some order on her surroundings, but after an hour or so she realised she was tired and hungry, running on empty, as her mother would have said. There was nothing in the house but mouldy cheese so she put her jacket back on, laced up her boots and headed back down into town.

It was 9pm. There was still time to grab a takeaway. The Thai place was playing dreamy music. Callis ordered a noodle dish and sat in the window on a high stool, wondering how busy Karl and Michel's bar would be and whether she wanted wine and company. She decided not. Waiting for her food, she leafed idly though a newspaper, taking in the gist of what was written. Her Norwegian was still not up to scratch. She had done the usual British thing, picking up easy words that overlapped with English, learning some polite phrases and enough chat to get by in shops and bars and restaurants. But for work, friendships or political conversations, she still often resorted to English, taking for granted the near-fluency of so many of her colleagues and acquaintances.

The newspaper was full of bears: photos, discussions of the proposed new law, histories. She plugged away at translation with the help of the dictionary on her phone. On page seven there was a piece about a meeting in Oslo to form an expert group for the reintroduction and protection of bears. She found herself wondering if there was some way to make a good name for the acronym BEAR. Bear Ecology Assessment and Restoration, perhaps. She asked the waiter if she could clip the cutting out of the paper. He shrugged permission. Scotland needs this, she said to herself. But first, Norway. This is where to start. This is where to learn.

At the 24-hour store, she bought bread, cheese and coffee for breakfast, then went home. With a cup of tea, she sat back on the sofa and called Stig.

'Hi Stig, did you hear what's happening here?'

'No, what?'

She raved to him about what Karl had told her about the bears.

'How did you get into the lynx programme?' she asked him.

'I just got asked to join in, they thought my PhD work was relevant.'

'Damn, do you think I can persuade someone that vegetation dynamics is relevant to bears?'

'Maybe.'

'I mean, the whole climate change thing has to be a major risk. And there are bound to be habitat requirements specific to bears. I've got to, I don't know, I've got to do something about bears. I'm sick of doing a job that's just ancient history. I make all this stuff up for grant proposals about it being relevant to today, but I don't really believe any of it any more.'

'So join in. Write to someone. Phone them up. Don't tell me. I'm in Scotland.'

'I might have to go for a total change of life: job, home, everything.'

'Go to bed, Cally,' he said.

She flicked off her phone and smiled around at the sky-blue walls of her living room. Eventually she took herself to bed. For the first time since her mother's death, sleep swallowed her willingly.

She dreamed that she had snuggled into a bear's winter den

and lain down next to the sleeping bear, rolling into its warm, hairy body, wrapping herself in its musky pelt, feeling its fur rubbing against her skin, its heart thumping slowly, deep in its body. The bear was not alone: it was suckling a tiny baby, not a bear cub but a human baby, eyes and fists tight closed in an ecstasy of milk-sucking. She watched the infant until it woke and when its eyes opened they were her mother's eyes, and as they recognised each other both of them began to cry. The baby's voice grew to a wail and she, worried at what the bear might do, tried to withdraw, but there seemed no way out of the cave. She woke to her own baby-like whimpering, face wet with mourning.

She began the day at home, in the doldrums, doing nothing much, mind flitting from task to task, drawing up lists, tyrannising herself with trivia. After breakfast, she worked herself up enough to call the bear reintroduction group number from the clipping she had taken the night before. It switched to voicemail so she left a message offering her services and giving her work number. Then she wrote a resignation letter to the Institute and emailed it to Yuri, reflecting that the last time she had seen him he had asked her to let him know her plans. This probably wasn't what he was expecting.

After that she couldn't settle to anything, and tricked herself out of the door for a walk, on the excuse of having no fruit in the house. With a bag in her pocket she set off, and let herself go the long way around to the shops. She plodded up the lane behind her house and into the forest, following the wooded path that wended up the hill. Her breath deepened and she increased her pace, feeling the need to pant, to push herself on. She took her jacket off, tied it around her waist and kept climbing.

A couple of kilometres up, through spruce and birch woods, she came to a waterfall, a white spate, gushing on to black gleaming rocks, splashing the ferns and mosses gathered around it as if to appreciate the spectacle. She stood letting its roaring force fill her with energy then allowed its momentum to carry her back home, deviating for only a couple of minutes to pick up essentials from the corner shop by the tram stop.

As soon as she was in the door, she knew she couldn't come up with any more sidetracks. She would have to go into work eventually. It might as well be now.

🐾 🐾

Striding from the back door down the main corridor to her office, she saw Maria, the Institute receptionist, clock her arrival. She had taken off her coat and just fired up the computer when there was a knock on her door. It was opened without needing a response from her.

Yuri shut the door behind him. 'Welcome back,' he said. 'How are you?'

It was a friendly enough opening gambit. She was prepared for a storm and thought she'd rather endure it sitting down, so she offered him a seat, stalled him while she made coffee, chatting about the funeral, the ferry crossing, not much caring what she said. She knew she had to go.

'I am surprised to get your message,' he said. 'I hope you change your mind. I do not want your resignation. Your work is important, Callis. To us. I don't want to lose such a valuable member of the team.'

She looked him in the eye and wondered if this was a purely professional speech. A predatory look had been in his eyes ever since that one night, that one mistake, drunk on vodka after a leaving do for a colleague. She had known he was drawn to her and had let the flattery of being fancied by her boss carry her along. Naked, she had discovered something reptilian about him. Her refusal to repeat that night had soured their previously collegiate friendship. She had insisted when he asked her outright to come back to his flat after a post-work session in the pub, that she was merely standing by a pledge she had made to limit her indulgence in sex to one-night stands, but it cut no ice with him. He still stood half a metre too close with a visage full of expectation.

'Perhaps you can explain to me your reasons for resignation.'

In his Russian accent the word was portentous, with its rolling r and hard g. Ressick-nation. 'Losing your mother, I understand, it is a difficult time. It is hard to be away from your homeland. If you need more time off work, you can ask. More vacation, for example, it's no problem.'

'It's not my mum,' she said. 'At least, not directly.'

'So what is it? I did not know you are unhappy. Is there something you want change about working here?'

She shook her head. 'No. It's been a great place to work. You, the team, you've all been really nice.' She had a glimmer of the disruption her departure would cause: the projects she was involved in, all the lab work that would need to be tied up or handed on to someone else. And then she remembered it was all, literally, ancient history and she was giving it up to go and save the bears.

Yuri was looking at her as if he was the one who was grieving. 'So, you have been offered something else?' he said.

'Um, not exactly.'

There was a knock on the door and Maria stuck her head around it. 'Dr MacArthur.' Callis nodded. 'Professor Eldegard from the National Science Institute is trying to reach you. She phoned here twice this morning. She says she responds to your message and wants you to call her urgently.'

'Thanks, Maria.'

She handed across a slip of paper with a phone number on it and tiptoed out to start a rumour.

'What is this that is urgent?' Yuri gave a pained smile. 'Palaeobiology is not so often urgent.'

'I don't know what it is until I've spoken to her. Obviously.' It came out sounding more petulant than she had intended.

'A job?'

'I don't know.' There was an uneasy silence. 'I'm sorry, Yuri, I might as well come clean. This is going to sound crazy, but I need to join the campaign to bring the bears back.'

He relaxed suddenly, as if she'd put a weapon down. 'You join campaigns, it's no problem. It's not reason for resignation. I am sure many others in department feel same way. We can have some little debate about it. I am Russian, I am not sentimental about bears. But it's not big deal. Some...' he paused, seeking the word, 'activism is quite OK, I think.'

'Yes, but I wasn't just thinking of a little activism. I was thinking more of giving it all I've got.'

He reached out and touched her lightly on the arm. 'Callis, perhaps you are maybe being hasty. What is it you plan? Street theatre?'

'No!'

'Your science expertise is very important here. Your historical work is crucial for us to understand how the climate is responding post-420. You have many opportunities here in the Institute. We can make many things possible for you, I think.'

Callis looked down at her feet. Yuri was confusing her, repeating her own arguments for the relevance of her work to the current crisis, referring to the atmospheric carbon dioxide threshold of 420ppm, long touted as the maximum tolerable level, but now exceeded. Perhaps she was being too hasty.

'I have spoken with Anja Eldegard. She will understand,' he said.

Callis stared at him, outrage flooding out reason. She didn't know what to say. Had he only been pretending not to know what was going on?

He got to his feet. 'You can retract resignation, you know?' He stood, waiting, mouth pursed shut.

'What do you know that I don't?' she said.

He raised both hands. 'You call Anja Eldegard. I stay?'

'No!'

'OK, come talk to me after.' He left.

Callis was sweating. She took a deep breath and reached for the phone.

'Professor Eldegard, Callis MacArthur here.'

A sonorous voice responded in impeccable English, with just a trace of a Nordic accent. 'Ah good. The vegetation dynamics expert who wants to give it all up to save the bears.'

She found a smile breaking out. 'Yes.'

'You're hired.'

'What?'

'I don't suppose you could be here for a meeting tomorrow morning? We have a roundtable with the Energy and Environment Minister. A vegetation expert with a passion is just what we need, especially an international expert. I've read your work, Dr MacArthur, and I've spoken with my old friend Yuri Zeveris and you come very highly recommended, though I think he will fight to keep you. I'd like to welcome you on to my team, if you'd be willing to join.'

She grasped the arm of her chair, needing its solidity to hold on to. Something fizzy was unbottling in her stomach. 'Um, of course. I'd be delighted. What team, exactly?'

'Oh, I thought you knew. It's the Norwegian government's expert group on Ecological Restoration, which has been set up to advise the Energy and Environment Committee. I've sent you the remit. We all know it's about bears really, that being the hot political issue as it were. But they can hardly have an advisory body on bears alone, hence the general title and the need for people like yourself to broaden it out beyond the charismatic megafauna.'

'So you need people with interests in habitat and such like.'

'Exactly. And I gather you're good on climate change, likely impacts on various ecosystems, that sort of thing?'

'That was my PhD, yes. It's a core interest of mine.'

'Perfect. You're just the woman we need. And you did say you're keen on bears?'

She could hear the smile down the phone. 'Mad about them! Always have been.'

🐾 🐾

She gobbled down the relevant email. In it Professor Eldegard explained that the post was a secondment rather than a position of employment. She also offered to help persuade Yuri if he proved unwilling to release her, suggesting that he would be amenable once he appreciated the kudos the position would bring to the Institute. The implication was clear that she should not give up her current post. The roundtable was next morning at 9am in the *Storting*, Norway's Parliament.

It was the opportunity of a lifetime, if she could persuade Yuri to let her take it up. She was bursting to tell someone her news. Realising that the window blinds were down, she stood up and opened them. The old roller snagged where it always did. Impatiently, she unfurled it and slowly rolled it up again. There was no view to speak of, just the back of the next block and a mass of piping. But the sky was blue.

She reached for the phone and called her father. It rang and rang and just as Callis expected the message service, he picked it up.

'MacArthur.' His voice was hoarse.

'Dad, it's me. Are you all right?'

'Hello, love. I'm fine.' He sounded tired, sad. 'Good to hear you. What's doing?'

She poured it out as succinctly as she could manage.

'Well, congratulations, quine. A government commission.'

'Och, it's not quite.' She liked the phrase, though.

He made her explain what little she understood about the workings of the Norwegian Parliament, the *Storting*, and the role the expert group would play.

'Well, quine, your mother would have been proud.'

It cut right through her. The gap between the high she had been on and the pain of missing her mother set her teetering, one foot on joy and one on sorrow. 'Dad.'

'Aye. I mean it. She'd've been proud of you. As I am. I've probably not said it enough.'

'Thanks, Dad.' She felt her heart swelling up into her throat.

'And what does your boss say, what's his name, the man in the moon, Yuri Gagarin?'

She laughed. 'Zeveris. Yuri Zeveris. He's, um, I'm not sure he's going to like it.'

'Have you not asked him?'

'Well. Kind of.'

'It's a good job you've got there. Don't do anything that'll jeopardise it.'

'Um.'

'Och, Callis, mind you don't let flattery get the better of your senses.'

The bubble inside her chest deflated.

'OK, Dad. I'd better go.'

She put the phone down and sat looking at it. She took a deep breath and felt tears welling up. She bit them back, hard. Work. She would just focus on the work.

Turning to her in-tray, she took the first sheaf of papers off it, but couldn't take a word in. Damn it. She had to do it. It was an offer too good to refuse. Her father had never understood that kind of thing anyway.

She checked the night train to Oslo. There were berths available.

Before she could lose confidence, she strode along the corridor to Yuri's office and tapped on the door. She blurted all she could remember about the meeting the next day in Oslo and how she had to go to it. She couldn't not go. And was that all right? Could she have his permission?

He stared back, one finger crooked under his nose, his blue eyes impassive. Callis began to feel like a teenager asking to stay out late. She elaborated on the need to attend the meeting the following day, repeating what Anja Eldegard had said about kudos, then petered out.

He put his hand down on his desk. 'So you retract resignation?'

She nodded and gulped. 'Yes.'

'We will assess how much time this role will take. When you return from Oslo.' He turned his head towards his computer. The interview was over.

She slipped out of his room, but as she was leaving he said, 'Perhaps I can buy you dinner before your train?' He had turned back to her, his smile avuncular.

Callis, taken aback, could think of no immediate reason to refuse. 'OK.'

'We can meet at Macbeth.'

The Scottish bar was a long-term Trondheim institution. 'I'm not *that* bothered about the Scottish thing, you know.'

He shrugged and pointed to himself. 'Maybe not. But I like whisky.'

What was he plotting? 'You can get whisky anywhere.'

'You want to meet somewhere nicer. The Brittania then, I'll book a table.'

The Brittania was an excessive choice, but the luxurious hotel's restaurant did have a good reputation and it was convenient for the station. 'OK,' she said.

'Nineteen hundred. I will expect you.'

Back in her office she found herself annihilating tasks in minutes that had been stagnating for months. All day she had colleagues coming up to her with commiserations for her loss. She batted them off one by one with her news about being a government advisor on bears, but each one left a mark.

Mid-afternoon she went home and changed out of her jeans into her best leather boots and skirt, topped by a patchwork jacket she had bought several years back and hardly ever worn. She packed light.

On the way back to the Institute she stopped on a whim at Michel's salon and asked if she could get her hair done. He gave her a slot right then. She didn't know what she wanted, as ever. She had never really latched on to the idea of hairstyles. Hers was ginger, ragged by default because she rarely took the trouble to get it tidied up until it grew down into her eyes. It had reached that stage.

Michel made her smile, gave her coffee and a biscuit, told her that it was the colour of fox's fur and asked if he could cut it short. They talked bears and he growled and squealed and strutted while she laughed and trembled under his hands, letting herself sink into the luxury of his fingers on her scalp, massaging her neck, feeling as if electric currents were sizzling beneath her hair follicles.

By the time she emerged, groomed and renewed, Yuri was waiting for her at the hotel. She hurried there, not sure what to expect. He was at a table close to the door, with two glasses and a bottle of champagne. Not whisky after all. He waved the waiter over with a plate of fish roe.

'You deserve,' Yuri said, when Callis made protestations at the expense. 'Not real caviar, but as good as they have here.'

As they clinked glasses he said, 'You have new hair. It is very beautiful.'

Callis managed to smile and accept the compliment, while something inside her cracked. The champagne must be going to my head, she thought. She became acutely conscious of his perfect teeth, the point of his tongue once as it licked across his upper lip, the clusters of stubble above and below his mouth, his Adam's apple bobbing over the open shirt collar as he spoke. Flashbacks to their night together kept intruding, making her feel embarrassed all over again.

They talked bears mostly. She showed him the programme of the meeting the next day. He put his hand over hers and she left it there until she had to move it, feeling its weight pressing down on hers. He did not seem to notice that she did not touch the fish roe, or was too polite to comment.

She got out her phone and sent a message to confirm that she had officially retracted her resignation and he messaged back accepting the retraction. They clinked glasses again and downed the last of the champagne. 'Now, dinner,' he said, picking up the menu.

They ate well, but her food became harder and harder to swallow as his arguments against the proposals for more bears mounted up. As he got more drunk, his scorn at the attempt grew stronger. 'This is small country,' he said, repeatedly. 'Too small for bears. Bears and people make conflict. It is inevitable. You can see in Russia. Bears must be hunted. They need big forests, much bigger than here. This is too small country. Tomorrow, you will hear many people talk in Oslo. But it is political talk. You are ecologist. You must think like scientist. Not stupid dreams and politics. Anja Eldegard, she is dreaming. Do not listen. You must be rational.' He rolled the 'r'. 'Rational. This is too small country.'

She argued in vain, her grasp on reasons why bears might feasibly survive being brushed aside by Yuri. 'This is too small country,' was a fixed point from which he was immovable. His certainty rocked her. And between his assertions about the impossibility of bears expanding their range, he smiled his blue-eyed smile and insisted on the importance of her work to the Institute. 'You are one of us,' he said. 'We need you here, for real science. Tomorrow, you will see Committee of Dreams. And you come back to Institute of Truth.'

Callis played with the ring she had slipped on to her little finger, a Celtic knot she had not worn for years. She bit back her response that the 'Institute of Truth' had an Orwellian ring to it. She could almost pity him, he seemed so desperate to persuade her.

'I'm going with an open mind,' was all she said.

After their plates were cleared away, he refused to let her chip in for the bill. 'It is my pleasure.' He helped her into her jacket like some nineteenth century gentleman and picked up her luggage.

She was tense as wire as they walked towards the train. At the end of the platform he put her bag down and gave a little bow to her. 'Perhaps some other time we can be more...' he paused, 'longer together. Good night.' He turned, without waiting for a reply, and paced out into the darkness.

Professor Eldegard met Callis off the train, somehow picking her out of the crowd and pouncing on her with a jocular shout of 'Callis, *velkommen*!' She was tall, with short grey hair, and dressed in plain, loose brown slacks and jerkin. But over them she wore a calf-length knitted coat, in a traditional red, blue, black and white pattern, with big bone buttons. As they marched to the *Storting*, Callis had found herself needing to jog to keep up with the professor's stride, her swinging cloak sweeping aside anyone who might obstruct her way.

She was physically intimidating, without doubt, standing a head taller than most men, but this was offset by her wide, easy smile and when she turned her shrewd dark eyes on Callis, the younger woman felt an instant sense of protection. At the *Storting*, people stood aside to let her sign Callis in at the security gate, and they coursed on downstairs and through underground passages to another building, then up to the pine-lined committee room. Professor Eldegard sprawled into a lavishly padded seat indicated by a nervous-looking official, who nodded a terse acknowledgement as Callis was introduced and seated next to her. With winks and waves, the professor greeted many of the others already gathered.

Minister Thorsinn marched into the committee room at two minutes past nine, took the seat reserved for her at the head of the oval table, laid her file down and started proceedings without drawing breath. She was open to all and any suggestions to reduce the public outcry. If a programme to release some 'replacement' bears into the wild would help then she would have no objection in principle. She was willing to support Bjørn Bakker's bill. She nodded acknowledgement to the MP who nodded back. There would be those who would oppose this move, arguing that persecution of the bears had been inevitable, and any future bears would meet the same fate as the last. She believed they were wrong and bears had a future in Norway. The Environment and Energy Committee and the *Storting* would take any actual decisions but she hoped that they would be guided by the expert group and agree to an accelerated expansion of the residual population, and possibly also an introduction of some new genetic material.

She paused and circled her gaze around the table, meeting the eye of each person as if gauging them. 'I have full Prime Ministerial backing. If we can bring bears back, we will.'

Callis noticed herself holding her breath, and let it out in a long slow exhalation, blinking at the minister's performance. She guessed that what was going on was the closest thing to resurrection any normal human being, particularly a politician, could achieve. The symbolism was incredible.

Those seated closest to the minister responded, turning the general thrust of what she had said into suggestions of specifics. There was a proposal to set a release date of the following Easter. A nice addition to the symbolism, Callis thought, but that would mean less than a year to find some bears, decide where and how to release them and plan a monitoring and protection programme for the ensuing years. It was a tall order, but the table was stuffed with power and eminence. The country's greatest scientists, most famous naturalists and broadcasters, and environmental activists Callis had only dreamed of meeting one day, were all there around the table. It did not seem quite real that she was among them.

'Our vegetation specialist, Callis MacArthur, will identify some suitable locations for release,' she heard Professor Eldegard say to the minister, 'taking into account both historical factors and future pressures such as climate change.' She glowed. I get to choose the site, she thought. How cool is that? And then she remembered Yuri. He would be scornful of the proceedings.

'Very good.' The minister and professor nodded to each other.

'How long will that take?' They both looked at Callis. Suddenly she wished that she had not got on the train to Oslo. She had no idea what such a task might involve. It could easily be several years of work; a team of PhD students could devote themselves to the question for much of the next decade; a whole new institute would be required for trans-European collaboration involving hundreds of scientists. And they had eleven months for the whole thing.

She swallowed. 'Two months should be sufficient,' she replied. 'Perhaps three to be realistic, allow a bit of slack.' A bit of slack? She must be insane.

The grey heads bobbed with approval, moved on to the tricky matters of farmers and funding. There was much consideration of the compensation to be used to pay farmers for any livestock used, and the benefits of the Swedish incentive scheme that required farmers to protect their livestock and paid them to do so. Callis intervened at one point suggesting grants to upland farmers for bear habitat enrichment measures such as planting fruit or nut trees. This was noted with agreement. Otherwise, she sat, hands sweating, stomach churning at the utter ridiculousness of even thinking of surveying Norway's entire land cover and determining the most welcoming places for bears in a mere ninety days. At all, for that matter.

They broke for lunch and Professor Eldegard, ('Anja, please, we're colleagues now,') led Callis along to the dining room.

'We are glad to have you in the team, Callis. Not afraid to speak your mind, that's what we like. Positive input, good, very good. It's going well. We've got the farmers on the defensive, the public's all on our side. If we can keep it positive for a few months we'll get the Bill through Parliament.

'You and I can put our heads together about locations. We'll need a methodology to put before the Executive. Can you put some thought into that? Evidence from other countries will be important, most important. I can give you all the leads you need: Romania, Slovakia, Russia, Sweden, Finland, France. A whirl around some of those will be essential for you to make a strong case, don't you think? Are you free later? I should run you through some names. It would be good to have you out there straight away, really, before we meet again in a fortnight. Yes. If you could at least visit Romania – they have more bears than anyone else, you know – size up the habitat ideals, and hit Finland and France to find out about their experiences with bear range expansion...' The professor reached for her notebook and scribbled names down in it. 'My secretary will give you contact details, and do travel arrangements if that would help. Make sure you mention me, the panel, all that. Yes? And if you could sketch out a methodology for site identification by, say, next Monday?'

Callis wondered how forced her smile looked. 'I'll do my best,' she said.

'Excellent. Look, I'd better eat with the minister. Good to have you on the team.' She pumped her arm, sighted her next target and was off.

Callis had two weeks to visit Finland, France and Romania. The names she was given by Anja were in obscure corners of each country: Kuhmo on the Russian border with Finland; Evian on Lake Geneva in the French Alps; and Brasov, in the Carpathian mountains, Transylvania. If she had three months, it would have been an adventure, three weeks might have been fun. Two was a logistical nightmare.

She perched on a chair in Anja's office, scanning travel websites on her phone. 'I suppose flying's out of the question?'

'Callis, what's it going to look like?' the professor said. 'Government climate change advisor flies to Romania on bear research. I don't think so. We have to be squeaky clean, I'm afraid. Ask one of the office staff to book you on a train.'

They tried every route they could think of but couldn't fit all three into a fortnight, so Callis dropped the French trip. She headed back home to Trondheim on the night train, knowing she would have barely thirty-six hours to persuade Yuri that her role on the Bear Panel was a credible interpretation of her job description and to get leave to devote the next three months to choosing the bears' reintroduction site.

The next morning, she went straight from the train to her office at the Institute. She was ploughing her way through unanswered mail when Yuri knocked on the door and entered without waiting for an answer. He looked pink-cheeked and flustered. He asked her how the meeting had been.

'Fascinating,' she said.

He raised his eyes.

'I need to go to Romania and Finland to find out about bear habitat.'

'I will not stop you taking leave.' He sat on the arm of the chair nearest to the door.

'Can this role not be considered part of my job here?'

'Of course not. You are hired as palaeobiologist, not wildlife tourist.' The tone of his voice was light, as if he might be joking, but his eyes were steel.

'Oh.' Callis wondered how to crack open this statement, wishing she had asked a less direct question. 'I'll be going tomorrow. For two weeks. I guess I'll take it as leave, then.'

'Will you have dinner tonight?'

She looked at him. He had a fake look of nonchalance, but under it she sensed something else. What was it? A kind of longing? Was she hoping their drunken fling might be repeated?

'I've got to pack for tomorrow and sort out all this!' She pointed at the mountain on her desk. 'I've the same at home.'

'So I bring you something and we eat at your house. You must eat.'

She relented and he grinned. Callis felt as if she was sitting on an Aberdeenshire beach, sun on one side, cold breeze on the other.

'Give Maria any work she can do. She is happy to help,' he said.

'Thanks, Yuri. See you at eight.'

After tackling the urgent work, she wasted an hour on Fem-Comm, where Diana had posted an animated polar bear, 'to watch over you'. It was wearing a T-shirt with '*Independence*' on it, chanting 'Freedom, freedom'. Callis silenced it, deleted its shirt, and gave it a heart-shaped balloon saying '*Love*'. Within minutes Diana had posted her another Independence Bear, but this time it was saying 'Fe-Phi-Pho Freedom'. Callis silenced it and stripped its T-shirt, but this time gave it a white dove cooing 'peace'. Diana turned it straight back into the Independence Bear, now stamping its feet in time with the chant. Callis sighed, gave up, and went home.

Yuri arrived at her flat wearing pointy shoes and jeans, a woollen sweater and a crisp collar, failing to look casual. She handed him a bottle of beer and he sat watching her sorting her mail. Shortly after he arrived a delivery man knocked at the door with rice, curries, samosas and popadoms.

She had called Karl and Michel, not wanting to face Yuri alone for the whole evening, and they arrived with a crate of chilled Kingfisher. Yuri kept the food warm while Callis got herself organised. Then she sat down and filled them in on the previous day, winding Karl and Michel up into glee at the reality of having to choose a site for the bears' return. They tucked into their curries with gusto, clinking beer bottles for the return of the bears. Yuri was quiet.

'It sounds like something is really going to happen,' Karl said.

Callis nodded. 'There's definitely political will. But the crunch will be after the recess when the Environment Committee looks at the detail. There are lots of people out there who think it's a crazy thing to do. It'll be a fight between Grizzly and Teddy.'

'Let's hope Teddy wins,' said Michel.

'What do you mean?' Yuri looked at him, shaking his head.

Michel started explaining as if Yuri hadn't understood the words. 'The farmers' argument is that bears are grizzly, big, scary and fierce, and the conservationists want to remind us of how much we love teddy bears.'

'Will the bears eat your children or cuddle them?' Karl said.

'Exactly. Do we love them or fear them most?'

Yuri gave Michel a withering look. 'There's a long way between love and fear.' He emptied his bottle and got up to get another from the fridge. 'Don't you think, Callis? Anyone want more beer?'

'Why not.' Callis left the first question unanswered.

After beers and eating, they did the Russian thing and started working on a vodka bottle. Yuri's toasts became more personal, his banter more suggestive. Eventually Karl hauled Michel to his feet and they made a boisterous exit.

Yuri caught Callis as their wave of hilarity receded, kissing her full on the mouth in the hallway.

She pushed him away hard. 'No,' she said. She remembered the night they had spent together. She had kissed him, touched him and felt nothing but the rub of flesh on flesh, the heat of mere friction. Scrape against him as she might, no flames kindled at all, not even a spark.

He tried to put his arm around her and she heard herself

saying, in a voice more confident than she was used to, 'Yuri, I need to make it clear that night was a one-off.'

'Oh.' He looked at his feet, then at a point just above her head. There was a long silence, during which he seemed to turn to bronze.

Callis thought of Diana. This was how it was done in Fe-Phi-Pho: direct and to the point. She felt hollow inside. Now she had to deal with the job issue. It wasn't a good moment, but there was no time. 'About this bear panel...' she began.

'No, not about it. Nothing about it. I do not agree. Am I clear?'

'But...'

'No but.'

'My job description says only that I need to do research on vegetation dynamics. Which is what I am doing for the panel. And it will be good for the Institute.'

He switched his gaze to the cupboard to the right of her head. 'In my country we learn difference between vegetation and animals quite young.' He pronounced vegetation as if with a double 'g'. 'I see education in your country is defective. Bears are not veggetation.'

Callis stared at him hard, wondering what he was thinking, sensing his anger and feeling a twinge of fear.

Suddenly he met her gaze, and smiled. 'Callis. Don't make this mistake. We have new pollen from Finnmark, it is important development on climate change impacts. You are needed here for our analysis work.'

'I can still help with it. The technicians know what to do and I'm not going to be vanishing off the earth, I just need some time for the panel.'

His smile remained but seemed to thin. 'It is not only time. What about commitment? Focus?'

He reached towards her but she stepped aside. 'You should go. I need to get my head together before the train, make sure I've got everything,' she said. He offered to take her to the station to see her off, but she refused.

Sighing relief as she shut the door behind him, she leaned

her back against it and shook her head. She wondered if she should feel guilty, but didn't. More than anything she felt like chuckling. No regrets. For once in her life, she was clear about what she did not want. Once was quite enough, thank you, just like it should be, according to Fe-Phi-Pho. And as for the job, the more he pushed her, the more certain she became.

🐾 🐾

The journey to Romania began with the night-train to Oslo, then a twenty-hour ferry trip to Kiel followed by two more days and nights on the train. The bear committee budget stretched to a first class berth so Callis had peace to sketch out some ideas about a methodology for site identification. Fortunately communications were good for most of the journey, and she discovered that the government's entire data library was available to her with no access constraints. She spent half the trip downloading data layers and brushing up on her geographical information system skills, wishing she had spent some time to spend face-to-face with the geeks in Oslo before she had left. Still, they seemed to be able to perform miracles via cyberspace.

Her plan took shape. The basic methodology would be to decide where the bears would like to live, then rule out where people wouldn't like the bears. Hopefully there would be somewhere left, to focus in on other factors like climate robustness, ecosystem integrity and landscape connectivity; the hard stuff that might make all the difference for their long-term survival. The challenge for the next fortnight was to come up with the six priority habitat attributes for the bears. After that she would crunch the maps and look at geopolitical constraints.

Brasov was a shock after Oslo. Callis felt as if she'd gone back in time as she got off the train into the crumbling concrete station, and swayed like a mariner on solid earth after seventy-two hours of constant motion on the rails.

She was met by Valentina, a bleached blonde who shook her

hand firmly, welcomed her in strongly accented English, and whisked her to a parked car with shaded windows. They sped out of town, Valentina gesticulating ambiguously at landmarks as they hurtled by. Callis felt vertiginous and exhausted.

'Where are we going?' she asked, as Valentina swerved to avoid an oncoming log truck while overtaking a bus.

'You go to hunter cabin. You want to see bears?' She sounded impatient.

'Yes, that's right. And I need to meet with Petr Scazia.' She had vaguely recognised this name when Anja had recommended him, and wondered, not for the first time, if it was him she had heard on the radio talking about the shooting of the bear the morning after her mother died.

'Yes, yes, Petr, of course,' Valentina nodded vigorously. 'What you want to eat?'

'To eat? Um anything is fine, really.'

'Sausage? Cheese?'

'Do you mean for a meal, or…?' Callis was baffled.

'I take you to hunter cabin. There you need food. We stop in Rasnov, go shopping. Yes?'

'OK. And how long will I be at the hunter's cabin?'

'I think you go away on Thursday at seventeen o'clock. Yes?'

'Yes, I think so, back on the train. So I'll be at the cabin until then? When will I meet Professor Scazia?'

'The professor? I don't know. I am just pick you up, take you to hunter cabin. I am told get food. That's all I know. You have money?'

'I've cash euros.'

Valentina nodded.

'So, I will be at the cabin for three nights?' Callis said.

Another nod.

'And, um, is there a phone there?'

'I think you have cell phone. Yes? Here.' She screeched to a halt at the start of a row of inauspicious-looking buildings, remnants of the Soviet era, concrete stained with damp. Valentina burst out of the car. Callis struggled with the handle, the door creaked open and she clambered out. It was surprisingly hot in the May sun.

'Market, this way.' Valentina strode up the street, disappearing down a cutting. Callis followed, and sure enough, the alley was lined with stalls. Headscarved women were selling vegetables under red-and-white-striped awnings: lettuces in all their organic variation, glossy radishes, baskets of muddy carrots and potatoes, strings of onions and clusters of garlic.

'What you like?' Valentina said. 'Grow here. No chemicals.'

'This is great! I've not seen a real food market like this for years.'

Early cherries, boxes of individuals, gave off sweet smells of sunshine. The nearest stall holder waited patiently for her to begin choosing, smiling a gap-toothed grin as Callis beamed over her vegetables.

Valentina grabbed a handful of green pea pods. 'You want?'

'Oh yes, I love peas.' She stuffed them into a paper bag proffered by the stallholder. Callis grabbed a large and succulent-looking cabbage and Valentina chuckled as she handed it over.

'Good,' said Valentina, smiling. Callis took a bag and started loading up courgettes, potatoes and bunches of herbs.

'Good food!' she repeated. Valentina laughed as if she had grown it all herself.

After the market they went to a grocery and stocked up with local cheese and sausages and several plump loaves of bread.

'Vodka? Wine?'

'Yes, yes please.'

They staggered back to the car laden with sufficient food to fatten up a bear for hibernation. Valentina's retail-fuelled good humour retreated behind her driving frown. She set off again at a breakneck pace up a narrow road out of town, past a big factory belching fumes.

'What's that?' Callis asked.

'Paper factory.' They drove alongside the mill and the unmistakeable rotten-egg whiff of sulphurous emissions from the wood pulping process began to percolate into the car. Valentina switched the car ventilation from inlet to air conditioner to ward off the stench. As they reached the main gate a sign read, "RomFor Ecopaper".

'Centre of Eco-Crime,' said Valentina.

'Are they having a big impact on the forests here?'

'Terrible,' she said. 'We fight them. They buy permit for destroy everything.' She rubbed her first two fingers against her thumb to indicate cash. 'Our politicians want one thing only. Our forests all for sale. It terrible.'

They slowed behind a tractor with a trailer full of hay rakes and swarthy people in checked shirts and jeans. Valentina blasted on her horn for it to pull over and let her past. The hay-cutters stared sullenly as the car overtook them.

'People cut hay by hand here still,' Callis remarked.

'People here very poor.' Valentina took a sharp left turn off the road on to a rough track that forced her to slow down at least enough to avoid the worst of the potholes. They drove between fields with stooks of hay.

'It's early for hay,' Callis said.

'No, May is normal first time.'

'How many cuts each year?'

'It depend on rain. Two, maybe three.' Valentina gesticulated to the right. 'Bears.'

Callis looked around, excited at the prospect of seeing a bear so soon, but all she could see was the track, lined with fruit trees.

'Look, trees broken.' Valentina pointed out where branches hung, snapped from the trunk, whole sections of the tree reduced to smashed wreckage. 'Bears eating plums, later, July, August.' The trees, Callis eventually understood, were planted for the bears, to try to keep them away from the fields of maize and beans.

The fields ended in an abrupt line and forest stretched onwards to the high horizon, up the steep-sided valley and beyond, layer upon layer of green, hazing out into misty mountains. Valentina pulled up in a sloping compound and stopped the car beside a cabin sheltered by a huge beech tree. The wooden building appeared big enough to house a modest conference of hunters.

'So. You are here. I pick you Thursday at fifteen. OK?' She pointed to her watch, tapped the three. Callis nodded. 'Here Theo.'

A khaki-dressed brown man with a gun on his back was wandering towards them. Callis could see another wooden cabin further off into the woods, down the track. 'Theo,' Valentina announced as they got out of the car.

'Hi, I'm Callis.' She shook his hand. He eyed her town boots, jeans and patchwork jacket, then looked her in the eye and gave a shy smile.

'*Vy govorite po-russki*?' he asked.

'*Po-russki nyet*, sorry.'

'*Français? Allemagne?*'

'*Français, un peu. Pas bien.*'

'*Moi aussi! Vous voulez voir l'ours?*'

'*L'ours. Oui. Grrrr.*'

He grinned. '*Bon. Nous allons marcher à huit heures. D'accord?*' He did a walking sign with two fingers and pointed at the eight on his watch.

'*Huit heures, oui. Bien.* Er, Professor Scazia?'

'*Petr? Oui. Il est là-bas.*' He pointed up beyond the cabin, into the woods.

Valentina was unloading bags and food and dumping them unceremoniously on the ground. She got back in the car. 'I sorry. Going now. I late. Bye bye,' she said, out of her window.

'Thank you,' Callis said. 'See you on Thursday.'

'Yes. Good luck for bears.' She smiled a warm smile. 'Ah, water.' She said something in Romanian to Theo, who nodded.

'*Le bain,*' he said to Callis. '*Viens.*' He picked up the two heaviest bags and led her into the cabin. There were several dormitory rooms, one showing signs of occupation.

'Petr,' said Theo, pointing to an empty bed.

Callis dumped her luggage in another room and continued to follow Theo around. A massive wooden table dominated one room, another contained some basic kitchen items: a two-ring gas hob, wood stove, cupboards, sink. Theo turned the tap. It sputtered, dribbled, then gushed into the grimy porcelain. Next to the kitchen was a small tiled bathroom with a ceiling-height wood-burning stove to heat the water for a primitive shower unit. A toilet with no seat and a small pink sink completed the mod cons.

'*Parfait*,' she smiled. He took her outside to show her the shed where firewood was stored, and another with a diesel generator.

'*Lumière*,' he said, grinning at who knows what private joke. He shrugged when she clearly hadn't got it, then took her by the elbow back into the house, showing her a cupboard with a stack of candles, firelighters and matches. Another cupboard beside it contained blankets, sheets, towels and pillows. He filled her arms with everything she might need to sleep comfortably and waited while she took them to her chosen bed. Then he left her to it. '*Huit heures*,' was his parting shot.

Callis sat down on her bed, exhausted. It was three o'clock, time for a nap before dinner. She liked it here. It was quiet, just a mutter of birdsong and a distant sound of water. All the sharp edges of her life seemed softened here; Diana, Yuri, her father, all seemed far away. An old tune came to her, one of those mournful Highland melodies her mother used to sing, like a lullaby. Listening to the thread of notes, she lay down and let thought slip away.

🐾 🐾

She woke to a sound of breathing so close she was awash with terror. She opened her eyes. A dark-haired man was standing next to the bed.

'You must be Callis,' he said. 'Sorry, I alarmed you. I didn't know you were here. I was snooping about to see where all the food had come from. You shouldn't leave it lying around. Bread especially, the bears love bread. We try to keep them out of here.'

'I feel a bit like Goldilocks,' she said, sitting up. It was a stupid remark, she realised as soon as it was out of her mouth, but he just smiled.

'Excellent. We'd better find you three bears.'

'Professor Scazia?' Callis guessed. Feeling rather compromised to be making his acquaintance in her T-shirt and knickers, she held her hand out.

'Petr, please,' he said. 'Sorry. I'll leave you to your snooze.'

'No, really. I'm awake. I'll get up.'

'You must be exhausted after your journey.'

'It's a long way from Oslo to Brasov.'

'*Brashoff*,' he corrected her pronunciation. 'Would you like some tea?'

'I'd love some, thanks.'

'I'll go make some, then.' He paused at the door. 'I like you already.'

She got dressed and met Petr properly in the kitchen. He pointed to the kettle on the stove. 'Nearly boiled. Go out on to the deck. I'll bring the tea out.'

They sat side by side on the bench outside, backs against the cabin, looking out across the Strimba valley, a green luxuriance of oak, fir, beech, willow and fruit trees of all persuasions, all in spring finery, their blossoms fluttering in the late afternoon breeze. Callis breathed in the warm fragrance and listened to the hush of leaves, birdsong, a distant chatter from the river. Her head was ringing from the journey, but each mouthful of air breathed her back into herself, tension dropping away as the green soothed. She nursed her tea, revelling.

'It's lovely here.'

'Yes, it's a special place,' Petr agreed. 'I'm glad you could come. It's important for people to come here and see this. I think the world has mostly not heard of us, of what we have here, but I don't know any better place, not for bears anyway, except possibly west coast Canada.'

'Russian Far East?' Callis suggested.

'Hmm, maybe.' He looked sideways at her, then away. 'I prefer here. The birds don't sing in Russian here.'

They chatted easily. He was a comfortable man to sit beside.

'I need to understand where bears love to be,' she said.

'Anja filled me in. Don't let's waste time. Tell me what you think you need to know, I'll help in any way I can. For what it's worth, I think you simply need to watch some bears. Ask them what they like. They'll show you far more than I could ever tell.'

'I think I need to see maps, know some basics, numbers.'

'Satisfy the left side of your brain. Later. Let the forest whisper to you first, go and smell some blossom, watch the butterflies, feel the snow-melt water on your skin. Be a bear for a couple of days. Trust me. You look like a woman who needs to growl awhile.'

She looked at him. His gaze was smooth, green, luxuriant.

'You sleep in the afternoon. That's a good start,' he said, with an elfin smile. She began to fool herself that research and seduction could be combined, but then she thought of Yuri.

'I think I'll go for a little stroll,' she said.

He nodded approval.

'Is there a phone signal here?'

He pretended affront. 'What would we want with a phone signal? Bears don't use phones.' Then he relented. 'Is it urgent?'

She shook her head. 'Not really. Tell my dad I'm safe and sound.'

'Will he worry? You're an adult.'

She shrugged acquiescence. 'Three days off the hook. What a treat.'

'That's the spirit.'

'How do you speak to Anja?'

'I have my ways and means. Go for your walk. I'll make some food. Did you meet Theo?'

She nodded.

'Did he give a time?'

'*Huit heures.*'

'*Bon. Déjeuner à sept. Vous voudrais baigner, Mam'selle?*' He spoke French like his mother tongue.

Instead of agreeing that she wanted to bathe before dinner she invited him to use the informal '*tu*' form of address. '*Tu peux me tutoyer, Monsieur.*'

He laughed. 'Of course, all the bears use "*tu*".'

He studied her and she couldn't resist his gaze.

'Hot water would be great,' she said eventually. 'Three days on the train. Better smell sweet for the bears.'

'Your wish is my command.' He gave a little bow. 'They don't like perfume, though, so don't get too clean. I'll put the stove on. Go walk.'

She walked. Breathed. Smelled. Watched butterflies. She considered bathing in the snow-melt water from the mountains, but after testing it with one hand thought better of the idea and contented herself with listening to the river's chorus as it wound down the glittering leaf- and blossom-festooned glen. The woods were rich with curved fernheads unfurling, strawberry flowers and wild garlic among deep leaf litter. She returned to the cabin curious, hungry and full of anticipation of what *huit heures* would bring.

Shortly before eight o'clock they set out. Dusk was falling. Theo was in front, gun slung over his back, a huge flashlight in his hand. Petr brought up the rear, armed only with another torch. Both had the footsteps of cats, silent on the track. Callis' boots crunched and clicked on the stones. She tried to stay on the verge but sometimes the herbage was too thin and she would be forced back into the vehicle ruts. Even on the grass her feet seemed to be noisier than both of theirs put together. The more she tried to quieten her steps, the more chunks of stone seemed to get in the way, clattering as she kicked them. She endeavoured to divide her brain between her feet and observation of what was around her.

They were walking between trees, down towards the hay meadows where crickets scratched their evensong. The river chattered on their right, bickering as they approached, reducing to a murmur as the track wound away from it. Out in the forest, night sounds began. An owl screeched. Bats fluttered, their squeaking so high it seemed illusory.

Theo stopped and raised his hand. Callis halted behind him.

Something scuffled in the bushes a few feet away, then huffed and moved away.

'Wild boar,' Petr whispered. 'Sow.' Theo shone his light but Callis saw only swaying vegetation. The invisible pig rustled away. They walked on.

Callis was electrified with attention, all her senses stretching into the dusk. Night was emerging from the earth, rising through the undergrowth, up into the canopies of trees. Between their leaves the first stars gleamed. An owl swept past like a gloved hand brushing away cobwebs.

As they walked, Theo stopped from time to time to swing his beam around. Once, he flashed up a roe deer standing just out from the wings of the forest, frozen on a meadow stage, its eyes gleaming pearly in the torchlight. Later, he caught a fox trotting on some night errand. It was like watching the action on some urban closed circuit television: grainy glimpses of nocturnal happenings, snatches of inexplicable other lives.

Theo was flashing his torch with increasing regularity, becoming agitated. Petr stepped past her, tapped Theo on the shoulder and murmured in Romanian.

They turned back up the path, retracing their footsteps. Callis tried to resign herself to not seeing a bear that night. Any bear for miles around would, presumably, have fled from the combination of their smells and noise and glare. She concentrated on her feet. The zen of quiet walking, she reflected to herself, was one of many skills she had yet to master.

The river rewound its story on their left. The herbs on the verge gave up sweet smells as they trod, and a heady fragrance of blossom wafted down from a tree. Callis stared into the darkness and fought back her disappointment, but it seeped up and out of her eyes into a grieving trickle. She trudged along between the two men, letting tears fall, not wiping her eyes so that Petr behind her would not notice. Her inner voice chanted in time with her feet, 'I am too sad for this, I am too sad, too sad, too sad, too sad.'

A shape welled out from the shadow of a willow thicket

and loped into the path ahead, trailing a pungent musk. Petr grabbed her upper arm. Theo pointed with a beam. Her finger followed. The animal crossed into shadow on the riverside. They stood, frozen. It reappeared, moving in a fluid shamble up the path ahead of them, its big feet padding over gravel without the merest wisp of sound, swift and sure and... gone. Back into darkness.

Callis exhaled. The spotlit rump was indelible on her mind's eye. She strained into the black for another glimpse. The bear's scent hung in the air.

Theo's torch scoured the night, and then once again caught the bounding body, crossing a clearing up towards the edge of trees. There it stopped and turned its head, nose up, taking one last dismissive sniff, before plunging into the forest.

Petr reached for Callis' hand and gave it a quick squeeze. She turned towards him, beaming, then realised her expression would be in shadow. She felt Theo touch her arm. He gave the thumbs-up sign in the light of his torch. She thumbed back.

Now her feet were light. The way back to the cabin was a blur, her mind filled with the images of the hairy body and the rhythm of its steps.

After they returned and Theo headed home, Petr and Callis shared a bottle of wine on the cabin deck, looking out across the stretch of darkness that was the river into the deeper dark of the forest beyond. The moon rose, a dented lantern. It turned the black sky to grey, paling the stars.

Callis didn't want to talk. She sat back, listening to the night noises, indeterminate scufflings out there in bear-land. In her imagination, she followed the animal back into the forest. She pictured it poking its way through the night woods, foraging, taking any opportunities that might arise for food, browsing on juicy green vegetation, crunching on a squirrel's hoard of nuts, rooting for tubers of ferns. The forest was a great feasting hall to a bear, full of the season's specialities: a frog here, slugs there, perhaps a mouse, a rich mixture.

Petr seemed to understand her quietness. No doubt he'd

seen countless visitors breathe out after the long suspense and thrill of their first night walk. He poured them each a second glass of wine. They clinked a toast. 'To bears.'

'Tomorrow I'd like to walk in the forest,' she said.

'Of course.'

She yawned. In the dark she could barely make out his features, but somehow she could hear him smile. 'I thought I would be buzzing with excitement, having seen a bear,' she said, 'but I'm sleepy.'

'Good.' He ruffled her hair. 'The excitement was out there. There will be more adventure tomorrow. We'll put you to bed soon, sing you a lullaby.'

His whisper was spiced. She sipped her wine.

'I wonder if…' She stopped.

'What?'

'Nothing. I was thinking of home.'

'Your home. In Norway?'

'Scotland.'

'Ah, Scotland. Beautiful.'

'You've been?'

'Yes, of course. I took some bears there, oh, what, six years ago now.'

'Bears? You took bears to Scotland?'

'To Glenmathan. You know it?'

'Yes, I was there recently. I saw a mother with cub, it was lovely.' The memory of the bear sighting was still fresh – and it was good to have hit on something positive to recall from her trip home, in among the misery of the funeral and the fall-out with Diana and Frances. 'I hadn't realised the Glenmathan bears were from here.'

'Yes. So do you know my friend, Luke Restil?'

'Not really, but I have met him.' She remembered the tall man who had greeted them that morning, the way he had acknowledged her half-intelligent question about bears from the back seat of the 4x4, how moving it had been to see bears in her home country, even if they were behind a fence.

'Luke's great. He spent a lot of time here on the large carnivore project. Glenmathan's only a wildlife reserve of course, not like your plan in Norway, but it could be a real home for them one day, don't you think?' It was as if he had known what Callis had been thinking and spoke it aloud. 'Bears should roam wild again in Scotland, in those great glens. I felt it strongly when I was there. They would do so much good.'

'How do you mean, they'd do good? They're hardly going to be cuddling people.'

He looked at her, one eyebrow raised, long enough to make it plain what he thought of such a remark. 'It looked to me as if their contributions would be more than welcome.' His tone was that of a lecturer.

She bit back a trite comment about shitting in woods and wondered what he might be getting at. 'Excuse my ignorance, Professor.' He raised the eyebrow again. 'What contributions?'

'Seeds, mainly.'

'Seeds?'

'Yes. Seeds.'

Callis was looking at him blankly. 'It's amazing how few people understand this,' he said. 'After the ice age, how do you think the fruit and nut trees managed to recolonise Europe? How did all those oak trees make their way up into northern Scotland? Acorns don't blow in the wind, they need to be carried, same for all the fruit – brambles, raspberries, cherries. And what better seedbed is there than a big mound of bear crap? And did you know that we should thank the bears for apples? Over thousands of years they've eaten the biggest, fruitiest, sweetest, yummiest fruit and spread their seeds around. They're the masters of selective breeding. So if you look around at all the fruit in this forest, which all the other birds and animals can enjoy as well, it's in large part thanks to the bears.'

'I didn't know that.'

'Well, well, well, you botanists don't see the forest for the trees.'

'I'm not a botanist.'

'What are you then?'

'I normally say ecologist.'

'Well, good. Bear ecology fact one, they spread seeds.'

'Do they eat much fish here?'

'Some, not a huge amount. But it forms an element of their diet. It's not like America, where the bears pull the salmon out of the rivers in huge numbers, capturing all those nutrients and fertilising the forest. But they do their bit for the ecosystem here, too.'

'What else do they eat?'

'Let's go and see tomorrow.' He took her glass. 'More?'

She shook her head.

He corked the bottle. 'I'll wake you for a dawn walk.'

'Yes, fine.'

He went inside. Callis got to her feet. He reappeared with a candle for her. 'Sleep well.'

'Dawn.' Once more Callis juddered awake to see Petr standing over her with that not-saying smile. He handed her a mug of tea as she struggled into a sleepy sitting position.

'You're tired?' he sat down on the end of the bed.

'Hmm. I'll be OK once I'm awake.'

'How long do you want to walk?'

She blinked blearily.

'I think you're too tired. We'll keep it short.'

'I'll be fine once I wake up.' She rubbed her eyes. 'Honestly.'

'No. You'll need to sleep later. I can tell. It's not a problem.' He shrugged.

She sipped the tea.

'How are you about a gun?' he asked.

She shook her head. 'I'm not big on guns.'

'Will you be worried if we do not carry one?'

'Should I be worried?'

'Some people are,' he said. 'Most people are.'

'I've read that you're only at risk if you come between a mother and a cub, or between a bear and its kill.'

'Yes. They can get a little grumpy if you disturb them when

they're eating.'

'There are worse ways to die.'

'Many.'

They understood each other. She finished her tea. 'Thanks.'
He took the cup.

'Ready in five minutes,' she said.

She dressed and took a hasty turn in the bathroom. Petr was
waiting for her, calm on the deck, a small rucksack beside him.
He slung it on to his shoulder.

'Breakfast,' he smiled.

They set off upstream, facing into the breeze flowing down
the glen, following a track that hugged the bank. The world was
all dew-spangled spiders' webs caught between grass blades and
freshly dropped blossom. As they walked, the sun rose, creep-
ing down from the uppermost miraculous golden green tips of
beeches on the opposite side of the river. Birds twittered in high
branches. Here at ground level the shadows remained cool.

The path was wide enough to walk side by side. Petr seemed
to adjust his stride to hers, his arms swinging loosely as he
padded along. She noticed he had a camera on a belt and for a
moment she regretted her decision not to bring her own on the
trip. She had decided her phone would do, but she had even left
that in the cabin. What the hell, it was the experience, not the
record, that mattered. She found herself relaxing, a sense of flu-
idity coming into her body as she paced and breathed. Rounding
a bend, he pointed ahead: a red hind was grazing in a clearing. It
caught wind of them and melted away.

He pointed out an anthill, a huge mound of fir needles and
leaf litter, with a dent in one side. 'See that hole, that's a bear.
They love ants. The grubs are high in protein and fat and we
estimate they might account for as much as fifteen per cent of
a bear's protein intake. You don't often see a fully intact mound
in the woods here. It must be a constant nightmare for the poor
ants.'

'Fifteen per cent,' Callis said. 'Wow.'

As they moved out of the forest shade into the space the

deer had occupied, the warm sun was sweet. Bees and butter-flies guzzled on the herb-rich under-storey. Scent billowed in the morning warmth and the last drifts of mist dissolved. A grasshopper scraped an inscrutable song.

They strolled on up the valley. As they came out of another dense overhang of fir trees, there, in the river, was a dark, hairy animal.

Callis stood, not daring to breathe. A breeze touched her face; they were downwind. The creature dawdled in the shallows, its back to them. Petr reached for his camera. The noise of the river trickling among stones hid the sound of his movement. The bear was oblivious to them.

Petr took a cat-step sideways, towards Callis, and whispered, 'White Scar, female, five years.'

Her fur was rough, shaggy. She seemed close enough to reach out and scratch. Callis imagined the touch of pelt under her fingers and became aware of the animal's primeval smell. The river skittered and splashed at full volume. The moment was endless, the world complete.

She stood feeling a thrill root through her into the ground beneath her feet, so powerful it seemed as if it must surely make the earth tremble and give them away. But the bear just lumbered on upstream, muscular step by hairy-legged step, her rump an impossibly beautiful, dark, wonderful, scruffy, big roundness. After a few metres she raised her head, ears like a teddy, furry and round, but alert.

Callis held her breath. The bear's nose, a sharp point not at all like a teddy's, lifted, sniffing. Her shoulders tautened. She sniffed again and was off, up the far bank, into the dark vegetation. Hidden.

The river sang. Callis gazed on, in rapture, her eyes watery. So close! So close! To be so close to a bear! For the bear to be so scruffy, so real! To be so bear!

A camera clicked. Petr lowered the lens from his eye. It was pointing at her. He was smiling, too.

'You're beautiful,' he said.

She shook her head, blushing. 'No, she's the beautiful one.' She pointed to the bear-shaped space in the riverbed. It hung like a chiming bell, its emptiness loud and portentous.

He chuckled.

Callis hugged herself. She wanted to bounce and cheer. 'Thank you,' she said.

'What for?' He was putting his camera back in its case around his waist.

'For showing me the bear.'

'Me? I didn't do anything. Thank her!'

'I'm so excited.'

'You're like a little child.' He smiled. 'And that's a compliment.' She could tell. 'Can I hug you?'

'Of course!' He stretched his arms out. Callis crushed herself to him, squeezing her joy between them. Her hands crossed behind his back. He smelled of wood smoke. His arms slowly wrapped around her. He felt bigger than he looked. Powerful. He did not squeeze, just held her, lightly. She felt a tension in her shoulder muscles release. He rubbed his chin slowly across the top of her head and made a deep sound, a short, animal groan, like hunger.

Callis pulled away. There was no sign in his face of anything that could be the source of such a sound. He looked serene, fluid.

'Did you see her move when she smelled us?' he asked.

'Yes, amazing speed. She was there one moment, then gone.'

'Faster than an Olympic sprinter,' he grinned. 'If a bear chases you, forget it, you can't run away.'

'It's the way she looks so floppy at rest and then all that flesh is suddenly rippling muscle.'

He nodded.

'She scampered away like a dog,' she said.

'No, not like a dog, like a bear.'

She giggled. He took her arm. 'Come on, breakfast time.'

'Where will she be now?' she asked.

He gestured up into the forest, the looming fabric that cloaked the riverbank up as far as the ridge line, and said. 'She'll be way away up there. She'll put distance between us. They don't like to encounter humans.'

'Will she be looking back, watching us?'

'I doubt it, but who knows?'

'Do you think she knows you, like you know her? Is she thinking, "There's that handsome Petr with a strange woman"?'

He laughed. 'What's the ugly brute doing with *Scufiţa Roşie*, you mean.'

She looked blank.

'Little Red Riding Hood.' He grinned and tugged her along the path towards the next sunny clearing.

After breakfast they walked on, up the river valley. Callis kept her eyes peeled for more bears but perhaps White Scar had warned them off. They did see a pine marten, its yellow chest like egg yolk spilled down a bib, bright eyes scrutinising them from a fallen beech trunk before bounding off into the undergrowth. Beside the path grew a profusion of raspberry, strawberry and bramble. Everything seemed to be in flower. The woods were diverse stands of fir and beech giving way to giant sycamores and oaks along the river's edge. Sometimes, rounding a bend, they would get a perspective on the forested slope, with its rich tapestry of greens, rowans, hornbeams, ashes, willows, birches and hazels jostling for position.

By mid-morning Callis was flagging and they turned back and strolled down the valley for lunch and an afternoon snooze. They had the perfect excuse: this was what the bears would be doing, too.

🐾 🐾

Callis woke from her doze without prompting and lay listening to Petr's faint snoring in the room next door. She got up and by the time she had splashed water on her face, Petr was also up, in the kitchen, chopping vegetables. They ate a quick dinner of pasta before setting out for a hide a few kilometres upstream.

For the first kilometre they took the same path as that morning, then broke off up a tributary of the Strimba river.

They followed its valley, winding and twisting up a steep slope. Callis was glad it was now the cooler part of the day. Even so she was sweating hard. Petr stripped off his shirt. Balls of moisture formed and rolled down his back. After an hour he stopped where the path crossed by a wooden bridge over the river. A short fall trickled into a pool.

'I need to cool off,' he said. 'Coming?'

He dropped his pack, untied his boots and peeled off his trousers. Naked, he splashed into the water. It looked too delicious for Callis to refuse. She contemplated stripping naked but, with British prudery, kept on her sweat-drenched T-shirt and knickers.

He shook his head. 'You've got your clothes wet. You'll get cold later.'

'I'm shy,' she said. 'And anyway they're already sweaty.'

'Bears don't wear clothes to swim,' he chided.

'They keep their coats on.'

He chuckled. 'You're a funny one.' He rolled over to float outstretched from a black mossy rock, his buttocks white and touchable. He stuck his head under the water, then pushed forwards towards the waterfall, letting it pound him before emerging with a gasp and shaking himself like a dog.

Callis wallowed tamely, her T-shirt billowing. She would have to take it off to dry, baring herself then, anyway.

'I can see through it, if you were wondering,' he said, as if reading her mind. 'Very nice!'

She splashed water at him, blushing, but liking him for it.

'Do you have something else to wear?' he asked. 'It'll get cold later.'

'Yes, I brought a fleece. It's in my pack.'

'Why are you shy?' he asked. 'There's no need to be here. Just me and the bears.'

'I don't know why.'

'Are you scared of me?'

He was sitting, dripping on a slab, his hair sleek, his brown face shiny with wet, dribbles of water trickling down his chest, hair just visible between his legs, thigh raised. He is gorgeous, she thought. Any sensible woman would be throwing herself at that body. The sudden image of Yuri's scrawny frame came to mind and the very idea of bathing in a forest pool with him made her want to cackle. And then she couldn't help but think of Malcolm, whose body she could barely picture, except it was bigger, much bigger, than the one before her.

'More of men in general,' she said, 'rather than you in particular.'

'Why?'

She wondered where this conversation was going, where she wanted it to go.

'I'm not sure. Apart from drunken one-night stands, I haven't had much experience with men. I don't know what they're look-ing for.'

'What are you looking for?' he asked.

She looked at him again, felt herself starting to lose her foot-ing. She floundered on to her front, felt the T-shirt balloon stu-pidly on her back and rolled back again. What was she looking for?

'I'm looking for someone who's satisfied with me, I guess.'

'You have to want more than that, no?'

'Really. I want to be enough for someone. So they don't want something, someone else. So they're satisfied.'

'But what about you? What about your satisfaction? Your own needs, your own appetite?'

'I haven't thought in those terms.'

'I recommend it.' He smiled that warm smile. She wondered what exactly he recommended. She let herself think momentar-ily of what it might be like to touch him. To feel him touch her. It would be like touching mercury. He was too perfect to contem-plate, and far too dangerous. She rolled over again.

He was hauling himself up the rock, water sweeping from his skin. 'We'd better get to the hide before it gets much later,' he said. Dusk was clambering up the trees. The last glimpses of sun had abandoned the pool. 'I'm not watching you, don't worry,' he said. 'Here, dry yourself on this.' He tossed her his shirt.

'Are you sure? I'll get it wet.'

'Take it.' He was emphatic. 'Take what you need. It's allowed.' He stepped into his jeans and put his back to Callis to tie his boots. Then stood, waiting. She dried and dressed, her attempt to hurry thwarted by damp skin.

He grinned. 'Let's go see the bears.'

She gave him his shirt back and he put it on. She felt bad, although he didn't appear uncomfortable. She squeezed out her T-shirt and knickers and strapped them to the outside of her pack. They walked on.

Five minutes further up the track they diverted on to a small side-path towards a wooden hut raised on stilts. He motioned her to silence. They tiptoed towards it and up the ladder to the door, which he unlocked without making a sound. Inside were two beds, a bench, two plastic chairs and windows on all three walls. Beside the door, a cupboard, which he rummaged in, extracting two small sacks and a gun.

'Stay there,' he said, heading out of the door.

Callis felt the shudder of his movement down the steps. He emerged into the space in front of the hide, gun on back, shaking the contents of the sacks out into an old tin drum and a wooden trough in the middle of the clearing, then a scattering under a pine tree a few metres from the building. Alert as a marmot, he gathered up the sacks and retreated. The hide swayed again as he clambered back up the ladder, soon reappearing in their stilted retreat.

They sat on the wooden bench by the front window. Callis willed herself to settle. A few birds chirruped over the faint trickle of a stream. The breeze had dropped and the trees stood still and silent. Callis became aware of her breath slowing. She fought the urge to cross her legs, desperate not to fidget.

Petr nudged her elbow and pointed into the gloom under the trees at the far side of the clearing. A form swelled out of the shadow and lumbered into clear view. Callis clutched the narrow windowsill and held her breath. A big bear, much bigger than the one they had seen earlier, was heading straight for the old tin drum to investigate the treats Petr had offered.

Callis dug her fingers into the seat of the bench. The bear stuffed its head in the drum and scoffed up the contents, then swaggered over to the trough, close to the hide, so close they were able to watch the big long tongue slurping at its contents and see its shaggy coat, greying and baggy as a borrowed suit. After emptying the trough, it stood up, front paws on the structure, as if about to preach from a lectern. Callis stifled a laugh, trying not to make a noise or sudden movement that might give them away. The bear turned its head and sniffed before slumping back down and strolling over to lick up what it could find under the pines. It did a thorough job of cleaning up the food, unhurried but watchful, before merging back into the shade of the forest.

Darkness was settling out of the woods. Soon, peering out, it was impossible to distinguish animal from shadow. Callis rubbed her eyes, her cheeks sore from smiling. Petr lit a candle then lounged on one of the beds.

'He was lovely!' breathed Callis.

'That was Old Grey,' Petr said. 'He was the top bear until last year.'

'And what's the food you put out?'

'Chocolate,' he grinned. 'Bears love chocolate more than anything.'

Callis rummaged in her pack and produced one of the bars of Divine that she had brought for some unpredictable moment of need. He rubbed his hands. 'Real chocolate!' He closed his eyes, leaned towards her and opened his mouth. He groaned ecstatically when she placed a chunk on his tongue. He chewed and swallowed. 'More!' He made the stupid face again, mouth wide, eyes screwed tight. Callis had an urge to touch his tongue with her finger, or even her own tongue, just to trick him, but resisted and gave him more chocolate instead, laughing. He savoured it with exaggerated glee, then opened his eyes and leaned towards her, planting a swift kiss, lightly, on her lips. 'Thank you. For that, you deserve some cognac. You like cognac?'

'I'm ambibivorous.'

'What's that?' He looked concerned.

'It means I drink anything. Like ambidextrous.' He shook his head. 'It means you can use both hands, like for writing, not right-handed or left-handed.'

He nodded. 'Ambi…'

'…bivorous. Yes, I'd like some cognac.'

He beamed at that. 'Good. Take some.' He handed her a bottle out of his bag and a chipped teacup from the cupboard. 'Take as much as you want.'

She poured a generous measure and then some. He was giving her his fatherly smile. She passed back the bottle and said '*Slainte mhath*.'

'Slann ze jar?' he said.

'*Slainte mhath*. It's how we say "cheers" in Scotland. *Slainte*.'

'Slanj' he repeated.

'Meaning health. *Mhath*.'

'Va,' he echoed.

'Good. It's Gaelic, our old language.'

'*Slainte mhath*.' He clinked the bottle against her cup, then sat back, stretching his legs out on the bed. 'You drink well.'

'Yes, I learned to take a drink from my father. Maybe I take a few too many.'

'And not only for pleasure maybe?'

'You're getting to know me.'

'I hope so. I'd like that. Taking a drink is OK.'

'But only for pleasure?'

'Especially for pleasure.'

They supped in silence for a while, then talked about the three bears they'd seen. Callis emptied her cup and asked for a refill. 'Will Big Grey still be out there?'

He nodded non-committally. 'Maybe.'

'Is it safe to walk?'

'It's safer in here. Do you want to walk?'

She shrugged. It dawned on her that he might not intend going back to the cabin. 'Can we sleep here?'

'Of course.' He gestured to the bed he was sitting on and the other with its blanket roll neatly in the corner.

'And will there be bears here in the morning?'

He gave that nod. 'Maybe.'

'Toilet?' She asked. He pointed to the bucket under the bed. It would be an intimate night.

She crossed to where he sat, face half lit by the candle, reflected in the window, and watched herself sit down beside him on the bed. He put an arm out to welcome her, and stroked her as if she were a little rabbit or a mouse, his fingers gentle on her hair, her neck, rhythmic, soothing, calming.

'I could drive you crazy,' he said eventually. 'Be wild and free, but take care of yourself.' He carried on stroking her hair, his paws ambling from crown to nape in a hypnotic motion.

Callis let her hand creep on to his thigh, where it lay, tongue-tied. His touch murmured its thunder on her neck and she said nothing in reply. It dawned on her that he would not move upon her, would not force a pace, and she did not know how to carry on. It was as if he lay floating out on some vast body of water, and she was stranded on the shore with no clue how to reach out to him, how to take the plunge. She had only ever been to bed with men who knew what they were aiming for and she had been content to get there with them. Her sex life, such as it was, had been led, she realised, entirely by male appetites. She had received phone calls, letters, invitations to dates. She had said yes, and yes, and sometimes no, but she had never asked or offered, never led. She had responded, been towed along, but had never driven and never sought. Now she felt she might give it all, but here she was, not being asked for anything, with a man who had stolen the passive role.

She wondered if she should ask his permission but knew already what the answer would be. She forced herself to take a deep breath and before she could let go of the courage it mustered, she reached her hand up to his cheek and drew his mouth to hers. Her tongue tasted brandy, chocolate and the darkness of him.

'You're beautiful,' he said, for the second time that day. He cupped her face in his hand, his eyes soft, still, unflustered.

'What do you want to do?' she whispered.

'Anything. Anything you want.'

She pulled away. He was like a dog endlessly returning a stick. 'But what do *you* want?' Her voice was a croak.

'I want everything,' he shrugged. 'But I am more curious about you, about where you might want to take me, what your taste might be.' He paused and smiled. 'Are you here because you think that's what I want?'

She shook her head.

'Good.' he said. 'Promise me you won't do anything because you think I want it.'

'OK. The problem is I'm not sure I'm... My own appetite, I'm not sure I know what it is. I'm not used to thinking like this.' She got up and stood by the window, peering out into blackness.

'It's not about thinking.'

'I think about everything.'

'Sometimes you need not to think, just to feel, just to be, to let yourself be.'

She looked at his reflection in the window. He was gazing back at her. 'A masseuse once told me I'm too cerebral.'

'Cerebral?'

'Use my brain too much, analyse everything.'

He nodded.

'I don't suppose bears analyse so much.'

He shook his head.

She stood staring out into nothing for a long time, and when she turned back he had stretched out, eyes closed, a model of relaxation. She watched his long, slow breaths, then tiptoed to the other bed, unrolled the blanket and lay in the flickering candlelight. Her pulse thumped in her head and her mind grated itself on questions: Could she join him now? Was that what she wanted? Was it freedom she really needed, or love? Which was she most frightened of?

Part *Two*

I woke to Petr's eyes, two pools of serene green. 'Listen!' he whispered: a scraping, scratching noise came from below the hide, which was rocking a little.

He glided upright and beckoned to me to approach the window. The scratching sound stopped, then re-doubled. The hide juddered.

I hauled myself awake and, still wrapped in the blanket, joined him, peering out of the front window. Down below, a huge male bear was rubbing himself against the post holding up the right side of the hut, back scratching in an ecstasy of friction. Petr grinned and stretched in imitation of the animal.

The bear dropped to four paws and sauntered out into the clearing, lifting his head to scent, then pausing to chomp some dandelion flowers. He checked out each of the places where Petr had left treats the night before, licking hopefully under the pine tree, sticking his head into the drum, rocking the trough, like a teenager ransacking larder shelves.

'No chocolate for breakfast,' said Petr.

The bear took his time, making do with something to snack on from a fallen branch, a beetle or a slug perhaps, and another mouthful of a fern. Turning a stone, he dug determinedly for a while, munching.

'What's he got?' I asked.

'Roots.' Petr shrugged. 'Worms maybe. Grubs.'

The bear looked round at them, muddy snouted, rubbed its face in a grassy patch, huffed and lumbered off into the trees, his dark pelt merging with the shadows.

'He's huge.'

Petr nodded, rolling his bedding into a neat bundle. 'That's Big Black. He's the top male. You're lucky to see him. He doesn't visit here often.'

'How big is he?'

'300 kilos or so.'

'That's massive.'

'Yes, exceptional, even for here.'

I unwound myself from the blanket and rolled it up. I felt calm and well rested. Brand new, as Mum would have said, a new woman. 'How old is he?'

'Eighteen years old, maybe twenty. The old grey we saw last night, he was top male for years, but Big Black is dominant now.' Sitting on the bed, he reached for his boots.

'Do they fight?' I asked, following suit.

'Maybe. Not much. They know who's biggest, strongest. Last spring I saw Big Black chase Old Grey off a deer carcass. It was a wolf kill, and Grey had pushed them off but Big Black fought him for the meat. Old Grey conceded. Knocked off the pedestal. There's nothing to gain for him continuing to fight and lose, so he stays out of Big Black's way. The younger males, too.'

'And what about the females? How do they behave with him?'

'Oh, he's dangerous. He'll kill their cubs if he can. They'll steer well clear unless they're in season.'

'And then?'

He looked at me as if to indicate it was obvious.

'Well?' I said.

'He bites her, scratches her, generally throws his weight around acting like a thug, and she growls and bites back a bit until he overpowers her and then afterwards she gets the hell out of there and won't speak to him. If she is unlucky enough to bump into him again over the next couple of years he'll try to eat her babies. He's a bastard.'

'Typical man.' I regretted it as soon as it was out of my mouth.

He looked put out. 'Not all men want to be fathers, you know. Some of us are motivated purely by aesthetics.' He frowned at me. 'We can learn a lot of things from bears, but romance is not one of them.'

This was a different person speaking from last night. I saw I had annoyed him. He seemed to be waiting for a reply, but I didn't know what to say. There was, somehow, more information here than I had expected. It needed thinking about, chewing over. We packed our bags in silence. I found myself regretting what had not happened the night before. I wondered what might have been possible if I had not been afraid.

Without debate we were leaving the hide. I watched as Petr made last-minute checks, considered the gun and decided to leave it, then led the way out of the hide. At the top of the steps, he scoured the woods, then descended, agile as a squirrel. I clambered after him and dogged him back to the main path where we could walk side by side.

'Are you hungry?' he asked.

I nodded.

We struck a fast pace back to the cabin, where Petr made omelettes and I laid the table. Over the food, we conversed in the sane tones of colleague scientists, as if there had been no talk of being bears. Petr considered what else I needed to see to equip me for the site selection back in Norway. I said little, just prompting with questions from time to time. Petr decided it was important for me to see a winter denning area.

'I think the den sites are perhaps the most important constraint, particularly for breeding success,' he said.

'Surely food supply is more crucial.'

'You've seen the forest, you've watched them browsing, fishing in the river, digging, all that feeding behaviour. I've told you about their hunting and scavenging skills. If there is food there, they will find it. They are very versatile. In Scotland you have not much good forest but many deer. That's fine. The bears will adapt.'

'It's Norway I'm looking at, not Scotland.'

'Not yet, maybe, but you must look at Scotland. It's your home country.'

My dream sparked. If Petr Scazia thought bears in Scotland was possible, that made it something more than a crazy whim.

'Are you serious?'

'Why not?' His eyes gleamed.

We were back on shared territory.

'It would be wonderful to bring them back, after a thousand years, but it's not exactly likely.'

'You are independent now, no? No more Queen?'

'Well, we still have her, in fact. She's ancient now. But yes, we aren't ruled by a government in England any more.'

'Bears are the symbol of rebirth. They seem to die in the winter cold, then every spring they cause a miracle.'

'I've heard this idea before. Are you saying we should use bears as a symbol of rebirth of the Scottish nation?' He stirred his coffee and said nothing. I felt the idea taking root.

'Symbolism is everything,' he said. 'Conservation of big mammals is all about finding channels for fear – we instinctively fear carnivores. We have to convert that, transform it, into love. Fear and love are quite close, I think.'

'Do you really think so?'

'Yes. Religion is based on this idea. Conservationists can learn a lot from priests – mixing fear with reverence. In the old days, right back to the Neanderthals, and everywhere on earth where there were bears, there were cults who worshipped them. The ancient Greeks kept it up. You must know all about that with a name like Callis!'

'Yeah, some.' I somehow wasn't at all surprised that he knew the story of Callisto, who was turned into a bear, and then into the Great Bear constellation.

'Anyway, worshipping them, revering them, was definitely useful for the bears. I think we need to get as close to that as we can again. It's all about symbols, about awe.'

'That's what has been lost in Norway.'

'Not just in Norway, everywhere. You will need to get it back to some degree if you want reintroduction to succeed.' He tossed back his coffee. 'Lecture over.' He grinned. 'On a more practical level you need to identify somewhere with good winter accommodation, so we'd better go and have a look at what we have here to give you some ideas. It'll be quite a hike. Are you up for it?'

'Of course.'

We packed food, waterproofs and survival kit for an expedition into the wilds then set off. As we walked Petr appeared to shrug off the scientist role and return to the creature of yesterday, loping up the same path as on our first walk out, smiling in the sunshine. It was the shallower slope of the main river valley and we made good progress. I could already feel myself starting to benefit from all the exercise and time in the forest. My senses were quicker, my muscles responded to being used with a glow of well-being, I was more alive. We walked in companionable silence, with only the odd gesticulation at a striking butterfly or a pause to appreciate a birdsong.

As we walked deep into bear habitat, I stuffed impressions into my brain like a hamster filling up its cheeks: bright white strawberry flowers catching the sun, the pungent crush of wild garlic, a spatter of water from a stream tumbling down the steep slope to the river valley, the cool shade of fir trees, a gold and red flash of a butterfly, a muddy wallow made by wild boar, the cronk of a raven flying over, a fur-filled fox scat.

After a few hours the track ended abruptly at the confluence of two even-sized streams, both cascading down from much steeper ground. We took a small path beside the northerly flow. It soon petered out. Clouds billowed down from the mountains. There was a rumble of thunder. We continued alongside the stream as best we could, where it splashed down from a precipitous crag. I made a scrambling struggle of the ascent, hanging on to trees, checking every foothold, puffing with exertion and lashing sweat. I thought of the bear we had seen two days ago, bounding like a puppy up the riverbank, just as steep as this. At the top, the stream levelled a bit and we pushed through a wet tangle of swampy forest to the foot of another crag. Petr stopped and pointed up the rockface.

'See?'

I shook my head. 'What?'

'The cave mouth,' he said. I couldn't make it out. 'Up at the top end of that crack, where the fissure comes in from the right.'

I saw it. 'It's tiny.'

'Yes. Hard to think a bear could get in there, eh? Are you up for the climb? It's not as hard as it looks, we can go up the side there and along that ledge.'

We hauled ourselves up and peered into the cave. Petr shone a torch to reveal that it was remarkably tight-mouthed but opened up into a more substantial space within. A scuff of old leaves was scattered among the dust on the floor. It looked dry and snug.

Above the forest canopy, the ever-present breeze had worked itself up into wind, and there was more thunder. A few fat drops of rain squeezed their way between the dense leaves.

We carried on upstream. The next cave was in an even more precarious position and we decided not to try to climb up to it. A third, not used every year, Petr explained, was easier to reach. It had a more substantial opening and though it had a deep litter of dry leaves on the floor it was clear that moisture dripped in from above, especially once the rain got going outside.

'Good bed of leaves,' I said.

'Yes, but that shows it is exposed to the wind. Where leaves can get in, snow can, too.'

'I'm starving, and we're going to get wet.'

'One last stop,' he said. 'It's close.'

We made our way back to the stream, followed it upwards around a couple of bends and then crossed it and headed towards a dramatic outcrop of rock. A quick scramble brought us out under a huge overhang with an almost level shelf several metres wide underneath it. It too was half a metre deep in dry beech leaves. I collapsed on them and rolled. It felt as soft as a feather mattress.

Petr laughed at me. 'Look,' he said, pointing to crude paintings on the underside of the limestone ledge.

All I could manage was 'Wow.'

'The historians say people have used this shelter for millennia,' he said. 'Not bears. It's no good for the winter, far too exposed for a long winter sleep. They'll use it in summer sometimes maybe, to shelter. Like us, now, same thing.'

Rain was beginning to fall in earnest. We tucked into bread and cheese. My shirt and trousers were gummy with sweat. In a sudden urge, I began stripping them off.

'What are you doing?' Petr was shaking his head.

'Cooling off.' I stood just beyond the lip of the overhang, where the rainwater streamed off. I let it pour over me, sweeping it down my sweaty legs and washing the leaves out of my hair.

There was a flash of lightening and an almost immediate growl, then boom, of thunder. Petr was beside me. I shifted so he could get the full force of the water spout and stood outside, letting the rain fall fresh, sweet and delicious on my skin.

'I feel like I'm part of the forest now,' I said.

'We are,' he said. 'Hopefully an intelligent part.'

'I'm not sure about intelligent.'

'You sure look like a wild animal now.'

Another flash and crash made me jump. 'It makes me want to scream. Such energy.'

Petr laughed as I revelled, eyes sparkling. The mountains thundered.

With some sort of girl-guide good sense I had brought a towel. Petr's pack contained a sleeping bag, which he unfurled on the beech leaf mattress. We dressed and lay there, dried and languorous, watching the storm. Later, we gathered water dripping off the overhang and ate again. Dusk began to fall.

'Walk back or stay?' he asked.

'Are you serious?'

He stretched out his legs. 'We're dry here. We have enough to stay warm. Water. Food.'

I drummed my hands on my knees. I'd never done anything like it. A mad adventure.

'Stay.'

He nodded. 'Good answer.'

In a pause in the storm, we sought out birch bark to light a fire and gathered wood: it was mostly wet, but we found some dry enough to start a fire under the overhang. Stacking sticks around the birch bark, I was glad I'd got the knack of firelighting on my many camping trips as a child. My dad was good for something. I looked up and caught him eyeing me.

'You seem to be settling into the forest,' he said, as if I'd achieved some special status.

'I feel free,' I said. 'You set me free.'

'No. You set yourself free.'

'You helped.' I bent down and squatted beside him.

He rumpled his chin and nodded. 'Maybe I helped a little.'

'Shall we light the fire?'

'Not yet.'

He shuffled over so I could share the sleeping bag. We sat watching the lightning as the thunderstorm roamed around the mountains. He told me stories about his life and interrogated me gently about mine. I told him about my mother, and cried; we talked about love and fear; he related the trauma of his upbringing by Romanian parents in exile, who could never settle; he showed me the traditional dance his grandmother had taught him so he wouldn't forget his origins; I confessed to the tricks I had developed to avoid ever having to dance with my father; we laughed.

As we talked, night crept in. I was stirring the leaves beside me when Petr stilled me with a hand on my thigh. I felt his body lock.

The musk was like a wet shout in the darkness, a scent barking out of the night, pungent and damp. A big animal moved, just outside of the overhang, passing from the right, across the front of the cave, between us and the stream. Close. Very close.

My stomach was like a fist.

The thunder and lightning had stopped but rain guttered from the roof and the stream roared in its bed. The animal could have been trampling noisily, we would not have heard it. But the smell of a bear, especially a wet one, is sufficient signal for the deafest creature. Invisible and soundless, its scent beamed its fierce greeting.

I reached for Petr's hand and he squeezed, then released. My pulse raced. Love and fear: indistinguishable.

Petr rummaged in a pocket and handed me a lighter. I reached over to the unlit fire and sparked a flame on to the birch bark. It sputtered and caught. Light and shadow loomed and danced on the roof, and the world outside the rock shelter switched sheer black in contrast to the flames.

The musk faded. Out there in the darkness, the wet bear gave up its plan to shelter on the ledge under the overhang.

I shivered, drunk with emotion. Petr offered me his jacket. I shook my head so he put it on. I fed the fire with the dry twigs and laid a branch on, then moved to sit close by him, wrapping his arm around my shoulder and huddling in to his body heat.

Through the night we woke often, one or other of us disentangling to throw more wood on the fire. The rain stopped, the sky cleared and stars showed themselves as sparkles on twigs. Small animals scuffled darkly on their night business. An owl hooted nearby for a while. I heard its wing beats wiping through the night, sweeping up hunting messages and scents.

I listened to the forest's starlit night chatter, which seemed richer in meaning than any human language, a meaning that could not be articulated, only felt. For once I did not seek to understand. It was enough to lie there, simply being in the forest, listening to rustle, hush and snap; a squeak, a whisper; nothing. Petr held me, his heart a drumbeat beneath the forest's song.

When we woke the sun was climbing down the trees from the highest leaves, lighting the tree trunks inch by inch. We brewed some tea, then let the fire die.

It was a beautiful morning, crisp and bright and sparkling. The whole world was washed clean by the rain. The forest soil exhaled heady wafts of life. Clouds of moist breath feathered on the forested slope beyond, just visible from between the trees. I let my mind roam the expanse of wooded land, miles and miles around in all directions, the vast Carpathian mountain wilds.

'You go today?'

I nodded. He turned away, a furrow across his forehead I hadn't seen before. He started packing up the sleeping bag.

We walked back to the cabin, finding little to say. There, he lit the stove and after the water heated, he offered me the shower, while he made some food.

Then there were formalities with Theo, lunch, packing. I was inarticulate with confusion. It had been just three brief days. Just three. I tried to convince myself nothing had happened, but I knew I was transformed. I put my town boots, skirt and patchwork jacket on, and sat on my bed with papers on my lap, trying to project myself back up the train line to my work in Norway and to re-instate the formal methodology for site identification into the forefront of my mind. Petr occupied himself with domestic chores, packing away foodstuffs in the kitchen, banging cupboard doors.

The day fizzled towards the hour I was due to leave. The time came, and with it, Valentina's car. Petr and I barricaded ourselves behind bad humour and allowed Valentina to prevent an intimate farewell. He gave me a collegial hug and I was on my way.

🐾　🐾

The train journey north passed in a blur. I tried to concentrate on analysis of the data the tech guys in Oslo had sent me, but hours seemed to go by when I did nothing but lie on the bed in my berth, my mind flitting between my mother and the men who seemed suddenly to have disturbed my life. As the train tracked along the foothills of the Carpathian mountains, fantasies of a life with Petr flowed, then clotted. I listened to a Sibelius symphony on my phone, to see if that would get me in the mood for Finland, and wallowed in its unashamed emotion.

From Budapest to Vienna I chewed over my experience with Yuri. And then thoughts of Malcolm took over. I agonised about the night I spent with him, trawling my memory for glimpses of what, in my drunken state, I had said and done. I kept returning to that hug, the following morning, the way he had held me, his sheer physical strength. That alone was a comfort. Petr Scazia wasn't the only man who could hug like a bear.

All this churned up thinking about men wasn't exactly in tune with my spinsterly pact with Fe-Phi-Pho, but I persuaded myself I hadn't actually broken the rules yet. Waiting for my connection at Vienna I typed a message to Diana and Frances. 'Hey D&F, still chaste and enjoying freedom in the wild woods of Europe.' I tried changing the wording, 'your trusty friend, enjoying freedom in the forests of Europe', then scratched it completely. Why was I trying to be conciliatory? What exactly had I done wrong anyway? The memory of the teddy bear weekend put me back into a sulk, which lasted through Germany, almost all the way to the ferry to Helsinki, and was only conquered by burying myself in geographical data.

Finland could not have been more different from Romania. There were still mounds of grey snow at the sides of roads. It rained all the way to Kuhmo as I travelled by bus from the train station at Kajaani, and it poured almost without a break throughout my three-day visit, not passionately like the Transylvanian deluge, but as insistent as a bad headache. I was given an apartment furnished in blond, utilitarian pine, next door to the Kuhmo Friendship Park museum.

Next day I met Kuhmo's senior ecologist. Drima Raito was short and balding, and he softened the effect of his white collared shirt and office trousers with a sweatshirt stretched over his belly, emblazoned with a smiling wolf. In his cluttered office, he tried to charm me into understanding the Friendship Park's importance. For thirty years he had been studying the migrations of bears across the border from Russia and he worked hard to cram a decade's worth of his conclusions into each day of my visit.

We began with historical data and the Cold War period when he had commenced his research. We pored over maps and charts and watched his animated (prizewinning) Xelsia power-show about post-Soviet impacts on the migratory behaviour of charismatic megafauna of Fennoscandia. I took copious notes.

At night we drank cold beer, ate reindeer steak and I made excuses to retire early. Feeling somehow obliged to use all the facilities provided, I sat sweating in the stuffy electric sauna cubicle in the bathroom of my apartment. Afterwards, I slept deep, black, inscrutable sleeps.

On the third day, a tall man appeared in the doorway of Drima's office. 'Hey, boss!' he said.

Drima raised his eyebrows and put down his pen. 'Tanka, you're back.'

A woman poked her head between the doorframe and Tanka. 'Païvi, too,' she said, winning a smile from Drima. She slipped into the room and gave him a light hug. She looked a few years younger than me, a blonde, sequinned pixie dressed in pink skin-tight leggings and a multicoloured cycle top.

Tanka strolled in behind her. He was ageless, his hair cropped convict short, white or blond, so very pale it was hard to tell which, and dressed in loose combat pants and camouflage jacket.

Drima offered coffee and Païvi followed him out. Tanka took off his jacket and sprawled in a chair near the door. He was wearing a skin-tight T-shirt with a STOP sign slapped over an image of a felled tree and a slogan he told me was Chinese for 'logging = death'.

Drima and Païvi returned with drinks and we were all intro-duced. It turned out Tanka was a national authority on rare lichens of old-growth forests, and he and Païvi had just returned from a month-long survey of a forest area just north of the Kale-vala National Park over the border in Russia.

'Did you see any bears?' I asked.

'Yes, some few,' Tanka nodded. 'Six, I think.' He looked to Païvi, who nodded.

'Six in a month, that's not so many,' said Drima. 'My guest here has seen as many in three days in Romania.'

'Romania?' Tanka looked intrigued. I explained about my trip.

'Bears are the coolest animals,' Païvi said. 'They're like Mother Earth's messengers. You see them out there in the forest, but only when you really need them, only like when you need to know something. I really believe that. And it's not just in the forest, you know. Tanka, do you remember that Taiga Terror meeting, when the bear came right down to the conference centre?'

He nodded indulgently.

'We were, like, getting nowhere, you know?' Païvi continued. 'Talking each other's butts off, making no decisions whatsoever, and this bear comes strolling out of the forest and across the lawn, like, right outside of the conference window and it climbs up this birch tree and starts snacking on the buds. This was spring, you know, when the sap's rising. They just love those tips.' I made a mental note. 'And we all just shut up and watch the bear and this First Nation American guy stands up...'

'Chief Garry,' Tanka interjected, as if I might know him.

'Yeah, like, Chief Garry stands up and says in his teachings the bear is the symbol of courage and steadfastness. And then the bear came down from the tree and wandered back off into the forest, and wow, that conference, it just turned around. We stopped bullshitting and hit the plans, you know, radical stuff, these big ideas came pouring out, it was amazing. So much energy. And all from that bear, y'know. I really believe that.'

'That's cool,' I said. 'No wonder I'm mad about bears.' After two days of rain and maps I felt as if the sun had come out.

'You fucked up bad in Norway, huh?' said Tanka.

'You could put it like that,' I laughed. 'I'm on the team to bring them back.'

'Really?' He looked me up and down as if I didn't appear properly kitted out for such a role. 'Are you all academics?'

'Some naturalists and government, too,' I said.

He shook his head. 'Don't say. And farmers' representatives. And forest industry.'

'Farmers, yes. Not industry, as far as I'm aware.'

'Activists? Grassroots people? Sámi?'

'Not yet, as far as I know. It's early days.'

'It's never too early,' he said. 'Predator expansion only works if it's bottom up. They should know this by now. Norway's so fucked up. They treat farmers like nobility – they've grown into nation of, how do you say it, barons.' He pronounced it like a Russian, with the emphasis on the second syllable. 'Lords of Land. To Vanquish Nature by Plough and Dominate with Guns.' He paraded like a mock soldier. We all laughed.

Païvi said, 'Humans, bloody humans, we think we know what's best. But we know nothing sometimes, nothing but how to load a gun. How to kill. How to break things. How to destroy. How to try to take control. But nature isn't like machines. It doesn't go when we say go. It doesn't steer. It doesn't stop and change direction when we push a pedal here, turn a switch there. It doesn't need us to fuel it up or fix its carburettors. It's alive, like us.'

No one had anything to say to this.

'Where I'm from it's much worse than Norway,' I said, eventually.

'Where?' Tanka asked.

'Scotland.'

'Aah, Scotland!' His eyes lit up and he leaned towards me. 'That's great!'

'Why? Talk about barons, we've got the most inequitable land distribution in Europe. The countryside is completely dominated by rich farmers. Our ecosystems are trashed, especially the woods, we've no forest worth the name, and the rivers are all dammed for hydro-electricity, we've far too many herbivores and no big predators at all.'

'But she's independent now, yes?' Tanka said. 'You can change everything. No longer English colony, is what I hear.'

'What's this?' Drima looked blank.

'We had a referendum on independence,' I said. 'We've had the pro-independence party, the Scottish National Party, in government for years now, and finally the people have voted yes, let's go for it, leave the United Kingdom, take control of our own affairs.'

'Interesting. Will it make a big difference?'

'Well, I have wondered whether we might be able to start at least talking about reintroducing bears. We have a lynx programme.' Tanka and Païvi were nodding vigorously.

'The bear is like symbol of rebirth,' said Païvi.

'Yeah, people keep telling me this,' I grinned. 'After our great political hibernation of hundreds of years, let's be reborn and bring back bears.'

Tanka asked, 'Do you have good habitat?'

'I don't know. Like I said, our forests are rubbish. Do you think bears need old-growth to flourish?'

'No. She likes it, of course, and core areas are important, but bear is omnivore and she'll survive. Look around you here – we have no old-growth left in Finland, hardly none anyway, but we have more bears here now than any time in history. Tourist boom, ban on hunting, big protected zone in Russia, it adds.'

'What's most important?' I asked.

'Ban on hunting is single biggest factor, I think.'

'I've heard people say bears are good at helping restore damaged ecosystems. Any truth in that?'

'Yes. I agree with that,' Tanka nodded. 'She eats what there is plenty of, does some gardening, helps balance.'

'Gardening?'

'She breaks up fallen wood, spreads nuts and seeds and spores, turns stones, a bit of digging, all of this is good for diversity, this is true, Drima?'

'Absolutely.' He nodded vigorously.

'We need to study the habitat issues, I guess,' I said.

'And people's opinions. That's like way the most important thing for bear survival,' said Païvi.

'You should propose to do study with Norway and some other countries. European Commission love this kind of joint project, even if Norway still isn't officially in Europe.' Tanka surprised me. One moment an eco-warrior, the next a diplomat. It was a good idea, and I told him so.

As if needing to reassert his more radical side he said, 'If that doesn't work, you can speed things up with some little direct action. We find she's very helpful here from time to time.'

'What do you mean?'

'Well, sometimes there are border fences to stop animals going where they want. I don't think bears are using wire cutters very good. Her paws are too big, you know. Sometimes she needs helping hand.' He winked.

Drima said, 'I am not hearing this.'

'Unfortunately, Scotland's on an island. They'd need swimming lessons, not wire cutters,' I said.

'Yes, it would be challenge,' Tanka grinned.

'But not impossible,' Païvi giggled.

'Are you two subversives here for anything in particular?' Drima asked.

Tanka dug a Geo out of his pocket and waved it at him. 'Inventory results. Can we use couple of terminals? We put them straight into database, if you want.'

'OK, use the west lab.'

'Good to meet you.' Tanka rose and swung his jacket off the back of the chair, pulled out a card and handed it to me. 'Maybe have some beer later?'

'I leave tonight, have to get the night train from Kajaani,' I said, with genuine regret, rummaging for my card. 'We'll meet again, I hope.'

'I'm interested if you make progress in Scotland,' Tanka said. 'Good luck in Norway. I hope some bastards don't shoot your bears.'

'Me, too. Thanks.'

Païvi gathered up the mugs and with a 'Ciao', they were gone.

Drima and I returned to the study of vegetation patterns and bear movement correlations for the remainder of the afternoon. But I was haunted by the premise that human opinions constrained the success of any bear population more than the quality of the woods.

Anja Eldegard met me at Oslo station.

'It's very kind of you,' I said. 'I hope I'm not putting you to any trouble.' It was Saturday evening.

'Not a bit,' said Anja. 'This is my husband, Per.'

A round smiling father-bear shook my hand. A more matching couple it was hard to imagine: both dressed in black velvet suits, they clearly featured in the same fairy story.

'We were in town for a concert, so this is good timing. And if you stay with us, I won't have to go anywhere tomorrow to meet you, and we really need to put our heads together before Monday,' Anja said.

Per grabbed my bag and led us off to a parked car. It was electric and purred quietly out of the city, through the suburbs and onwards to a gingerbread house in the woods. I was yawning and grateful to be shown to my room as soon as we got there. I slept under a gingham quilt, presumably in Baby Bear's bed, and woke to the sound of a violin, and sun streaming in through the window.

Downstairs, Anja was presiding over a breakfast table laden with breads, cakes, jams, cheeses, meats and preserves. 'Eat!' she demanded. I ate.

'Per is playing Bach,' Anja smiled. 'That's always a good way to begin the day, I think.'

'He's very good,' I said. 'It sounds complex.' Sweet toned threads of melody twisted and looped from the room next door. 'Beautiful.'

Anja beamed at me. 'Yes. The most beautiful music.'

We ate on wordlessly, listening. I was grateful not to have to speak and guessed that Anja hated breakfast-time conversations as much as I did. Not a woman for small talk and that suited me fine.

After breakfast Anja declared it time for work. We moved to the back of the house, to a large table in a conservatory.

'Petr Scazia was very impressed by you,' she said, getting a large map out of a tube and unfurling it across the table.

'Likewise,' I said, feeling the blush rise, hoping it was not too obvious. I helped Anja pin down the corners of the map with pots of pens and paperweights.

'I'm glad you went in person,' Anja continued. 'Petr says, if we need to, we can release some of the bears they have at their rescue centre. You didn't get there?'

'No.' I had to keep my eyes down, feeling my face turn the same colour as my hair. 'We spent the three days I had in the forest, watching bears, exploring their habitat.' Was I trying to convince myself that was all that had happened?

'Excellent. Much more important for your role in this. And I'm not sure if Romanian bears would be a good idea. Perhaps we should just be bringing some over the border from Sweden, hastening their expansion, as it were. On the other hand, some new genetic material might be a good idea. Anyway, there's no need for you to get embroiled in the logistics of finding bears. We need to keep you focussed on locations.' She tapped the map. 'Let's see where we are. You've chosen your criteria, I take it? I must say I like your methodology. Very clear, simple. Even the minister should grasp it. Well done.'

I sighed relief.

'Can we do the first stage yet, do you think? Identify the suitable habitats?' Anja looked up at me. 'I recognise the geopolitical constraints task is a bit tougher, but if we could have the ecological frontrunners for the meeting tomorrow that would be very useful.'

'I've got about twenty sites. The GIS guys have been incredibly helpful – let me get my data stick.'

'What for?'

'I can plug into your computer, show you the analysis.'

'I've no computer here, I'm afraid.'

'You what?'

'No computer. I'm old-fashioned. I work on paper here. I don't like machines at home.' Anja looked sheepish, putting her

118

hands out in a gesture of offering. 'Bears don't use computers, do they?'

'I can see why Petr and you get on.' I grinned.

Anja smiled back. 'Oh yes?'

'The three days I spent with him I never used my computer, my phone, not even electric light.'

'But you still learned enough?' She looked concerned, as if I might be criticising.

'I learned more about bears in those three days than I could have learned at a desk in a lifetime.'

Anja relaxed.

'I'll go and get my phone. I've done a heap of analysis on the long train journeys to come up with the site selection. It'd be good to go through it with you.'

'Can we not just do it on this map?' She was like a big kid, in danger of sulking if we didn't play with her favourite toy.

'Of course. I just don't think I can remember the sites I've picked out off the top of my head. I've never been to some of them. And I think the justifications might be important. But the map'll really help me to get a sense of the locations, the big picture.'

'OK.' Anja looked mollified by the 'big picture' comment.

She is more sensitive than she looks, I thought, as I made my way to the bedroom and back; strange how our vulnerabilities show at home. I wondered what Petr's home might be like, then pushed the thought away. I needed to stop thinking about him. There was nothing but frustration to be gained from a crush on a Romanian scientist. I had to forget it. Forget him.

Anja had drawn both chairs round to the side of the table so we could work with the map. We spent the morning sticking notes on it, colour coding for habitat attributes. I had chosen winter cave sites as the top criterion, indicated by geology. Then large intact forest as number two. General vegetation diversity third. Ant nest distribution fourth. Then I had ruled out the wettest areas, and added a preference for high elk density.

'Why the rainfall criterion?' Anja asked.

'Call it a hunch that bears don't like to get too wet.' The memory flared of the wet bear seeking shelter that night, and I quickly stamped on the spark.

'And the elk? Won't high numbers mean repressed vegetation and conflict with the third criterion?'

I explained the theories of Petr and Tanka that the bears would exploit the available niche, helping to restore balance to the ecosystem, flourishing where excess herbivores indicated a shortage of top predators. 'So I think the elk numbers are a good indicator of where the bears might be able to do most good.'

Anja paced the room. 'It's an interesting approach. There may be some challenges tomorrow. I hope you're ready for them?'

I expounded the theory of seed dispersal and Anja smiled at me. 'You did learn a lot from Petr.'

I laughed in acknowledgement.

'Have you got references?'

I nodded. 'I've done some other scenarios, too,' I said. 'For example, if I drop large forest area, move vegetation diversity up the ranking as a proxy for it, and add in a migration factor, then there are a couple of other sites.'

'Migration factor?'

'The likelihood that some will trot west over the border from Sweden, or from Finland or Russia into Finmark.'

'It happens, certainly.'

'That changes the picture dramatically. Suddenly, instead of all these southern plots, there are several northern sites.'

'All in Sámi territory.'

'Yes. It could make a huge difference to the socio-political analysis. The question is whether forest habitat is essential or if they'll survive in a more mixed mosaic landscape, which is where we get our highest diversity.'

'What if you keep the migration factor and lose one of the others, like the rainfall or elk or ants?'

I ran the various scenarios. There was less variation. A dozen sites were featuring on all versions, strong on all criteria. With all seven criteria, these twelve sites dominated.

Anja said, 'OK. How about we settle on the seven criteria, including migration. Seven's a lucky number anyway. Happy?'

I nodded.

Anja pointed at my phone. 'Let's get this to Paul Undset, the ministerial advisor. Can you send it on that? Then he can brief the minister before we meet tomorrow. No surprises. We need it to go smoothly. The Bill goes to the Parliamentary Committee on Wednesday.'

'Already? Wow.'

'Politics works at a different pace to science, that's for sure,' said Anja. 'When they want something they get in their sports cars and race it through. When they don't want it they can spend years unable to find the ignition key. It's very frustrating. But at the moment they are motoring and we will just have to try to keep up.'

'So about these twelve sites. Should I go and check them out? I've never been to some of them.'

Anja sat back in her chair and rocked her head. 'Maybe a good idea, but it's time-consuming.'

I thought about what Tanka had said and turned to Anja, trying to make eye contact. 'What about local people, local knowledge, people on the ground? We need to consult them, surely, get them involved somehow.'

She shook her head. 'Don't worry about that. That's not your problem. You stick to the identification issue.' She tapped the map. 'We'll deal with public relations separately.'

I turned further towards the professor. 'I think I should check out the sites, get a feel for what the criteria combinations look like on the ground.'

Anja must have seen I was insistent. 'OK. You'd better get an itinerary worked out. Try to have a firm conclusion two weeks from now. That'll still leave us time for geopolitical constraints.'

'I'll need to do some historical and future variability analyses, too. Look at resilience, run some climate models, that kind of thing. We could do that in parallel with the geopolitical constraints work.'

'Can you have that analysis all done by July 15th?'

I took a long breath. 'I can try.'

'Then we'll still have a month to make the decision and persuade the minister before the *Storting* comes back into session after the summer recess. That's when the Bill will go to the full *Storting* and, if they are still in favour of the idea, having a few specific locations agreed by then will be important.'

I gulped. It was all moving very fast. I was responsible for decisions in Parliament.

'I was wondering,' I said, 'would there be any advantage in getting some other countries involved in this?'

'How do you mean?'

'Well, it might be useful if the methodology was tested in other countries, say one with and one without bears, see how the maps look elsewhere, get more confidence in the method by testing it somewhere else.'

Anja nodded. 'Could be, yes. I can see the merit in that.'

'It might attract European funding if it involved partnerships with EU countries.'

The professor widened her eyes. 'You're serious. Where do you have in mind?'

'Well, Scotland's my obvious first choice for no bears. For places with, there are all sorts of options. Finland might be good – same latitude, or Sweden, or both, and we could get the Sámi Council involved.'

'There could be a problem…' She scratched an eyebrow.

I pressed on. 'France then? They've recently reintroduced successfully. We could learn a lot from them.'

'Yes, but if our criteria don't predict well?'

'We learn.'

Anja's hand slipped to her chin. 'Hmm. Finland's better. Or Romania, any model should really be tested there.'

'Both?'

'But the timing is impossible. European bureaucracy is legendary. Though…' She furrowed her brow. 'I did hear something recently about a rapid turnaround process for small projects with political relevance – they're calling it something like the hot science fast track. Leave it with me. I'll sound out some of the others, and put it on the agenda for the team meeting after the minister has left.' She put her hands on the table. 'Good. That's us, then. Time for lunch, I think. Then a walk, or a snooze. Whatever you do on a Sunday afternoon. Make yourself at home. I walk, alone. Don't take it personally, please, but I need a regular dose of solitude.'

'Me, too. I'll send the sites to Dr Undset,' I said.

'Yes, do that. Then let's eat and afterwards enjoy the rest of the day.' She rubbed her ample belly and headed off towards the smells of cooking.

I searched my phone for Undset's address and sent him a copy of the map, a list of the criteria and a brief explanation.

A message had come in from Dad. I felt a pang of guilt. I'd hardly been in touch for the past fortnight.

Had a trip to hospital on Thursday. Minor op. No need to worry. Your boss has been in touch. Good guy. Don't let that commission interfere with your job. Love Dad xxx

No need to worry, indeed. He couldn't have alarmed me any more if he'd sent a telegram saying HELP!!! And what was Yuri up to? I went to lunch, anxiety bunched in my gut like a fur ball. I pleaded tiredness and got away as soon as I could, grateful for Anja's call for isolation. In my room, I called Dad, getting only the answer machine, and left an insipid message. I lay down for a snooze, but tossed and turned, unable to sleep.

Before dinner, I called again. He was in high spirits after an afternoon coaching at the football club.

'So how did you hear from Yuri?' I asked him.

'Oh, he's on the board of PiNor, and they're going to sponsor the juniors.'

'What, PiNor the timber company?'

'Yes, I believe so. We applied to them a while back. They've built a big board plant not far from here.'

'They're part of UPP, you know. They've got a hellish reputation.'

'Well, I don't know anything about that. All I know is I get a letter of congratulations from your man Yuri Gagarin and so I sent him an email and he phoned me up.'

'He's not my man. And it's Yuri Zeveris.'

'Aye, well.' He sounded aggrieved that his attempt at a joke had fallen flat.

'I had no idea he was involved in the corporate world.' Surely a board position at UPP shouldn't be a surprise to one of his closest colleagues. I wondered what other secrets he had up his sleeves.

'Aye, quine, and he's spending their money well, if you want my opinion. More like that, I'd say.'

'Anyway, how was your hospital visit?'

'Ach, it's nothing to worry about, like I said, maybe we can chat about it next time you're home.'

The meeting with the minister went smoothly and I caught the night train back to Trondheim afterwards. Next morning, I went straight to the Institute and directly to Yuri's office. I needed to sort out my position. If I was going to carry out the site assessment properly given the time constraints, I wouldn't get much else done.

Yuri was sitting at his desk with, as always, three neat piles of papers in front of him. Apart from three chairs, a single bookcase of ecology texts and a filing cabinet, the office was devoid of the normal trappings of a researcher's work, and there were no pictures on the walls at all, nothing to reveal the man's personality. Or perhaps that was the point.

'My favourite researcher,' he said, getting to his feet.

I stayed by the door. 'Hi Yuri. My dad says thanks very much for the football sponsorship. I don't know if you knew it was him, but the Moray Juniors are very chuffed with the new kit from UPP. I didn't know you were on their board.'

He put his hand on his hip and waved a hand. 'It is pleasure to be generous with someone else's money!' he laughed.

I wondered how false my grin looked. 'Actually the reason I'm here is I've been asked to spend the next three months working full time on the bear project. We had a meeting with the minister yesterday and they want me to lead the release-site identification.'

'Well, you'll just have to say no.' His desk was a barricade, behind which he refused to hear of me spending so much as a day more on the bear issue. He spread his hand flat on the file in front of him. 'When politics and science mix, politics win always. You tell Professor Eldegard no, and you tell her I said so. It is anti-science.'

I stood gripping the door handle behind me. 'I need to do this work.'

He shook his head.

'It *is* science,' I said. 'It's the best kind. It's actually going to make a real difference in the world. I've never had that chance before.'

He looked away, as if not listening.

'I think Professor Bergen will support me.' I didn't know where that came from.

He turned his head, slowly, but there was curiosity in his eyes, and a black glint of suspicion. 'I doubt it. Don't make a stupid mistake,' he said. 'You have a good career. Don't throw it away.'

'I'm not,' I yanked open the door. 'Thank you for nothing,' I muttered.

I pulled the door closed behind me and took a deep breath, then stalked up the corridor to the Institute Head Office. I told the secretary, 'I need to talk to Professor Bergen'.

'She's away until next Thursday. At a conference in Alaska, then at a wedding in Oslo. You could try a message?'

I nodded. 'I'll do that. Thanks'.

I went to my office and began working my way through my inbox, most of which I seemed to find easy to toss into the recycling bin. Unlike Yuri's, my office was stacked with piles, no, heaps of papers relevant to the various projects I was working on, plus a few that were the result of simply emptying out my inbox on to the floor to make way for the latest influx of post. You would think I was trying to make myself believe my work was important through the sheer volume of dead trees I could amass about it. Diana would have had a fit if she saw it, I thought. And really, what was there in all of this that mattered to me as much as being on the bear panel?

Thinking of Diana led me to reflect on Frances. I thought of phoning her. Then I realised that Stig was likely to understand my dilemma better. I called him and explained the situation.

'I can't advise you,' he said, rational and cautious as ever, 'but it sounds like a brilliant thing to be involved in. Can't you get the Oslo professor to talk your boss into it?'

This was a useful reminder. Anja had promised she could try to talk to Yuri if he was proving difficult.

'Thanks, Stig. You're a star.'

'I've done nothing,' he said. 'When'll you be in Scotland? Gi' us a call and I'll take you to see my lynx.'

'Serious? That's brilliant. Not for a few weeks, if I take this on. I'll have to go to all the potential release sites. But I'm going to have to get back to see my dad sometime. He's worrying me. And he's in cahoots with my boss, and that's worrying me even more.'

'I got your message about the feasibility study. Let me know if it comes off, you can count me in.'

'So you reckon someone at your research institute might be interested in collaborating? That's magic.'

'Aye, like I said, I'm up for it and my prof loves anything with money attached. Get yourself to Scotland and I'll set up a meeting.'

I fired up the computer on my desk and uploaded the maps from my phone, then started plotting a route around the trial sites. I would do the work anyway, even if that meant defying Yuri.

I couldn't get back to Scotland for the next few weeks, as I tore around Norway sizing up the sites my analysis had picked out.

Most were suitable, a couple really captured my imagination, but I didn't have long enough to really appreciate them. I vowed to go back if I could.

Anja turned out to have contacts in every region and made introductions by phone wherever I went. She said she had put the concept of the joint European study to some people and was getting a good response. There was a feeling that we should involve people from areas with high densities of bears as well, she said, and did I think Petr Scazia might take part? I agreed to contact him, and Anja promised to try to bring Yuri round to the idea of me being on the bear panel while I was away travelling, though I didn't fancy her chances much.

A high mountainous region near Røros, remote and beautiful, stood out as the preferred site from an ecological point of view. Most of the area was owned by a co-op of farmers, so in mid-June I arranged to meet their board of directors.

I found myself seated on one side of a boardroom table faced by four substantial men, bristling with hostility. A glass of water was placed before me, as if to indicate the level of hospitality I merited.

The chairman, who was the biggest of the four and had the largest moustache, skipped any kind of welcome. 'We will make it clear and simple,' he said. 'Any import of bears to here is completely impossible and we will use our right to protect our livestock and shoot any bear on sight. We have written to the minister to make this clear already and we intend to complain in the strongest possible terms. It is outrageous that we are being singled out like this.'

I slipped my hands off the table on to my legs. 'I'm sorry. There is no intention to single you out. This is just one of twelve sites where I am exploring the ecological suitability for bears.' I felt from some of the looks I was getting that some members of the board could well mistake me for a bear, and deal with me accordingly.

'This is not a *site*. This is our home. It's where we farm, and it is obvious to us that ecologically, and in every other way, bears and farms do not mix. They are completely incompatible. A first grade school kid could tell you that. Bears eat sheep. They are predators. What kind of ecological suitability is that?'

'I am sure the minister will listen to you.'

'But are you listening? No one is listening. The fact that you turn up here with your ecological nonsense means no one is listening. The newspapers are full of lies about farmers.' The chairman's fury met with nods from his colleagues. He was clearly referring to the boycott of the Svenson's meat chain that had gained huge popular support as a way of protesting about the death of the bear.

I tried to think of a suitable platitude and wished I could be anywhere else.

'We will fight this all the way. You go back and tell your minister that.'

I retreated as soon as I could. From my hotel room I called Anja in Oslo to tell her what had happened.

'You'll get a better reception in some of the other sites,' she said. 'Don't take it personally. You're an easy target but it's not you they're angry about.'

I tried to thicken my skin and carry on. I spent most days either on trains, on the road, or, where possible, walking in the chosen regions, trying to get a feel for the ecology, the potential for bears, and avoiding meetings with potentially aggressive landowners.

Just north of my preferred option, in the Blåfjella-Skjækerfjella national park, an enthusiastic ranger walked me out to some promising caves. I assured him the site would be considered, and that evening I wrote a postcard to Petr:

Spent the day looking at rock shelters. Next winter maybe a bear will be sleeping here. Thanks for all you showed me last month. I learned more about bears than I would have believed possible in 3 days! We're planning a study of good habitats for bears, across Europe. Would you like to join in? I'll email details. Ciao, Callis.

At one of the sites in the far north I met Brigid Aikio, a representative of the local Sámi organisation. She collected me from the bus station in an old Mercedes Benz and drove me out into an open land of swamps with barely any tree cover. She stopped the car at a rise with a view of low hills, on which she pointed out some distant dots: reindeer, belonging to her family.

We strolled over to a bench and sat in the sunshine. I asked about bears, and Brigid told me they had been there within her lifetime. 'Bears here were very strong until pseudorabies came.'

'Is that what others are calling Aujeszky's disease?' I asked.

'Yes, it wiped them out. It is a tragedy. We are very sorry. We have many legends about the bears. I am a descendent of the bear, you know.' She looked at me with a shy smile. 'Shall I tell you?'

'Oh, please.'

Brigid linked her hands together in her lap, and began. 'My grandmother's grandmother, or possibly her grandmother, was walking in the forest after she had been fruitpicking. We don't know her name now so let's call her Brigid, like me.'

I looked the Sámi woman up and down as she spoke. She was small, white-haired and tan-skinned and wore a checked shirt, leather jacket and rubber boots. Her voice was soft and lilting and reminded me of the way my mother used to tell fairy stories to me when I was little.

She continued, 'Strolling along, Brigid tripped on a root and spilled her berries. A handsome hunter appeared from among the trees and helped her to refill her basket. He invited her to come with him to his house, and she was curious, so she followed him. He lived in what looked like just a simple shelter under a cliff, but once she was inside she saw that it was really a huge network of caverns and corridors under the earth. There were many other people arriving and all came wearing fur coats, which they hung up as soon as they entered. They were all very friendly to her.

'She loved it there and she stayed for the whole winter, agreeing to become the wife of the hunter. In the spring she was pregnant by him and she was very happy. But then she noticed that the people were starting to leave, putting on their fur coats and going back out into the world above ground. Without a fur coat, she wasn't able to leave. She was a prisoner.

'At first she was furious, but when she gave birth to two sons she was so delighted by them and they kept her so busy she did not have time to be angry any more. Her husband brought her good food and in the autumn all of the people came back into the underground place and it was once again full of life and fun. This went on for some years, and she grew used to the lonely summers and joyful winters.

'Eventually, by peering out of the door, Brigid discovered that these people she had been living with, when they went out into the world she came from, were bears, and she deduced that her husband must be a bear, too. What then were her sons? One summer she was so lonely she decided to escape, and so when her husband went out seeking food she tricked him by only pretending to close the door behind him. He had grown trustful of her and didn't check. When he had gone, she opened the door and ran away, back to her village, taking her sons with her. They grew up to be great hunters, just like the bears.'

'And one of them was your great-great-great-whatever grandfather?' I swatted at a mosquito.

'That's what I was told!' She scratched her head. 'Come on, they're biting. I'll show you some more of our beautiful bogs.'

As we drove, we talked about the various compensation schemes for livestock hunted by bears in Russia, Romania, Sweden and some other countries, and Brigid explained how she thought such a system should work for reindeer. I promised I would raise the issue with the rest of the team, but I wasn't optimistic such an area would be the chosen site.

'Bears sometimes wander over the border from Finland or Sweden,' Brigid said.

'And what happens to them then?'

'The last few have all been shot. The fear of pseudorabies is very strong.'

'Is it also fear of them killing the reindeer?'

'Not so much, I don't think so, though there are some people who say why should we pay with our reindeer to feed bears. But even when they are shot deliberately, the animal is treated with respect, its eyes closed, a blessing spoken, that sort of thing. The story I told you, it's one of many. The bear is a good guy in Sámi culture.'

'So is there a chance they could be allowed to live if, say, they were vaccinated?'

'Yes, possible,' she said, 'though there are some people who will defend their right to hunt to the very last, and remember there are many people in our community who are not Sámi or who don't believe the legends any more. Some people, even Sámi people, would not mind if there is total decimation of the species.'

'That's depressing.'

'Not everyone is like that.' The car pulled up back at the bus station. 'It was nice to talk with you. Good luck with your project.'

I failed to spend even one night in my own house. I had exchanged numerous messages with Karl and Michel while I had been travelling and wanted to spend an evening with them, but in the end I arrived back in Trondheim on the day of my ferry booking to Scotland. I stopped in to pick up mail and swap dirty laundry for clean clothes. It felt like someone else's home.

It was a glorious day and I had spent so much time on trains, I decided I deserved some fresh air. Once out of the house I found myself drawn to the waterfall in the forest.

It was as delicate as macramé. The last time I had been here it had roared with meltwater. This trickle was a gentle surprise, its rhythms mesmerising. I stopped and watched it whorl and spatter, the rocks gleaming black as ink. The pool, overhung with rowan blossom, was tantalising. As my breath slowed, I edged towards it. I don't know how long I stood there in that leafy window of warm sunshine, listening to the splashing song of the fall.

On a sudden whim, I stripped off my clothes, piling them in a heap on my jacket among the woodland flowers. Stepping on to the black slimy stones to stand under the water shower, breathless, I shrieked, then let the cold batter my face into a smile. It was enough. I was out again, and back in the sunshine. It felt glorious.

I dried myself with my shirt, regained the respectability of dress, then strolled back down the slope with a glitter in my eye. The world shone back.

There was only time for a quick dash to the office, where I ploughed through the mountain of mail that had accumulated in my absence. I hoped to avoid Yuri. When there was a knock on my door, I took a deep breath. It was his secretary, Maria.

'Callis, it is good to see you. You are very absent recently.' She frowned disapproval at the heaps on my desk.

'I can't believe what's happened to my life. This job. It's incredible. You won't believe where I've been.'

'I've heard a couple of things,' she said. 'How long are you back now?'

'I'm not. I'm off on the ferry tonight to see my dad in Scotland. He's not well. And I've to see if I can persuade the Scots to join in our project and look at bear reintroduction.'

'Is that right? I am sorry about your father.'

'What? Oh thanks. Nothing serious, he says, but I'm not so sure. Anyway, yes, we're planning a joint project looking at using our methodology in other countries. The funders sound interested, but we need partners.'

'Well, if you have time,' Maria leaned forwards as if not wanting to be contaminated by the clutter, 'you might like to attend to this.' She handed me a brown envelope, turned on her heel and closed the door smartly behind her.

I looked at the missive. It wasn't exactly smoking, but Maria's manner left me in no doubt that it did not contain good news. It would have to wait, I decided, until later. I stuffed it in my bag with various other things I would need to attend to, and set off to the ferry terminal.

I opened the letter in the new departure lounge. It was from Professor Bergen.

Dear Dr MacArthur

    I am writing to notify you that a formal grievance has been made concerning yourself by another member of staff of the Institute. In accordance with Norwegian law and Institute policy, a full investigation of the matter of the grievance must be undertaken. As part of this investigation you are entitled to an impartial hearing. I would therefore be grateful if you would contact me as soon as possible to arrange a suitable time for such a hearing. You are entitled to bring a legal representative.

Yours sincerely

Professor L Bergen

There was also a handwritten note.

Dear Callis,

It would be useful, I think, if prior to the formal hearing we could have a chat – informal and preliminary – about the allegations that have been made about you. Please could you drop into my office as soon as you can? I understand that your government work is keeping you away from the Institute a great deal, but I should like a brisk resolution of this matter.

Yours

Liza

I read both sheets of paper three times, then folded them back into the envelope, feeling my temperature rise, blood racing. It was Yuri. It had to be. What was he up to?

I found a quiet corner away from most of the throng of travellers, and called Professor Bergen's direct line, not really expecting an answer at this time of day.

'Liza Bergen.' The voice was weary.

'Professor Bergen, it's Callis MacArthur.' Despite the note, I couldn't quite bring myself to call her Liza. The matriarch of the Institute might like to think of herself as an approachable woman, but she was still a distant authority figure to me.

'Callis, thanks for calling. Are you in the building?'

'No, I'm at the ferry terminal, on my way to Scotland. I've just opened your letter...'

'Oh, that's a shame. I was hoping we could have a quiet chat, in person, you know.'

'I'm sorry, but I'm not back until next week. Can you please tell me about the allegations?' I kept my voice low, hoping none of the seated passengers were listening.

'I'm sure it's a simple mix up, but I would like to get it clarified as soon as possible. The person concerned has involved a lawyer, so we're having to do it all by the rules, but really, I'd rather we could sort it all out in a friendly manner.'

'Yes, but what's the complaint, exactly?'

'It's a claim that you've misused data, basically that you have taken credit for work that is someone else's.'

'And who is it that's claiming this?'

'I can't tell you who has lodged the grievance, I'm sorry. I know that's awful for you, and I imagine you'll be trying to guess, but I have been told I must allow them to remain anonymous.'

'Is it Yuri?'

'I'm sorry, I can't say. Will you come in and see me as soon as you get back?'

'Yes, of course.'

'Do you know what it's getting at? I'm afraid it's completely out of the blue to me. I had no idea there was a problem, until I got the lawyer's letter.'

'I haven't a clue, sorry. I'll rack my brains, but I can't think of anyone who might think I've stolen their work.' An announcement started up on the tannoy and people began getting to their feet and heading for the gangway. 'I've got to go, my boat's loading.'

'OK. Thanks for calling. Have a good trip.'

On the ferry, I blessed the expenses budget that allowed me the privacy of a cabin to myself, allowing me to nurse my thoughts in peace. I racked my brains to think if any of the angry farmers

I had encountered in recent weeks might have raised the grievance. But the letter said it was a member of the Institute staff. It had to be Yuri. What was he up to? Could this be about me taking up the position on the panel? Was he going to get me for insubordination? Anja had said in a recent message that he was proving 'awkward', but she was going to persist in her efforts to persuade him my new role was a benefit to his department. I suspected she wasn't making much progress.

Despite these worries, I surprised myself by sleeping well and woke to the ship's horn announcing the approach to Aberdeen. Dad was waiting for me, looking like he had just had a bad sea crossing himself. He hugged me to him and I felt his once-sturdy body now frailer than my own. In the car park he asked me if I wanted to drive. 'Get used to the car. I've put you on the insurance, thought it might be handy for you to get around.'

'I'm on expenses. I'd intended hiring, if I need to.'

'Ach, just use mine. I've little need for it these days.'

I took the keys. He was proud of his car, a Nissan Sunburst electric with hydrogen cell backup for long journeys. He and Mum had bought it with his golden handshake for their trips around the Highlands, when the new wind-generated hydrogen plants were being hyped as the new oil boom.

'It's a nice car to drive,' I said, once we were on the main road, heading home. I saw him nod appreciation, knew I'd said the right thing. The wipers swished rain out of our view.

We talked weather for a while, the latest flooding after weeks of record high temperatures, then he said, 'Sounds like your commission's taking you all over the place. I can't imagine you're getting much real work done.'

So, it had begun already. Would he needle me all weekend about my job? I decided to ignore the dig. 'I think it's nearly over, that bit,' I said, 'but it's been amazing. Romania was a total treat. I wish I could've stayed three months, not just three days.'

'You went all that way just for three days? That's daft.'

'I couldn't stay. I had to cover Finland as well in time for the next meeting with the minister.'

'What is it you were doing? Finding bears to take to Norway?'

'Not really, just finding out where they like to live, so we can choose the best place for their return.'

'And what's this meeting you've got tomorrow?'

'It's to see if anyone in Scotland would like to be involved in the project and look at bear reintroduction here.'

'Oh aye,' he snorted. 'The farmers'll love that one.'

I turned the windscreen wipers up to maximum and bit my tongue.

I took the turning to home and we didn't speak again until the car was parked up outside. The houses had been built in the Fifties by the Forestry Commission: good quality timber buildings, a brief dalliance with Scandinavian construction that had, inexplicably, failed to catch on. Perhaps this was why I had thought I might feel at home in Norway.

'Shall I put it in the garage?' I asked.

'No, I'll do it later.' We got out and he made for my bag out of the boot, but I got there first. He didn't look strong enough to lift a football, let alone a suitcase. I waited until we were ensconced inside, sitting in the comfy chairs in the living room, Dad in his high-backed chair, Mum's still with its tapestry cushion. I sat on the sofa under the window. There was dust on the skirting boards, but otherwise the place was tidy. Once we had drunk our tea, I asked about his operation.

'Och, I'm fine,' he said.

I realised I would have to drag the information out of him, and did: diagnosis, prostate cancer; prognosis, pretty good. He would be kept under close observation but they thought it had been caught early enough to stave it off.

'It's my ticker they're a bit more concerned about,' he eventually conceded.

'Do I have to give you the seventh degree?' I sighed. 'Come on, tell me. You're my dad. I care. I love you. I want to know how you really are.'

'You don't.' He shook his head.

'What do you mean?'

'I'm missing your mother.'

'Of course you are, Dad. I am, too.'

'I'm not, well, there are some things I don't know I can cope with. I never was much of a homebody.'

'You could get a cleaner.' I thought of Malcolm, for the first time in ages. Perhaps I might contact him, now that I was actually back in the same country again.

'It's nothing a cleaner could help with. Believe me, quine. I'm a mess since your mother died. Not even surgery'll heal that. It ripped me apart, losing her.'

I went to sit beside him, hugged his head to my shoulder. He let me stroke him as he wept like a lover, brokenhearted. I'd never seen him cry; never, that is, until now. I began to glimpse a side of him I hadn't ever imagined.

'I'm sorry, Callis.' He pulled a handkerchief from his trouser pocket.

'No need to be sorry.' I was crying now, too, into his thin hair. I hadn't known we had it in us to be so open.

'I'm glad you're here,' he said, blowing his nose, wiping his cheeks and eyes and pulling himself upright. 'Thanks for coming home. It's been hard going since the funeral.' He nodded and swallowed between words.

I felt as if a cat was kneading me with its claws out.

'I'm sorry I couldn't get back sooner,' I said. It sounded crass after his disarming honesty. 'My life seems suddenly to have gone into overdrive.'

'And is Yuri happy now? He seemed concerned you were going off on a bit of a tangent with this government job. You don't want to do anything to upset him, you know, he's a good boss.'

I took a deep breath and said nothing.

'Did I tell you he says we might be able to wangle sponsorship for a minibus for the team?'

'No, but Yuri is full of surprises.'

He turned to me, eyeing me curiously.

I tried a change of topic. 'Have you seen much of Auntie Marjory? She told me she'd look after you.'

'Your aunt is as disreputable as ever. Now stop changing the subject.'

'OK, but please let's not talk about Yuri.'

He continued to scrutinise me. 'You look well. Your skin's clear. You suit your hair short.' Since when had he ever noticed, let alone commented, on my hair? 'Have you got a new man, is that it?'

I couldn't hold his gaze. 'Not exactly. It must just be my work. I've been to some amazing places, met some amazing people in the past month.'

'Including a man?' he insisted.

'No!' I giggled, feeling myself blush at his interrogation. It was like being fifteen again.

As if he could read my mind, he said, 'Well, if there's no a man in your life, you should look up Malcolm Johnstone while you're here. He's been asking after you and he's got a look in his eye. I met him in the town last week, and he's here this weekend, visiting his mother. It's her 70th birthday. You should go and wish her many happy returns and put her son out of his misery while you're at it.'

'Are you matchmaking?' I pretended affront, trying not to think about the night in April. He gave me a grin I hadn't seen in years.

I got up to make some more tea. He followed me into the kitchen and sat at the table watching me as I fussed unnecessarily over tea caddies and sugar cubes.

The rain had stopped and the sun was out. The world was glistening outside. I opened the kitchen window and let the scents of the roses beneath it waft into the room, then sat down and poured the tea.

A bee buzzed into the kitchen through the open window and landed on the yellow tablecloth. We watched it rub its front two legs in front of it as if wringing its hands and then rub them over its swivelled head, like a cat washing its ears. 'Your mother would have squashed that by now,' he observed.

'No, she wouldn't. She'd have put a glass over it and tipped it out of the window. She only squashed flies.'

'Bees, flies, same difference,' he muttered.

'No, they're totally different. Bees make honey.' I could hear myself regressing to around seven years old. How did parents manage that? One moment you're feeling proud to have grown up so fine and the next minute you're back in primary school.

He reached for a newspaper. 'Same difference.'

I flicked the bee away before he could hit it. 'Now it'll be buzzing around all day annoying us.'

'It'll go out the way it came in.' The bee battered itself against the closed window. 'Eventually.' I took the newspaper from him. 'With a bit of help.' I guided the bee back out of the open window.

'The roses smell gorgeous,' I said. Another bull's eye.

He got to his feet. 'I've a mind to do some weeding,' he said. 'I've not really felt much like it, since…'

'I'll give you a hand, if you like.'

'It means killing wild flowers, you know.' A half-grin.

'I agree it's hard for a botanist to understand the concept of weeds.' I smiled back. 'But I'll try.'

We were going to try to be kind to each other after all. He pottered out, and after deciding that thinking about Malcolm, or Petr, or Yuri, should be avoided at all costs, I pottered after him.

After lunch, I checked my phone and skimmed my messages. Among the junk and newsletters there was one from Professor Petr Scazia. I left it waiting in the inbox while I deleted rubbish and sent apologies for meetings I would miss. I thanked an editor for the peer-review comments on a paper I'd submitted to the Palaeobiology Society Bulletin. I wondered for the thousandth time what the grievance was, which data I was being accused of misusing, and which, if any, of the various papers currently in the process of publication contained the problematic claims. Then I stared at the bold symbols of the unopened message. It bulged back. I clicked it open.

Dear Callis

It seems only a moment since you were here. Of course I would like to work further with you — it is not often I encounter someone with such

139

openness to new ideas and ability to assimilate knowledge so rapidly. It was a pleasure, to be continued, I hope.

Unfortunately, I am not willing to become a partner in the consortium as you suggest. I have been involved in these EU projects before and swore never again. The bureaucrats have too much control. Also, the project seems just to be a desk study and I've never seen the point in them. No bears in the office, as far as I can tell. Contact me again if you have plans for work out in the forest.

Please don't take this personally. Perhaps, if you're at the IBA conference this autumn we could do some plotting there.

Petr

I felt a stone in my stomach and my face scorching. I only realised now how much I had hoped, expected, looked forward to his involvement. We needed Romania. I should ask him if he might recommend a Romanian who would be willing to be involved, but I couldn't bring myself to respond to what felt like a snub. What really hurt was that it was true. It *was* just a desk study: no new data would be gathered, the work was theoretical, not out in the field. The EU rules explicitly ruled out fieldwork costs.

I searched for 'IBA conference' on the Internet and felt even more stupid. The International Bear Association, of course, a whole world of professional bear researchers I didn't even know about. No wonder Petr didn't want to work with me. I was just an amateur with overblown ideas.

The house had just become a trap that I had to escape from. I had boots in my bag, and waterproofs. I dug them out, and dressed for a walk.

Dad was weeding again. He looked up from the border under the kitchen window as I passed.

'I'm off up the hill,' I said. 'Need to stretch my legs.'

'Aye, catch the weather. Don't go off the path.'

Don't do this. Don't do that. It was his perpetual refrain. I opened the gate at the bottom of the garden on to the back lane. He was no longer a policeman, maybe, but it was still part of his character. Don't give up your job. Don't do anything to threaten your job. Don't so much as think differently from the person in authority over you.

At the end of the road was the edge of a large plantation of Sitka spruce. Through the kissing gate, I followed the forestry track up into the trees.

I felt his obedience trained in, from childhood. It was the value he most espoused. Daddy's girl was good and didn't break the rules. And now here I was, a grown adult, still cowed by his instructions. No doubt he meant them kindly enough. But 'don't cross your boss' meant 'don't follow your dream', and 'follow your dream' was always Mum's mantra. What would her advice have been right now? Chances are she'd have fallen in behind Dad, not to cause open conflict, but then quietly, behind the scenes, she'd have said, 'follow your dreams'. How much bedroom diplomacy she must have worked, bringing Dad around from his absolute 'don't do that' position. I wondered how she'd managed it. I remembered his determination that I must not go off to work in a foreign country, and how, when I got the post-doctoral fellowship in Trondheim, he had, miraculously, come round to it. What had Mum said to persuade him?

Now instead of Mum, he was having backroom chats with Yuri. All of a sudden he was a hero, having helped his beloved football team to their splendid new strips and now, seemingly, maybe also able to wangle sponsorship for a new minibus. It unnerved me to think the two men were talking to each other. Was it just a coincidence, and if not, what was Yuri up to? Was he trying to win me round to giving up the bear job? If so, it was a really strange way of going about it.

Panting, I reached a clear-cut area. Massed foxgloves had sprouted among the brash, the plush rosettes of their foliage beneath spears of buds, their first purple flowers opening like finger puppets. Mum had told me they were sleeping bags for pixies, who cuddle bumble bees as we do teddy bears. I'd never forgotten the image. I smiled at the memory but then remembered my most recent experience of a sleeping bag, out in the Romanian forest, with a real bear, and I found myself back at the message from Petr.

I stomped on, up the hill, towards the moor, where clouds were thickening again. That would be right. It would rain. I would carry on walking anyway.

The following afternoon Stig had offered to take me out to the lynx reintroduction site. He collected me from the house in a Land Rover and we drove south into the hills, over a pass where plantations of conifers flanked both sides of the road. Stig slowed, gesturing on down the road.

'I stay in the next village that way, but this is where we go off-piste.' He indicated left and turned on to a forestry track. Two miles on, he halted and jumped out to open a gate.

'I could have done that,' I said.

'Go on then,' he said, pausing on the other side.

I got out to close it behind us and we drove on. Shortly afterwards Stig pulled up and switched the engine off. He reached for his coat, put his finger to his lips to indicate quiet, and pointed to a raised hut among the trees. We climbed out and approached the hide. I tried to soften my footfalls, look in all directions at once, peel back my ears for any sound and remember to breathe. While Stig unlocked the door, I pulled my phone out of my pocket and switched it to silent.

The hide was positioned at the edge of dense Sitka spruce plantation, looking out into mixed, pretty young-looking native woodland. After we'd been in the hide for an hour and a half, we had still seen nothing but a couple of squirrels. The trees were in full leaf and the undergrowth here was thick: bracken knotted among brambles. There could have been anything moving around out there for all we would see of it.

For the first hour, the small wooden hut had been dense with excitement, as the landscape outside had slowly given up its secrets. I scoured the slope up from the hide for any sign of movement. At first, as I scanned the hillside, each grey rock was possibly a creature and the shade patterns lengthening under trees all potentially concealed what we were looking for. My eyes tracked backwards and forwards, trying to learn the view out of the window off by heart, so that any change would become more obvious. I looked and looked, as if it was possible to peel the visible away and reveal a hiding animal. Instead, whatever was hidden remained obstinately obscured by ever amassing details of foliage and stone.

Nothing moved except eyeballs. I found my shoulders tensed around my ears, and had to make a conscious effort to loosen them. I fiddled with a broken toggle in my pocket. My lower back was sore from sitting on the uncomfortable bench by the hide window.

'Nothing doing,' Stig murmured.

'Not a twitch,' I whispered.

I scratched at an insect bite on my ankle and yawned.

'You had enough?'

I breathed out hard. Then sighed, and nodded reluctantly.

'Sorry mate, another day.'

I nodded again. I had a momentary vision of throwing a childish tantrum, stamping my feet and howling, 'I wanna see de puddy tat.' I thought better of it. I wasn't sure I could make it seem convincing as jest, not real.

I unwound myself from the bench, rubbing my lower back, arching my shoulders. Stig appeared as loose and calm as when we had arrived. He had sat, silent, watching, alert but peaceful, while I had twitched, itched and shuffled. That man is made for watching, I thought. He reminded me of Petr. His movements were graceful and noiseless as he swung the door to the start of its creak, ushered me out then followed. He closed the hide up, locked it with a quiet click and tucked the key away in a hiding place above the door. Then he drifted down the wooden steps to ground level and stopped, waiting for me to fall in behind him for the walk out in the greying dusk.

The air was still among the trees, a dor beetle droned past and a distant woodpecker drummed. The scent of moss wafted a seduction from somewhere unseen. Stig stood motionless, intent on something to his right. His hand, I realised, was pointing in a subtle gesture to a ghost under a pine tree, a grey smudge in the gloaming. The blur ambled out from the tree shadow and took on the form of a pale foxlike body, but too tall for a fox. Its head lifted, scenting. Pert ears over a cat's face, glimpsed for a second, and then, long legs running, gone.

Straining into the half-dark I looked and looked, my face taut with wonder. Lynx! It was a lynx! It had been no phantom. It was real, and here, hunting in the woods.

Stig grasped my hand and gave it a squeeze.

'Female,' he mouthed. How could he possibly tell, I wondered? But I didn't question that he knew. What else had he seen that I had not? Watching him observe I saw a heightened form of seeing. Could I learn to tune in to the world like that? To attune to animals, to life, to being, without interference from abstract thought, emotion, ego, all the clutter clogging up my brain: the stresses of deadlines, tasks, duties, obligations, negligences, failures, bitterness, grief. Perhaps it was already happening and I hadn't noticed. For a moment, I looked into the woods, just looked, and felt my life shed some of its triviality, like a tree losing leaves in autumn.

Stig was off, padding along the track, out of the woods, back to the Land Rover. The night was thickening. As the startling door-light blazed, it cast the world into total dark. I scampered after him.

'Good one, eh! She didn't want you to leave disappointed.'

'Beautiful.' I was as close to speechless as I had ever been. I clambered into the seat beside Stig, and fumbled with the seatbelt.

The engine juddered into noise, and Stig raised his voice over it. 'That's Lara, she's three years old. I'm hoping we'll see her with young in spring. She's been mixing with males a fair bit and she should be old enough for a litter.'

'How do you know it's her?'

'Size, colour, markings, just like you know your house cats. She's got a smashed right ear from a fight last year. Her pelt's pure grey, no mottling like a lot of them.'

Stig reversed the Land Rover back on to the track, eased into first gear, then up into second.

'How many are there now?'

Stig was keeping the pace slow, avoiding the worst of the ruts. We splashed through a puddle.

'Eleven females now, eight males. Four of the females bred this year. I think we might have seven young left: two have pairs, one has three and the other lost them all.'

'How?'

'Fox probably, maybe raptors, maybe she just couldn't feed them, lost them in a river, hard to tell. It's tough out there for kittens.'

'Ah, I'd love to see them.'

'Yeah, they're cute. Hard to spot though, the mothers keep them well hidden.'

We stopped at the gate and I jumped down, opened it and gave a queenly wave as Stig drove through. It clunked shut and I climbed back into the cab.

'So, it's working, the reintroduction?' I said.

He turned to me as if to gauge my tone. 'Aye. If you mean they're still here. Breeding, settling in. It's early days, though. Plenty opposition out there, yet to be convinced they aren't going to ravage farms and steal their babies.'

Stig slowed to nudge over more ruts in the track. On both sides, Sitka spruces towered, blackening out the sky.

'The foresters are pleased though. I'm getting good support for the reduction in roe deer damage on the new plantings. Give it time.'

'Brilliant.'

'Aye, wolves next. That'd make a real difference.'

'Are you serious?'

'In my dreams.' I shot him a sideways look but he was concentrating on the track.

'What about bears?' I ventured.

'What about bears?'

'Could we reintroduce them? Bring them back to Scotland?'

We reached the end of the forest track and Stig pulled up. 'Do you want a lift home or do you fancy a pint at the Cask?'

'Do the aforementioned big furry animals shit in the woods?'

He hit the indicator and turned left.

In the pub, I put a pint of Big Cat Ale down on the table in front of him and sat down opposite. He snapped his phone shut.

'Big Cat beer, has to be a good sign,' I grinned.

'Aye, I guess so. Unless it's just to wind the farmers up. How's your farmer, anyway?'

'Shut up!'

'Frances warned me it might be a sore point. Sorry, I just put my foot in it, didn't I?'

'No. There's nothing to put your foot in. We had a one-night-stand after my mum's funeral, then I've met a rather delicious Romanian and failed spectacularly to manage even one night with him. Otherwise my lovelife's a washout. Shall we stick to talking about whether we can we bring bears back?'

'Yeah. You're serious.'

'Course. I'm pretty obsessed with bears these days.' I liked the way he smiled at me then, eyeing me with those piercing blue eyes, stroking his beard.

'To be brutally honest I don't think there's the habitat.'

His body language had changed completely since we hit human civilisation. The languid attentiveness had tightened up. His eyes darted for threats. There were other men in the bar, three of them lined up along the counter, two at tables, all watching the football on the plasma screen, eyes trained like guns on the sport, periodically sighting round for trouble or predators, firing volleys of sarcasm at the game or each other.

'All right, Jock,' Stig had said as we came in.

'Aye,' had been the barman's response. Stig didn't really belong here, I could see that.

He drained his beer halfway in one swig. I supped, wiping the froth off my lip. 'Good beer,' I said.

'Aye, not bad.'

We chatted about mutual friends and I probed for news of Frances and Diana. Stig didn't know what Diana was doing but he had heard all about our spat at Fenwick from Frances. According to Stig, she was feeling sorry for me.

'Well, you tell her to get in touch with me, then,' I said. 'I'm sorry to snap, but she knows all my numbers.' The idea of being pitied by Diana and Frances infuriated me.

We fell silent and drank. Towards the bottom of my pint, I had to ask. 'Can the habitat be restored?' I wondered if I was pushing it.

'For bears?'

'Yes.'

'Do you want another pint?'

'Twist my arm.' I handed him my glass.

With a full pint in front of him he talked. 'The thing is, bears need a lot of feeding, especially to build up for the winter. They need an easy source of food: good woods, you know, rich in nuts and berries, full of toads and slugs and anthills.'

'Yeah.'

'Fish must have been a big part of their diet in the past, but the summer runs of salmon are so feeble now and hydro dams have screwed up half the rivers.'

I shook my head. 'According to the people I've been talking to, fish don't feature much in European brown bear diets. North American brown bears eat a lot of salmon, but our salmon are a different species and don't die after spawning, so there isn't the same fishing frenzy you see in places like Alaska. In Sweden and Finland bears eat elk – I was told they take the stupid one-year-old ones – so if they don't get lots of nuts and fruit, they'll just eat more meat.'

'I'm not convinced that would work in Scotland.'

'Why not? We've got loads of deer. Too many deer.'

'But more than likely they'd take sheep or find their way to grain stores on farms. They like to roam a bit, keep moving, need some space. Our woods are so fragmented they'll keep busting out to farmland, that's the problem. They'd be in constant conflict with people, just like Norway.'

'But…' I stopped.

'What?'

'There are two quite separate issues, aren't there? The bears need habitat, food, a place to live that's ecologically ready for them. But they also need a human society that will tolerate them, even welcome them. In Norway, habitat's not the problem, it's society, the bloody farmers and the law that let them shoot bears on their land. Here in Scotland, we're bringing predators back and mostly I think folk are ready to see them here, but you say the habitat's no good.'

'Not no good, just not rich enough and big enough to ensure the bears stay out of harm's way.'

'But if society could ensure no harm if and when they come on to farmland?'

'Aye, right. That'll be the farmland where they grow flying pigs.'

'But the lynx are here, we're going forwards not backwards.'

He drained his pint. 'You really are serious, aren't you?'

'Deadly!' I grinned, picked up his glass, and my own, and got up. 'Another one?'

'You're mad.'

'About bears, yes.' I walked over to the bar. 'Two more Big Cats, please,' I said to the barman, giving him a two-pint smile.

'Miao, miao.' He took the glasses from me and put a clean one under the tap.

'No pussy jokes, now.'

'Would I?' he smirked.

'I saw a lynx today,' I told him. 'That's why I'm getting drunk. We should bring back bears, too, don't you think?'

'No, thanks. I like to be left in peace when I'm fishing. I don't want some old grizzly breathing down my neck.'

'Aw, killjoy. Just take a spare rod and lend it to him. They're not very good at fishing.'

'Aye, that'll be right.'

The following Monday, I met Stig at the lobby of the Scottish Land Institute. I was relieved to find him in jeans and a rugby shirt. I hadn't known whether to dress up for the meeting and had opted for the comfort of casual clothes. He led me up to the boardroom, where his boss was already helping himself to coffee.

'Peter Harsel, Callis MacArthur.'

We shook hands and I watched myself being appraised while Stig poured coffee. His boss was not much older than him, if at all, but was sharp-suited, shiny-shoed and sported a navy-blue institutional tie. I began to wish I had worn something smart, after all. The door opened and an older man walked in from a military mess room of an earlier century, complete with polished bald head, handlebar moustache and tweeds.

'Sudbury,' he announced in a plummy Home Counties accent. 'You must be Dr MacArthur. Delighted.'

Professor Sudbury and Dr Harsel sat like an army general and navy lieutenant opposite Stig and I, and proceeded with an interrogation so lacking in logic that I soon began to despair. I had sent various documents beforehand with the intention that we would work our way through them, in order; the key document being a concept note outlining the proposed EU project. But without so much as glancing at it, they proceeded swiftly to page seven of the thirteen-page sample funding application form, which I'd expected we might get around to in the afternoon, if we managed to agree on certain principles and core ideas.

'Risk assessment and amelioration,' boomed Professor Sudbury, a man, I realised, who would only have a first name to close friends and family, and possibly not even them. 'Key issue, I think, for us, here.'

'Absolutely key,' Harsel nodded vigorously.

'Surely we need to be clearer first of what exactly the risk is to be assessed?' Not very well expressed, but, I hoped, a logical remark. I wondered if I would ever get a chance to make a proper introduction to the study idea.

'Well, risk of damage to the reputation of the Institute, naturally.' Sudbury got up and paced, as if seeking a mantelpiece to lean against to pontificate with greater stature. 'We cannot be seen to be scaremongering. There'll be media all over it. The first scent they get of wolves, they will all howl.' He chuckled.

'There is no suggestion of wolves,' Stig pointed out.

The professor ignored him. 'Far too many horror films, not to mention Little Red Riding Hood.'

Harsel waded in. 'There's a real risk it will undermine our other programmes, reduce our credibility in the agriculture sector.'

I was getting sweaty and probably looking red in the face. I tried to keep my voice calm. 'Professor Sudbury, Dr Harsel,' I breathed, 'there seems to be a misunderstanding of what is involved here.'

'Large Carnivore Reintroduction.' Harsel poked the three words on the title of the document in front of him.

'That is an example of a successful project application under the same Habitats Directive Programme we are proposing to apply to, but it is just an example to give us some ideas, to act as an inspiration, if you like.' I tried to smile and hoped my grimace wasn't too canine. 'It's clearly much more ambitious than anything we could realistically do in Scotland, or indeed Norway. The reality in France and Spain is very different to here.' I kept smiling, speaking slowly, as if to idiots. 'Very different. What we are proposing is much less ambitious. We are proposing merely to look at the ecological feasibility of introducing bears, not actually to introduce them, of course. We're nowhere near that stage.'

'The idea is to start with just a desk study,' Stig threw in. 'to better understand the constraints that exist here in Scotland, with respect to bears. No intention of looking at wolves at all.'

'No wolves whatsoever?' said the professor.

'None whatsoever.' Stig and I shook our heads gravely. Sudbury looked reassured.

'Still, bears are dangerous carnivores,' Harsel jibed.

'They're omnivores, actually, mostly vegetarian,' I threw back, 'though we of course recognise that they could pose a modest risk, for example to farm livestock, so we would need to carefully assess those risks. I think that is the kind of risk assessment the funders would be expecting to see under section seven there.' Sudbury still had his document open at that page. 'But before that, don't you think we should look a little at the concept note for the proposal, work out if we see eye to eye on the overall objective, for example, and discuss just what it is we might be trying to achieve here?'

'Quite right,' Sudbury said. 'Lead us through it, Dr MacArthur.'

'Please, call me Callis.' The charm was working. I leaned across the table and reordered the papers in front of him. 'This concept note has been drawn up by a government commission involving Norway's most eminent ecologists and natural scientists, farmers' organisations and so on, chaired by Professor Anja Eldegard who, as I'm sure you know, is Head of Natural Resource Management at Oslo University. She asked me to give you her regards, Professor Sudbury.'

He nodded sagely.

'But of course it is not set in stone.' I smiled at Peter Harsel, who was stony faced. 'And we need Scottish expertise to ensure that the methodology we are testing is not coloured too much by the particular political situation we are facing just now in Norway.' I explained about the recent loss of bears and the public fervour for their return.

'There'd be a public outcry if you tried to bring bears here, I'll tell you that for a fact. The farmers would never tolerate it.' Harsel's hands were fists on the table in front of him.

'Actually I have a letter expressing support for the project concept from the National Farmers' Union of Scotland. Shall I read it to you? It's from John Mackay, Chairman.'

'John Mackay?' Harsel opened his eyes wide and laid his hands flat. 'What does it say?'

'It starts by thanking us for the chance to look at the concept note. Then it says,' I read from the email I had printed that morning, still not quite sure I could believe its contents, ' "We would be very interested to learn about the ecological issues around bear reintroduction and to contribute to a study of the constraints and potential impacts of such a reintroduction. It will be important for such a study to gauge the public opinion surrounding this issue in light of the recent downturn in the Norwegian agricultural sector. We see potential opportunities as well as threats and welcome the opportunity to participate in further discussion of this issue." And then there's some stuff about their ecological policies.'

'Well, well, well,' said Sudbury. 'More coffee anyone?'

Malcolm was waiting for me in the snug, with a full pint in front of him. He was in jeans and a sweater, dressed down compared to the last time. I made a mental note of comparison with Petr – Malcolm was burlier, and no less attractive. Spotting me, he leapt to his feet to buy me a drink.

'Sit down! I'll get it,' I said. 'You can get the next round.'

I was surprised how comforting it was to see him. The chat was easy, easier than I'd expected. I found myself talking about Mum. He talked about his dad's death a few years back. Conversation moved on to music, a remarkable congruence of tastes. Then we got on to bears.

'It's a pretty crazy project you're setting up,' he said, sitting back, his arm along the back of the bench seat, not quite touching me.

'Where did you see it?' I cringed at the idea that the media might have got hold of it already.

'NFUS. I'm on the exec committee for my sins. Got into it through the Young Farmers. Your project came up at the last meeting.'

'I got a nice response from someone Mackay.'

'John, aye. I wrote that.' He grinned.

'You wrote it?'

'Aye. It caused a bit of a stooshie in the meeting. There's a knee-jerk reaction from some of them if you so much as mention big hairy things with teeth.'

'Cows are big hairy things with teeth.'

'You know what I mean. I'd been keeping an eye on the news from Norway since your mother's funeral, just out of interest. Your timing was good. There'd been an article about the boycott of that Norwegian meat-chain in the Scottish Farmer the week before.'

'Svenson's? That made the news here, did it?'

'Aye. I read some bits out at the meeting. The committee didn't like the sound of a groundswell of public opinion against Norwegian farmers, so we agreed to support the impact study. I argued that we've nothing to lose, and it's important to influence your thinking. We've got to keep our beady little eyes on you, haven't we! I persuaded them it'd be better to be inside shaping what you're up to than having to react to the results.'

'Oh, good for you.'

'Anyway, as a result I got the job of writing the letter to you. I thought you'd spot my email address.'

I pulled my phone out of my bag and flicked through my email files until I found it.

'There you are. mj@nfus.sco... bla bla bla, "Cheers Malcolm". Shit, sorry. I totally missed it. I mustn't have clocked the address. It's obvious really, not that many Malcolm Js around. It never crossed my mind it might be you.'

He shrugged. 'Nae bother.'

I felt bad about it, as if I'd blanked him on a street. I said so.

'Look, I'm not worried.' He put his hand on my arm and looked me straight in the eye. 'You're here. I'm here. You didn't

153

spot my email. Big deal. I enjoyed sending it. I got my kicks – you missed yours, shucks, eh?'

'It won the day at my meeting at the Land Institute yesterday, if that's any consolation. They were dead set against the idea, said the farmers would crucify them for even saying the word "bear" in public. Then I read out your letter and they all back-pedalled like crazy. Stig was most impressed.'

'They were opposed to it? But they're all sandal-wearers, aren't they?'

'Don't you believe it. Tweeds and brogues all over the place.'

'You're kidding me. So they're not all like you?'

'Not a bit. I was the mad ecologist just dropped in from Viking Land. I may as well have been wearing a horned helmet.'

He chuckled. 'It'd suit you.'

I punched him on the arm.

'Ow. I'm breakable.'

'Oh, aye. Get us another pint before I cause a riot.'

'You learn that in Norway?' He looked at my empty glass.

'Aye, marauding, pillaging and getting stocious, first year study. It cost me a fortune, the getting stocious module especially, but I got a distinction.'

He shook his head and headed for the bar.

'I got you a pint of Red Rider. Seemed appropriate. Is that OK?'

'Is that the one with the axe-wielding warrior?'

'That's the one.'

'Thanks. I'm actually a very sensitive Viking.'

'Aye, I know. I remember how you looked when Brian McCabe stole your teddy.'

'I'd probably still cry if you stole my teddy. Look, I really appreciate you getting NFUS support, it's brilliant.'

'Entirely selfish. You always were besotted with bears, nothing'll change that. You haven't got a cat in hell's chance of getting them back here, but if you want a job in Scotland and this is the option, who am I to stand in your way? I'll be honest, I'd like to see you back here. I could put up with seeing a bit more of you.' He gave me another of those direct looks and I tried, but failed, to hold his gaze.

'I think we'll get bears back,' I murmured into my pint.

There was an embarrassing pause.

'Naa. Nae chance.'

'I'm confident.' I flashed him a glance.

'You're mad.'

'Aye, mebbe. I'm still confident. And I wasn't angling for a job. I've got the best job going in Norway.'

'Oh?' He looked unconvinced. 'Your dad'd love it if you were back here, especially at the Land Institute.'

That shut me up.

A ginger-haired head peered into the snug. I pointed and laughed. 'Jimmy Black, fancy seeing you!'

'Is that really wee Callis MacArthur? A little birdy told me you were here. How the hell are you? Did you know a bunch of your old classmates are playing pool in the back bar? And Malcolm sire, is this a secret tryst or are you up for an old school pool challenge?'

'No secrets from you, Jimmy,' Malcolm said. 'I've not quite made my pass yet, but I'm working up to it, that's if she doesn't get in first. She's been in Viking country, you know. I've got as far as a confession for marauding and pillaging and I'm wondering what else she might get up to.'

I feigned affront. 'Modern Vikings require prior and fully informed consent, signed in triplicate.'

'Just show me the dotted line.'

Jimmy put both hands up in front of him. 'I'll leave you two lovebirds in peace then, shall I? That's if Vikings do peace?'

Malcolm pushed back the table. 'Nah, I think she deserves a thrashing on the pool table.'

'Well, you're welcome. Whatever.'

We joined the throng. I was blushing to my collar. I played a disarray of fluky brilliance dotted among utter rubbish and was wiped off the table within minutes. Malcolm lasted a bit longer.

I went for a round of beers and he came to help carry them, leaning behind me as I stood at the bar. I could feel the whole length of his body pressed up against me, his breath on my hair, his arms one on each side of me clasping pint glasses. He stood there longer than he needed to and I felt his warmth soak in, knowing the next step was inevitable, finding comfort in the press, hoping that we would find more excuses to stand close together like that, closer than necessary by far, just to feel our bodies wishing to work like one. And my so-called friends in Fe-Phi-Pho could, well, they could take a running jump. I had other pals.

In the toilet Catherine Sinclair said, 'So how long have you and Malcolm Johnstone been an item?'

I had never been close to her at school. She had always been a bit prim. Now she was heavily made up, as if her real face didn't match her soul or her expectations of life, but I was drunk and friendly.

'We're not,' I said.

'You look like you're together,' she said. 'He can't take his big eyes off you.'

The toilet door swung and banged behind her. I stood looking at myself in the mirror. I was flushed. My hair did suit me short, it was true. I thought of Petr and of Yuri, and wondered what my next night with Malcolm would be like. I pulled a face at myself and returned to the beery clamour.

Later, he walked me to Dad's house, and I invited him in for coffee, but he refused. 'I'd better get back, it's Mum's 70th tomorrow. And I'm a bit drunk to meet your father,' he said.

'He'll probably be in bed.'

'No, he won't, he'll be watching *Newsnight*, waiting up for you. Another time. There will be another time, won't there?'

'Of course,' I said. He bent down and kissed me on the lips.

'Is that a promise?'

I nodded, greedy.

'When are you next in Scotland?'

'I don't know. It depends on the project. It's a busy job. I'll be sure and let you know as soon as I do.'

'Come and stay at mine again. I'll show you the bright lights of Inverness.'

'Oooh.' Deep sarcasm.

'It's all right, the Sneck. Cosmopolitan Heelan' Capital. Stuffed full of Weegies and Poles. Excellent bar scene. An alky like you'd love it.'

'Calling me an alky?'

'You're shit-faced everytime I see you.'

'Yeah, like twice in twelve years.'

'Three times in as many months.'

'Aye, so it is. That was a nice kiss, have you got any more?'

'Plenty where that came from.'

'Show me.' He showed me.

It was odd to part with unfinished business. 'You've got my email address,' he said.

The ball was in my court. I left it there, not sure what move to make, waiting for some witty inspiration to strike, sending no message rather than something bland. And life, on my return to Norway, was hectic.

🐾 🐾

On my first day back at the Institute I had a brief, cold meeting with Professor Bergen, who explained that the grievance was indeed from Yuri. He was claiming I was using pollen samples collected by others, then writing up the results as if it was my own work. He cited three recent papers. It was a cheat. Of course I had used pollen data collected by researchers around Norway, but I was sure they were all referenced and acknowledged. I didn't think I'd done anything wrong, and if I had slipped up at all in referencing it was accidental, not deliberate. But the very accusation of data theft made me toss and turn in bed at night, rage alternating with despair at what this might mean if I couldn't prove my innocence.

In an email to Yuri, copied to Professor Bergen, I demanded that he give chapter and verse about the data misuse but he merely said I was evading the claim and it was up to me to prove I had permission to use every piece of information I published.

Meanwhile he continued a campaign of deprecation of my work as 'derivative', flawed and unscientific. I started to dread entering the Institute: conversations with once-friendly colleagues were strained and my pollen analysis work ground to a halt as I wrote to source after source, seeking written permission to cite their work and use their data. After this drudgery, it was always a relief to turn to work on the EU funding proposal for the study of the feasibility of restoring predator populations, despite the horrible Euro-jargon and mind-bogglingly complex financial arrangements.

In the end it was Malcolm who took the initiative in making contact.

Hullo Callis. Just wondering how you're doing. Hope all's well with you. I've just heard I've lost my job. It turns out the dairy's been losing money down the drain for two years, bled dry by the supermarkets, same old same old. Four of us are out on our arses, hoping NFU contacts will come up trumps. Got some harvest work up in Easter Ross and I've put my name down for a croft in Sutherland. Getting sick of working other ****s land. Don't hug too many bears. When are you next in Scotland? It'd be good to see you. Malcolm.

Hi Malcolm.
Fucking supermarkets. Fucking landlords. Sorry to hear your bad news, hope you find something better. I'm up to my eyeballs in work here, submitting the proposal for joint project - thanks to your support - and waiting to see if the Norwegian Parliament will pass the Bill to bring bears back. Life as a government advisor is cushy - covering the length and breadth of the country on expenses, but no time for a trip

to Scotland in the near future. If you've got
time off and want a holiday, you're welcome to
come marauding and pillaging.

  Bear Hugs.

Callis.

  I'll take you up on that. Especially the
bear hugs. M.

🐾 🐾

In early August there was a second, rather longer conciliation
meeting, a valiant effort by Professor Bergen to keep Yuri's grievance out of the legal system by resolving it within the Institute.
It did not go well. Yuri stonewalled and kept up his accusations,
alleging there were disgruntled academics from other institu-
tions whose work I had misused, but refusing to give names,
and insisting, still, that I prove all my data use was permitted.
Professor Bergen's nervousness about the Institute's reputation
seemed to limit her sympathy and she tended to agree with Yuri
that, given the circumstances, I should gather more evidence in
support of my claim that all my source material was freely given
and fully referenced.

Tedious weeks went by but eventually I delivered what I
believed to be a comprehensive report on all my data use since
coming to Norway – frustratingly, several people from whom I
had received pollen samples had not yet responded to my requests
for written permissions, but at least I had proof of asking for these.
Writing the EU project proposal was light relief by comparison.

The Sunday after I submitted both documents I found
myself at a loose end. It had been the wettest summer on record
and today was a particularly grey rainy day, a tidying up day. My
inbox was, as usual, full of rubbish. There was a message fester-
ing in there, one bad apple, making them all seem sour.

I went on to FemComm, anything to avoid the real problem, and noticed that Catherine Sinclair had posted a photo of

159

me from the pub in June, and that I'd been unfriended by both Frances and Diana. I'd never much liked online networking anyway. Half of my 421 so-called friends I'd never actually met and most of the rest I hadn't seen since university, and even then 'friend' would have been stretching it.

Email couldn't actually be any worse. I filed, responded briefly or deleted, trying to be systematic, and made good progress. The one difficult message at the top became more and more prominent. Eventually it was the only one left. I had to deal with it.

```
Callis
    As agreed at the meeting on Thursday, I am
willing to drop my complaint about your misuse
of data when you resign from the Bear Reintro-
duction Working Group.
    Yours
    Yuri
```

His adamant misnaming of the group infuriated me.

```
Dear Yuri
    I remain convinced that I have not misused
any data and mystified by your complaint. I am
sorry, but I am not willing to resign from the
Parliamentary Expert Group on Ecological Resto-
ration at present.
    Yours
    Callis
```

I cc'd the message to Professor Bergen.

🐾 🐾

The Bear Bill, as it had become known, was put before the Parliament on 22 August, so I went to Oslo for the debate. The minister was confident that it would pass, because the majority coalition had promised support. However, the farmers' lobby had been working hard and they were there in force at the *Storting*, ranks of portly men and power-dressed young women. The academics and conservationists were thin and shabby in comparison. Fit and casual, I tried to tell myself.

It was a tense afternoon, waiting for decision time. I was offered a tour of the *Storting* but declined, instead killing time in a café nearby, watching rain stotting down on the pavement outside, and tourists hunched under umbrellas, unimpressed with the Nordic capital.

In the end, getting through security to get back into the building took so long that I missed the actual moment of the vote and wondered why I had bothered making the trip south. The Bill was passed by only four votes due to a mass of abstentions from the Christian Democrats in the coalition. Only the Greens voting for the Bill, from outside the coalition, won the day, which they were quick to point out, as was the media. One newspaper headlined 'A hippy victory'.

Although the opinion polls still showed strong public support for the return of bears, it appeared to be waning. There were grumbles from various parts of the country about inadequate consultation on the locations that had been shortlisted for the releases.

'We have to win some local support for our top sites,' I said at our team meeting the next day. I managed to persuade Anja to launch a consultation at each of the twelve sites on the shortlist. I volunteered to attend public meetings and explain why particular sites had been selected, and I soon had a punishing schedule of site visits lined up for September.

Then Malcolm's next message arrived.

Taking time out mid-September. Tromso Music Festival 20, 21, 22. Will bring horned helmet. Up for it? M

I rescheduled my third week and buzzed the festival number.

```
Hi Malcolm.
   I have 2 tickets for Tromsø. Book the ferry.
   Bear hugs waiting.
   Callis.
```

```
Arr Trondheim 16 Sept. How the fuck do we get
to Tromso? Hurtigruten boat? M
```

His message had a link to the *Hurtigruten* website. '*The World's Most Beautiful Voyage.*' It would take three days and looked ravishing. I made some enquiries and did some more rescheduling.

```
Hi Malcolm
   Sounds like a holiday, but I can make it work
and put it on expenses. Deluxe cabin booked and
paid for.
   Hugs
   C
```

```
Jammy! M
```

It was a ridiculously luxurious cabin, all things considered. A porthole window on the bathroom door and some fancy knotwork in a frame hinted at nautical, but if it weren't for the roll of the boat and the way the view flowed past the huge picture window, it could have been a five-star hotel, not a ferry. I sat on the bed.

'How'd you wangle this on expenses?' Malcolm asked. 'Some job you've got here.' He stood silhouetted by the window.

'I have to meet some folk in Tromsø and we'll stop off for a night at Harstad so I can be harangued by the locals.'

'Where's that?'

'Just a bit south of Tromsø. At the north end of the Lofoten Islands, supposed to be spectacular scenery. We're looking at there as a release site. Hoping the wildlife tourism guys will carry more weight than the farmers. There's a serious spat going on there, apparently.'

'So you're going to sort them out?'

'No, I'm going to listen and learn.'

Malcolm nodded.

'But first,' I said. 'We have the best part of forty-eight hours to chill out and watch Norway go past the window.'

I got up and joined him looking out, put an arm casually around his waist. We had hugged when I met him from the Aberdeen ferry but kept a platonic distance as we had checked in for the *Hurtigruten* and eaten dinner in a harbour restaurant waiting for departure time. Now in the privacy of the cabin I wondered what I had been thinking of to spend two nights locked in a cabin with a man I barely knew, or only knew as a primary school kid. Had been quite intimate with as a primary school kid, in fact, but never since, until that one, drunken, grief-stricken night. Perhaps for good reason. What if we didn't get on?

He bent down and kissed me. It felt OK. He was quite tasty, really.

'What's the view like from the bed?' he said.

'Perfect. Do you want a drink?'

'Not really. I was thinking about something more along the lines of marauding and pillaging.'

The boat rolled. We stumbled towards the bed, grabbing each other and giggling. Once we began, we discovered a hunger fired by almost two months of anticipation. Quite tasty became quite satisfying, then more substantial, then delicious. Our bodies rocked with the swell of the boat. We took our time.

While Malcolm slept, I thought of Petr, that burst of newness in the danger of the forest, my self laid bare. It felt like a dream. This was different. It was physical and fun.

Malcolm and I revelled in each other, talking, telling, peeling off layers of stories to reveal ever more of ourselves. We moved from familiar to intimate. We laughed, kissed, played, bathed and slept as a single body. We swayed hand-in-hand for meals on trays in the ship's cafeteria and stood wrapped around each other out on deck. We even indulged in the outdoor jacuzzi, lying giggling in the bubbles, watching fulmars and black-backed gulls wheel and soar in the wake and sea eagles beam across the ship like pirates.

The beer was bland and expensive and our bodies more intoxicating. We frequently found ourselves back in our cabin, indulging in our private view.

On the second night he told me he loved me. The next morning I said I loved him, too.

At Harstad we found it hard to stand on solid earth and wobbled our way to the Clarion Hotel Arcturus and a somewhat less luxurious room than we had grown used to.

'No fluffy bath robe,' I grumbled as I peered out over the harbour with its cluster of brightly painted wooden houses, pleasure yachts and fishing boats at anchor. A grey seal bobbed curious, circular ripples in the still water, and a raft of eider ducks made letter patterns as the outsized ferry boat honked its horn and disappeared around the headland.

The phone rang. 'Dr MacArthur?'

'Yes.'

'Reception here. Anders Pederson is waiting in the lobby.'

'I'll be right down.' The fun was over.

I returned to the hotel six hours later, bruised by two long meetings with pro-bear and anti-bear campaigners and a public presentation at which I had been ritually whipped and beaten with questions from an odd mix of fishermen, shopkeepers and retired urban executives, before being given a large bunch of flowers, a bottle of aquavit barely big enough for a single shot, a hand-carved wooden bowl and a standing ovation.

Malcolm had spent the day alone and though he'd attended the public meeting he had understood little of the rapid-fire exchanges in Norwegian between irate members of the audience.

'I couldn't make head nor tail of it, but they sure feel strongly about it all,' he said, bringing drinks from the bar to a table with a view out across the harbour and the black skerries beyond.

'They seemed to like you, anyway,' he grinned, pointing to the flowers. 'A few too many to wear in your hair at the festival. Not sure I can fit them in my tent.'

I laughed for the first time in hours. 'Thanks. God that was tough.' I felt my shoulders unclench. 'I never would have expected people to get so upset by this. It really brings out the testosterone in some of these blokes.' I shuddered at the memory of one man standing in the town hall, red-faced, his right arm pointing at me like a gun, poking his finger like a bayonet, shouting, 'You have no respect for us, for our livelihoods, for our safety, for the safety of our children.'

'You know the guy in the hall, the furious one, the one in the red-checked shirt?'

Malcolm nodded.

'He was right on one count.'

'What was that?'

'Roughly translated: fuck off home and see what Scottish farmers say to releasing fucking bears in their fucking villages.'

'They'd probably say, fuck off back to Norway.'

'You don't think they might say, "Oh good, enhanced biodiversity will bring economic opportunities for us to diversify into ecotourism," or something like that?'

'Nope.'

'Ah well, better stick to Norway for the time being, eh? At least here I only understand half the swear words.'

'And you get scenic boat rides between jobs.'

'True.'

'If you release bears on an island like this, will they swim over to the mainland?'

'Yes, we hope so.'

'Ah. No chance keeping them on the Isle of Rum or somewhere, then?'

'Not a chance. They'd do great at triathlons except they don't ride bikes very well.'

'Ha ha.'

I yawned. 'Knackered.'

'I see that. Bed time.'

'Goody.'

'Not that knackered, then?'

'Nope.'

Tromsø's bear debate was a bit less defensive but they were further removed from any of the proposed release sites and the town was packed full of ecotourism businesses and naturalists. I was given an exquisitely carved wooden bear and fox. I had been told it was from a local folk story about how the wily fox tricked the bear into ice-fishing with its tail, which froze off, thus leaving bears ever since with nothing more than stumps.

I joined Malcolm for dinner after the meeting, considerably more cheerful than the previous night.

'That one went a bitty better,' I said. 'And now I'm off scot-free for three whole days. Time to go wild at the festival.'

We had one more night of expenses-paid luxury in the Rica Ishavshotel looking out across to the world's most northerly cathedral. Next morning we stashed all our good gear in the left luggage room and light-packed it over the bridge and out of town to the world's most northerly music festival. We set up the tent among an encampment on a field, thankfully not yet a mud bath, and prepared to party.

While southern Norway was flooding, the north, unusually hot for the time of year, was having perfect festival weather. We stripped to shorts, vests, sandals, shades, and smothered each other in suncream, then stripped some more. Eventually we peeled our sweaty bodies back out of the tent and headed out towards the music. We danced madly to the Zen Grasshoppers and collapsed with a beer when some Swedish band we had never heard of came on.

We wandered off along a line of stalls for every environmental organisation imaginable, from eco-warrior bands like Earth First to WWF's global 'Panda' brand. I gazed lovingly at willow baskets made by the local Tromsø community woodcraft association and Malcolm seemed to be seriously considering buying a T-shirt from the local branch of the farmers' union with a horned helmet logo and the words '*Farmers are Hard*'. I told him it would be like having a T-shirt saying '*Farmers are Trying*', but that seemed to make him more rather than less keen. Then I heard the sound of a ram's horn: a weird, high-pitched wailing, like a voice from a previous millennium, a sound hand grasping down the fjord from the mountains, seeking help.

'Utla!' I grabbed Malcolm by the hand. 'Come on, it's Utla.'

'What are you on about? What the hell's "Utla"?'

'Listen.'

That call again, the call of a hollowed-out, curled horn of a mountain sheep. 'It's Utla, they're a bunch of old Norwegian hippies, but they're great, you'll love them.'

I dragged him away from the farmers' stall, but not before he'd completed his transaction. He tore off his sweaty vest and stuffed it in his pocket, pulling on his new '*Farmers are Hard*' shirt as we headed for the main stage.

'I hope you don't regret that,' I said, though he did look good in it, bright white and lean against his harvest muscle tan.

A thumping drum kicked up behind the horn. I tugged his hand and ran. We kept moving forward, stomping as we hit the loose outskirts of the crowd. I fell into step with him and we shifted into a single unit, his arm around my shoulder, mine around my waist, pushing inwards until we reached the throng. Even then, I wanted to get closer to the stage. The horn wailed and warbled. The drum pumped a perfect heartbeat.

'It's pretty weird,' he said in my ear.

'Wait, they've not started up. It's Viking music.'

I stopped pushing and then Håkon Høgemo started up a tune on his fiddle and Malcolm squeezed me. 'You never said it was fiddle music. Weird fiddle.'

'*Hardanger*.'

'Sounds like a Shetland tune.'

'Now you know where the Shetlanders got it from.'

'Let's get closer.'

He stood behind me and we started weaving forwards through the crowd. We got close enough to see Terge Isungset still banging on his biggest drum, its pounding eerie with the mourning fiddle sound. Then the stringed instrument stopped abruptly and there was an echoing silence, in which someone in the crowd whistled. Then all hell broke loose with a romping melody on Karl Seglem's sax, backed by a complex syncopation of percussion and thick chord harmonies on the big *Hardanger* fiddle.

Malcolm paused. I turned back to him. His mouth was open, a wide grin forming. We shifted our forward pursuit into a skipping, swaying lilt. This was hoedown farmer music, harvest dancing music, passionate rural land music. They reached the climax and stopped, then flew into a reel, another that could easily have been from Shetland. We danced like we had in primary school, laughing as we did so.

'Thank you, Mrs Mackay!'

'Aye!'

And then, stop. Cheers. Roars. Silence from the band. A weird creaking, as if from a glacier. Then an impossible sound of a waterfall, a trickling stream, a waterfall again, a gushing river, then back to the trickling stream. Isungset was conjuring sound from what was apparently just a random bundle of sticks, one of many of his strange collection of forest instruments. The other players made bird songs, weird sounds from the hills, ice creaking and rocks groaning, and then they launched into a springlike song.

We bounced and birled. We were nearly at the front. I was exhilarated both by how brilliant Utla were and by how much Malcolm was loving them, too. We grinned and hugged in the crush, not losing each other, no question of that, sharing the heat, the beat, the passion, the fashion, the fun, the sun, the music… and there was Tanka, jumping like an idiot just in front of us.

'Tanka!' I yelled. No way he could hear me, but Païvi did. She and I spotted each other at the same moment. Païvi grinned and poked Tanka. He turned. I elbowed forwards. 'Hey Tanka! Hey Païvi!'

'Hey!' Tanka bawled. 'Wild!' No need or possibility of conversation.

'Favourite!'

'Yeah.'

Malcolm looked Tanka up and down. I saw Tanka check the T-shirt. Wait for it, I thought.

We jumped about and sweated more than seemed humanly possible in an hour. We shouted ourselves hoarse. We danced and danced. And sadly, it was, despite encores, eventually, reluctantly, jubilantly, over.

'Fucking magic.' Malcolm was blown away. 'How come they're not massive in Scotland?' He was sweaty and beaming.

'Beats me,' I said. 'Best band in Norway, in my view.'

'They don't need to get better than that. They're amazing. That drummer guy, how many arms has he got?'

'Not to mention the fiddle.' Païvi was there.

'Exactly. Jimi Hendrix reincarnated, that's what I think.' Tanka slapped me around the shoulder.

'With some sort of mad Viking Miles Davis thrown in for good measure,' Malcolm grinned at Tanka. 'Who's the guerrilla?'

'Who's the farmer?' Tanka asked in return.

They both looked at me. They were both right. Tanka was in camouflage gear, tall, scrawny, hair spiked, ears, nose and eyebrows all sporting hardware. Malcolm was fresh off a haystack, sun-drenched brawn in rugby shorts and trainers, and the T-shirt didn't help. I looked at Païvi. We laughed.

'Tanka, this is Malcolm, the sexiest farmer in Scotland, and this is Païvi and Tanka, Finnish eco-warriors.'

'Hey.'

'Hey.'

'Pleased to meet you.'

'You Scots are so polite.'

'Thank you,' I said. 'It's a national custom. Good to see you guys. Beers, food, party!'

We partied, ate and drank copiously. We danced more. Then Tanka said, 'It's too hot. We're going back to our tent, in forest, you want to come?'

'Sure.' I looked at Malcolm. 'Fancy cooling off?'

'Totally. It's blistering out here.'

We followed Tanka and Païvi out of the festival compound and into the forest behind.

'How'd you wangle this?' Malcolm asked. 'We tried coming up this way and got sent straight back to camp in the field.'

'A friend of ours is running security out here. It's no problem.'

Malcolm nodded. He looked impressed.

They were camped on a little rise in the woods, with as much of a view as it's possible to get in dense birchwood. I sat with my back up against Malcolm, who leaned against an old spruce tree. The throb of the festival was just below us, the cheers of the crowd like a motorway roar. The cool of the forest was bliss. Just below us was a white van with Taiga Tunes emblazoned on the side. Païvi skipped down to the vehicle, opened up the back door and rummaged among stacks of musical equipment including two huge speakers. She opened up the bottom of one speaker and crawled inside it, then emerged with a growl and grinned in that elfish way of hers.

'The woofers that only go woof if you bring a dog,' Tanka said.

Païvi returned with incense to keep the mosquitoes and midges at bay.

'Are you guys in a band or something?' said Malcolm.

'Yeah, Taiga Tunes, it's our band. That's our band car,' said Tanka.

'Truck,' Païvi corrected. 'Two of the others could not be here this weekend so we're just audience for a change.'

Tanka was busying himself with a brew over a Trangia stove.

'What's that?' Malcolm said.

'Forest food,' grinned Tanka. 'Magic.' He wiggled his fingertips.

'Count me out,' Malcolm deadpanned.

'How about you?' Tanka looked at me.

'I'm a government official, remember?'

'So what? You're not working. You need to relax!' Païvi said.

'True, especially after what I've been through recently. I'll be glad if I'm never shouted at by anyone ever again for consulting with them, not to mention having to find the precise source for every single grain of pollen I've ever looked at down a microscope.'

'Time to check out of the race and party!' Païvi did a little jig.

I couldn't help but melt. I so wanted to play with these guys. I wasn't sure why, I barely knew them, but they made me happy. 'Go on then, I'm up for a little trip,' I said. 'Not too strong now, it's been a while since I had mushies.'

Malcolm shot me a concerned look.

'Have you ever?' I asked him.

He nodded. 'Tons as a teenager. Never again. I vowed. Never again.'

'Do you mind if I do?'

'You go ahead. You're your own woman. I'm just not up for it any more.'

'Bad trip?' Tanka asked as if he'd not understood.

'Yeah, man. Bad trip. Count me out. I'm cool, don't worry about me.'

'I'm not worried about anything.'

Païvi and I laughed.

'What's so funny?' asked Malcolm.

'It's an Utla song,' I said.

Tanka hummed, pouring his brew into three tin cups. We sipped and screwed our faces up as we swallowed, then laughed again. And again. And again.

Later – who knows how much later as time had ceased to function as normal – we strolled down to the festival zone. Malcolm headed off to buy beer. I wandered among jewellery, funky clothes and smoking paraphernalia. I became deeply absorbed in the patterns on a display of silk scarves, stroking them until the stallholder asked me to leave them alone if I wasn't buying. I had begun to feel lost and was wondering where everyone else had gone, when Païvi appeared, as if from nowhere, holding a string on the end of which was a big balloon in the shape of a bear's head. She soon spotted Malcolm and had me giggling once more.

We watched a couple of bands then, as night fell, returned to the safety of the woods where Tanka had gathered wood and lit a fire. Païvi tied the bear balloon to a branch of a nearby tree so the rest of the bear appeared to be hidden behind the trunk. She related an adventure she had had when a bear had raided the food store on a camping trip, climbing up to a high branch where they'd stashed their food bag. Tanka followed with a tale of a bear that learned to open the doors of 4x4s.

'We should have left some mushrooms,' said Païvi. 'I was told by a Cree leader you should always leave some food out for the bears to stop them needing to raid to get their share.'

'There are no bears here,' I reminded her.

'But they're coming back, and we should remember how to behave towards them, we should prepare.'

'Prepare for bears!' Tanka said. It was the perfect toast. He, Païvi and I thunked our cans together, chortling, then put them down. I wasn't really interested in drinking. Malcolm emptied his can and popped another one open, drinking in a determined manner while the three of us tranced out to the flames.

Three cans later, Malcolm announced he was bored. 'Bears, bears, bears. I'm here for the music. Are you coming?'

'It's dewy here,' I said. 'Loud enough for me. Come back and tell us how it looks.'

He shrugged, opened a new can, and loped off back down to the melee. Tanka put another log on to the fire. We lounged, listening to the music beyond the trees, watching the fire, sometimes laughing together with a kind of understanding that belied the short time we had known each other.

Malcolm did not reappear. Hours later, as a chilly dawn broke, I made my way back to the tent, and found him there, asleep.

I was shivering, coming down. I slipped into the sleeping bag beside the snoring body, hungry for his warmth. I stretched my front into contact with his back and felt him stir.

'Grrr,' I said, pretending bear. He shrugged away, and I let go of him, as if he had stung me.

I rolled on to my back and lay like a corpse trying to focus on my breath, then abandoned myself to a flow of images. I was lying among soft, damp sphagnum moss. A shaggy bear lumbered between tall trees in a dense forest, stopping to smell and nuzzle at a fallen trunk. It was getting closer, nearing, nearing. Now its nose was nudging my foot. Now it was standing over me, snuffling my face. It was breathing me in. With each exhalation, I felt myself dissolve into the bear. As I breathed in it would lift its head, then lower its snout back to my mouth for my out-breath. As each lungful of air released, I became lighter. My flesh vaporised, melting into breath. The bear gazed at me, nostrils twitching, as I disintegrated. It licked its lips, and took a final swig of breath, and I was gone, sucked up into the big hairy animal. Its flesh was mine, mine was the bear's. I looked up into the trees, where light glittered down between a lattice of branches into a world full of pungent scents and tasty delicacies – frogs, slugs, mushrooms, roots – and a symphony of birdsong.

I didn't really come round for the rest of the day, though I got up around noon and enjoyed the rest of the festival in a benign daze. I slept like the dead that night and woke, bleary, to Malcolm complaining about the cold, starting to strike the tent before I was dressed, setting a pace for our departure 'before the crowd gets going', as he put it. There was a calm centre to me now that let me ignore his pointed comments about my slowness. I was bear. I packed my bag and smiled at him until he hugged me.

🐾 🐾

I managed to squeeze a weekend off work in late September and Malcolm met me in Shetland. In October he went to a farmers' meeting in Oslo and visited me for a few days afterwards. I found myself developing an appetite for him. The prospect of a job in Scotland was starting to appeal.

By November the Norwegian bear release sites were fixed. They would begin in Jotunheimen, one of the biggest national parks. It was a brave decision, because the park was such a popular recreation area, and it needed ratification by the Environment Committee.

I was sitting next to Anja in the big comfy chairs, my phone on the table in front of me, with all the data to hand if it was needed. Minister Thorsinn tapped her coffee cup and the various chats came to an abrupt end, heads swivelling to attention. Everyone knew how important this meeting was.

'Good morning, ladies and gentlemen. Thank you for coming. As you know, the Ecological Restoration Bill, which everyone seems to be calling the Bear Bill so I'll use that shorthand for convenience, has its second reading next week, and there are some amendments tabled that we need to consider carefully. Some are, I believe, extremely helpful in clarifying the intention and scope of activities that are already being planned, and enabling others in future. However, some of the amendments could, if passed together, be mutually contradictory, and our lawyers are anxious that such legal tangles are avoided. Mrs Schwarz is here to advise us on these points.'

She gestured to a big woman in a red suit and loud glass jewellery, a chandelier in human form.

The meeting got underway, soon reaching the 'helpful' amendments, one of which would specify the process of the 'accelerated population expansion'.

'So the preferred release site is Jotunheimen?' the minister asked Anja.

She nodded. 'After much deliberation, yes.'

'Minister, can we please discuss alternatives to this?' I recognised Brigid Aikio, the Sámi representative I had met up in Finnmark.

'I don't want to open a can of worms,' the minister said.

Brigid pressed on. 'There are sites up north in Sámi territory that meet the ecological requirements better than Jotunheimen, with far fewer tourists, on the border with Sweden, sites that could pose at least as much opportunity for a successful release. Surely it would be a good idea to spread the risk and include one of these sites, perhaps in addition to Jotunheimen. I can see why you want to use the heartland of the country and restore the bears to the central highlands, that this is a gesture of confidence...'

The head of the Parks Service interrupted. 'It is also practical, we have a strong network of wardens and conservation bodies there. We can't staff a project so effectively up north.' Everyone knew the recent history of Sámi and park authority conflicts.

'I think we must go with where our advisors have decided,' the minister said.

'There's nothing to stop future reintroductions in Sámi lands,' said Anja. I agreed with Brigid that the northerly sites were ecologically preferable. I had been through this with Anja on more than one occasion.

'But why not now?' Brigid lifted a document from in front of her and held it upright so everyone could see its title: *Living with Reindeer Predators*. 'We have done a lot of work on how to manage carnivores, how to live in harmony with them, we want to work with you.'

'Thank you, Ms Aikio, that is admirable, but the advice seems to be that we should start first in Jotunheimen.'

'...And continue to exclude the Sámi.' She put the document back on the table, raising her eyes in exasperation.

'This is not about excluding anything, the Bill will enable future work and we encourage you to bring your proposals forward. We commend the work you have been doing. No, there is no desire to exclude anyone at all. Now, does anyone else have anything on the Jotunheimen release site?'

The Agrarian Association representative stood up, the chairman from Røros with the big moustache. 'How exactly are the bears going to be contained inside the park?' He sat again immediately and the minister turned to Anja.

'Professor, would you like to speak about that?'

Anja put both of her hands flat on the table, one on each side of her papers, and looked directly at the farming representative. 'Each bear will be tagged and we will know their exact whereabouts at all times,' she began. She then explained, step by step, our proposed methods for trying to avoid conflict between the bears and neighbouring communities. Then she handed over to the head of the Parks Service to spell out their security procedures.

The farming representative nodded along. He knew all of this and we knew he knew. We had been through it in a heated meeting just two days previously. But everyone accepted, as the stenographer typed away in the corner, that it had to go on the official record, just as, I realised, Brigid had intended with her earlier questions. The point was not, at this stage, to win the argument, it was to be recorded as a voice of dissent, or a voice suggesting a better solution, only to be rejected. I now saw there was a method in the Sámi opposition, which up to now had seemed pointless. Brigid was doggedly pursuing a process that seemed, to me at least, more principled than the performance now playing out between the Parks Service and the Agrarian Association.

'And do we actually have any bears to release?' the minister asked.

Anja nodded. 'We'll bring in some bears from Sweden and, to introduce some genetic diversity, after intensive discussions with Professor Scazia of the Carpathian Large Mammal Project, we have sourced a male bear from Romania, and two females from Slovakia.'

I found myself irritated that Anja should have been having any intensive interactions with Petr without my knowledge. It didn't seem fair after he had rejected the invitation to take part in the feasibility study. Then I chided myself for my pettiness. This was different, I had to admit. It certainly wasn't desk work.

It was agreed that we would do staged releases, beginning with six animals – three male, three female – in the southern uplands in May of the next year. The committee discussed whether there should be an effort to keep the exact location secret but as the Agrarian Association would inform all of its members in that area, it was going to be common knowledge, at least locally.

The difficult work, for me, was over. Now I would just have to sit on my hands and wait for spring, hoping that public opinion did not worsen. I took the chance for an extended trip to Scotland. Professor Bergen was happy to give me leave of absence from the Institute, and I was glad to see the back of the place for a while.

🐾 🐾

I met Stig at the Broken Hart. I had spent the morning in a meeting with Professor Sudbury and Richard Thin from the Scottish Government's Environment Department. Stig was sitting in a booth nursing a pint.

'So,' he said, as I joined him with an orange and lemonade. 'Not having a celebratory drink, I take it?'

I shook my head. 'Later. There's work to do first.'

'How did it go?'

'Richard Thin was good, asked really constructive questions, was very interested in the Norwegian experience. He was much more positive and helpful than his curt, abbreviated little messages led me to expect. He'd read the papers, unlike your Prof, needless to say. He's hopeless.'

'Tell me about it.'

'I told them both you should have been there. Richard totally agreed. Professor Sudbury didn't have a leg to stand on. If Harsel can't be bothered to even send an apology, he's not going to help the project any. I made that clear. And Richard agreed you'd handled the lynx project with utter panache and visionary strategic leadership.'

'Get lost.'

'"A steady hand", was how he put it, I think. Oh yes, and "sound".'

'"Sound", eh? Praise indeed from His Thinness.'

'So you'll be project leader for Scotland.'

Stig raised his fist and punched a small invisible creature on his right. 'Yes! Starting when?'

'What are you doing this afternoon?'

'Let me guess. Brainstorming possible sites to evaluate as bear habitat?'

'Spot on. Richard wants to join in. OK with you?'

'Spying already.' Stig took a swig of his pint.

'No, I think he might be genuinely interested. He has that look in his eye. Shall we get some food?' I reached for the laminated menu.

'I've ordered,' said Stig.

I got up and placed an order at the bar for wild mushroom risotto and salad. When I sat down again Stig said, 'So you think Thin is genuinely on side?'

'Yeah. People love bears, you know, loads of people do.'

'Ah. Bless. Come to think of it, I could picture His Thinness cuddling a teddy bear at night. Unlike Arsehole.'

'Is that what you call Harsel?' I laughed.

'Aye, what else? So when do we really start, in terms of money?'

'The project application had 1st November on the form so I'm assuming we can run right away. I've not seen the documentation, but I got a message on the ferry over to say that we'd got the green light. If they'd said "no" or "later", I'd still have wanted to meet to discuss plan B. My plans don't depend on EU support, that's for sure. Anyway, it's good news we've got the dosh, it makes it easier for everyone to come on board. We should start making some other contacts, too, broaden it out. How would you be about that? I was thinking some kind of reference panel, to give us feedback, be a sounding board, a bunch of sympathetic folk who we could use to get the idea gently percolating out there, help head off the screams and howls of protest from people about not being consulted.'

'Yeah, definitely. Some of the lynx advisory panel might well be interested.'

'I've got a tame crofter on the NFUS board I could pull in.'

'Who's that?'

'Malcolm.'

'Crofter? Since when?'

'Oh, you didn't hear? He got one of the new crofts in Sutherland, those woodland crofts in Ben Mor forest.'

'Nice one.'

'Yeah. Another big reason to come over. I'm going there with him at the weekend to put a shed up – we got a bargain out of ScotAds. You'll need to come up sometime.'

'I can see why you weren't waiting for the EU answer. You and Malcolm getting serious?'

'Let's just say the North Sea's awful wide these days.'

'What's my sister got to say about that?'

'Fran's not speaking to me.'

'Do you want me to talk to her?'

'What's the point, Stig? I've broken the code.'

🐾 🐾

My first view of the croft was enough to put me off. It was a cold blue day when Malcolm picked me up from Dad's house, but it became steadily greyer as we drove north and west. Malcolm had borrowed a trailer to tow the shed and we had intended making a start putting it up when we arrived, but the wind was punishing and ruined any prospect of holding walls steady. I looked around with horror at the Sitka spruce plantation, a wall of identical, alien trees, crowding in on all sides of the clearing.

We unloaded the panels and lashed them to the foundations Malcolm had built on his last visit – huge beams roughly cut from some of the trees that had been felled to make the clearing. When the rain started in earnest, we opted for lunch in a pub. The Altnacaelgach Inn was shut, so we carried on down the road to the hotel at Inchnadamph. While we waited for the soup, I got up to look more closely at a display board about the Bone Caves, learning with delight that bears had once roamed this land, and that the most recent bear bones in the whole of the UK had been

179

found there, which meant that it was likely that the last bear in Scotland had lived here, in Assynt, probably about a thousand years ago.

This changed everything. I found myself looking out of the window not just at hills and moors, but at potential bear habitat! Plus, there was no doubt the weather was clearing up.

As we drank our coffees, a couple of the other new crofters called in for a pint, and we got chatting. Before long we had four more hands willing to help with shed erection, and after lunch, we headed back to the croft. By dusk, the roof was on and an unfamiliar sense of neighbourliness seemed to have been built along with the shed. We drove back to Moray in the dark, the Blazing Fiddles on full volume. Half-dozing in the passenger seat, my hand on Malcolm's thigh, I smiled at the thought that Diana and Frances were missing out on the best things in life.

🐾 🐾

Working from Dad's house, or Stig's spare room, seeing Malcolm whenever possible, I set about the background research for the feasibility study. At least Yuri's attacks were doing me the favour of giving me time to spend with Malcolm.

With Stig's help, I gathered Scottish data, testing the same criteria as we were using in Norway. Over the course of a couple of weeks, I built up the layers in the GIS to produce a map of Scotland showing red for zones unsuitable for bears, through to green where the biophysical opportunities seemed best. There were four green areas: the pinewoods in the Cairngorms, the wooded straths to the north of the Great Glen and two areas in the west of the country, one up north centred on the Coigeach and Assynt mountains, the other down in the oakwoods of Argyll.

The next step was to field opinion on these areas. Stig and I decided a meeting of the reference group would be a helpful first step, followed by some visits to sympathetic landowners, before opening up the study to wider consultation.

The reference group met in the boardroom at the Scottish Land Institute. Stig had dressed formally for the occasion and looked starched and uncomfortable in a grey jacket, pale blue shirt and mauve tie. I was in the cream linen skirt and jacket I thought of as my '*Storting* suit', which I had had dry-cleaned specially for the occasion.

The turnout was even worse than we had feared, a total of eight people, including Stig and myself. I recognised the names of only two of them: Luke Restil, the landowner of Glenmathan, and Robert MacFadyan, the son of a big Aberdeenshire farmer with a bad reputation for harassment of raptors and an outspoken opponent of predator conservation. He was representing the farmers' union, along with a young woman called Carole Smith. There were only two people from within the Institute plus a painfully shy young man from the Scottish Wildlife Trust. Stig read out a list of apologies from the great and good of Scottish conservation and the question begged itself why everyone who mattered had failed to appear.

'I'm afraid we're clashing with a free lunch at the zoo,' said Stig. The Royal Zoological Society of Scotland was renowned for its buffet lunches, mostly due to the lavish provision of free booze. The farmers' union pair looked stony-faced, not getting the joke. I gave a wan smile.

The meeting got under way and it soon became clear that we were trying to push a boulder uphill. The friction from the NFUS staff was enormous. The Land Institute people were both junior and new to the Institute and seemed nervous about contributing; Harsel and Sudbury were both at the zoo. The SWT project officer made an early blurt about his work in one of the areas that appeared feasible – the northwest – and then sat, trembling like a snared rabbit.

Luke Restil was the only person in the room who appeared to be enjoying himself. He sprawled in his chair, as if it was primary school furniture, eyeing the rest of us with the glee of a national jockey at a village gymkhana. As soon as he had arrived that morning, I had recognised him as the tall man who had leaned into the 4x4 on our photo safari during the teddy bear weekend. He showed no sign of knowing me at first but, after accepting a cup of coffee from Stig, he turned to me and said, 'You've been to Glenmathan. I never forget a face.'

I nodded and smiled. 'I saw a mother bear with cub that morning. Very exciting.'

'Good, good.' His long arm reached for a biscuit. 'Excellent plan, this.' He took the Bourbon in one mouthful and grinned, munching.

I warmed to him immediately. He was a big kid, a breath of fresh air among the academics and policy workers who filled my days. He beamed when I told him we had a mutual acquaintance in Petr Scazia.

'Gem of a guy,' he said. 'Should get him involved in this project – no one more expert.'

I still smarted at Petr's rejection and couldn't bring myself to admit it to Luke, so I just said. 'I wish.'

As the mood in the room hardened against the proposal in front of us, I was comforted by his presence. He laughed at Stig's jokes and bounced in his seat as I presented the map, showing by his loose body language that he was with us and open to our ideas.

'I'm really interested in that big green patch you've got on the map up in the northwest. I mean, we're there just off to the east, and there's this gap in the middle that's also pretty green.' He was stabbing at the forests in the Oykel River catchment. 'It's perfect territory, if you ask me. We've been looking at it for years.'

'You're saying we should extend that northwest area?'

'Yeah. Bring it across all the way to Glenmathan. After all, we've already got bears. It's logical to include us in the area you're studying. We're happy to share our experience of how they're doing. They love it up there!' He looked mischievously at the NFUS staff and opened his mouth as if to say something else, then stopped and looked back at me, a gleam in his eye. 'Broaden out to include more sympathetic landowners.' He gestured to the guy from the Scottish Wildlife Trust, who nodded assent.

'I think you'll find plenty of crofters and farmers in the area who are not what you would call sympathetic, not by a long shot,' said Robert from the NFUS. 'You'd better listen closely to them, I suggest.' He wore an expression that was almost a snarl. His female colleague sat rigid, fingernails biting into her chair arms.

'Yes, OK, thanks very much.' Stig nodded fast. 'That takes us on quite neatly to what I'd like us to discuss now. The issue of risk management and livestock compensation schemes.'

I suddenly became aware of the smell of sweat. 'Perhaps we could have a little break first, have a cup of tea, make ourselves comfortable?'

There were nods all round. I got to my feet and headed for the door and the solitude of the toilet. It was not going well.

As I emerged from the Ladies, Luke Restil was standing in the corridor with his jacket on. He pumped my hand. 'Must dash. Best of luck. If you'd like to hold something a bit more convivial, we're happy to play host at Glenmathan. All the best.' With a carefree wave, he breezed out.

Oh, to be so free. I gazed at a photograph of a wooded glen on the corridor wall, then pushed my longing aside and returned to the meeting room.

🐾　🐾

I watched Christmas approach with dread. The family celebrations had always been managed by Mum: the whole ritual decoration, gathering, gifting, feasting complexity of it had been led by her. With no captain at the helm, I was sure Dad and I would just drift along and be miserable. The very idea of trying to cook a turkey filled me with horror. I considered boycotting it altogether and finding an excuse to return to Norway, but I was haunted by the image of Dad alone with a spruce tree in a plant pot and a supermarket ready-roasted chicken. I had an inconclusive conversation with him one Sunday about options for dinner out in some country pub but in the end we were spared by Aunt Marjory, who invited us to spend Christmas with her.

The morning we were due to leave, a stack of mail arrived. I had asked Karl to forward my post and in among the cards was a handwritten letter. I didn't recognise the writing and the postage mark was blurred. I opened it in my bedroom.

Dear Callis

I hope that all is well with you. I haven't heard from you for many months. I wonder if you are angry with me for not joining in your EU project. If so, I am sorry. I have struggled and tried hard to resist making contact with you again, thinking that nothing good would come of it, but in the end I realise that I have to say what is on my mind, to make my confession. So here it is.

I often reflect on those brief three days we spent together in the Strimba valley, and wonder what might have happened if we had not behaved with such professional restraint.

You seemed shy from the start. Whenever you looked at me you had a startled look in your eye. You looked at me as if I was carrying a loaded gun, as if I was dangerous. I wanted to protect you. It was a fatherly feeling, not something I have a reputation for. At the same time, I wanted to put you in danger, to prove to you that you could cope with it, that you could overcome the fear.

Make no mistake, I wanted you too, to take you to bed, from the moment I saw you. While you were sleeping, the lines of your face like an etching – perfect – I looked at you for a long time. I'd never seen anyone so delicate. It was like looking at a flower bud. When you moved I felt certainty, utter certainty, that I could bring you into bloom, that I could be a rootstock for you, give you direct contact with the earth.

I've never met anyone who made me feel so animal, so male. And yet, when you looked at me all I saw was fear: those pale eyes, with their little spark, your chin jutting forward with bravery. You placed your feet apart like a cowboy ready for action. I learned that you were a tough creature, really, physically, despite your appearance. I was desperate to hold you.

I felt it was possible to touch you like a father does, and I tried, and it was a pleasure, but it felt wrong, too. That was not what I wanted really. What I wanted was to fuse myself to you, melt you into me, but I was scared of how hot that passion might burn. I was scared of hurting you. That was my fear. What I suppose I am trying to say is that I loved you from the moment I saw you.

Perhaps you think it is strange of me to write this to you now, but I am less frightened of being strange than of being forgotten, and as you know, I do not believe in keeping secrets.

Have a happy new year.

Your friend,

Petr

Dad was shouting that it was time to leave. I folded the letter up neatly, returned it to its envelope, creased it in half and buried it in the inside pocket of my suitcase.

I was intrigued to see where Marjory lived. I hadn't been to Dad's sister's house for years, and it wasn't the place I remembered, which was a ground floor tenement flat in central Dundee. Now Marjory lived in some style in a stone house high up on the north side overlooking the city, with a splendid view out to the Firth of Tay. It was one of those sturdy well-to-do Presbyterian houses, complete with tall privet hedge, a garden of tortured rose skeletons and a rounded faux-turret corner window in the living room and guest bedroom.

Marjory more than filled the place from her first chimes of welcome to her full-throated singalong to the TV when *The Twelve Days of Christmas* came on. A huge fir tree, dressed from floor to tip in silver tinsel and red baubles dominated the dining room and glittering streamers decked the entire house. After a very large glass of pink Cava – there was no question of asking for anything else – I found myself almost able to smile.

As well as Dad and I, Marjory had invited another friend of hers, Anne. She worked as a librarian in Crieff, lived alone and gave little else away about herself, but I found we shared an interest in botany, and we spent a contented hour in discussion of how moths and butterflies were responding to climate change, and the invasion of alien plants across the country. Anne's knowledge of the spread of giant hogweed and Himalayan balsam was prodigious.

The other guest remained in the kitchen for most of the pre-dinner preparations. At 2pm he emerged with a huge turkey on a platter, and proceeded to carve it into impressively wafer-thin slices. Jack, it turned out, had served as a cook in the merchant navy for fifteen years before being 'land-locked', as he put it, 'for getting a wee bit carried away with the herbs and spices in the Far East'. I let my imagination do what it could with this information. Jack's conversation always left me alternately guessing and knowing more than I really wanted to. I watched with amusement as Dad made an effort to relax his policeman's shoulders, but Jack's repartee and a generous refill of wine soon won him round. Marjory even consented to turn the telly off while we ate.

In the kitchen afterwards, while I washed up, Marjory plucked my concerns out one by one, while dismembering the remains of the turkey. It was a relief to talk to her.

'I can't get Dad to stop going on about my job in Trondheim, as if it's the only job I'll ever have.'

'He thinks your boss is the bee's knees.'

'I know, but that's just because he somehow wangled that football club sponsorship out of him. He can't understand that actually the man is a total bastard, excuse my French. He's trying to turn all my colleagues against me. I just don't get it.'

'Run a mile, love. Life's too short to scrap about work.'

'My sentiments exactly.'

'I'll have a word in your dad's ear. On the quiet. Don't you worry.' She took a drag on her cigarette and blew smoke up towards the rattling extractor fan. 'More importantly, do I hear you've a man tempting you back to Scotland?'

I grinned at her. 'The walls have ears?'

'Who is he? Is he dishy? Has he asked you to marry him?'

'No!'

'He's not dishy? Ditch him, a girl with your looks deserves a handsome man.'

I laughed. 'OK. He's fit. He's a farmer. You'd have seen him at Mum's funeral. And there's no marriage on the cards.'

'Yon big fella? Well, I hope you're happy together. I've never been a great one for marriage myself, but a woman deserves a bit of romance, that's what I've always believed. I've followed my heart and I can't see it's done me anything but good. I've had fun, that's what matters. And he's fit, you say?'

I flicked bubbles from the bowl at her as she sucked on her fag, pouting like a cabaret queen.

Jack edged into the kitchen and reached for one of Marjory's cigarettes.

'Well, good for you, Cally,' Marjory said, catching his hand. 'And all I get for my trouble is a pot-bellied sailor!'

He slung an arm around her ample waist. 'Aye, hen. All you get is me and I get all I can, isn't that right?'

I grimaced into the washing up to the sound of kissing. 'Are you two not too old for that?'

'Ach, Miss Prim. Your Aunty M could teach you a thing or two, I'll bet.' He chortled like a boat engine, then choked into coughing.

'Go and confess your crimes to Derek,' said Marjory. 'We're having a girls' talk.'

'Don't mind me.'

'Go on, get the malt out. We'll be through in a minute.' She pushed him out of the door, then turned to me.

'I'll speak to your dad, love. Your mother used to get me to have a word with him sometimes. He's a stubborn old bastard, but he'll see sense in the end. You trust to your instincts and don't let anyone bully you. Sometimes I think the most important thing to be able to do is to walk away. Do you know what I mean?'

🐾 🐾

Malcolm and I drove out to the croft one January morning. It was a grey day as we set out. Malcolm had bought a classic Land Rover as a symbol of crofter status. We battered up to Evanton in it, pursuing an advert for an old caravan, so cheap I couldn't believe it would have wheels. But it did. It had everything – a cooker, a heater, even a tiny shower – and I fell instantly in love with it. Malcolm failed to see the charm, and tried in vain to argue in favour of bigger, newer models, or the option (his preference) of a motor home. But my determination prevailed. The caravan was mine.

'Can I keep my caravan on your croft?' It was meant as a joke but it came out sounding more pointed than I intended.

We squabbled for a while about who would drive. In the end I persuaded him that as I had an advanced driver's licence I was competent with a trailer, and we set off in the rattly vehicle towing the caravan across the country.

Two hours later, the caravan installed in the clearing beside the shed, we were drawing up a list of all the things we needed to make it comfortable. There followed a shopping raid on the Lochinver Fish Selling Company, one of those West Highland stores that sell everything for boats and houses, including kitchen sinks. As we ate a late lunch in our newly furnished home, the sun came out, sinking into the southwest sky, low-angled beams levering under clouds, prising them apart and squeezing shafts of eye-piercing brightness into the clearing.

'Shall we go for a walk?' I said.

'No, I'm going to try to work out how to connect this thing up to a battery. You go.'

I pulled a hat and gloves out of my bag, tugged on my new Lochinver Fish Selling wellies and set off. Beyond what I was already thinking of as 'our' clearing we were surrounded on all sides by a plantation of conifer trees, mostly Sitka spruce. I followed the trickle of water that oozed out of the ditch running along the track. A mat of sphagnum moss glowed amber, russet and jade in the low sun. I peeled my gloves off and bent down to touch it, stroking it like the pelt of an animal, marvelling at its velvety softness, the spongy denseness. It made me wonder how different a bear pelt would be under my fingers, and whether that was something I would ever feel.

I looked up. The sun chequer-boarded between trees. White lichen shone among the moss like a scatter of snow. Along the streambed a gap had been left in the forest, a corridor without trees, forming a natural passage. I followed it, trying not to plunge into the stream's deep channel in the peat, detectable only by sound, it was so smothered by moss and rank heather. I picked my way along, squelching, enjoying the bounce of the deep moss underfoot, until eventually I reached the edge of the plantation at the shore of a loch.

It was cool now. I breathed little clouds and my knees were damp from the long heather. I stood among stones at the uneven edge of the water, looking out across the grey-green reflection-blur of trees. Fish made circular ripples that radiated across the loch. Looking out at the surface, I let myself be absorbed by its pattern of rings, the shuffling shadows where two circles interfered. Just how people interact, I thought, blurring each other's identities. I put my gloves together on a boulder and sat on them. On the bank, a heron stalked and paused, mesmeric in its watching poise.

My phone bleeped. The heron swivelled its head towards me, then, as I pulled it out of my pocket to answer, it flapped up like an old coat shaken off its hanger and beat away with a derogatory squawk to the far end of the loch, off to some undisturbed fishing corner.

I hit green. 'Hello.'

'Cally, it's me.' Stig sounded tense. 'Can you talk now?'

'Aye, you've frightened the heron off. I'm by the loch near the croft. It's beautiful. Can't think where I'd rather be for a chat. What's doing?'

'Um, not sure. I've had an email. Thought I'd better call you.'

Something about his tone made my stomach clench. 'What kind of email?'

'It claims to be from Dr Yuri Zeveris, at your institute in Trondheim. It's kind of official looking, and it's got an attachment in legalese.'

I swallowed. 'Accusing me of data theft,' I said.

'Yeah. You know about it?' Stig sounded relieved.

'No, but I'm not surprised. He's determined to spread these crazy accusations. He's got it in for me. I don't know why.'

'God, why didn't you say before?'

'I dunno. I hoped it could be sorted out by the Institute. Can you forward it to me?'

'Yeah, sure. What're you going to do?'

I held my head in one hand, the phone pressed to my ear with the other. 'Call my professor, I guess. I don't really know what to do. I mean…'

'Is there, um, you didn't, did you? The data, is there any truth in it?'

'Christ, Stig, not you as well. Who do you think I am? It's a complete work of fiction.'

'No. I didn't mean… I'm sure you wouldn't…'

'He's a bastard. I used to think he was OK but since I joined the bear panel he's been a total…' Smarting, I tailed off. There was silence for a while.

'Is he jealous?' Stig said.

'Do you think? Of the bears?'

'Envy makes people do some pretty weird stuff.'

'Is that experience talking?'

'Just observation. People are pretty green about what you're pulling off.'

'What people?'

'Well, like, you should hear Fran.'

My pulse raced. 'What's she saying?' The wound was as raw as ever, fresh, untouched by any explanation or compromise. Frances' rejection still cut as sharply as it had that day after our trip to Glenmathan. I had tried to deal lightly with her unfriending me on FemComm, but it really hurt. Blood rushed up my neck, into my cheeks, flooding me with resentment. 'What's she saying?'

'Oh, the usual feminist rant about independence. I reckon she's jealous of Malcolm, you know. You used to be her bosom pal and now there's a man in the way.'

'But what's she said?' I fought for control. I couldn't bear the thought of Stig and Frances discussing me. 'She won't talk to me at all.' I could hear myself close to whining and tried to choke down the emotion. Diana being hateful was somehow easier to bear, but Frances had been my friend forever.

'Och, I can't remember,' Stig said.

I let the lie roll between us like the ripples on the loch.

'I tell you who else is seething with envy,' Stig continued. 'That Fenwick model lassie, Julia whatserame, the toff.'

'Why on earth?'

'She used to be an item with your Malcolm. Rumour has it they were even engaged, so I hear.'

'You're making this up.' I felt like pinching myself. The hand clamping the phone to my ear was freezing. 'You'll send me that message from Yuri.'

'Yeah, um, yeah.' A pause. 'It's gone.'

I looked at my inbox. It was there. 'OK, Stig, thanks. Better go.'

'Nae bother. See you, Cally'.

'Yeah, thanks, Stig.'

'Take it easy.'

I pressed the red button with a stiff finger and sat looking at the phone, then opened the new message. I froze as I saw what Stig had omitted to mention. The message to him was not from Yuri, at least not directly. The original message had been forwarded to a substantial list of people with the question 'Can anyone shed any light on this?' I checked and double-checked that I was not included in the list of addressees. It was gossip deliberately sent behind my back. The sender: Dr Peter Harsel. Yuri chose his accomplices with skill. I looked at the list of people who had received it: Sudbury, Thin and several other Scottish Land Institute addresses. It was all, apart from Thin, in house. I scoured it for the other people in the reference group, but I was spared. He had stopped short of including the farmers' union, thank goodness, or the landowners in the site assessments, at least on this message. But who knew who else would have been blind-copied?

The attached message from Yuri was curt.

I believe you are currently involved in a project with Dr Callis MacArthur. You may find the
attached of interest.

How many people would be too busy to bother opening the
attachment? Too few, no doubt.

A shiver shook me out of myself. I put the phone to sleep and
got up. My gloves were damp now so I stuffed them in my coat
pocket and tucked my hands up my sleeves. Dusk was pouring
out of the forest. The loch retained an eerie, almost purple glow.
I turned my back on it and set off, watching my feet, back into
the shadows of the trees.

Easter arrived at last. I managed to wheedle a place for Stig at the
release of the bears as Anja Eldegard eventually agreed that his
experience with the lynx releases in Scotland, coupled with his
role on the Scotland Bear Project, meant that he might actually
be useful, quite aside from the signals of good co-operation it
would send to the EU funders.

The six bears were being released in two bursts, three at a
time, each in different locations, to give them a bit of peace and
quiet. It was also safer to deal with one animal at a time.

'If one gets into difficulties, you don't want two more dozy
bears blundering around with hangovers while you try to revive
it,' as Anja had put it.

The first bear had been set free on the previous day. I was
sorry to have missed day one of the show, but they had done the
first release by helicopter so numbers were kept to a strict minimum. The minister had to be present for the symbolic first bear
reintroduced to Norway, and I had lost my place to a photojour-
nalist whom the minister had insisted accompany her.

Today's two releases were happening from a truck. Anja over-
saw the crate handling, setting a slow but efficient pace, thinking
ahead, smoothing the way. She and Stig seemed to have an instant

rapport and Sorn, the Jotunheimen park manager, a stout man in khaki fatigues with a rifle over one shoulder, showed clear respect for her, falling in behind all her suggestions.

When I had met Sorn previously he had talked about 'my park' and 'my staff' with an arrogance I had found unpleasant, but today I saw a different side to the man. He deferred to Anja's leadership without question, co-operating as the four of us heaved the crate on to a trolley and slid it up the path into a clearing.

In a beige lamb's wool sweater and freshly laundered cream slacks, Anja seemed somehow to possess both bulk enough to help with the heavy work yet also the delicacy to avoid the merest smudge on her clothes. She looked just as comfortable in the forest as she did in the *Storting*. Bare eyed, she pointed out a woodpecker at the far side of the clearing that I had a struggle catching sight of with binoculars. I felt scrawny and inelegant by her side, but was charmed as ever with her breathless smile of anticipation.

'I'm so happy about this!' she whispered to me. 'To be actually here, releasing the bears! It's so exciting.'

I nodded and shared her glee. The bears brought out the best in all of us.

As we watched her poking fearlessly into the opened crate containing the tranquilised bear, it transpired that among Anja's many skills and qualifications, before becoming Professor of Natural Resource Management at Oslo University, she had been a large carnivore vet and had held down the top job at one of the country's biggest wildlife parks. 'Yes,' she winked, 'when I was your age I was a high flyer, too.'

There was a viewing hide on stilts where we were going to wait while the bear came round. We all crammed together inside the tiny wooden structure.

'How long before she will wake?' Sorn asked Anja.

'I gave her a shot of Temazepam at around nine; it should wear off after maybe ninety minutes. If there's no sign by 10.25, I'll go and see how she's doing.' She tapped her watch, which said 10.16.

I was restless with anticipation, shifting in my seat, toes twitching.

'Relax,' Stig smiled at me.

'I can't, I'm too nervous.'

'Here she comes,' said Anja.

Sure enough, a snout was emerging from the crate, sniffing warily, followed by the rest of a head, ears up, twisting like furry satellite dishes. Her eyes seemed glazed, though that could have been my imagination. Her step was definitely drunken, as she stumbled out of the wooden container she'd been trapped in for the duration of her journey from Slovakia, from the sanctuary where she had been reared since being found as a cub. Would she have the instinctive knowledge to survive here? Only time would tell.

She shambled away from the box and plumped down. Her long tongue licked at her face and she scratched the slightly bald patch on her right shoulder with her left paw.

'Don't scratch too hard there, Bjorna,' Anja whispered. 'It's not quite grown over. I hope... perhaps we should have waited longer.'

'What's that?' I asked.

'It's the chip, for satellite tracking.'

She gestured with her fancy GPS, flicking the screen into tighter zoom, pointing to a pulsing yellow bear icon. 'It'll go green when she's fully awake, yellow when her heart slows, like when she's asleep in winter, and red if it stops. It's going green.'

Bjorna rubbed her face in a clump of grass in front of her, then lifted her head and yawned a huge cartoon yawn. We all ah'ed like happy children with a new puppy. With murmurs of 'she's lovely' we watched as she rolled on the forest floor, crushing the flowers and moss.

'She's happy to be out of the box,' I said.

'Welcome to Norway,' Anja said, gravely, tipping back a silver flask, which she passed to Sorn.

'Welcome to Jotunheimen.' He took a swig then handed it to Stig.

'*Slainte Mhath*.'

And finally, me. 'Good luck, Bjorna.'

The bear gave another yawn and got to her feet. She moved towards a patch of wild garlic, tearing a few leaves off and munching. Anja nodded.

'She'll be OK,' she said. 'She's coming round now.'

'Bet she's got a headache,' Stig said. He nudged me. 'You're very quiet.'

'Me? I'm gobsmacked.'

It had really happened. The bear, less wobbly now, explored the vegetation in the clearing and then headed towards the stream that ran past the right side of the hide. We all shuffled as smoothly as we could to that window, hoping our movement would not spook the bear. At the stream, she drank copiously, smacking her lips as if getting rid of a nasty taste.

'I feel just the same with a hangover,' I murmured.

'That's pretty close to what she's feeling,' Anja said. 'She'll come out of it soon.'

'Where's Ono?' Sorn asked.

She zoomed out on the GPS and showed us the map. A second bear, green this time, pulsed on the screen. It was the animal from the previous day's release. We all peered in towards it.

'About a kilometre away, a bit more. And the third release will be 2K upriver.'

'Do we need to get going?' Sorn said. 'I'm worried about the bear out there in the crate.'

'As soon as I'm happy with Bjorna, we'll go.'

The bear had emerged from the stream, dripping, and continued to bumble off, soon shifting out of view of the front and side of the hide. Sorn opened the door a fraction, peered out and exclaimed, '*Faen!*'

'What?' Anja joined him, peered out of the crack and shook her head.

'What is it?' I asked.

'She's going to check out the vehicle,' Anja whispered. 'There she goes.' She swore under her breath in Norwegian.

'She can smell the other bear, maybe?' I asked.

Anja nodded. 'I'll have to scare her away. She's going to trash the truck.' I hunkered down and looked out of the door between Anja and Sorn's legs. Sure enough, the bear was up on her hind legs, pushing the truck and rocking it.

'Hey Bjorna, stop that!' Anja shouted. The bear stopped, like a naughty child, then carried on rocking the vehicle. She nodded to Sorn, who stepped out of the door on to the narrow porch at the back of the hide at the top of the steps, flicked the safety catch on his gun, pointed it skywards and let it off. The crack reverberated around the clearing. The bear went scampering for cover, high-tailing it into a scrubby willow and bramble thicket. Trampled vegetation snapped a round of applause as she charged off.

'Sorry,' Anja said, whether to us or the bear, I wasn't sure, but I thought it likely it was the bear.

'OK, we have to move fast now,' she said. 'Let's go.'

We obeyed, filing down the steps of the hide and marching to the truck. Anja jumped up and peered into the crate. 'She's OK, still asleep.'

'She'll be dreaming of a stormy night on a boat,' Stig said, as he opened the back door of the king cab to let me get in first. I clambered up. Sorn was driving. Anja secured the tailgate, then took the other front seat. All in the cab, we began jolting and juddering our way up the track along the edge of the park to the third release point.

'She's following the truck,' Anja said, anxiously watching the flashing bear icon on the GPS. 'Damn. We were assured they were not habituated.'

'How do you mean?' I asked.

'Often bears that have been been captive learn to associate vehicles, sometimes just a particular kind of vehicle, with food. That can obviously cause problems when they're released.'

'Maybe she's just following the other bear, now she knows she's there. Maybe she wants to release the other bear prisoner.'

Anja smiled at me indulgently.

'Better that than an Isuzu fetish,' she said.

'She's dropping back,' She said after a while, and a little later, confirmed it. 'She seems to have stopped. Fingers crossed.'

As Sorn pressed on up the track, I hung on to the handle above the door, swinging as we picked a way over ruts and splashed through puddles. We pulled up in a grassy spot beside the river. Anja told me to stay in the truck while the others got out and manoeuvred the crate off the back, then Sorn and Stig returned.

Anja opened the door of the crate, undoing the clasps, lifting the wood and wire gauze up and back, lowering the bottom section of the door flat to the ground. She reached into the box to check eyes and pulse, then got to her feet, and retreated to the truck.

'OK, let's back off.'

Sorn pulled the truck away to the edge of the grass, and turned round, ready to drive back down the track.

'A few minutes to wait, I think. She's still quite heavily sedated.'

'Let's hope she's awake before Bjorna turns up,' Stig said with a grim smile.

'Is she still coming this way?' I asked. Anja nodded.

It was a pensive wait, but eventually a head blinked out from the crate and a sleepy bear lumbered out into the sunshine. Anja's flask did the round again and we toasted this new arrival with another nip.

This one was called Ra. She was smaller than Bjorna and had much darker fur. She had a deep scar on her right side from an attack by a big male that had happened in captivity. 'A mating scar,' Anja explained. 'They're quite common.'

'She's much more timid than Bjorna,' I said. She appeared to be very cautious, sniffing and standing to survey the clearing, shifting rapidly into the cover of trees.

'Good,' said Anja. 'Their fear of people is going to be their best self-defence.'

Ra rubbed her face in vegetation, rolled and drank from the river, then headed off out of sight. She was much less entertaining

197

than Bjorna, but Anja appeared to be happier about this. Once her icon on the GPS had turned a healthy green, Anja said, 'Right, let's be off.'

'What about the crates?' Stig asked.

'I'd planned to leave them till tomorrow, but I suppose, since she has headed off...'

The four of us got out again and cleared the crate back on to the truck. As the tail went up, Anja said, 'Quick, in the truck. She's here.'

Sure enough, Bjorna lumbered into view on the track and headed for the vehicle, apparently not only unafraid of it, but attracted.

'Trouble,' Anja said.

We sat and watched as she strolled up to the truck, ignoring us inside. She put her front paws on the tailgate and gave it a good rattle.

'What does she do if you start the engine?' Anja asked Sorn.

Sorn fired it up.

Bjorna bolted for cover, scampering with surprising speed into the shelter of trees.

'Good,' Anja nodded. 'OK, let's get out of here.'

As we bumped back out of the park, Anja watched the GPS anxiously.

'Is she following?' I asked.

'No, doesn't seem to be.'

Anja handed me the tool and we passed it between us on the back seat.

'Ah well, maybe it was just the other bear,' I attempted to reassure Anja.

'Let's hope so.' She nodded but her frown suggested it had not gone as well as she had wished.

'When does the male bear come from Romania?' I asked.

'A week today.'

'I wish I could be here,' I said. 'But there's a debate in the Scottish Parliament about the Habitat Directive and our reintroduction programme. I need to be there.'

'The release will be the same routine,' Anja said. 'With the added excitement of three bears already wandering around out there. Hopefully the language barrier won't be a problem between the Slovakian females and the Swedish and Romanian males. I think your friend Petr Scazia may be coming with them. If he can't sort out any romantic problems, no one can.'

I blinked. 'Sorry I won't be here.' I stared out of the window and we fell quiet for a mile. I was relieved to be spared the awkwardness of having to see Petr. I still owed him a response to his letter. Despite trying to ignore it, his words haunted me. *I am less frightened of being strange than of being forgotten.* No chance of that. *But when you looked at me, all I saw was fear.* Spot on, Petr, if a bit too close to the bone.

I forced my mind back into the present and, with a grin, elbowed Stig. 'We did it! We really did, we brought back the bears!'

Anja turned an elated smile on us. 'Yes. Let's hope we look after them better this time.'

🐾 🐾

When Malcolm swept me up at the ferry terminal, he was sexy in black jeans and white Hard Farmer shirt. The drive from the ferry terminal to the croft at Ben Mor was more than three hours, even in the Jaguar – not quite the convenient forty minutes of the trip to Dad's house. I felt a bit guilty about not going there first, but it had been ages since I had seen Malcolm.

As we drove, I watched the landscape go by. After miles of farmland and woods, we emerged on to the open Sutherland moor. I understood why Assynt is called 'God's Own Country'. The mountains were still tipped with snow, the deep claret birches blurring to green on the lower slopes, a first flush on the limestone grasslands. The lochs reflected a perfect blue sky. Malcolm's hand occasionally reached over from the steering wheel to touch my leg or hand. My shoulders and thighs unclenched as if I had been physically holding myself together not to be overwhelmed by the ache of missing him.

'There's a surprise waiting for you at the croft,' he said.

'Oooh.'

He grinned.

'Don't give it away. I like surprises.'

It was a chainsaw sculpture of a bear, life size, on its hind legs, like a sentinel at the end of the track down to the croft. I hugged it. 'It's so beautiful, I'm going to cry.'

He was pleased I liked it so much. I could tell by the small grin, the smug look that reminded me of how he had been in Mrs Cameron's geography classes, with his hand up, full of the right answers.

He had been working hard on the croft. The track in was levelled and gravelled and the area we had picked out for a possible future house site had been transformed from a stand of Sitka spruce to several dozen stumps and an impressive woodstack.

'Was there any decent timber in it?' I asked.

'Hardly. A couple of trunks were OK. Jason has taken them, the rest's rubbish, just firewood. There's some good stuff down the slope there. We could take some of it out for the sawmill one day but we'd need to set up a winch to get it out.'

'Have all the crofts been allocated now?'

'Aye, all twenty. We're officially a community. And the outline planning permission came through.'

'Already? Wow, that was fast.'

'Aye, it's green lights all the way.'

We wandered around the site, talking sewage soakaways, solar panels, garden, trying to visualise what the clearing in the forest would look like as a home. 'It's easier to picture now the trees are down and the space is made,' I said, but it still seemed unreal. Was my time in Norway over? Now bears roamed free again, was my work finished there? Was it time to shift my centre of gravity back to Scotland, focus my attentions on this thing with Malcolm and put my efforts into the real issue, bringing bears back here? The totem pole bear was a kind of symbol, a lucky charm.

'There's loads of decisions to make, how it should be laid out, where to bring power in to, loads of stuff like that,' Malcolm said.

We padded hand-in-hand, populating the space with ideas about practical things like running water and a chicken coup. We ran amok with dreams of a sauna, summerhouse and pond.

'I'm hungry,' I said.

'Beans on toast?'

'Yeah.'

In the caravan, its little bed was inviting in the corner, and after lunch, I said. 'I think I need a snooze after lunch to recover from my sleepless ferry journey.'

'Why sleepless?'

'I dunno. I just must have been too excited about seeing you.'

'Yeah, yeah.'

But he was showing no reluctance about the snooze, stepping out of his jeans. 'Not as excited as I am about seeing you.'

I was naked in seconds and soon pinned to the bed. He wrapped himself around me, giving me the strength of his torso and warm muscle.

'You're a lovely cuddle,' he said. 'I've missed you.'

'You're a big soft animal, aren't you?' I said.

'No,' he replied. 'I'm not soft at all.'

🐾 🐾

Next morning, I woke to my phone's bleep. I reached for my bag and switched it off. 'It's Sunday and this is the West Highlands,' I mumbled and rolled over.

We woke again later to a beautiful clear blue sky and a breeze ruffling the tree tops. Over breakfast, we were talking about how to gradually clear the Sitka spruce from the croft, to replace it with native trees, when it came on the radio.

'One of three brown bears recently released into the wild in Norway has been shot.'

'What?' I jumped up and turned the radio up, then grabbed my phone.

'Sven Jorriksen, the farmer who has admitted to shooting the bear, said, "The bear had been terrorising local people since its release last week." A spokesman for the bear release team described it as "a tragic setback".

'Fuck, fuck, fuck.' There were messages from Anja and Stig. I was joining late into a frantic debate about how to handle the crisis, and there was little I could do to help from Scotland. It was Bjorna, who did indeed have, it turned out, a passion for four-wheel drive trucks. Unfortunately, there were plenty of them at Boverdalen, within a fairly short walk, for a bear, from the release site. She had reached the nearby village on Saturday and hadn't lasted two hours.

I was livid. 'She was tagged. Why the hell didn't someone get her out of there?' I railed at Malcolm. 'What were the park authorities thinking of?'

'Calm down,' he said. 'It's not that big a deal, is it?'

I turned my back on him, and fired a message off to Anja. One came straight back.

```
It's my fault. We didn't have a clear line of
authority for this kind of crisis. Sorn was hav-
ing a day off. The deputy park manager thought
he needed clearance from us to stungun one of
'our bears' but he only had our office number
and of course there was no one in on Saturday.
The local vet couldn't be found, and turned out
to be in Lom, too drunk to drive. Anyway, by the
time they reached me it was too late. Jorriksen
had taken his gun to her. I take responsibil-
ity. All the local park staff team should have
had training to handle a situation like this.
We should have had it covered. I fucked up.
    Anja
```

I was gutted to see her putting her head on the block like that.

```
The whole team should share the responsibility,
including the park management. There's nothing
```

to be gained by pinning blame on one person
(other than Sven Jorriksen).
    Cheers
    Callis

He claims he acted in self-defence. And I was
responsible for risk assessment. The buck stops
with me. Urgent that we meet tomorrow re release
of males. Anja

Apologies. I'm in Scotland for the Parliament
debate on reintroduction on Tuesday.
    Cheers
    Callis

Bad timing. Can you video-link to us? Anja

I'll find some bandwidth.
    Cheers
    Callis

I spent the afternoon making frantic enquiries about where I could get access to broadband and sufficient privacy to take part in a video conference, and the following morning I borrowed the Land Rover and drove the four miles to the Altnacaelgach Inn. I perched in the corner of the lounge. Anja and Sorn peered out at me from the screen I had borrowed to link to my phone. Sorn was slumped, head propped up with one hand, the other holding a pen, at work on an elaborate doodle. Anja smiled her benign smile and brought everyone up to date.

It was a grim meeting. The farmers were on the front foot with the media. One of the vehicles Bjorna had taken a liking to had a child in it, whose parents were featured hourly being hysterical in front of TV cameras. The bear team was being accused of lack of planning, being too hasty and not consulting the local community. Anja was firefighting as best she could but, she admitted with resignation in her voice, 'I am a scientist, not a politician, not a PR person.' If anyone on the team would take a fall for this it would be Anja.

'We have to postpone the release of the males, there's no question of that,' she said.

'But what's the point of having two females out there alone?' I asked.

'Postpone, I said. I don't know for how long. Hopefully it will blow over in a couple of weeks.'

'And Jorriksen, what's happening there?'

'He has been arrested and charged with breach of the Animal Protection Act and will be released on bail.'

'And public opinion?'

'Disaster,' said Anja. 'Not good, anyway. There's some footage of Bjorna, well, it's not helping...'

Sorn cut Anja off. 'The story of park staff panic is all over the media, we're being made to look like fools.'

'Let's say we need to make some progress with our public relations.'

'And the other two bears?' I asked.

'Both fine, living quietly in the forest,' Sorn said. 'They each have someone near them full-time, monitoring.'

'We don't foresee any more problems with them,' agreed Anja. 'Bjorna was a rogue. We are asking serious questions of the sanctuary in Slovakia, why this behaviour was not predicted. They must have known. They are a little embarrassed and our relationship with them is, shall we say, strained right now. That's another reason to postpone the release of the males. We need much tighter checks on the individuals, their pasts. We cannot afford any more delinquent bears. I will continue working on that. Anything else?'

'Just wish me luck in the Scottish Parliament tomorrow.'

'Yes, of course. Do you get to speak?' Anja asked.

'I talk to the committee responsible tomorrow morning. Stig, too. Then it's debated in the chamber in the afternoon, and I'll just have to listen then.'

'Best of luck,' said Anja.

'Thanks.'

🐾　🐾

The session with the Environment and Rural Affairs Committee was held in a wood-panelled room around a huge rectangular table. Stig was asked to speak first about lynx and got off quite lightly. The tide seemed to have turned in his favour. There had been reports of livestock kills, lambs mostly, but he got in first with statistics and detailed the procedures for complaint-handling and compensation. He had figures from community consultations showing opposition going down. I had to admit his presentation was flawless. The politicians were clearly impressed.

Things were not so easy for me. The presentation I had prepared played heavily on Norway; things had been going so well there. Now that had all changed, but completely reworking the presentation would have taken time I didn't have. I wished I had more material on some successful introductions, like France and Germany, but had to make do with what I had. I decided to go for 'Lessons Learned From Norway', driving an argument that the original reason for the loss of the bear had been insufficient understanding of their ecological benefits, and that the shooting of Bjorna had been due to insufficient consultation with local people and training of park staff. I argued that in Scotland these things could be done much better, and concluded on an impassioned note, suggesting that bears could become a symbol for a reawakening of the nation after a long sleep through a colonial winter of rule from London, signalling Scotland's rebirth, embracing natural diversity, symbol of courage and perseverance.

The atmosphere in the room was cool. There were some nodding heads and some of the Greens and radical nationalists seemed to like the idea. But there were many blank faces.

Fergus Irvine began the attack. 'We need much more fact and much less fancy, in my view,' he said. 'You brushed rather rapidly over the fact that the Norwegian people have been forced into a hurried release programme that is clearly going completely wrong. Would you elaborate on that?'

I withered. I wished I had Anja Eldegard at my side, and tried to imagine how she would respond. 'As I said, I believe that the process in Norway was carried out too fast, and with insufficient consultation. I think we can learn valuable lessons from there and my recommendation would be for a much more participatory and slower process in Scotland.'

'Yet I understand that you were part of the team who planned this disastrous process in Norway. Why should we trust you? It seems to me that a slower process would simply mean longer and more lucrative contracts for those involved, more expense and quite frankly, for what? To introduce a dangerous animal into an already crowded landscape.'

The Liberal Democrat MSP Stewart Lyon spoke up. 'I agree with Fergus. We have neither the desire nor the space for bears in Scotland. There's not been room for them for a thousand years. You're living in cloud cuckoo land. Norway has four times the land area of Scotland and roughly the same population, and even there they don't have room for such dangerous animals.'

I tried to stay calm. 'Can I point out that the distribution of population in Scotland is entirely different from Norway, and the Highlands of Scotland, in particular, have a significantly lower population density than anywhere in Europe, including all of Norway.'

The Liberal clasped his hands. 'Yes, but that is something we are trying to change, my dear. We don't want to drive even more folk out of the Highlands due to fear of bear attacks. We've had quite enough of Highland Clearances, or hadn't you heard?'

'That risk is very low, in fact,' I said, but I was met by jeers and calls to watch the news from Norway. I struggled to point out that in Norway, no one had been so much as injured and it was the bear that had been the victim, but the politicians had made up their minds by putting their fingers in the air and testing the direction of the wind blown up by the media. There was no way I would bring them round. I pointed out that the ecology of the Highlands was profoundly out of balance, the ongoing problem of deer numbers and their damage to vegetation, not to mention risk to car drivers, could be helped by the presence of bears, but I felt pinioned into a role of mad scientist with no grasp of the real world of public opinion.

'This is putting ecology before common sense,' was one riposte. 'Anyone who can claim deer to be more danger to the rural public than bears has clearly misunderstood the basics of predator-prey relationships,' was another. Even the Labour MSPs, who had been silent until that point, laughed at that.

The chairman, Simon Miles, said, 'It would seem to be fool-hardy, given the current climate of opinion, to promote the reintroduction of bears, but that is not to say we cannot con-tinue to look into the issue and to try to understand the ecol-ogy and economics better than we do. As Dr MacArthur has pointed out, there is significant support from the general public and a requirement from Europe to give it due consideration, as we have done for the lynx, with considerable and some might say surprising success. Perhaps we can propose continued sup-port for the large carnivore programme, recommending greater weight to be placed on the lynx aspect of that programme, and by implication that would mean a lesser role for the bear and, though we have not discussed it directly, the wolf, wolverine or whatever else once roamed these isles.'

There were thumps on tables and many nodding heads.

'In that case, I propose we move on to the next item on the agenda. Thank you Drs MacArthur and Morrison.'

I sat down next to Stig, feeling heavy enough to crash through the parquet floor to whatever gloomy cavern of trolls must lie beneath it.

The debate in the afternoon was no better, except for the Green MSP from the Highlands and Islands, Eleanor Morrison, who did us proud. She talked most positively about the potential benefits of more top predators, bears included. She reminded the chamber that 'under the European Habitats Directive's new terms we are obliged not just to consider the reintroduction of our missing species, but actively to plan and implement reintro-duction programmes.'

Fergus Irvine was itching in his seat. 'Will the member give way?' he butted in. She let him speak. 'Is the Green member completely insensitive to the risks that people will face if such animals are released? These are large, dangerous animals, as the experience in Norway has shown.'

The Green member came straight back. 'There is no cause for scaremongering. In fact there are fewer fatalities in Europe from bears than from rams and bulls, but I haven't noticed any-one suggesting that cattle and sheep are too dangerous to roam about the countryside. I urge you to vote for our amendment to this bill and to extend the reach of our national ecological res-toration programme not only to include lynx but also the other missing top predators, wolves and bears.'

The voices of opposition were strong, however, and after several references to Goldilocks and Little Red Riding Hood, both bears and wolves were consigned to remain wild only in fairy tales. The amendment adding a specific mention of lynx to the motion's otherwise anodyne wording about the Ecologi-cal Restoration Bill was passed by a substantial majority but the Green amendment to further include all top predators, was voted down. The chance of getting bears into the wild in Scot-land in the next decade appeared to be zilch.

I tried not to feel sorry for myself as Stig and I left the visi-tors' gallery after decision time, but I was gutted. Stig was look-ing pretty chuffed with himself as we set off to the pub. I turned my phone on and a flurry of messages came in. I switched it to audio and listened to the first as we walked down the narrow wynd at the back of the Parliament building with what looked like bundles of sticks framing the windows of the MSPs' offices. The concrete of the much-acclaimed building was water-stained and tatty.

'Callis, bad news, I'm afraid.' It was Anja. My heart sank. 'We've found the third bear we released, Ra, in a snare. She's going to be OK but we have had to have her compounded so we can tend her wounds and keep an eye on her. We have no idea yet who set the snare. Obviously it's illegal, but it looks as if we have a campaign to harass the remaining two bears. Ono is being closely monitored. Armed guards for the released animals is hardly what we envisaged for the return of bears to the wild, but we have no other option at this stage. Anyway, I wanted you to hear this from me before anyone else gets to you. If the media ask you about this I'd be grateful if you'd make no comment. Oh, and I hope your day in Parliament went better than ours here.' I grimaced.

Next up was Malcolm. 'Hi sexy. Heard the Parliament on the radio just now. Hope you're not too gutted. Give me a call.' A number I didn't know was next. 'Hello Dr MacArthur, this is Sue Lloyd from the *Sunday Times*. I was hoping to get your comment for a piece on the reintroduction of bears issue. Could you give me a call?'

Anja: 'Callis. Need to talk. Need you back here next Monday.'

I booked the ferry and sent a text message back: `Bad day for bears.`

Part *Three*

I'm on the train just north of Perth. Stig has changed for Aberdeen and to be honest I'm glad he's gone. He can't understand how frustrating yesterday in Parliament was for me.

It's a filthy morning. Rain is lashing against the window and I'm finding it hard to do anything but sit here in a dwam, staring out at the Perthshire woods, daydreaming about their natural residents lumbering through them. Just before Pitlochry, a message arrives. It's from Tanka and Païvi.

Sorry is not enough to say how bad we feel about yesterday. Is it time for direct action?

Although, obviously I can't say yes, I'm immediately caught up in imagining various crazy and illegal methods of moving bears into Scotland. I shake myself by the mental collar and get out a book. It's something Karl recommended to me, by Derrick Jensen, but I can't concentrate on it at all. It's too angry and I'm furious enough already. I can't cope with someone else's indignation. I put it down and think how to reply to the message for a minute or two, then begin a reply. 'Thanks.' I peter out. I can't seem to frame anything to answer the question, so in the end I just send the one word reply, and return to Jensen and his analysis of how most people are in denial about the destruction we are wreaking on the planet.

The train passes Blair Atholl and heads into the hills. The landscape up here is totally denuded of trees, and I can't help thinking the seed-dispersal services of some bears would do it a world of good.

I change at Inverness for the train north, and at Lairg station there's a taxi, thank goodness. I'm absolutely not in the mood for chat, but as we head west, the driver regales me with stories of the old post bus service which used to meet the morning train and deliver passengers as well as mail all the way to Lochinver. I'm sure on a good day he's quite funny, but I'm having a sense of humour failure, big style.

It's 2pm by the time I get home. As I walk up the track, I try to keep my town shoes out of the mud. There's no sign of Malcolm at the caravan. I make a cup of tea and take it down to one of the trunk-stump stools at the foot of my wooden bear. The sky is glowering with rain clouds but it holds off, just, as if gritting its teeth.

As I finish my tea, there's the purr of Malcolm's Jaguar. He jumps out and strolls over. As he bends down for a kiss, it occurs to me that he might not actually have stayed here while I was in Edinburgh. I wonder where he would go instead.

'I guess that's as close to a bear as you're going to get here, then,' he says, patting the wooden carving. 'You must be gutted.'

'I'm putting a brave face on,' I say. I lean back to look at him and he kisses me again. All of a sudden I just want to abandon myself to animal instincts. I can't think of anything subtle or suggestive to say, but 'I missed you' is enough.

Afterwards, lying in the caravan, I give him a blow-by-blow account of the Parliament debate. 'It seemed like everyone was against it. The toffs were out in force, making a mockery of the idea. It was hard to believe we had the support of the farmers' union.'

'Well, we never actually supported the reintroduction, did we? We were just going along with the process. We wanted to keep an eye on you!'

He's lying on his front, propping up his head on his hand, a grin on his face. I stare at him until his face becomes unfamiliar. Going for a walk, alone, is suddenly imperative. I get up, throw on some scruffy clothes and stomp off into the woods.

At first, all I can think of is the failure of the Bill, the failure of the release in Norway, the failure of my job at the Institute. I trip on something and stumble. The woods are a blur through angry tears. I'm thwarted everywhere. All my best efforts have come to nothing. Nothing. It's all impossible.

I march on. The sphagnum moss slurps and squelches. My tears run out, leaving only rage. Rage against the institutes and governments I've lavished so much time on for the past year. The official channels of science and politics loom, no longer channels at all, just huge obstructions to my dream. My impossible dream.

But it won't die. My dream of bringing bears back to Scotland is all I have. I'm not going to let them take that away from me. And if bears are going to make it back to Scotland, it is clearly not going to be by act of Parliament or by the benign activities of a team of scientists. Through my fury, Tanka's words echo like a mantra. 'Is it time for direct action?'

Down at the lochside, after blowing my nose and letting the sight and sound of the ripples calm me down, I call him.

'Hey, Mad About Bears!' he says. Hearing his odd lilting voice I smile for the first time in days.

'Hi Tanka, where are you?'

'Kirkenes. Païvi says hi. You're in Scotlandia.'

'Yes. How did you know?'

'We saw you on TV last night. The Russians love Scotlandia Parliament.'

'What do you mean, Russians? You said Kirkenes, no?'

'Yes, just over the border. With our band, Taiga Tunes. The big woofers are growling nicely. You know the song *Waltzing with Bears*?'

'No.'

He launches into song. In the background I can hear Païvi's voice, too, joining in. It's a ridiculous song about Uncle Walter who sneaks off at night to go waltzing with bears. '*Wa-wa-wa-waltzing*,' they warble.

My rage is dissolving with laughter. Then Tanka says, 'Shall we come waltzing to Scotland? It's good time of year, don't you think?'

'Are you serious?' I giggle at the idea.

'I am joke always, but if you ask, do I mean this question, yes.'

This takes some deciphering. I know I should think about what he's suggesting but I seem to have no belief left in the official ways of doing things. That's all darkness, but here is light. I turn towards it, instinctively.

I take one breath, knowing if I wait too long I might miss the moment and, like a surfer catching a wave, I make my choice. 'OK.'

'Majestico! We will arrive in Aberdeen ferry on Friday, eighteen hundred. Can you meet us?'

'Sure. I don't know how but yes, I'll be there.'

'Excellent. Get ready to waltz baby. Ciao.'

He cuts the connection and I sit there staring at my phone, picturing their van, eco-warriors up front, its back jammed full of guitars, a drum kit, microphone stands, cables, jacks, plug boards, an amp and two huge speakers. Clearly today, they have bears in the band. Russian bears, by the sound of it.

I wonder who I can tell, if anyone, that I'm expecting a van-load of crazy Finns to arrive off the Friday ferry with bears in the back. I shouldn't really tell anyone. The fewer people who know, the less chance of the story getting out, the fewer people looking for them. What should I do? What do I need to get ready? I have to tell Stig, of course, he has a right to know, after everything we've shared, though it could incriminate him. No, I can't risk telling even Stig. After some thought, I conclude that I definitely can't tell Malcolm.

I will need to find a precise spot for the release. Two spots, one for each bear, somewhere remote but accessible by van. From the feasibility study I know the areas with the best potential habitat and of them, Glen Affric stands out by miles: by far and away the best, most intact, forest in Scotland, backed by a big, roadless, core mountain area, thick with deer. It's ideal. I should go there to suss out a drop-off point. I'll be able to squeeze in a visit on Friday morning before heading to meet Tanka and Païvi off the ferry.

On the way back to the clearing, I notice spring details I must have failed to see before. Primroses and celandines, wood sorrel and bluebells embroider the grass and fists of bracken are unclenching everywhere.

Malcolm asks me what has cheered me up, and I tell him about the flowers. He looks doubtful, but leaves me to my dreaming.

Then on Thursday evening I get a message from Tanka. 'No can do tomorrow, woofers not allowed on ferry.'

I call him but only get voicemail. I ask him to call me and let me know what has gone wrong, but instead I just get a text question back:

When will you be in Norway?

I reply, 'Oslo, Monday'. I've got a meeting with Anja and the rest of the team, then who knows what I'll be doing. We make a plan to meet up in Trondheim as soon as I can get back there.

🐾 🐾

While the data theft investigation is pursued I'm suspended on full pay from the Institute, and Yuri insists my room should be used by someone else, so my return to Trondheim begins with a day spent clearing personal things out of my office. Ana, Professor Bergen's secretary, helps take boxes out to a taxi, tiptoeing around as if I might explode. I've completed my third and final journey to my flat from where the taxi dumped me, and I am thinking about whether I need some food, when the Finns call.

I arrange to meet them at Karl's bar, and set off straight away. Païvi is waiting for me, elfin on a big comfy couch with a splendid view out over the harbour.

'What have you done with Tanka?'

'He's checking out boats. Do you know anyone here with one?'

'Yeah, Karl and Michel, the guys who run this place. They love sailing. What happened on the ferry?'

'Customs man. He opened the back of the truck and said he smelled something. We told him it was our dog. He said we'd need to quarantine it. We managed to back off before he looked too close.'

'No way, close shave or what?'

She smiles that pixie grin. 'No problem! We have a new plan, but we need your help. It might be a little more complicated. But fun. Are there fishing boats here?'

'There must be. Karl and Michel will know. They know everyone at the harbour.' I lower my voice to a whisper. 'Where are the bears now?'

'We took your advice on the best release site, unlike the Norwegian government. The Sámi are once again living with big predators, thanks to Norway's customs service.' Païvi uncrosses her legs and stretches her toes out. She's wearing plimsolls like the ones I wore in primary school. Everything about her is small, seemingly innocent. 'It means we'll have to go back to Russia for more bears, but that's OK. It's worth it.'

Not for the first time I wonder how all of this is financed, whether the bears that Païvi and Tanka acquire are freely given or not. I guess not, but what do I know? I pluck up my courage and ask. 'Where do the bears come from?'

'A rescue centre. It's very sad. There are so many cubs left when mothers are killed by hunters.'

'Do you buy them?'

She looks at me as if I've asked a ridiculous question. 'Of course.'

'Is it rude to ask how much they cost?'

'No, but I won't tell you anyway, so there's no point asking. Don't worry. We won't charge you. We're doing Scotland a free service. For the fun of it. For the earth. And for the bears. You should see the place they're in. Even Scotland's better than that kind of captivity.' She rubs fingers through her spiky hair.

I begin to doubt that Païvi really is younger than me, as I've always assumed. I realise I have no idea if she is 17 or 70. She could even be an actual pixie.

'So you're going back to get more bears?' I say.

Païvi nods, frowning at me as if I'm stupid.

I continue thinking out loud. 'And you're looking to charter a boat.' I step through the thought process. 'So you'll need me in Scotland to sort out...' I tail off, my mind racing. I have no idea about what a boat might involve, or where two crated bears could be smuggled off it.

As if reading my thoughts, Païvi says, 'You just do the same as you would have done last time. Don't worry about our arrangements. We'll go to the Rock Ness Festival, assuming we're ready in time. Will you be going?'

'I could be, I guess. Tickets might be a challenge so close.'

'No problem. Security will let us in.'

I remember the Tromsø festival. These guys clearly don't go in the front gates of anything.

'Shall we meet you there?' Then, as if she's reading me, 'Or do you want to come with us from here?'

As soon as she says it, I know I do. I do! It's crazy, probably criminal, certainly dangerous, but I've never wanted anything more.

'It kind of depends what boat we can get.' She's giving me time. 'But we like you.'

I'm grinning from ear to ear. I've been invited to party with the cool kids. 'Are you serious?'

She crosses her legs, yogi style, folding herself neatly into the couch. Her eyes twinkle. 'Here's Tanka.'

The lanky Finn strides in, his eyes sweeping the room in one systematic arc, and raises his hand with a, 'Hey, Mad About Bears!' He says it as if it is one word: Madaboutbears. It dawns on me that this is the name they call me by, how I am referred to when I'm not there. Two big steps and I'm in a carnivore hug.

'I am starve.'

'She's joining the band,' Païvi says.

Karl walks over, proprietorial in response to the combat-clad apparition who has invaded his space.

'A band? What do you play, Callis?' he asks.

'Whistle.' It's been a few years since I played the flute, or my penny whistle, but it's not an outright lie. 'Karl, meet Tanka and Païvi, friends of mine from Finland. Karl's the landlord of this fine establishment.'

He shakes hands. 'What can I get you?'

'Fish?' Tanka asks.

'Cod fresh from the fjord?'

'Wonderful.' Tanka lowers himself into a chair and looks instantly at ease. 'I like it here!'

Karl leans on the back of the chair and relaxes into the well-practiced role of painstaking host.

By dessert the Finns have established who, down at the harbour, they should open up discussions with on the possibility of their band, Taiga Tunes, hitching a lift across to a northern Scottish port. I watch, in awe. Then I have an idea: Jack Magee. I call Aunt Marjory.

She's blown away to hear from me. It's all hen and ken and jeezo, it's hard not to cry. I love my Aunt Marjory. I pour out my sorrows about my job. 'Get yersel back here, Cally, they don't deserve ye,' she says. 'Your father talks with too many company men, always has done, lets his head be turned.' So my dad's talking about me behind my back, too, but not everybody's fooled.

Jack's there and I ask to have a word.

'I'm just wondering, I know this is a crazy idea, but is there any chance of bringing my stuff over by sea, and helping out the band at the same time? It'd make coming home into an adventure.'

'It sounds like the kind of job I might do, and for you, hen, it's no trouble. Trondheim to Invergordon, I've not done that trip for a year or two.'

When I explain about the two large dogs in crates, he starts to hedge. Tanka gestures to speak with him.

'Allo? I am dog man,' he bellows. 'Big fat dogs, fierce, but don't worry, we make sure they sleep all the way.' A rapid dialogue full of laughter ensues. Tanka scribbles notes, and arranges to call again. He seems pleased.

'That is our man. Good contact, Madabout. Cool buddy.'

I call Anja to explain my suspension. I find her sympathetic. 'I knew Yuri Zeveris wasn't keen on the role but it's no need to start a vendetta against you. He is a childish man,' she says. 'It must be very upsetting for you. I'll check, but unfortunately, this probably means you can no longer be officially on the Committee.'

'I guessed as much. How's Ra?' I ask.

Ra, the wounded bear, is still in captivity. As some sort of parting consolation, Anja suggests we go to see her. She sets up a visit to the wildlife park north of Oslo where the animal is recuperating. I take the train down and she meets me at the station and drives us out to the reserve.

The bear is in a compound normally used by an old wolf, by the look of the photos on the heavily barred door. I wonder what they've done with the wolf.

Ra has been darted and after she is unconscious, Anja lets me stroke her. I'm supposed to be watching for signs of life while Anja checks all the wounds, and re-stitches one the bear has rubbed open. I hold Ra's head on my knee, its weight as heavy as a child, and stroke the ears of the sleeping animal.

My excuse for being here is that I might never get the chance to be so close to a bear again, but really I want to watch how Anja handles the anaesthetic and listen to what she has to say about the vital signs. I want to be clear about the indications of the bear being OK and coming round. I wish we had a vet involved in our escapade.

As Anja talks about the drugs and fiddles about with syringes, I reach out to feel the neck pelt. It is rough and thick on the outside, but downy and soft closer to the skin. Its texture lulls me. Anja, whose mouth is pressed tight, checks the stitches in the shaved area at the top of the bear's left hind thigh. The wound seems to be healing. She takes the bear's pulse and seems satisfied.

I wonder how the Finns will cope with two sedated bears on a boat. It seems at once both a ridiculous and marvellous enterprise to be involved in.

'OK, we'll leave her now,' Anja says. 'She is waking.'

'That's quick,' I say.

'Yes, just a little sedative this time.' She rubs Ra's back. 'Just a little sleep.'

The bear's right front paw waves sleepily as I lower her head on to the grass and get up. I don't want to leave her, now that I've got so close.

Ra rubs her face with her paw and rolls on to her front. A little groggy, she gets up, walks a few paces then sits down again, scrapes at the bandaged upper thigh with the other hind leg, then scratches her head. Sniffing, she swings her snout round, stares warily in our direction, then strolls out of her confines into the wider compound beyond. She finds some melon that we left out for her and sets to eating it, apparently none the worse for her sedation. She cracks the melon like an egg and chews into it with gusto, juice running down her jaw and chest. She moves to sit with the melon on her belly, like an otter with its catch, chomping and slurping with evident pleasure. We giggle at her and she seems unperturbed.

'How long before she goes back out to the wild?'

'I am hoping we can release her by the end of next week, if the stitching is good. I don't want her to stay in here too long, but it is all politics now. All politics.' Anja shakes her head and looks at me. 'You are tense. You're very disappointed about this, I'm not surprised.'

I wish I could tell Anja the real reason for being strung out. I'm burning to let someone in on the secret I'm holding tight, but of course I can't. Not one word to anyone, not even Malcolm. That's the deal with being in the band. So all I say is, 'Yes.'

I think about the bears that will now be roaming up north. How will they be getting on? How long will they remain hidden? Will they... I don't want to contemplate what might go wrong. Anja finishes putting away her vet kit. I watch the various swabs and knives, forceps and needles, and feel wholly unqualified for what I am about to attempt.

On the way back to Trondheim, I go out to the lobby between carriages. Swaying to the rocking of the train, I call Malcolm. At first he says it isn't a convenient time, then it sounds as if he excuses himself from wherever he is. I talk up Rock Ness. He is reluctant to go, especially when I tell him I'll be coming with Tanka and Païvi, and will be arriving with them by boat.

'Maybe you and your druggy mates should just go together,' he says.

'They're not my druggy mates. They're no druggier than the average punter at the festival, less likely to be off their head on booze, anyway.'

'Makes a change for you, I suppose.'

I bristle.

'Well, it's an offer. They're going and can get you a free pass if you want to come. I'd like it if you were there.' I explain I might begin playing penny whistle with them and he gets a bit more interested in that, but my nervousness only increases. He says he'll think about it.

I snap my phone off and turn left towards the restaurant car in search of a cup of tea. Or perhaps I might have a beer. When I get there, I choose the beer and take it back to my seat, where I sit, musing that I am becoming a fabricator even to my own boyfriend.

When it comes to secrets, there is another one I am keeping for a more appropriate time. I haven't bled for six weeks and I did a pregnancy test just before setting off on this trip. I wonder how he will react to the news that he might be a father.

Is it all worth it? Yes, I think, it's just for this while, a temporary secret, just a bluff, but it rankles me, having to conceal, and then suffering the consequences of not being understood.

Malcolm rings the next morning, agrees to go to the festival and apologises for being grumpy the night before. He's funny and warm and I forgive him everything. I'll see him in less than a week if everything goes according to plan.

🐾 🐾

At the jetty, Karl is fielding enquiries from the harbour master about the Scottish boat, its cargo and its unconventional crew. Karl and Michel have already been brilliant, helping me to pack up the contents of my flat, letting me redirect everything to their address and offering to post anything I need to Scotland. But down at the shore they come into their own. There's a customs boat in the harbour today. Jack calls it 'The Grey Man,' appropriately enough as every surface is painted with gun-metal sobriety. One of the navy blue-uniformed officers strides over, rifle across his back, and shakes hands with Karl and Michel. He points at the two crates on board, and nods and smiles as Karl speaks. I can barely breathe. Tanka passes a box of food to me and I busy myself with stowing it in the little galley on board, grateful for the chance to turn my back. When I look again, the customs man is strolling back to his boat, chatting to the harbour master.

Karl winks at me, and gestures me over. He takes a book out of his pocket. 'Something to read on your trip,' he says.

It's called *The Monkey Wrench Gang*. I read the cover, briefly, and have to get off the boat to give him a hug. I turn to Michel, who gives me three kisses like a Swiss gentleman. Then Jack shouts, 'All aboard's goin aboard,' and I scramble back on deck. The engine steps up a gear. Païvi and Tanka are at each end of the boat. Karl and Michel wave us away, returning Jack's salute from the wheelhouse and tossing the big loops of rope up to the Finns as we cast off from Norway, heading homewards.

Jack Magee's boat is an impressive gin palace, beautifully fitted, 'And she's fast,' he says, 'I don't call her Queen Marjory for nothing.' He lifts his Merchant Navy cap to stroke the bald head under it and winks at me. He was quiet, even rather terse, as we were loading up in the harbour, but now we're under way he is a jovial captain, complete with pipe and blue jersey. There is even a stuffed toy parrot perched in the corner of the wheelhouse. 'You can guess who gave me that!' he chuckles.

We pass an easy night, the four of us, as if we've been sailing as a crew for years. I cook and follow instructions but there isn't much to do. Anything nautical Jack and Tanka seem to be able to communicate about with barely a word. On deck, Païvi keeps almost constant vigil with the bears, saying she's worried that they might overheat in their boxes. The crossing is easy, blessed by a calm sea. It all seems to be going well.

The bears have to be sedated before we arrive at Invergordon harbour to avoid attracting attention to the crates as we unload them from the boat. In sight of land in Scotland, Païvi gets out a small case of medical kit. She handles the hypodermic with ease and confidence, then looks up and sees me watching her. 'I'm getting better at injections. I just imitate my father,' she says.

'Your father?'

'He's a vet, and his father was, too. It runs in the family. It needs to, they don't teach anything practical at vet school.'

'In Finland?'

'Of course. My father wants me to take over the family prac-tice. I guess I might, eventually, if the time seems right. Mean-while I'm getting lots of good experience that I can't put on my CV!'

I must be gawping at her.

'Why are you shocked that I'm a vet?' she asks.

'I always just thought of you as, well, as an eco-warrior. I've been dead worried how to look after them.'

'You have a PhD and a job as a government advisor,' she points out. 'We are all onions.' She looks to see if I understand her. 'Have many levels.'

I nod.

'You play the whistle, too,' she says.

'I am large, I contain multitudes.'

'Exactly.'

She is human after all, and that somehow makes her more magical than if she had been waving a wand.

As soon as we reach land, Tanka sets off to collect the van we're hiring to transport the bears. Back in Trondheim we debated long and hard about who should do this, me arguing that, as a Scot, I would draw less attention than he would, and Tanka insisting that it is his responsibility, and should anything go wrong, he doesn't want a paper trail to lead back to me. Eventually he and Païvi prevailed.

It should have taken him no more than an hour to reach the garage and return with the vehicle. Three hours later, the tension on the boat is reaching fever pitch. It's well into the evening. What can he be doing? Jack has been a hero but he wants rid of us, and Tanka has still not appeared with the van.

'I'm not too happy about sedating them again. Can't we wait and see?' asks Païvi.

'I can't have your fucking circus animals coming to life on the pier. It's more than my life's worth. You'll have to shift, ken?'

Païvi shakes her head, crouches down, and peers into the crates. She straightens up and signals me over. She whispers, as if trying not to wake sleeping children. 'Hansel is still out cold, but Gretel is showing distinct signs of life. We should have been at the first release point by now.'

Where is Tanka? I pace back and forth, like I'm the one in a cage.

As Gretel starts to roll and make a distinct grunting sound, Jack scratches his forehead and turns away with a sigh. Païvi stands with her hand over her mouth, thinking. Then she kneels for her vet kit bag and, with her back turned, delves into it. I can't see what she's doing but she turns back with a loaded syringe. Opening the small access hatch on top of the crate, she reaches in and parts the fur of the sleepy bear, jags it with the needle and slowly plunges the drug into it. The bear shifts and huffs again, then falls silent. Païvi closes the hatch and puts the needle back in her bag. Jack nods approval.

At last a white van approaches the pier with Tanka behind the wheel. Païvi takes a fat envelope out of her pocket, gives it to Jack and clasps his hand, saying something quiet to him that makes him smile and shake his head. Then we swing into action.

Tanka and Jack slide one crate off the deck, on to a trolley and into the van, then the other, while Païvi and I scamper back and forth with boxes and cases and musical instruments and band gear. It's just a matter of minutes before the boat is unloaded. Jack gives me a whiskery, smoky kiss and tries to land a skelp on my bum.

'Thanks, Jack, you're a star.'

'Off with you,' he says.

It isn't far to Glen Affric, not much more than an hour's drive, and there is still plenty of daylight. It turns out Tanka had to go to Inverness to pick up the van, hence the delay. Nothing sinister, but still, my nerves are jangling. Païvi puts Utla on and I try to focus on the wild music. It helps, a bit. Excitement begins to bubble inside me.

As we weave along the twisting road, the last evening sun plays through the birch leaves, highlighting the granny pines on the south side of the glen. We pass a couple of cars heading in the opposite direction, walkers returning home after a long day out, or perhaps an evening tryst. I hope the spot I've chosen is unpopular enough to be deserted. We don't need to find someone camping next to the release site.

The first site is up a forestry road. Tanka picks the padlock on the gate and leaves it looking secure. We lurch our way up the ruts into the pine plantation. Inside the forest, the dusk is deeper. A mile from the road we stop at a fork in the track.

Païvi dives into the back of the van. Hansel is showing the first signs of movement. Gretel is slumped in deep sleep, mouth slightly open, head tilted on one side. Païvi chews her fingernails as Tanka and I ease Hansel's crate towards the tailgate. It's tough going and I wish I was stronger. Hansel isn't a particularly big bear but shifting 150kg of crated animal is no easy business.

Now I appreciate how Jack's wordless muscle power has helped us so far.

Tanka works calmly and efficiently, setting up a ramp, giving me instructions. It works surprisingly well, his system, taking full advantage of gravity. It's evident that this is by no means the first time he has done this operation.

With the crate on the ground, Païvi prizes open the grill, then we back off with the van and watch from the vehicle as Hansel makes his first tentative steps in the wild for eighteen months.

The bear sniffs the warm Scottish air. I sniff, too: the scent of honeysuckle and rowan blossom is rich gold and sweet like honey. My elation is pure fire.

'Welcome to Scotland, Hansel,' I say. Tears prickle my eyes. I can't quite believe what we've done.

The bear stretches languorously and looks around, eyeing the vehicle. Then, with none of the slow wake-up I witnessed in Norway, he turns his back, steps purposefully into the thick undergrowth of willow and bracken and is gone. There's no time to relish his furry form – we're left with just an empty crate and the knowledge he's free in the woods. Tanka and I look at each other. He raises an eyebrow and smiles. There's no need for words.

Païvi is crouched in the back of the van, tugging her lip with her fingers.

'Problem?' Tanka says.

'She's not breathing.' Païvi sits back on her heels, a tear rolling down her cheeks. 'It was that second injection, it must have been too much for her.'

The sickness comes slowly, like a rising tide, a flooding cellar. Païvi is talking about the drugs, something about the mix of ketamine and xylazine hydrochloride, but her voice seems to be coming from far away. Nausea drenches my calves, knees, thighs. I wobble, take two paces and vomit beside a foxglove. When I stand up, Tanka is there, not quite touching me. I find my handkerchief and wipe my face. My eyes are watering but I'm not crying. I blow my nose.

I feel a bit better having thrown up. My head clears. I go and stand at the back of the van, where Païvi is squatting, her hand in the hatch on top of the crate, stroking the bear, which hasn't moved. I peer in at her. Her mouth is still slightly open, head still askew. She has the appearance of being lost in a dream.

'Are you sure she's not just snoozing?' I ask.

Païvi sniffs and shakes her head.

'Is there an antidote?'

She tosses her head again. 'You can use Yohimbine hydrochloride as an antagonist if you want to wake them up fast. But I don't have any.'

'She looks so peaceful.' I feel Tanka's hand on my shoulder.

Gretel is a small animal, pale brown, her fur flecked with reddish, foxy tints, her nose pert and friendly. I gaze down at the bear, through the blur of tears. She still appears only to be sleeping.

'What are we going to do with her?' Tanka asks. I have no idea, other than to wait for her to wake up. Or for me to wake up, whichever comes first.

I lean against the van. Hansel has snuffled off into his new home and now only the crate suggests he was anything other than a fantasy. I wonder if the drug has overtaken him again and he is lying somewhere nearby snoozing, to wake later, looked down on by a curious owl or squirrel. I hope he'll be all right, and will steer clear of the humans at Cannich down the road or the noisy visitors who throng the Dog Falls car park and walk the loop tracks through this last fragment of Caledonian pine forest. Will he make his way out of the forest on to the scrub and moorland above the treeline and meet the many deer up there? I wonder when he will make his first kill, whether he will be seen, who will be the first to notice his scat, spoor or scrapes on trees, whose sightings will be given credibility, what Scotland's reaction will be.

I help Tanka load the open, empty box on to the van beside Gretel's. Païvi has almost crawled in beside the bear to try to revive her. Now she sits slumped and miserable on the tailgate.

'I wish I smoked,' she says.

'We have problem now, hiding body.' Tanka is, as ever, thinking practically. 'We must bury her. We need spades, and some place not attract attention.' He looks at me. This is my country.

'Well, we simply cannot get a spade at this time of night. Not till tomorrow.' I ponder the options, but only one seems really secure. 'We should go to Malcolm's croft. We can bury her there in the forest, no questions asked.' Except by Malcolm, of course. I'll have to tell him. Having kept the bears a secret, how will he react to my arrival, with the plan having gone awry? Will he be hurt that I have kept it secret? I'm pretty sure he has kept plenty of secrets from me.

We don't talk much on the way to Ledmore. The road is narrow and twisty to Beauly and on to Maryburgh. By the time we turn on to the Ullapool road it is as dark as it gets at this time of year and the headlights gleam on the white birch trunks of the forest between Contin and Garve.

'It's taiga forest,' Tanka murmurs. 'Hansel will be happy to be here. He will feel at home.'

At Ullapool we turn north and by the time we swing up the track to the croft, first light is already starting to creep into the eastern sky. We pull up by the sculpted wooden bear and Tanka says, 'Païvi, look at the bear.' She nods like an obedient child being introduced to a relative she does not remember.

🐾 🐾

Malcolm emerges from the caravan. 'Hello?' he says, sleepily. Then, 'What are you doing here?' He's looking at me, as I clamber down from the van, leaving the door open, and then, seeing the Finns, he says, 'What the hell's going on?'

Tanka jumps down from the cab. 'Hey Malcolm.' Païvi sits motionless in the van.

'We've got a bit of a problem,' I hear myself say. It's a ridiculous statement, I know, so I cut to the chase. 'We've got a dead animal we need to bury.'

'You hit a deer? We'll eat it.'

'No, it's a bear.'

His eyes bore into me, black with incomprehension. I feel like I'm in the headmaster's office. Then the van headlights switch off. The space between us stretches into darkness.

'It's two in the morning,' he says.

'Shall we have a cup of tea?' I say. When in doubt, my mother always said, have a cup of tea. I can't believe I've said it.

'Or maybe a glass of something.' Tanka rummages in a bag and produces a bottle of whisky, which he thrusts towards Malcolm. 'Sorry to disturb so late, man.' He grins his charismatic best.

Malcolm manages an inhospitable grimace. There are midges biting. 'Let's go in,' he musters.

Païvi heaves herself out of the cab and we all pile into the caravan. It's as tidy as ever.

'I didn't tell you what we were doing,' I begin.

'No, you didn't, did you?'

Tanka scratches his head and Païvi looks away. It's too confined a space for an argument.

'Go on then,' Malcolm says.

He pulls glasses out of the cupboard above the table and pushes the bottle towards Tanka, who pours three serious drams. It's a good single malt, though everyone seems oblivious. Païvi shakes her head. I think about the pregnancy test and waver, then see the cloud in Malcolm's face and take the glass. We clink and *slainte*.

I sip gingerly, then fill Malcolm in on some aspects of the bear release plan. I don't elaborate or use names and try to keep to the bones of the story, omitting all reference to Hansel. It's a one-bear version of the tale. I talk about how awful it is for the bears in captivity in Russia. I tell him we hoped, if it went OK, to bring another bear later, but clearly it hasn't, so… I peter out. He's glaring at me as if I'm a stranger.

'Will you help us cover our tracks? I mean there's no harm done, really. We just need to bury the bear somewhere quiet…'

'I had no idea you could be so fuckin' stupid.'

I sit on my hands. I can feel my face redden, eyes smarting. It's worse than the headmaster.

'Yes, I was stupid. I've made a stupid, ugly mistake and I'm sorry. So can we bury the bear here? Right now we need a solution, not a telling off. If you can't or won't help, we'll go somewhere else.'

It's as if I'm talking to someone far away. Someone I no longer want to touch. The bond between us hangs loose, twisted and useless. He doesn't understand about the bear.

'Can it wait until morning?' He looks between me and Tanka. Païvi is in her own world.

'Until first light,' Tanka says. 'We need to borrow something for digging.'

'There are tools in the shed.' Malcolm stares hard at me. 'Find somewhere up the back, away from the decent timber, in the rubbishy lodgepole pine or somewhere. And make sure it's too deep for a dog to find.'

Tanka thanks him and says, 'I'll get a couple of hours sleep before we start.'

Malcolm gestures to the cushioned benches in the caravan.

'No, we'll leave you in peace.' Tanka stands up. 'We're happy in the van.' Païvi nudges along behind him and the two of them escape, leaving me alone with Malcolm. I envy them. The atmosphere is dense and brittle.

'I can't believe...' He leaves it hanging.

'What were you thinking?' He downs his whisky and turns away. He somehow manages to make the few yards to the other end of the caravan seem a long distance. Once there, he steps out of his jeans, tugs off his shirt and gets back into bed, his back to me.

'It's about bringing something back,' I say. There's no response.

I stay where I am, and sit up, cradling the tumbler of whisky, musing, looking out of the window as a slow dawn hides among the trees. Tears roll down my face. One drops into the glass. I take a little sip and feel it burn, then push it away. I notice that Tanka did not finish his, either.

A silver, trembling moth presses itself against the window. I can't imagine why it would prefer the electric light inside here to the broken mother-of-pearl moon in the dark sky.

I sit until Malcolm snores and then pad outside to the tool shed. He keeps everything orderly and clean in here, too. As quietly as I can, I pick out two spades, then I follow the stream up the gulley to find a grave site for the bear.

We bury her near a holly tree. It's hard to find a place where the ground is not too rocky and in the end we pile stones over the grave as well as earth to keep it secure. Païvi weaves a little hoop of rushes and flowers, a mini wreath, and lays it on one of the rocks.

'Will Malcolm forgive you?' she says.

'I don't know.'

'He doesn't like bears.'

'No.'

'Madabout,' Tanka says. 'You need a man who likes bears.'

I nod. It's Petr who comes straight to mind, sitting on the rock beside that forest pool, dripping. But then I think about what's growing inside me.

Can I survive on my own? I've broken what Malcolm and I had. The look in his eye last night said everything. I can't go back on it, undo it. I can't unsee the contempt he eyed us all with. I don't really believe what we've done is wrong, but it has breached some line I didn't know was there, some boundary of the acceptable.

'I wonder what Hansel is doing,' Tanka says. Païvi looks up at him and he puts an arm around her.

She leans into him. 'He needs a mate. We mustn't give up.'

I'm crying again. 'Here, Madabout.' Tanka reaches out and gathers me into his hug. Païvi wraps her little arm around me, too. My friends. 'We don't give up, OK? We need to get Hansel a mate. We can't leave him only free bear in Scotland, if we must set her free from Edinburgh zoo, we must.'

Through my tears I find myself giggling. I pull away from the hug and blow my nose. 'There are some bears much closer than that, you know.'

Tanka lifts a questioning eyebrow.

'Only a few miles that way.' I point up the glen, past the Cromalt hills, east towards Glenmathan.

'You're joking? Can we go and see, please?'

'Later, maybe. It's really tough country. Crags and knolls and bogs. We'd need a map and compass. I've never been all the way up to the fenceline.'

'I'm hungry,' says Païvi.

'Me, too.' I lead the way back to the croft. It's full morning when we get back and there's no sign of Malcolm. A note on the caravan table says, 'Gone home to Moray.' The word 'home' stands out a mile. I scrunch the note into a ball and bin it.

'He's gone to cool off,' I say to Tanka. I look in the cupboard. There's bread, eggs, enough for breakfast. I wonder when he'll come back. Whether I'll wait for him.

We agree to cancel the Rock Ness gig. None of us is in the mood. Païvi makes the call, then Tanka asks about Glenmathan. We look at maps and begin, addicts that we are, to plan. I explain that I know Luke Retsil, the landowner, from the reintroduction feasibility study and we decide to pay a visit. When I phone, Luke's at home and happy to be called upon.

🐾 🐾

We drive to Glenmathan the next day. By road it seems a great distance, all the way east to Bonar Bridge and then westwards again, up the wooded glen. At the huge security gates at the edge of the estate, I speak into an intercom and the barrier slides open with a clang. As we drive up to the big house, I point out to Païvi and Tanka the hill where I saw the bears on my first visit. As I do so, I realise it's on the west side, in the general direction of the croft, appropriately enough.

I'm not sure how pleased Luke Retsil is to see me. It's been a while since our paths crossed. He stretches out in his armchair as if he would rather be rowing or riding and surveys the three of us with some suspicion while telling us the story of his acquisition of the large Highland estate and the creation of what he terms a 'wildlife reserve' containing all of Scotland's original predators. It's clearly a well-rehearsed and often told story.

He begins to relax as soon as we establish that he and Tanka have mutual acquaintances in land management. They both spent several years in Poland in the post-Soviet era and worked with some of the same people on conservation of traditional hunting forests. Tanka imitates one particularly dim District Forest Officer's insistence that beavers are only good for hats, and Luke laughs and slaps his thighs.

Having established that the Finns are friendly, he turns to me. From his questions he seems to assume I'm a government employee, and thus potentially a thorn in his side, despite my role in the bear reintroduction study. But when I mention Romania he sits up and takes notice.

'Of course, you know Scazia!' he says. 'You told me last time we met. Have you seen him recently? I tried to get him to visit but he said he won't come, said he's nursing a broken heart as a result of some Scottish woman. It's not you, is it?'

I hope I'm not blushing too hard. I tell him I've not seen Petr for a year and that I'm officially on the staff of the Trondheim Institute of Environmental Sciences, but currently 'on a kind of sabbatical'.

He still looks a bit suspicious. 'What did you think about the Ecological Restoration Act?' he asks.

'Well, obviously it was good news for lynx, but I was really gutted by how far short it fell from what we really need.'

He nods. 'Absolutely. Toothless nonsense.'

I decide to press the point. 'I mean, how are we going to reverse the ecological decline of the Highlands without bears and wolves to help? We're fooling ourselves if we think stalking can keep deer destruction under control.'

Luke grimaces. 'I quite agree.'

I know I'm starting to rant, but I can't help myself. I have to get this off my chest. 'I can't believe the Parliament's narrow-mindedness. You know they completely ignored what all the conservation bodies and most of the community-owners were saying. Even the evidence from the tourist industry was that a lot of people like the idea of big carnivores, but the toff lobby is too strong, and so we're still stuck in twentieth century ideas of how Highland estates must be run.'

As I rave on, Luke becomes animated, sitting forward in his chair, shaking his head and nodding in all the right places. 'It's a disaster for us here,' he says, 'at least in terms of what we really want to do. It means these bloody prison fences staying like they are for the foreseeable future.'

He explains for Païvi and Tanka's benefit that he had hoped the wolves, bears, lynx, boar and elk that he has introduced would develop viable populations that could be released further afield. Now the boar and lynx might conceivably be able to distribute further but the wolves and bears will have to remain captive.

'And the bears in particular are doing very well,' he says. I hope my wide grin doesn't seem inappropriate. 'They get a varied diet, breed well, but they really need more ground to roam. I've made offers on the neighbouring estates but no one's prepared to co-operate. It's a crying shame, really it is.'

'What would happen if one got out?' Tanka asks, his face all innocence.

'Well, we can track them, of course. They're all chipped, so we'd have to follow it and try to recapture it before someone shot it. And, of course, I'm supposed to report such an event to the authorities.'

'And would you?' I ask.

'You know, since they knobbled the Restoration Bill...' He tails off and looks out of the window. 'Between you, me and the gatepost, what I would want to do would be just wait and see what it got up to.'

'Let nature take its course, as it were.'

He nods and we exchange a side-glance. I feel a jolt go through me, as if permission has been granted.

'Of course, it won't happen, so it's all theoretical.'

'Is there no chance of them breaking out of their prison?' Païvi asks.

234

'Not really, to be honest. The fences are top of the range. Though accidents do happen, you know. Windblown trees and snow are the main issues we don't have much control over, but the alarms would still go off. Look.'

He gets up and shows us a screen in the opposite wall. 'This is our animal monitoring system.' We watch the animals moving about, a scatter of blips on a map of the estate flashing as radio tags beam out co-ordinates. It's the same system we use in Norway, and I realised I've picked up much more from Anja than I appreciated at the time. Luke seems impressed by my questions.

There's a knock on the door, and a young man pokes his head into the room. 'Sorry folks, I've another visitor to attend to,' says Luke. 'You'll be very welcome here any time,' he smiles as we make our goodbyes. 'Really, please come again. It's such a pleasure to have knowledgeable, enthusiastic people visiting – I tire of all the naysayers sometimes.'

Behind the surface ease, I see a man who has ploughed a lonely furrow for many years.

🐾 🐾

Malcolm has indeed made himself scarce. When he fails to come back for three days, I call him. He says he's got a casual harvest job but won't tell me where, saying he doesn't want to see me. I hang around on the croft hoping to hear from him, thinking into the gaping space he has left in my life.

By July, I'm still officially employed (although still in suspension) by the Institute in Norway. I keep in touch with Anja. The government advisory team has disbanded, following a storm of protests and conflict between farmers and environmental groups. Anja has eventually managed to get permission for a controlled release, behind fences, of two males and two more females, at a site in the far north of the country, but everyone knows this is tokenism. Fences are fences. Anja's project has failed in spirit, though eventually all of its official boxes are ticked.

With the political situation in tatters, the partnership project between Norway and Scotland has effectively also failed, but Anja finds some funds to pay me to complete the paperwork, so I go through the motions of reporting on the site identification process, stakeholder consultation and feasibility assessment. In the arcane language of European bureaucrats it is impossible to distinguish success from failure. In document after document I tease out endless shades of grey.

I make a couple more visits to Glenmathan to see Luke Restil, the first a brief call, for which I have the excuse of getting him to fill in one of my consultation forms. He's one of the few landowners from whom I can guarantee a positive response to the idea of bears.

My second visit is at Luke's request, to join a team monitoring all of the bears, doing an estate sweep, guided by the GIS, to check up that those they haven't seen for a while are in good condition before autumn arrives. I manage to wangle to be on the northwest corner, nearest to Ben More. Luke and I ride out on the traditional grey Highland ponies called garrons. It's a blustery day. The wind in the birches and long bracken keeps up a constant whispering, an endless stream of breezy gossip.

At the far north of the estate, we sight three bears, two females and one male. I have my camera with me and take dozens of shots of the bears in the drama of searchlight sunbeams against dark clouds. The male is big, though only seven years old. The females are both cubless; the young five-year-old female is the older one's daughter and she has fresh scars from mating. If she has cubs in spring, they will be her first. The other, a fifteen-year-old, is one of the original releases.

Luke communicates the sighting to the rest of the monitoring team, then says, 'We saw her earlier in the year with a cub. She seems to be alone now. We think the male killed the cub.'

'Have they mated?' I ask.

'More than likely,' Luke says. 'It's becoming more and more of a problem, the males killing cubs. The females don't have the ground to get away. I've seen them like this before, looking out through the fence, it breaks my heart. See that craggy ground? It looks full of great hiding places, but they can't get out there.'

I look out across the hills that lead away westwards. Over the brow are the woods I'm coming to think of as home.

'But males killing cubs is quite normal, isn't it?' I say.

'Yes, but not in these numbers, we don't think. We think it's the first sign of overcrowding.' Luke shakes his head. 'Hard to believe they'd be too successful for their own good, isn't it?'

I wish we had tagged Hansel so we would have some idea of his movements. Instead, I'm trying to keep my ear to the ground regarding sightings, but there's no word. Through July, nothing. The deer stalking season begins and, in August, rumours start about bear scat, full of bilberries, being seen in Glen Strathfarrar. He's moved north, into more open country.

I live with dread for the news of a bear shot on the hill, but it doesn't come. I marvel at Hansel's ability to keep hidden, protected by his instinctive fear of humans, his sharp nose keeping him out of sight of walkers and stalkers.

Malcolm is about as elusive as the bear. He says he is back working at Fenwick Farm, having a busy summer, driving the monster combine harvester for eighteen-hour days, and has no time to visit the croft.

I'm hurt, but it isn't as if I'm unused to being single – until a year ago it was my normal state and I find I revert to solo life and keep busy. Once my grant reports are complete, I'm effectively a free agent.

Spending the long summer days on my own, I get to know the ground behind the croft up towards Glenmathan with the intimacy of home. I'm drawn to that land with a tug tighter than I've ever felt anywhere. I carry a notebook and spend hours sketching eagles, wild flowers, red deer, a stoat, a beetle, whatever I happen upon. It feels essential to try to catch them in images. I haven't sketched so much since school days. At nights I begin drawing out designs for panels, bringing all the sketches together into one whole celebration of the ecosystem. Always they have a bear at the centre. I create these pictoral webs of life, over and over, as if I'm attempting to cast some magic spell.

I find I like the caravan more and more. I've unpacked my boxes from Norway and installed some of my own things, cushions and comforts, bright colours and smells of home. It's a bit less orderly now than when Malcolm was here, but it feels more comfortable. The nesting instinct is strong, and being alone here is fine. I like being able to eat simply, sleep early and long, get lots of air and exercise. But it is Malcolm's croft. I know it can't last.

I can never bring myself to tell him that I'm pregnant and our time together has become so sparse it seems no great deceit. There comes the day in August when he says he wants to see me but hasn't time to get to Assynt.

We agree to meet for lunch in the Juniper Seed restaurant in Inverness. It's a neutral place. We sit at a table upstairs, looking out over the River Ness, flowing past in an unseemly hurry, full to the brim. My eyes are drawn to it and tugged rightward with its current, until it disappears past the window frame. It's either that or look at him. I let my eyes be dragged away again. When he says, 'It's over,' I know that what he actually means is, 'I don't love you any more,' and I realise I'm relieved. Whatever was between us withered the night Gretel died.

'I suppose I'd better move out off the croft,' I say.

He's facing out into the restaurant, watchful of the other customers. 'Doesn't bother me. It's your van. I don't think I'm going back. I've got a place at East Neuk, one of the Fenwick farms. It looks like they'll keep me on full time.'

I pick at the shared bowl of vegetables we've hardly touched. 'But it's your croft.'

'Ach, I only got it because of you. I knew you'd love it there. You always liked the woods.'

'Yeah, but...' I think about this. 'If I'm going to stay, I should sublet it or something, then.'

'Can I not just sign it over?' It's impossibly generous of him but he clearly means it. 'I'll come and get my stuff. If you can sort the bureaucracy, it's yours. I want shot of it.'

I take a deep breath. 'Is it the Fenwick House woman, Juliana Penville-Banks?' I pronounce her name Julie-Anna.

'Shooli-Arna,' he corrects. 'She hates people saying it like that.' He doesn't seem remotely surprised by my guess.

'Congratulations.' I just manage to bite my tongue before a sarcastic comment emerges. 'Quite a catch.'

'Well, it goes back a long way.'

'Oh really?' I stop eating. The gnocchi is too rich, anyway. 'How long?'

Malcolm chews his mouthful of steak, cutting as he eats. Between swallowing and inserting the next chunk into his mouth, he says, 'We've known each other since we were thirteen, and got engaged two years ago.'

I put my fork down. Inside it's like a match dropped on a pool of petrol, a wall of flame. 'Engaged? You mean you've been engaged to her all through this, us?'

'Well, I suppose, more or less, yeah, but I've known you even longer.'

I stare at him in disbelief, burning. 'You suppose?'

He pops another forkful of steak into his mouth.

'What was this about?'

He chews.

'You're telling me I was just your bit on the side?'

He shrugs, and shakes his head, swallowing. 'You're not supposed to get serious with men anyway, are you? Isn't that some sort of breach of your hippy feminist code?'

I push back my chair, and as I stand, pick up his half-full large glass of Shiraz and throw the contents into his face. I'm glad it's a white shirt. I hear the glass shattering on to the floor as I storm out, past the other diners.

🐾 🐾

I'm due to visit Glenmathan again when I get a message from Luke putting me off. Yuri has produced a new circular, full of all the same allegations, and it seems to be doing the rounds of an ever wider audience. I wonder if Luke has been one of its recipients.

I sketch endlessly, worrying whether I'm being paranoid, or whether I should be doing something in self-defence.

One rainy morning I'm in the caravan, and check my mail to find a missive from Yuri, just for my eyes, as far as I can tell.

```
Dear Callis
    Musical bears. Whatever next?
    Yuri
```

I ram my phone into my bag, stow the bag in a cupboard and get out of the caravan. He must somehow know about the band's big speaker boxes being used for smuggling bears and about my involvement. How? What else does he know?

I stomp off for a walk, taking my habitual track up through the plantation to the high point, marching until I'm breathless. At the top of the hill I wail into the wind. The Assynt mountains ranging the western horizon are mere stumps, their summits swallowed by cloud. Rain begins to spatter my face. I pull waterproof trousers out of my coat pocket and prepare for a drenching descent.

Before I'm halfway home it's lashing down and I'm soaked with sweat on the inside and rain on the outside of my clothes. I don't think pregnant women are supposed to do this sort of thing, but I don't really know. I want to ask Mum, but of course I can't. For the first time in ages, I'm grief-stricken again. I find myself tumbling into a pit of self-doubt. I've failed at my job, ruined my career, made a total mess of my lovelife, alienated my friends. What sort of a mother will I be? Sooner or later I'll be arrested for wildlife crimes and then even my dad won't want to know me.

When I limp, sodden, on to the croft, the post has come. There's a small parcel from Norway, inside it a slim book with a card from Karl, full of good wishes.

I change all my clothes and make tea. Rain batters the caravan roof. It's like living inside a drum.

The book, by Kathleen Jamie, is called *Findings*. I'm entranced. The wild rhythm of the rain suits the text. An hour later, reaching for my sketchbook, I find my tea has gone cold and the storm has eased to a finger-tapping on the roof. Outside, rain-laden trees are exuberant and lush, every leaf gleams, and dozens of birds have emerged and are hopping and flitting about in the clearing, each with its own story of the deluge.

I prop Karl's card up on the shelf, open the caravan door, and begin to draw.

At the end of August I visit my father for his birthday. I've bought him a book about eagles and I'm going to suggest that we visit the nearby bird sanctuary to see if we can spot any of the golden eagle young that fledged this year, but before I've been home half an hour the doorbell chimes. Dad answers it, and when I hear the voice in the hall, approaching the sitting room, I spring up from the sofa and back towards the kitchen door.

If Yuri is as surprised to see me as I am him, he doesn't reveal it with anything other than a slight pause in his tread as he steps into the room. 'Callis, it is pleasure to see you.' He tilts his head like a heron.

Aghast, I stay by the kitchen door. Nothing will persuade me to shake hands with the man. I want to tell him to get out. Instead, I say, 'Yuri, what a surprise.' Then indignation flares. 'What are you doing here?'

Dad frowns. 'I invited him.'

'I came wishing my good friend Derek happy birthday, and with good news for his football club.'

'More good news?' Dad claps Yuri on the back. 'Take a seat, and can I get you a dram, or a cup of coffee or tea or something?'

Yuri lowers himself on to the edge of one of the big chairs, feet together, then relaxes back into it as if it's the most comfortable thing he's ever sat in. 'Coffee is perfect,' he smiles at Dad, then sweeps his gaze round to me. I'm stony faced.

'You couldn't make us some coffees, love?'

It's a relief to be out of the room, though I want to put salt or worse in his drink. I resist, make him a weak, instant brew in a supermarket mug and select the blandest biscuit from the tin for his saucer. I pour what's left of this morning's freshly ground filter coffee into Dad's favourite cup with a chocolate wafer on the side. Then I go back through to the sitting room, deliver the drinks without a word and stand by the window with the sun behind me so Yuri has to squint to look my way.

'Are you not having any?' Dad says. He has a beseeching expression on his face, and it occurs to me that this meeting might be his idea of trying to help 'patch things up' between me and Yuri. I've never fully explained my suspension to him. He probably has no idea how vindictive Yuri has become.

'No, I'm fine. Quite jittery enough already,' I say.

Dad wrinkles his forehead at me. 'Did you hear what Yuri was saying?'

I shake my head.

'His company, you know, UPP, are going to match the funds for the new minibus for the squad, up to sixty per cent, and we know we can get the rest from the Lottery, so that's in the bag. Isn't that brilliant?'

'Brilliant,' I say.

Dad chunters on about the money already being transferred to their bank account, what a terrific sponsoring company they are, how well they understand the club's cash-flow situation, what a help the bus will be to the boys, the hassles they have been having with the old van, and Yuri sits nodding, his obsequious smile trained on Dad, not even glancing in my direction.

Dad finally pauses to take a slurp of coffee and Yuri takes a polite sip of his. I unclench my toes, thighs, shoulders and jaw, and breathe in.

Yuri looks at me. 'You are farmer now, I hear.'

'No, I'm still an ecologist. And I'd be grateful if you would stop telling everyone in the environmental world about your ludicrous claims against me.'

'I don't know what you mean.' He lifts his hand to shield his eyes from the sun behind me.

'Callis.'

I look at Dad. 'What?'

'Yuri's my guest.'

'Yuri's trying to ruin my career.'

'Nonsense.'

'It is not nonsense. Look!' I pull my phone out of my pocket, flick to the latest nasty circular about me that Stig forwarded on, and pass it to Dad. 'That's just one of the hate mails he's been sending.'

He peers at the screen.

'Open the file,' I say. It's the letter 'to all concerned', containing the usual allegations of data theft. It begins, 'I am disappointed to find Callis MacArthur to be an untrustworthy and duplicitous colleague.'

I pull the phone out of his hands and open an earlier message, then pass it back. 'This one's similar. He sent it about a month ago, to everyone involved in our European project.'

Dad reads the text, then looks first at me and then across the room to Yuri, whose smile is more forced.

'So I don't care if he's your special birthday guest or not, Dad, he's a monster and he's trying, and succeeding, to make my life a misery. I don't know why he's so keen on sucking up to you and spending UPP Forestry's petty cash on your club, but if I was you I wouldn't trust him as far as I could throw him.'

'You use harsh words, Callis,' says Yuri.

I snort. 'Thief, untrustworthy, deceitful – are those not harsh?' I turn to Dad. 'What do you think?'

'I don't know what to think, love. I don't like the look of these, but...'

'He's not produced a shred of evidence, you know. The Institute's done a full investigation and there's still nothing but his word that I stole anything. It's outrageous. You're outrageous.'

I point at Yuri, who shakes his head and addresses himself to Dad as if I'm not there. 'She is avoid truth, Derek, as usual. She does not understand scientists need only truth. She stupid girl, in love with fairy story bears.'

I can see Dad bristle.

I say, 'I do love bears, of course I love bears, I've always loved bears, haven't I Dad?'

He nods.

'And this government team role was the best job I'd ever been offered, the most exciting scientific challenge I could imagine being offered, except to do the same thing in Scotland, maybe, but you've had to go and ruin it all for me, make it a trial. I don't know what you're trying to do, but you won't crush me, you won't.'

'She not understand science at all, Derek.'

'You arrogant bastard.' I take a step towards him. 'Your version of science has nothing to do with reality. It is no help to anyone. You think because a task requires scientific information to be applied to an actual real world problem, like preventing animal extinction, then it is no longer rigorous.'

'It is not.'

'It is so!' I realise I'm shouting but now I've started I can't stop. I shake my finger at him and let all the months of frustration roar out. 'You have some crazy idea that scientists can't help with decision-making, and must just hide in the lab counting pollen grains. You seem to think that anything else at all is corrupt or false. Well, I think that's just a reflection of what you are. The fact that you can only see corruption and cheating, that's all about you. You wouldn't recognise an honest, passionate scientific breakthrough if it smashed your front windscreen.'

Yuri blinks at Dad. 'She is…'

But Dad's shaking his head and in his policeman voice he says, 'I think you'd better no' say any more about my daughter. If you don't mind.' He gets to his feet. 'I think enough's been said.' He bends to pick up his coffee cup, empties it and hands it to me. 'I'll show Yuri out.'

Tanka calls during the second week of September. 'Hey, Madabout.'

I grin into my phone. I never fail to cheer up at that voice.

'We're coming for equinox. It is time for pagan ceremony to open summer fence and let winter out for play.'

I grin even more widely.

He and Païvi arrive mid-morning off the ferry in Aberdeen. I spent the night with Dad, and have borrowed his car. He looks very grey, but after a forensic examination of all my correspondence with Yuri and the papers concerning my suspension he is at least on my side on that issue. When he started on an enquiry about Malcolm, however, I couldn't get away fast enough.

Tanka has a very heavy rucksack. I help him heave it into the boot of the car. 'What the hell have you got in there?'

'Traditional ceremony equipment,' he winks. Industrial-scale hydraulic wire cutters, it transpires, when we unload at the croft.

I let Païvi and Tanka use the caravan and, leaving them to settle in, go off to pitch a tent in my favourite glade, glad for the excuse to be deeper in the woods. They feel like my woods these days and it'll be good to sleep out here. I gather some late chanterelles, hedgehog mushrooms and a big cep on the way back to the caravan, where I find Païvi picking raspberries and Tanka padding around, scrutinising my garden.

'You're putting down roots,' he says. I nod.

'Are you living here alone now?' Païvi asks. I nod again. 'When is your baby due?'

I'm surprised, but somehow comforted that she can tell. 'Is it that obvious?'

'A little obvious,' Païvi giggles, handing me a particularly luscious raspberry.

I pop it in my mouth. 'February.'

Païvi hugs me and I want to sing or cry or both.

'Are they your drawings?' Païvi nods towards the caravan. 'In there?'

'The animals, yes. just some sketches I've been doing.'

'They're beautiful, aren't they Tanka?'

'Yeah, they are like wood carving or something, all the creatures of forest.'

'You're very talented,' Païvi says.

'You're lovely to me.' I'd forgotten what it felt like to have friends around.

I show them the latest message from Yuri.

'He's Russian, you say?' Tanka frowns. 'I bet it's that new sanctuary guy, Sasha, I don't trust.'

'And so?' Païvi shrugs.

'Yeah.' Tanka places his big hand over hers on the table. 'They arrest us for doing good for bears. So what?'

'It would be great publicity. Bring them on!' Païvi chortles.

'Don't worry, Madabout.' Tanka puts his other arm around me. 'You do nothing bad.'

I know various laws concerning wildlife crime and there are no doubt many regulations I don't know that I've already breached, but I stay quiet. I wonder what it takes to be as gung-ho as these two and wish I had it.

The next day is the equinox. I wake up in the woods early and the Finns already have a light on in the caravan. We set off just after first light. I know the area well enough now that I no longer need a map, though I carry it anyway, plus a compass in case the weather changes on us, but it's a bright, clear morning, with a fresh westerly wind. I set a fair pace and Tanka lopes along. Païvi skips across the rough ground beside him, humming a guileless tune. We make good progress.

We stretch out our arms in greeting to a passing buzzard and laugh as a raven flip-flops above us, croo-crawing at its soaring partner. We salute a stag, not yet roaring but practising his patriarch stance on the skyline.

It's a good eight miles to the Glenmathan fence line as the raven flies, tough going on such terrain, with no way of heading straight. We weave a circuitous route around bogs, lochans and craggy obstacles and make it to the fence by just after 2pm.

My legs are aching and my right heel has developed a blister. But it has stayed dry and for that we are thankful. I revive with food and a brew of tea, while Tanka surveys the fence, then unpacks his rucksack.

'How you managed to carry that, I don't know. You must be exhausted,' I say.

'I'm as strong as bear,' he growls and we laugh.

'Are those strands some kind of alarm?' says Païvi, pointing to two threads of cable running through the fence.

'Yes, no problem, easy to jump.' Tanka scrambles up to the top of the fence and attaches some red wires with crocodile clips to a couple of places, then clambers down and repeats the exercise on the lower alarm wire. He lays out his kit. 'OK.' He grasps the cutters and grins at me. 'You pump there, and I show you how it goes. Then you take over.'

He marches up to the fence and I start stamping on the foot pump. His cutters snip through the galvanised steel wire like scissors cutting wool. After half a dozen strands he stops and hands me the shears. I step up to the fence.

'Watch out for spring back,' he says. 'Take it about halfway up. And don't cut red ones.'

I grasp the clippers, a handle in each hand, and snip. It's as easy as cutting dead heads off daffodils. I work my way up from the bottom, and with each snip the wires spring aside, curling backwards from the gap like a tent door unzipping, leaving a growing triangle of space. I lop away my fury at the bureaucrats, the lawmakers, the naysayers, the pessimists, the critics, the farmers, the wingers, the doubters, the fearmongers, the apathetic, all the people who have done their bit to stop the bears coming back. I cut up Malcolm's duplicity and slash away Yuri's accusations. I chop them all aside, and what remains is a gap in the fence big enough for a large furry animal to walk straight through.

Païvi produces a newspaper bundle from her small pack and tips it out on to the moss on the outside of the fence. A tumble of chanterelles, raspberries and rowan berries fall out.

'*Ursus!*' Tanka booms in a deep voice.

Païvi giggles. I reach into the outside pocket of my bag and draw out the bar of chocolate I intended saving for that bit of the return journey when I would be completely knackered. I snap it in half, unwrap one piece and lay it among the mushrooms and fruit. I look up into Tanka and Païvi's quizzical faces.

'Bears love chocolate,' I say. 'More than anything. They do.'

I haven't let myself picture Petr for ages, but as the words come out of my mouth I recognise them as his and remember his daft expression, tongue out, eyes rolling, begging for a square of my bar of Divine. A shiver goes through me. Something clenches at my belly.

'Are you OK?' Païvi asks as I sit down.

'Just a bit dizzy,' I say.

Tanka is picking up the cutters. 'We better move,' he says. 'Long way back.'

'Are you sure you're OK?' Païvi looks concerned.

'I'm fine.' I get to my feet. We set off. At a high point we scour the land over the fence with binoculars. It's Païvi who spots the bear, the small brown shape in the trees near the fence line, coming in and out of view as she moves behind trunks and emerging further on, heading in the right direction.

'Can we wait and watch?' Païvi says. Tanka looks at his watch and shakes his head.

'Trust her, she'll find it,' he says. It's impossible not to believe him.

It's much harder going on the way back with tired legs. The weather, kind until now, carries out the west coast performance for which it is so famous. Clouds muster from the sea and a squall comes galloping across the muir. Led by a chilling wind, pewter clouds unleash a cold, battering rain over us, before cantering away towards Glenmathan. I picture the bear, imagining her sensibly sheltered under a birch tree, unlike us, stumbling across snaring heather.

But as fast as the weather deteriorated, it changes again and the clouds part to brilliant blue, with sunshine slicing across the hills, beaming and blinding. We reach the back of the woods as the last sunset lights glint. Bracken glitters, clusters of wet rubies hang heavy from rowan branches and birch leaves flutter to the ground. We brush our way through the drenching undergrowth into the dusk, weary now, and still two miles from home.

Tanka and Païvi have to be patient as I lumber along, slowing them down. Somehow they remain resolutely, insistently cheery. I don't know how they do it. I stumble, get up, slip on a rock and fall again, bruising my hip, staving my hand, and get up again.

'Come on, Madabout, nearly home,' Tanka cajoles.

I plod along, trying to be stoic, but shattered. I can't understand what's making me so feeble. Only the thought of the bear moving towards the gap in the fence buoys me up enough to keep moving. All the way home, inside my head, I'm still cutting the fence.

Dark is fully upon us when we reach the croft and I crash gratefully into the caravan, too tired for anything, but obedient as Païvi instructs me to take my wet clothes off. My bloody base layer shows the price I've paid for the day.

It's the start of the worst of nights, as I part company with the last vestige of Malcolm's role in my life. His baby, our baby, my baby has died, and all night I bleed, from womb and heart.

The tiny body is perfect – a little boy. I wrap him in a towel and clutch the bundle. I reach for Brown, the floppy velvet bear I made last year and cradle my little dead baby in our hug. Nothing can stop my weeping. Everything is over.

Through it all, I'm vaguely aware of Païvi at my side, and Tanka, like the presence of the bear, a stalwart comfort speaking from the shadows, sitting vigil through that dark time.

When a sliver of moon rises in the eastern sky, it's nearly dawn. I don't know if the others have slept at all. As the light strengthens, the truth of what I hold in my arms clarifies, and fades, and then becomes clear again. Just as I did the bear, I must bury this child.

Tanka seems to understand what's going through my mind. 'The little one will live in the woods with the bear,' he says. 'Shall I dig?'

I nod, drowning in the river of grief. Païvi makes a cup of tea, and by the time Tanka returns, I've managed to get up and put on clean clothes. I'm ready for the ceremony.

The grave is beside the bear. I place my baby in the hole, and Païvi hands me flowers. I lay them around the body, and then over it, and finally I cover the face with mallow blossoms and sweet peas. Their scent almost chokes me. When nothing remains to be seen of the little towel bundle, I stand up and take the spade from Tanka. I dig into the mound of soil and shake its contents on to the flowers. I try a second spadeful, but Tanka touches me gently on my arm and prises the spade from my trembling hand. He fills the hole with a few deft movements. As he reaches the last shovelful Païvi gives me a little rowan tree seedling, and I get back down on my knees and water it into the grave with my tears.

Tanka pats the soil firm. Then he and Païvi sing. I don't know the song but I understand its timeless sorrow. Their two voices, in unison, help me over the threshold of loss. Then they lead me back to the little caravan, and I stumble back into bed, and sleep.

I wake to a day of heavier, wilder squalls, rain slashing across the windows, the trees tossing their manes in the wind. In between showers, intense, baffling sunshine bathes the woods in unspeakable beauty, the earth laughing and crying at once. I let my own clouds wash through me and abandon myself to their ebb and flow.

I remember in the myth Callisto has a son called Arcas. He never knows her. At the end, when the god takes pity on them both, he turns them into constellations. Silently, I give my dead baby the name Arcas. I repeat it to myself: Arcas. I will find you in the night sky, my little boy, my son.

While I've been sleeping, Païvi has been investigating Yuri Zeveris. They may have sounded unbothered by his message, but she and Tanka were worried enough to want to get to the bottom of how their secret got out.

She's sitting at the caravan table with her phone. 'I've worked out how he knows of your link to us,' she says. 'The Rock Ness listing names you as a Taiga Tunes band member. But how he knows about the bears, that can only be the rescue centre in Kirkenes and I can't figure that out. He must know someone there. I've asked Elena and she doesn't recognise the name. She asks if we have a photo of him.' She is talking aloud as she browses. 'There must be a picture on the Institute site somewhere. Here we go, he... oh my God, he looks just like... it can't be. This is your boss?'

She flashes the picture round so I can see it. It's Yuri. 'Yes.'

'I know him. It's Anton Rushkov. Anton Alexandreyev Rushkov. He's a total criminal.'

Tanka looks at the photo over her shoulder, and shakes his head. 'I don't recognise. Who is he?'

'He's an illegal logging mafia man.'

'How is you know him?'

'I met him in Russia. He was in the middle of a huge forest corruption scandal in the Russian Far East. He was the frontman for a totally fake company that allowed timber to just disappear over the border into China. And when we got on to him he just disappeared, too.'

'Are you sure?'

'Yes, it's definitely him. We did a huge "WANTED OUTLAW" poster campaign, I'll never forget that face.'

'When was this?'

'It was before I met you. Years back, maybe twelve years? I was an intern at BROC, the Bureau for Regional Oriental Campaigns in Vladivostok, they were deep into illegal logging investigation. I bet Anatoly would love to check this out.'

'Anatoly?'

'He's a journalist, runs BROC, totally passionate about the forest, great guy. I've not been in touch for years. I'll ask him.'

She types furiously for a while, then says, 'If it is him, what's he doing in a Norway institute pretending to be a scientist? It can't be the same guy.' She turns to me. 'What is he like, your boss?'

I look across from my bed and sigh. 'Yuri? He's Russian. He's very charming. His English isn't too perfect but it's pretty good.

He's ambitious, I'd say. He knows loads of people in the forestry industry, always seems very well connected, lots of friends. He's on UPP's board and he enjoys spending their money. And he's a bastard if you don't do exactly what he wants.'

'A charming bastard, that's him.' Païvi laughs. 'Does he drink champagne?'

'Yes, and eats caviar.'

'Even in Norway.' She rubs her fingers together. 'If it is Rushkov, wow. I know some people in Greenpeace Moscow who would love to get their hands on him.'

As I sleep again, Tanka drives to Lochinver to do laundry and buy food, and then makes himself useful in the garden and at the stove. Meanwhile Païvi continues to research Yuri Zeveris, working her way through his CV, looking for gaps and anomalies.

I get up for dinner and Païvi tells us her findings. 'This guy is a fairy tale. From 2012 back it is all made up. Fiction. I'm sure of it. I bet if we ask the Russian Academy of Science about his doctorate, they'll deny all knowledge.'

'So ask them,' says Tanka.

🐾 🐾

Three days later the Finns have a ferry to catch. Païvi is reluctant to leave me, but I persuade them I'll be OK. I drive with them to the ferry then go to Dad's house to recuperate.

He's looking better, though he takes one look at me and shakes his head. 'What've you been doing with yourself?'

I tell him some of it, but not all, and agree to see a doctor. Rest is prescribed.

'You could have a look through some of your old stuff, and there's some things of your mother's I've been going through...' Dad says.

I spend a morning throwing out old ornaments from my bedroom. I manage to use up a whole day sorting bookshelves, sitting cross-legged on the floor rereading the stories from my childhood, wetting their pages. I drive myself almost crazy avoiding conversations about my job with Dad, who sits behind his newspaper whenever he isn't hiding in his shed in the garden.

I've been sorting out a load of camping and travelling gear that's cluttering up the garage, and packing some things I want to take back to the croft. In the pocket of my suitcase I come across the letter from Petr. I take it to my room, close the door, sit down on the bed and read it again, hearing his voice in his words. I can almost feel his hand ruffling my hair.

What might have happened if the trip to Romania had involved less, as he put it, professional restraint? It must have been hard for him to write such a letter. How different he is from Malcolm.

He says he doesn't want to be forgotten. I get out my phone, flip down to Scazia in the contacts list, then pause. Months have passed. My visit to Romania was more than a year ago. Is it too late? What on earth can I say? I fold the letter up again, slip it into the pocket at the back of my sketchbook, and go back to the garage.

🐾 🐾

After three days I arrange to meet Stig at the Cask. I think I might have to tell him everything. I'm bursting. But when it comes to it the need to keep the secret of the bears is far too intimidating. I can't risk anyone else knowing, so I keep quiet.

Over pints of Big Cat, Stig tells me the latest news: a stalking party caught sight of a bear in the mountains up behind Strathconon. A blurred photo is circulating on the Internet. I don't need to fake interest and hope my feigned surprise doesn't give me away too much. Fortunately Stig doesn't expect me to be anything but delighted, and I listen and try not to look knowing as he speculates about its source. Everyone suspects a Glenmathan escape. I catch him looking at me once, as if he has questions he would like to ask.

Once the second pint has loosened my inhibitions, I do tell him about Malcolm, and the miscarriage. Somehow I even manage to keep from crying, as he tries in his awkward way to express how sorry he is. Then he asks if he can tell Frances.

'Oh, why not,' I say, 'she'll no doubt say she told me so.'

A few days later, I get Dad to drive me back to the croft, and show him around. A letter from a lawyer has arrived, spelling out Malcolm's willingness to assign the croft to me, and that helps reassure him a bit about what I'm doing there. I call a solicitor who explains the bureaucracy and puts in place the slow wheels that will eventually make the croft my legal home.

There is also a card from Frances, a handmade design of a red flower, probably made by Frances herself. Inside she has written, 'I'm so sorry, Callis, to hear of the loss of your baby. If I can do anything at all to help, when you must be grieving terribly, please get in touch.'

I spend a lot of time beside the graves. The little rowan seedling has shed the last of its leaves.

I buy a car for sale in Ullapool, so Malcolm can have his Land Rover back again. I leave it for him to collect at a garage in Inverness, and get the bus back, thankful that I don't have to see him. What keeps me awake at night is what he might say about Gretel. I hope he will assume that my incompetence is total and that the Finns and I tried, failed and have been put off.

One bright morning in the middle of October I submit my resignation to the Institute in Norway. I'm not going back there now; I have to stay in Scotland, on the croft. I'll miss the Norwegian salary, but I've got some savings. Then I call Luke Restil and ask if he'll let me know if he is ever looking for more staff. He invites me for dinner.

🐾 🐾

Luke greets me at the front door as I pull up in my new car. I'm introduced to his wife, Sophie, who serves up an elaborate dinner and complains, wittily, about being a post-feminist drudge. I eat the food in a blur, waiting for the conversation to move beyond small talk. Once our chocolate pots are empty, Luke suggests we take our drinks into the lounge, the room we were in during the previous visit with the Finns.

'You'll be interested to see this, I think,' Luke says, flicking on the screen in the west wall. 'I'd like to ask for your confidence, Dr MacArthur.'

I can't quite judge if he is joshing me by the use of my title, but play along. 'You can call me Callis,' I say. I'm tempted to say Madabout, but restrain myself. I want to grab the map controller from his hand.

He zooms out to the whole estate view and I can't resist peering over his shoulder to see. He turns to make way for her. There, just to the northwest of the boundary fence, unambiguously *outside* the fence, is a little cartoon badger symbol, flashing, to a slow pulse.

'I didn't know you were tagging badgers.'

He turns and lifts his eyebrows. 'I believe one of their traditional names is Fern Bear,' he murmurs. 'We might be getting our icons a little bit confused. It's a frightfully complex system, don't you agree?'

'Extremely complicated,' I nod. I whoop inside myself, but remain soundless and, I hope, composed.

'I'd like to be able not to show the badger icons on the main display, since they're not our core species, do you know how to do that?'

I bend down, reach for the mouse and bring up the display menu, browse to find the badger configuration settings and uncheck the view checkbox.

'You just got yourself a job,' he says. 'We've been needing someone who can get to grips with our monitoring information. Is that something you can do?'

I assure him it is my bread and butter.

'I think we'll enjoy working together.' His voice is smooth, but his eyes dart about.

There is a lot unspoken, but I don't mind. I have access to the tool that will enable me to keep track of at least one of the bears I know is out there. All winter long I'll be able to watch the slow pulse of the sleeping animal, flashing orange on the screen, in amongst the hills between Glenmathan and home.

🐾 🐾

One day I walk out east and spy around the bouldery scree at the foot of the crag where the icon flashes. I don't want to get too close and disturb her. It looks like a good denning site.

The estate manager Steve, a gruff Yorkshire man, tells me at some length about a recent incident of fence damage. He assumes it was caused by 'right to roam' activists. He explains that ramblers and 'right to roam' campaigners have for years been demanding free entry to the estate, although most visitors willingly drive in through the main gates and stump up an entrance charge. I seem to remember being involved with some other Fe-Phi-Pho activists in the 'right to roam' campaign, wanting the right to walk amongst bears and wolves at our own risk.

The fence damage has been repaired and there are remarkably few questions being asked. 'Bloody ramblers,' says Steve. 'Bloody fence. Bloody nuisance.'

I'm issued with a contract. It points out that wilful damage to estate property is a sackable offence, if intended to thwart the objectives of the Estate Management Plan. I make a point of reading the Estate Management Plan and 'facilitating the restoration of the full quotient of Scotland's native fauna' is at the top. I content myself that a bit of fence-breaking seems to be not entirely inconsistent with my terms of employment.

I've got back into horse riding since starting work on the estate. Luke and Sophie ride every day and, increasingly, I go out with them. I like the way the other animals let us get much closer on horseback than on foot. I buy myself an Icelandic mare for my Christmas-Solstice-New Year present. The pony is dark and I call her Gretel. She is good company on the croft.

I suggest to Luke that in the interests of good neighbourliness a gate on the north-west corner of the estate might be an option.

There are gates on other corners: heavy, difficult structures with loud notices explaining that entry on to the estate, where wolves and bears roamed free, is entirely at the enterer's own risk. When I explain to Luke that I could ride to work from home if there was a gate into the estate, he agrees to put it in. I don't ride every day; it's a long way and hard going, but sometimes my monitoring work takes me out beyond the fence and it's good to have the cover story of riding home.

I'm not quite sure who knows that the little brown bear – for it is the five-year-old that has 'escaped' – is out there, apart from Luke and Sophie. So far it seems that the disappearance of the 27th bear is not gaining much attention. As long as she is in her den and the radio signal doesn't show up on the main Xmap system, there is no reason for anyone to find out, unless there is some kind of census of all the bears. It occurs to me that I could provide the carcass, or at least skeleton, of a similarly aged female bear, should that become useful at some point. I keep it to myself. No one seems to be counting.

I wonder where Hansel is hiding out. It's a good, cold winter. I'm pleased: less chance of bears waking up to wander around for food in warm periods.

🐾 🐾

Frances is sitting in the window of Yum Cafe when I arrive. The bus to Inverness was a bit late, but the cafe's just next to the station so I'm not too delayed.

'I'm sorry, have you been waiting ages?'

She gets up. 'You're here now. You look...' I can see her checking out my clothes. 'You look...'

I hug her. 'Like a crofter?'

She smiles and sits down, then reaches over to feel my patchwork jacket. 'A bit wilder than when I last saw you. Short hair suits you. Dykie. Diana'd die.'

'It keeps getting shorter. I'll get some tea. Want something?'

'No, I'm fine.' She gestures to her coffee.

257

I open my bag to get my purse, and get out the present I've brought her. It's one of my drawings, a wildcat hiding in among a thicket of rowan and brambles. It's wrapped in sheets of the *Scottish Wildlife* magazine. 'Sorry about the wrapping, I'm saving paper,' I say.

I go to the counter and order tea, while she opens her present. I knew she'd like it. She would have to have changed personality completely not to coo over it.

'Cally, it's beautiful,' she says. 'Have you seen one? In the wild, I mean, where you are now?'

I shake my head. 'I saw a big cat jump into the shadow by the road late one night, but I can't be sure that's what it was. I got the image from a book. Apart from the plants, they're from real.'

'You're talented,' she says. 'It's much more than good drawing, it's the whole design.' She traces her finger around the Celtic knotwork and leaf border of the picture.

'A bit hippy,' I laugh.

'But wait till you see this!' She's grinning as she passes over a glitter-wrapped package.

Inside is a sumptuous hand-embroidered little bag. I stroke it. 'Did you do this?' I ask, but it's obvious she did. 'Aren't we the crafty ones? It's lovely. I'll use it for my pencils. Thanks.'

We lean over and kiss, then sit, holding our gifts.

'How are you?' she says. 'I mean, after the miscarriage. Was it awful?'

'Yeah.' I pause. 'The broken heart's healing, too. Aren't you going to say you told me so?'

'We told you so.'

'I couldn't help it.'

'I've been so furious with you for being stupid, letting yourself get caught up. And sorry for you, too.'

'I know. Stig said you were pitying me. That only wound me up more. Anyway, you can have the satisfaction of being right. He was a bastard. A two-timing manipulative bastard.' I stroke the pencil case.

'So it's all over.'

'With Malcolm, aye.'

Frances raises an eyebrow.

'I'll make sure I fall in love with a good guy next time.'

She shakes her head.

'You're still pure, then?' I say.

She giggles. 'As the driven snow. Actually there's a rather tasty chap who I've been trying to get into bed for the past few months. Richard, he's called. But he's proving difficult. Insists upon my freedom from his clutches.'

'Sounds like your ideal man.'

'Don't worry, I'm still staunchly independent.' She sips froth from her coffee. 'By the way, Diana sends her greetings.'

'Is that right? Am I forgiven?'

'Forgiven? What do you think?'

'And you?'

'You're my pal. You're hopeless, but I still want to be your friend.'

'Thanks, Fran. How can I refuse an offer like that, you heartless cow?'

She clinks her latte mug against my teacup. 'Slit your wrists and hope you die.'

'Forever and ever, ah mental.'

'Ah mental,' she says, and I know it's fine between us again, really, fine. For the time being, anyway.

At Christmas I have some unexpected presents. One is a card with a letter enclosed, from Professor Bergen, telling me that Yuri Zeveris has been sacked after it was revealed to the Institute (she didn't say how, but I can guess) that his qualifications were fraudulent. 'He was not, it now transpires, who he led us to believe him to be.' She sends her unconditional apology for the suffering caused to me by my boss' behaviour and offers me my job back. I respond with thanks but decline the job.

I tell this story over Christmas dinner at Aunt Marjory's. I haven't seen Dad at all since the awful days after the miscarriage. He looks thinner. He's dismayed at my non-acceptance of my job back.

'I've moved on, Dad,' I say.

My aunt pats my lower arm then reaches for the Cava bottle and tops up all of our glasses. 'Quite right. Never go back, love. That's what I've always said. I just think it's super that you're back with us in Scotland. Isn't that right, Jack?'

Jack Magee raises his glass and an eyebrow, and says nothing.

My other end-of-year treat is a brand new top-of-the-range specialist wildlife Pentax with a huge lens, complete with camouflage cover. It's the prize for my winning shot of a female bear peering out through the fence at Glenmathan into a sparkling landscape of pools, rocks and a berry-laden rowan tree caught in autumn light. I called the picture 'Wistful', and though only I know it, it's of the mother of the animal whose icon I watch daily, pulsing in its hiding place. The photo is causing quite a stir in the media, reawakening some of the debate of earlier in the year, but now commentators are suggesting that the political decision to refuse any consideration of bear reintroductions may have been short-sighted. The wind of public opinion is fickle.

I'm not sure how much I'll use the camera in earnest. My interest in photography has waned as my sketches have grown in confidence, but it will be good to have it to take shots as material for my drawings. Adding to my glee at the photography prize, I spot among the runners-up a photograph of a sow and several piglets crossing a track, entitled 'Wild Boar'. The work has been captioned by the magazine as 'A Celebration of Motherhood'. I can only imagine the annoyance of its photographer, Diana Hunter.

I give Dad a framed copy of my winning photo, complete with its gold winner's rosette, and watch as pride overcomes all his other feelings, whatever they are. I'll never understand, I know that now, but I no longer mind. We have weathered another year without my mother. We will manage more.

After dinner, in the lounge chairs, Jack asks Dad about his football club. 'Well, I've decided to give up the coaching.'

I look up from the crossword.

'It's a young man's game,' he says. 'And how's the chandlery business?'

'Och, just the same.' Jack lifts his cap, strokes his bald head and puts the bunnet back on. 'Just the same, ken?'

'And you still have your boat?'

'Och, yes. There's aye someone needin' a wee job.' He winks at me, and I grin and concentrate on six across. 'Gizza clue, hen.'

'Six letters, starts with S, untold.'

🐾 🐾

Spring marches forwards. In February I notice the first pale primroses in the mossy woodland carpet. The bracken has died back and riding is much easier than through the autumn thicket. The days are starting to lengthen and I ride out more often, eyes peeled.

So it is, one warm, breezy Tuesday morning in March that Gretel stops and stares at a brown shape among the boulders at the foot of the crag where for months I have watched the yellow Fern Bear icon blip on its secret screen. I fasten my gaze on the bear, my heart pounding. Hardly daring to breathe, I lift my field glasses to my face and watch.

The bear shuffles around a large boulder and looks back over her shoulder, and there, emerging from the shadows, is a smaller version of her, a fluffy bundle of bear cub tottering out to join its mother in the spring sunshine.

I reach into my pocket and draw out my phone. Sure enough, the badger icon is green. I switch to silent and send a message to Luke. Fern bear plus cub emerging from den.

I feel the tremble as his response comes in. Freakin magic.

I start a new column in the monitoring sheet, record the time and location, and tap in 'playing'. Then I put the phone away and turn my full attention to the bears.

The mother leads her little one out to a sunny, brackeny patch where she rolls, scratching herself on the last of the bronze stalks. Her cub clambers up on to her belly and reaches for a teat. The new mother cradles her young, head back, eyes closed in what appears unambiguous bliss.

My eyes blur. I let the field glasses hang. A fat tear rolls down my cheek. I catch it with my tongue. Salty.

I take the phone back out of my pocket, tap in 'nursing' then open my address list and flash to a number I have skipped a thousand times, somehow never quite managing to hit the green button. I press it now, hold the phone to my ear and wait. Two long tones and then a pause. 'Allo?'

'Hi. It's Callis. I'm watching a mother bear and cub, in Scotland.'

'Beautiful!' I can hear his grin. 'So you still love bears?'

'More than ever.'

'Beautiful.'

I'm smiling so hard I might topple off the horse, but Gretel stands solid. 'You were right about everything.'

'Good.' That deep voice, the faint Romanian twang, how could I have forgotten? 'I met friends of yours recently in Russia,' he says.

'Who?'

'Tanka and Païvi.'

'My favourite friends, how are they?' The thought of the Finns is sweet as chocolate.

'Very good. Very cool people. They like you almost as much as I do.'

I remember the first time he said he liked me, when I was tucked up like Goldilocks in bed in the cabin in the forest. 'The feeling's mutual.'

'Which one?'

'All of them.'

'They call you Madabout. Madabout Bears. '

'Yes.' We laugh. I try not to jiggle the stirrups or grip Gretel too tightly with my calves. The sound of his voice makes my laughter flow so much, I miss what he says next.

'What?'

'I like the name. It suits you.'

'I'm sorry I didn't write back. My life's been a bit... complicated.'

'Is it simpler now?'

'Yes, much simpler.' There is a hot wind blowing through me.

'You didn't forget me after all.'

'No. Not at all.'

'Can I come and see them? Your bears?'

'Of course.' What else could make me happier?

'It's been a long time.'

I don't know what to say. 'Do you know where to come?'

'No.'

'Just come north. North of Inverness. I'll guide you in.'

'One cub, you say?'

'Yes.'

'I missed you.'

There is more in those three words of his than I can believe. 'Just come,' I say.

The mother bear rolls on to her side and the cub tumbles and scrambles back up, scrabbling at its mother's fur, up on to her shoulder, tugging at her ear. I chuckle.

'What are you laughing at?'

'The bears.'

'Tell them I'm on my way.' He hangs up. I keep the phone near my cheek.

'Petr is coming to see you.'

The mother gets up, sniffs at the wind and rears on to her hind legs, scenting. Gretel snickers in alarm, and steps back. The bear catches our scent or hears the horse, perhaps, and cautiously ushers her little one back into the safety of the scree.

'Keep tight,' I whisper after them. I turn Gretel away and head for the gate in the fence.

🐾 🐾 🐾 🐾 🐾 🐾

Acknowledgements

I'd like to thank the many people who have provided me with information, advice and opinions about bears and other carnivores, particularly Andreas Zedrosser and Jon Swenson of the International Bear Association, staff of the Carpathian Large Mammal Project in Romania, Kostadin Valchev in Bulgaria, and in Scotland, David Hetherington, Roy Dennis, Dan Puplett, Jonny Hughes, Alan Featherstone Watson and Margot Henderson.

Early work on the book was made possible thanks to a period of creativity funded by a writing bursary from the Scottish Arts Council. Thanks also to Jane Alexander, John Bolland, Maggie Wallis, Ed Group and members of the North West Highland Writers for invaluable comments on drafts. Sara Hunt and Craig Hillsley at Saraband have made the publication process a pleasure and I'm hugely grateful for all their work on the book.

Finally, thanks to Bill Ritchie, for being almost as mad about bears as I am.

Mandy Haggith